JUDITH McNAUGHT

A KINGDOM *of* DREAMS

POCKET BOOKS

New York   London   Toronto   Sydney

Pocket Books
A Division of Simon & Schuster, Inc.
1230 Avenue of the Americas
New York, NY 10020

This book is a work of fiction. Names, characters, places, and incidents either are products of the author's imagination or are used fictitiously. Any resemblance to actual events or locales or persons, living or dead, is entirely coincidental.

This Pocket Books paperback edition June 2010

POCKET and colophon are registered trademarks of Simon & Schuster, Inc.

For information about special discounts for bulk purchases, please contact Simon & Schuster Special Sales at 1-866-506-1949 or business@simonandschuster.com

The Simon & Schuster Speakers Bureau can bring authors to your live event. For more information or to book an event contact the Simon & Schuster Speakers Bureau at 1-866-248-3049 or visit our website at www.simonspeakers.com

Cover design and illustration by Lisa Litwack

Manufactured in the United States of America

10 9 8 7 6 5 4 3 2 1

ISBN 978-1-4391-9473-7

Praise for the latest
New York Times bestsellers of
Judith McNaught,
"One of the finest writers of
popular fiction."*

NIGHT WHISPERS

"Never miss a McNaught! NIGHT WHISPERS heads like the *Titanic* toward its iceberg of a climax—with shocking revelations. . . . Judith McNaught has written her most stunning work of fiction to date. Sexy, smart, and page-turning, this is a must-read."

—*barnesandnoble.com**

"A tender triumph that will leave readers awed. . . . The characters are warm and charming, and will long be remembered."

—*BookBrowser.com*

"McNaught has truly outdone herself with NIGHT WHISPERS. . . Equal parts romance and suspense, this is a must-read for mystery and romance fans alike. . . . You'll find yourself delighted with this excellent book."

—*Rendezvous*

"Curl up in front of your fireplace and enjoy."

—*Cleveland Plain Dealer*

REMEMBER WHEN

"[A] clever take on the ultra-affluent, ultra-cynical social scene of McNaught's hometown of Houston. . . . McNaught has a lot of fun with a marriage of convenience that turns out to be anything but."

—*Chicago Tribune*

"Delectable. . . . Romance blooms like wildflowers in the heart of Texas. . . . I loved *Remember When*."

—*Philadelphia Inquirer*

"Romantic, witty, and entertaining. . . ."

—*San Antonio Express-News*

Books by Judith McNaught

To toothless grins and baby toys;
To Little League games and tears
you wouldn't cry;
To fast cars, pretty girls, and
college football;
To compassion and charm and humor;

To my son.

We've come a long way together, Clay.

Special Notes of Gratitude . . .

To my secretary, Karen T. Caton—
For all the frantic midnights you worked beside me;
For never losing your patience or your humor;
and for never losing track of *me!*

and

To Dr. Benjamin Hudson
Department of History, Penn State University,
who gave me answers when I couldn't
find them anywhere.

and

To Dr. Sharon Woodruff
for her friendship and encouragement.

Chapter One

A toast to the duke of Claymore and his bride!"

Under normal circumstances, this call for a wedding toast would have caused the lavishly dressed ladies and gentlemen assembled in the great hall at Merrick castle to smile and cheer. Goblets of wine would have been raised and more toasts offered in celebration of a grand and noble wedding such as the one which was about to take place here in the south of Scotland.

But not today. Not at this wedding.

At this wedding, no one cheered and no one raised a goblet. At this wedding, everyone was watching everyone else, and everyone was tense. The bride's family was tense. The groom's family was tense. The guests and the servants and the hounds in the hall were tense. Even the first earl of Merrick, whose portrait hung above the fireplace, looked tense.

"A toast to the duke of Claymore and his bride," the groom's brother pronounced again, his voice like a thunderclap in the unnatural, tomblike silence of the crowded hall. "May they enjoy a long and fruitful life together."

1

Normally, that ancient toast brings about a predictable reaction: The groom always smiles proudly because he's convinced he's accomplished something quite wonderful. The bride smiles because she's been able to convince him of it. The guests smile because, amongst the nobility, a marriage connotes the linking of two important families and two large fortunes—which in itself is cause for great celebration and abnormal gaiety.

But not today. Not on this fourteenth day of October, 1497.

Having made the toast, the groom's brother raised his goblet and smiled grimly at the groom. The groom's friends raised their goblets and smiled fixedly at the bride's family. The bride's family raised their goblets and smiled frigidly at each other. The groom, who alone seemed to be immune to the hostility in the hall, raised his goblet and smiled calmly at his bride, but the smile did not reach his eyes.

The bride did not bother to smile at anyone. She looked furious and mutinous.

In truth, Jennifer was so frantic she scarcely knew anyone was there. At the moment, every fiber of her being was concentrating on a last-minute, desperate appeal to God, Who out of lack of attention or lack of interest, had let her come to this sorry pass. *"Lord,"* she cried silently, swallowing the lump of terror swelling in her throat, *"if You're going to do something to stop this marriage, You're going to have to do it quickly, or in five minutes 'twill be too late! Surely, I deserve something better than this forced marriage to a man who stole my virginity! I didn't just hand it over to him, You know!"*

Realizing the folly of reprimanding the Almighty, she hastily switched to pleading: *"Haven't I always tried to serve You well?"* she whispered silently. *"Haven't I always obeyed You?"*

"NOT ALWAYS, JENNIFER," God's voice thundered in her mind.

2

"Nearly *always*," Jennifer amended frantically. *"I attended mass every day, except when I was ill, which was seldom, and I said my prayers every morning and every evening.* Nearly *every evening,"* she amended hastily before her conscience could contradict her again, *"except when I fell asleep before I was finished. And I* tried, *I* truly *tried to be all that the good sisters at the abbey wanted me to be. You know how hard I've tried! Lord,"* she finished desperately, *"if you'll just help me escape from this, I'll never be willful or impulsive again."*

"THAT I DO NOT BELIEVE, JENNIFER," God boomed dubiously.

"Nay, I swear it," she earnestly replied, trying to strike a bargain. *"I'll do anything You want, I'll go straight back to the abbey and devote my life to prayer and—"*

"The marriage contracts have been duly signed. Bring in the priest," Lord Balfour commanded, and Jennifer's breath came in wild, panicked gasps, all thoughts of potential sacrifices fleeing from her mind. *"God,"* she silently pleaded, *"why are You doing this to me? You aren't going to let this happen to me, are You?"*

Silence fell over the great hall as the doors were flung open.

"YES, JENNIFER, I AM."

The crowd parted automatically to admit the priest, and Jennifer felt as if her life were ending. Her groom stepped into position beside her, and Jennifer jerked an inch away, her stomach churning with resentment and humiliation at having to endure his nearness. If only she had *known* how one heedless act could end in disaster and disgrace. If only she hadn't been so impulsive and reckless!

Closing her eyes, Jennifer shut out the hostile faces of the English and the murderous faces of her Scots kinsmen, and in her heart she faced the wrenching truth: Impulsiveness and recklessness, her two great-

3

est faults, had brought her to this dire end—the same two character flaws that had led her to commit all of her most disastrous follies. Those two flaws, combined with a desperate yearning to make her father love her, as he loved his stepsons, were responsible for the debacle she'd made of her life:

When she was fifteen, those were the things that had led her to try to avenge herself against her sly, spiteful stepbrother in what had seemed a right and honorable way—which was to secretly don Merrick armor and then ride against him, fairly, in the lists. That magnificent folly had gained her a sound thrashing from her father right there on the field of honor—and only a tiny bit of satisfaction from having knocked her wicked stepbrother clean off his horse!

The year before, those same traits had caused her to behave in such a way that old Lord Balder withdrew his request for her hand, and in doing so destroyed her father's cherished dream of joining the two families. And those things, in turn, were what got her banished to the abbey at Belkirk, where, seven weeks ago, she'd become easy prey for the Black Wolf's marauding army.

And now, because of all that, she was forced to wed her enemy; a brutal English warrior whose armies had oppressed her country, a man who had captured her, held her prisoner, taken her virginity, and destroyed her reputation.

But it was too late for prayers and promises now. Her fate had been sealed from the moment, seven weeks ago, when she'd been dumped at the feet of the arrogant beast beside her, trussed up like a feastday partridge.

Jennifer swallowed. No, before that—she'd veered down this path to disaster earlier that same day when she'd refused to heed the warnings that the Black Wolf's armies were nearby.

But why *should* she have believed it, Jennifer cried

4

in her own defense. *"The Wolf is marching on us!"* had been a terrified call of doom issued almost weekly throughout the last five years. But on that day, seven weeks ago, it had been woefully true.

The crowd in the hall stirred restlessly, looking about for a sign of the priest, but Jennifer was lost in her memories of that day . . .

At the time, it had seemed an unusually pretty day, the sky a cheerful blue, the air balmy. The sun had been shining down upon the abbey, bathing its Gothic spires and graceful arches in bright golden light, beaming benignly upon the sleepy little village of Belkirk, which boasted the abbey, two shops, thirty-four cottages, and a communal stone well in the center of it, where villagers gathered on Sunday afternoons, as they were doing then. On a distant hill, a shepherd looked after his flock, while in a clearing not far from the well, Jennifer had been playing hoodman-blind with the orphans whom the abbess had entrusted to her care.

And in that halcyon setting of laughter and relaxation, this travesty had begun. As if she could somehow change events by reliving them in her mind, Jennifer closed her eyes, and suddenly she was there again in the little clearing with the children, her head completely covered with the hoodman's hood . . .

"Where are you, Tom MacGivern?" she called out, groping about with outstretched arms, pretending she couldn't locate the giggling nine-year-old boy, who her ears told her was only a foot away on her right. Grinning beneath the concealing hood, she assumed the pose of a classic "monster" by holding her arms high in front of her, her fingers spread like claws, and began to stomp about, calling in a deep, ominous voice, "You can't escape me, Tom MacGivern."

"Ha!" he shouted from her right. "You'll no' find me, hoodman!"

"Yes, I will!" Jenny threatened, then deliberately

turned to her left, which caused gales of laughter to erupt from the children who were hiding behind trees and crouching beside bushes.

"I've got you!" Jenny shouted triumphantly a few minutes later as she swooped down upon a fleeing, giggling child, catching a small wrist in her hand. Breathless and laughing, Jenny yanked off her hood to see whom she'd captured, mindless of the red gold hair tumbling down over her shoulders and arms.

"You got Mary!" the children crowed delightedly. "Mary's the hoodman now!"

The little five-year-old girl looked up at Jenny, her hazel eyes wide and apprehensive, her thin body shivering with fear. "Please," she whispered, clinging to Jenny's leg, "I—I not want to wear th' hood— 'Twill be dark inside it. Do I got to wear it?"

Smiling reassuringly, Jenny tenderly smoothed Mary's hair off her thin face. "Not if you don't want."

"I'm afeert of the dark," Mary confided unnecessarily, her narrow shoulders drooping with shame.

Sweeping her up into her arms, Jenny hugged her tightly. "Everybody is afraid of something," she said and teasingly added, "Why, I'm afraid of—of *frogs!*"

The dishonest admission made the little girl giggle. "Frogs!" she repeated, "I likes frogs! They don't sceer me 'tall."

"There, you see—" Jenny said as she lowered her to the ground. "You're very brave. Braver than I!"

"Lady Jenny is afeart of silly ol' frogs," Mary told the group of children as they ran forward.

"No she isn—" young Tom began, quick to rise to the defense of the beautiful Lady Jenny who, despite her lofty rank, was always up to anything—including hitching up her skirts and wading in the pond to help him catch a fat bullfrog—or climbing up a tree, quick as a cat, to rescue little Will who was afraid to come down.

Tom silenced at Jenny's pleading look and argued no more about her alleged fear of frogs. "I'll wear the hood," he volunteered, gazing adoringly at the seventeen-year-old girl who wore the somber gown of a novice nun, but who was not one, and who, moreover, certainly didn't *act* like one. Why, last Sunday during the priest's long sermon, Lady Jenny's head had nodded forward, and only Tom's loud, false coughing in the bench behind her had awakened her in time for her to escape detection by the sharp-eyed abbess.

" 'Tis Tom's turn to wear the hood," Jenny agreed promptly, handing Tom the hood. Smiling, she watched the children scamper off to their favorite hiding places, then she picked up the wimple and short woolen veil she'd taken off in order to be the hoodman. Intending to go over to the communal well where the villagers were eagerly questioning some clansmen passing through Belkirk on their way to their homes from the war against the English in Cornwall, she lifted the wimple, intending to put it on.

"Lady Jennifer!" One of the village men called suddenly, "Come quick—there's news of the laird."

The veil and wimple forgotten in her hand, Jenny broke into a run, and the children, sensing the excitement, stopped their game and raced along at her heels.

"What news?" Jenny asked breathlessly, her gaze searching the stolid faces of the groups of clansmen. One of them stepped forward, respectfully removing his helm and cradling it in the crook of his arm. "Be you the daughter of the laird of Merrick?"

At the mention of the name Merrick, two of the men at the well suddenly stopped in the act of pulling up a bucket of water and exchanged startled, malevolent glances before they quickly ducked their heads again, keeping their faces in shadow. "Yes," Jenny said eagerly. "You have news of my father?"

"Aye, m'lady. He's comin' this way, not far behind us, wit a big band o' men."

"Thank God," Jenny breathed. "How goes the battle at Cornwall?" she asked after a moment, ready now to forget her personal concerns and devote her worry to the battle the Scots were waging at Cornwall in support of King James and Edward V's claim to the English throne.

His face answered Jenny's question even before he said, " 'Twas all but over when we left. In Cork and Taunton it looked like we might win, and the same was true in Cornwall, until the devil hisself came to take command 'o Henry's army."

"The devil?" Jenny repeated blankly.

Hatred contorted the man's face and he spat on the ground. "Aye, the devil—the Black Wolf hisself, may he roast in hell from whence he was spawned."

Two of the peasant women crossed themselves as if to ward off evil at the mention of the Black Wolf, Scotland's most hated, and most feared, enemy, but the man's next words made them gape in fear: "The Wolf is comin' back to Scotland. Henry's sendin' him here with a fresh army to crush us for supportin' King Edward. 'Twill be murder and bloodshed like the last time he came, only worst, you mark me. The clans are making haste to come home and get ready for the battles. I'm thinkin' the Wolf will attack Merrick first, before any o' the rest of us, for 'twas your clan that took the most English lives at Cornwall."

So saying, he nodded politely, put on his helmet, then he swung up onto his horse.

The scraggly groups at the well departed soon afterward, heading down the road that led across the moors and wound upward into the hills.

Two of the men, however, did not continue beyond the bend in the road. Once out of sight of the villagers, they veered off to the right, sending their horses at a furtive gallop into the forest.

Had Jenny been watching, she might have caught a brief glimpse of them doubling back through the woods that ran beside the road right behind her. But at the time, she was occupied with the terrified pandemonium that had broken out among the citi-

zens of Belkirk, which happened to lie directly in th.
path between England and Merrick keep.

"The Wolf is coming!" one of the women cried,
clutching her babe protectively to her breast. "God
have *pity* on us."

" 'Tis Merrick he'll strike at," a man shouted, his
voice rising in fear. " 'Tis the laird of Merrick he'll
want in his jaws, but 'tis Belkirk he'll devour on the
way."

Suddenly the air was filled with gruesome predic-
tions of fire and death and slaughter, and the children
crowded around Jenny, clinging to her in mute horror.
To the Scots, be they wealthy noble or lowly villager,
the Black Wolf was more evil than the devil himself,
and more dangerous, for the devil was a spirit, while
the Wolf was flesh and blood—the living Lord of
Evil—a monstrous being who threatened their existence, right here on earth. He was the malevolent
specter that the Scots used to terrify their offspring
into behaving. "The Wolf will get you," was the
warning issued to keep children from straying into the
woods or leaving their beds at night, or from disobey-
ing their elders.

Impatient with such hysteria over what was, to her,
more myth than man, Jenny raised her voice in order
to be heard over the din. " 'Tis more likely," she
called, putting her arms around the terrified children
who'd crowded against her at the first mention of the
Wolf's name, "that he'll go back to his heathen king so
that he can lick the wounds we gave him at Cornwall
while he tells great lies to exaggerate his victory. And
if he does not do that, he'll choose a weaker keep than
Merrick for his attack—one he's a chance of breech-
ing."

Her words and her tone of amused disdain brought
startled gazes flying to her face, but it wasn't merely
false bravado that had made Jenny speak so: She was a
Merrick, and a Merrick never admitted to fear of any
man. She had heard that hundreds of times when her

father spoke to her stepbrothers, and she had adopted his creed for her own. Furthermore, the villagers were frightening the children, which she refused to let continue.

Mary tugged at Jenny's skirts to get her attention, and in a shrill little voice, she asked, "Isn't *you* afeert of the Black Wolf, Lady Jenny?"

"Of course not!" Jenny said with a bright, reassuring smile.

"They say," young Tom interjected in an awed voice, "the Wolf is as tall as a tree!"

"A tree!" Jenny chuckled, trying to make a huge joke of the Wolf and all the lore surrounding him. "If he is, 'twould be a sight worth seeing when he tries to mount his horse! Why, 'twould take *four* squires to hoist him up there!"

The absurdity of that image made some of the children giggle, exactly as Jenny had hoped.

"I heert," said young Will with an eloquent shudder, "he tears down walls with his bare hands and drinks blood!"

"Yuk!" said Jenny with twinkling eyes. "Then 'tis only indigestion which makes him so mean. If he comes to Belkirk, we'll offer him some good Scottish ale instead."

"My pa said," put in another child, "he rides with a giant beside him, a Go-liath called Arik who carries a war axe and chops up children . . ."

"I heert—" another child interrupted ominously.

Jenny cut in lightly, "Let me tell you what *I* have heard." With a bright smile, she began to shepherd them toward the abbey, which was out of sight just beyond a bend down the road. "*I* heard," she improvised gaily, "that he's so very old that he has to squint to see, just like this—"

She screwed up her face in a comical exaggeration of a befuddled, near-blind person peering around blankly, and the children giggled.

As they walked along, Jenny kept up the same lighthearted teasing comments, and the children fell in with the game, adding their own suggestions to make the Wolf seem absurd.

But despite the laughter and seeming gaiety of the moment, the sky had suddenly darkened as a bank of heavy clouds rolled in, and the air was turning bitingly cold, whipping Jenny's cloak about her, as if nature herself brooded at the mention of such evil.

Jenny was about to make another joke at the Wolf's expense, but she broke off abruptly as a group of mounted clansmen rounded the bend from the abbey, coming toward her down the road. A beautiful girl, clad as Jenny was in the somber gray gown, white wimple, and short gray veil of a novice nun, was mounted in front of the leader, sitting demurely sideways in his saddle, her timid smile confirming what Jenny already knew.

With a silent cry of joy, Jenny started to dash forward, then checked the unladylike impulse and made herself stay where she was. Her eyes clung to her father, then drifted briefly over her clansmen, who were staring past her with the same grim disapproval they'd shown her for years—ever since her stepbrother had successfully circulated his horrible tale.

Sending the children ahead with strict orders to go directly to the abbey, Jenny waited in the middle of the road for what seemed like an eternity until, at last, the group halted in front of her.

Her father, who'd obviously stopped at the abbey where Brenna, Jenny's stepsister, was also staying, swung down from his horse, then he turned to lift Brenna down. Jenny chafed at the delay, but his scrupulous attention to courtesy and dignity was so typical of the great man that a wry smile touched her lips.

Finally, he turned fully toward her, opening his arms wide. Jenny hurtled into his embrace, hugging him fiercely, babbling in her excitement: "Father, I've missed you so! 'Tis nearly two years since I've seen you! Are you well? You look well. You've scarce changed in all this time!"

Gently disentangling her arms from about his neck, Lord Merrick set his daughter slightly away from him while his gaze drifted over her tousled hair, rosy cheeks, and badly rumpled gown. Jenny squirmed inwardly beneath his prolonged scrutiny, praying that he approved of what he saw and that, since he'd obviously stopped at the abbey already, the abbess's report had been pleasing to him.

Two years ago, her behavior had gotten her sent to the abbey; a year ago, Brenna had been sent down here for safety's sake while the laird was at war. Under the abbess's firm guidance, Jenny had come to appreciate her strengths, and to try to overcome her faults. But as her father inspected her from head to toe, she couldn't help wondering if he saw the young lady she was now or the unruly girl she'd been two years ago. His blue eyes finally returned to her face and there was a smile in them. "Ye've become a woman, Jennifer."

Jenny's heart soared; coming from her taciturn father, such a comment constituted high praise. "I've changed in other ways too, Father," she promised, her eyes shining. "I've changed a great deal."

"Not *that* much, my girl." Raising his shaggy white brows, he looked pointedly at the short veil and wimple hanging forgotten from her fingertips.

"Oh!" Jenny said, laughing and anxious to explain. "I was playing hoodman-blind . . . er . . . with the children, and it wouldn't fit beneath the hood. Have you seen the abbess? What did Mother Ambrose tell you?"

Laughter sparked in his somber eyes. "She told me," he replied dryly, "that ye've a habit of sitting on yon hill and gazing off into the air, dreaming, which sounds familiar, lassie. And she told me ye've a tendency to nod off in the midst of mass, should the priest sermonize longer than you think seemly, which also sounds familiar."

Jenny's heart sank at this seeming betrayal from the abbess whom she so admired. In a sense, Mother Ambrose was laird of her own grand demesne, controlling revenues from the farmlands and livestock that belonged to the splendid abbey, presiding at table whenever there were visitors, and dealing with all other matters that involved the laymen who worked on the abbey grounds as well as the nuns who lived cloistered within its soaring walls.

Brenna was terrified of the stern woman, but Jenny loved her, and so the abbess's apparent betrayal cut deeply.

Her father's next words banished her disappointment. "Mother Ambrose also told me," he admitted with gruff pride, "that you've a head on your shoulders befitting an abbess herself. She said you're a Merrick through and through, with courage enough to be laird of yer own clan. But you'll no' be that," he warned, dashing Jenny's fondest dream.

With an effort, Jenny kept the smile pinned to her face, refusing to feel the hurt of being deprived of that right—a right that had been promised to her until her father married Brenna's widowed mother and acquired three stepsons in the bargain.

Alexander, the eldest of the three brothers, would assume the position that had been promised to her. That, in itself, wouldn't have been nearly so hard to bear if Alexander had been nice, or even fair-minded, but he was a treacherous, scheming liar, and Jenny knew it, even if her father and her clan did not. Within a year after coming to live at Merrick keep, he'd begun carrying tales about her, tales so slanderous and ghastly, but so cleverly contrived, that, over a period of years, he'd turned her whole clan against her. That loss of her clan's affection still hurt unbearably. Even now, when they were looking through her as if she didn't exist for them, Jenny had to stop herself from pleading with them to forgive her for things she had not done.

William, the middle brother, was like Brenna—sweet and as timid as can be—while Malcolm, the youngest, was as evil and as sneaky as Alexander. "The abbess also said," her father continued, "that you're kind and gentle, but you've spirit, too . . ."

"She said all that?" Jenny asked, dragging her dismal thoughts from her stepbrothers. "Truly?"

"Aye." Jenny would normally have rejoiced in that answer, but she was watching her father's face, and it was becoming more grim and tense than she had ever seen it. Even his voice was strained as he said, " 'Tis well you've given up your heathenish ways and that you're all the things you've become, Jennifer."

He paused as if unable or unwilling to continue, and Jenny prodded gently, "Why is that, Father?"

"Because," he said, drawing a long, harsh breath, "the future of the clan will depend on your answer to my next question."

His words trumpeted in her mind like blasts from a clarion, leaving Jenny dazed with excitement and joy: *"The future of the clan depends on you . . ."* She was so happy, she could scarcely trust her ears. It was as if she were up on the hill overlooking the abbey, dreaming her favorite daydream—the one where her father always came to her and said, *"Jennifer, the future of the clan depends on you. Not your stepbrothers. You."* It was the chance she'd been dreaming of to prove her mettle to her clansmen and to win back their affection. In that daydream, she was always called upon to perform some incredible feat of daring, some brave and dangerous deed, like scaling the wall of the Black Wolf's castle and capturing him single-handedly. But no matter how daunting the task, she never questioned it, nor hesitated a second to accept the challenge.

She searched her father's face. "What would you have me do?" she asked eagerly. "Tell me, and I will! I'll do any—"

"Will you *marry* Edric MacPherson?"

14

"Whaaat?" gasped the horrified heroine of Jenny's daydream. Edric MacPherson was older than her father; a wizened, frightening man who'd looked at her in a way that made her skin crawl ever since she'd begun to change from girl to maiden.

"Will you, or will you no'?"

Jenny's delicate auburn brows snapped together. "Why?" asked the heroine who never questioned.

A strange, haunted look darkened his face. "We took a beating at Cornwall, lass—we lost half our men. Alexander was killed in battle. He died like a Merrick," he added with grim pride, "fighting to the end."

"I'm glad for your sake, Papa," she said, unable to feel more than a brief pang of sorrow for the step-brother who'd made her life into a hell. Now, as she often had in the past, she wished there were something *she* could do to make him proud of *her.* "I know you loved him as if he were your own son."

Accepting her sympathy with a brief nod, he returned to the discussion at hand: "There were many amongst the clans who were opposed to going to Cornwall to fight for King James's cause, but the clans followed me anyway. 'Tis no secret to the English that 'twas my influence which brought the clans to Cornwall, and now the English king wants vengeance. He's sendin' the Wolf to Scotland to attack Merrick keep." Ragged pain edged his deep voice as he admitted, "We'll no' be able to withstand a siege now, not unless the MacPherson clan comes to support us in our fight. The MacPherson has enough influence with a dozen other clans to force them to join us as well."

Jenny's mind was reeling. Alexander was dead, and the Wolf really *was* coming to attack her home . . .

Her father's harsh voice snapped her out of her daze. "Jennifer! Do you ken what I've been saying? MacPherson has promised to join in our fight, but only if you'll have him for husband."

Through her mother, Jenny was a countess and heiress to a rich estate which marched with MacPherson's. "He wants my lands?" she said almost hopefully, remembering the awful way Edric MacPherson's eyes had wandered down her body when he'd stopped at the abbey a year ago to pay a "social call" upon her.

"Aye."

"Couldn't we just *give* them to him in return for his support?" she volunteered desperately, ready— willing—to sacrifice a splendid demesne without hesitation, for the good of her people.

"He'd not agree to that!" her father said angrily. "There's honor in fighting for kin, but he could no' send his people into a fight that's no' their own, and then take your lands in payment to *him*."

"But, surely, if he wants my lands badly enough, there's some way—"

"He wants *you*. He sent word to me in Cornwall." His gaze drifted over Jenny's face, registering the startling changes that had altered her face from its thin, freckled, girlish plainness into a face of almost exotic beauty. "Ye've your mother's look about ye now, lass, and it's whetted the appetites of an old man. I'd no' ask this of you if there was any other way." Gruffly, he reminded her, "You used to plead wi' me to name you laird. Ye said there was naught you wouldna' do fer yer clan . . ."

Jenny's stomach twisted into sick knots at the thought of committing her body, her entire life, into the hands of a man she instinctively recoiled from, but she lifted her head and bravely met her father's gaze. "Aye, father," she said quietly. "Shall I come with you now?"

The look of pride and relief on his face almost made the sacrifice worthwhile. He shook his head. " 'Tis best you stay here with Brenna. We've no horses to spare and we're anxious to reach Merrick and begin preparations for battle. I'll send word to the MacPherson that the marriage is agreed upon, and then send someone here to fetch you to him."

When he turned to remount his horse, Jenny gave into the temptation she'd been fighting all along: Instead of standing aside, she moved into the rows of mounted clansmen who had once been her friends and playmates. Hoping that some of them had perhaps heard her agree to marry the MacPherson and that this might neutralize their contempt of her, she paused beside the horse of a ruddy, red-headed man. "Good day to you, Renald Garvin," she said, smiling hesitantly into his hooded gaze. "How fares your lady wife?"

His jaw hardened, his cold eyes flickering over her. "Well enough, I imagine," he snapped.

Jenny swallowed at the unmistakable rejection from the man who had once taught her to fish and laughed with her when she fell into the stream.

She turned around and looked beseechingly at the man in the column beside Renald. "And you, Michael MacCleod? Has your leg been causing you any pain?"

Cold blue eyes met hers, then looked straight ahead.

She went to the rider behind him whose face was filled with hatred and she held out her hand beseechingly, her voice choked with pleading. "Garrick Carmichael, it has been four years since your Becky drowned. I swear to you now, as I swore to you then, I did not shove her into the river. We were *not* quarreling—'twas a *lie* invented by Alexander to—"

His face as hard as granite, Garrick Carmichael spurred his horse forward, and without ever looking at her, the men began passing her by.

Only old Josh, the clan's armorer, pulled his ancient horse to a halt, letting the others go on ahead. Leaning down, he laid his callused palm atop her bare head. "I know you speak truly, lassie," he said, and his unceasing loyalty brought the sting of tears to her eyes as she gazed up into his soft brown ones. "Ye have a temper, there's no denyin' it, but even when ye were but a wee

17

thing, ye kept it bridled. Garrick Carmichael and the others might o' been fooled by Alexander's angelic looks, but not ol' Josh. You'll no' see me grievin' o'er the loss o' him! The clan'll be better by far wit' young William leadin' it. Carmichael and the others—" he added reassuringly, "they'll come about in their thinkin' o' you, once they ken yer marrying the MacPherson for their sake as well as your sire's."

"Where are my stepbrothers?" Jenny asked hoarsely, changing the subject lest she burst into tears.

"They're comin' home by a different route. We couldn't be sure the Wolf wouldn't try to attack us while we marched, so we split up after leavin' Cornwall." With another pat on her head, he spurred his horse forward.

As if in a daze, Jenny stood stock-still in the middle of the road, watching her clan ride off and disappear around the bend.

"It grows dark," Brenna said beside her, her gentle voice filled with sympathy. "We should go back to the abbey now."

The abbey. Three short hours ago, Jenny had walked away from the abbey feeling cheery and alive. Now she felt—dead. "Go ahead without me. I—I can't go back there. Not yet. I think I'll walk up the hill and sit for a while."

"The abbess will be annoyed if we aren't back before dusk, and it's near that now," Brenna said apprehensively. It had always been thus between the two girls, with Jenny breaking a rule and Brenna terrified of bending one. Brenna was gentle, biddable, and beautiful, with blond hair, hazel eyes, and a sweet disposition that made her, in Jenny's eyes, the embodiment of womanhood at its best. She was also as meek and timid as Jenny was impulsive and courageous. Without Jenny, she'd not have had a single adventure—nor ever gotten a scolding. Without Brenna to worry about and protect, Jenny would have had many more adventures—and many more scoldings. As a result, the two girls were entirely devoted to each other, and tried to protect one another as much as possible from the inevitable results of each other's shortcomings.

Brenna hesitated and then volunteered with only a tiny tremor in her voice, "I'll stay with you. If you remain alone, you'll forget about time and likely be pounced upon by a—a bear in the darkness."

At the moment, the prospect of being killed by a bear seemed rather inviting to Jenny, whose entire life stretched before her, shrouded in gloom and foreboding. Despite the fact that she truly wanted, needed, to stay outdoors and try to reassemble her thoughts, Jenny shook her head, knowing that if they stayed, Brenna would be drowning in fear at the thought of facing the abbess. "No, we'll go back."

Ignoring Jenny's words, Brenna clasped Jenny's hand and turned to the left, toward the slope of the hill that overlooked the abbey, and for the first time it was Brenna who led and Jenny who followed.

In the woods beside the road, two shadows moved stealthily, staying parallel with the girls' path up the hill.

By the time they were partway up the steep incline, Jenny had already grown impatient with her own self-pity, and she made a Herculean effort to shore up her flagging spirits. "When you think on it," she offered slowly, directing a glance at Brenna, "'tis actually a grand and noble thing I've been given the opportunity to do—marrying the MacPherson for the sake of my people."

"You're just like Joan of Arc," Brenna agreed eagerly, "leading her people to victory!"

"Except that I'm marrying Edric MacPherson."

"And," Brenna finished encouragingly, "suffering a worse fate than she did!"

Laughter widened Jenny's eyes at this depressing remark, which her well-meaning sister delivered with such enthusiasm.

Encouraged by the return of Jenny's ability to laugh, Brenna cast about for something else with which to divert and cheer her. As they neared the crest of the hill, which was blocked by thick woods, she said suddenly, "What did Father mean about your having your mother's 'look about you'?"

"I don't know," Jenny began, diverted by a sudden, uneasy feeling that they were being watched in the deepening dusk. Turning and walking backward, she looked down toward the well and saw the villagers had all returned to the warmth of their hearths. Drawing her cloak about her, she shivered in the biting wind, and without much interest, she added, "Mother Abbess said my looks are a trifle *brazen* and that I must guard against the effect I will have on males when I leave the abbey."

"What does all that mean?"

Jenny shrugged without concern. "I don't know." Turning and walking forward again, Jenny remembered the wimple and veil in her fingertips and began to put the wimple back on. "What do I look like to you?" she asked, shooting a puzzled glance at Brenna. "I haven't seen my face in two years, except when I caught a reflection of it in the water. Have I changed much?"

"Oh yes," Brenna laughed. "Even Alexander wouldn't be able to call you scrawny and plain now, or say that your hair is the color of carrots."

"Brenna!" Jenny interrupted, thunderstruck by her own callousness. "Are you much grieved by Alexander's death? He was your brother and—"

"Don't talk of it any more," Brenna pleaded shakily. "I cried when Father told me, but the tears were few and I feel guilty because I didn't love him as I ought. Not then and not now. I couldn't. He was so—mean-spirited. It's wrong to speak ill of the dead,

yet I can't think of much *good* to say of him." Her
voice trailed off, and she pulled her cloak about her in
the damp wind, gazing at Jenny in mute appeal to
change the subject.

"Tell me how I look, then," Jenny invited quickly,
giving her sister a quick, hard hug.

They stopped walking, their way blocked by the
dense woods that covered the rest of the slope. A slow,
thoughtful smile spread across Brenna's beautiful face
as she studied her stepsister, her hazel eyes roving
over Jenny's expressive face, which was dominated by
a pair of large eyes as clear as dark blue crystal
beneath gracefully winged, auburn brows. "Well,
you're—you're quite pretty!"

"Good, but do you see anything *unusual* about
me?" Jenny asked, thinking of Mother Ambrose's
words as she put her wimple back on and pinned the
short woolen veil in place atop it. "Anything at all
which might make a male behave oddly?"

"No," Brenna stated, for she saw Jenny through the
eyes of a young innocent. "Nothing at all." A man
would have answered very differently, for although
Jennifer Merrick wasn't pretty in the conventional
way, her looks were both stiking and provocative. She
had a generous mouth that beckoned to be kissed, eyes
like liquid sapphires that shocked and invited, hair
like lush, red-gold satin, and a slender, voluptuous
body that was made for a man's hands.

"Your eyes are blue," Brenna began helpfully, trying to describe her, and Jenny chuckled.

"They were blue two years ago," she said. Brenna
opened her mouth to answer, but the words became a
scream that was stifled by a man's hand that clapped
over her mouth as he began dragging her backward
into the dense cover of the woods.

Jenny ducked, instinctively expecting an attack
from behind, but she was too late. Kicking and
screaming against a gloved male hand, she was
plucked from her feet and hauled into the woods.

21

Brenna was tossed over the back of her captor's horse like a sack of flour, her limp limbs attesting to the fact that she'd fainted, but Jenny was not so easily subdued. As her faceless adversary dumped her over the back of his horse, she threw herself to the side, rolling free, landing in the leaves and dirt, crawling on all fours beneath his horse, then scrambling to her feet. He caught her again, and Jenny raked her nails down his face, twisting in his hold. "God's teeth!" he hissed, trying to hold onto her flailing limbs. Jenny let out a blood-chilling scream, at the same moment she kicked as hard as she could, landing a hefty blow on his shin with the sturdy, black boots which were deemed appropriate footware for novice nuns. A grunt of pain escaped the blond man as he let her go for a split second. She bolted forward and might even have gained a few yards if her booted foot hadn't caught under a thick tree root and sent her sprawling onto her face, smacking the side of her head against a rock when she landed.

"Hand me the rope," the Wolf's brother said, a grim smile on his face as he glanced at his companion. Pulling his limp captive's cloak over her head, Stefan Westmoreland yanked it around her body, using it to pin her arms at her sides, then took the rope from his companion and tied it securely around Jenny's middle. Finished, he picked up his human bundle and tossed it ignominiously over his horse, her derrière pointing skyward, then he swung up into the saddle behind her.

Chapter Two

Royce will scarce believe our good fortune," Stefan called to the rider beside him whose prisoner was also bound and draped across his saddle. "Imagine— Merrick's girls standing beneath that tree as ripe for plucking as apples from a branch. Now there's no reason for us to have a look at Merrick's defenses— he'll surrender without a fight."

Tightly bound in her dark woolen prison, her head pounding and her stomach slamming against the horse's back with each lift of the beast's hooves, the name "Royce" made Jenny's blood freeze. Royce Westmoreland, the earl of Claymore. The Wolf. The horrifying stories she'd heard of him no longer seemed nearly so farfetched. Brenna and she had been seized by men who showed no reverence whatsoever for the habits of the order of St. Albans which the girls wore, habits that indicated their status of novice— aspiring nuns who had not yet taken their vows. What manner of men, Jenny wondered frantically, would lay their hands on nuns, or almost-nuns, without conscience or fear of retribution, human or divine. No man would. Only a devil and his disciples would dare!

"This one's fainted dead away," Thomas said with a lewd laugh. "A pity we haven't more time to sample our loot, although, were it left to me, I'd prefer that tasty morsel ye've wrapped in yer blanket, Stefan."

"Yours is the beauty of the two," Stefan replied coldly, "and you're not sampling anything until Royce decides what he wants to do with these two."

Nearly suffocating with fear inside her blanket, Jenny made a tiny cry of mindless, panicked protest in her throat, but no one heard her. She prayed to God to strike her captors dead on their horses, but God didn't seem to hear her, and the horses trotted endlessly, painfully onward. She prayed to be shown some sort of plan to escape, but her mind was too busy, frantically tormenting her with all the gruesome tales of the deadly Black Wolf: *He keeps no prisoners unless he means to torture them. He laughs when his victims scream with pain. He drinks their blood . . ."*

Bile surged up in Jenny's throat and she began to pray, not for escape, for she knew in her heart there would be no escape. Instead she prayed that death would come quickly and that she would not disgrace her proud family name. Her father's voice came back to her as he stood in the hall at Merrick, instructing her stepbrothers when they were young: *"If it is the Lord's will that you die at the hands of the enemy, then do it bravely. Die fighting like a warrior. Like a Merrick! Die fighting . . ."*

The phrases ranted through her mind, hour after hour, around and around, yet when the horses slowed and she heard distant, unmistakable sounds of a large encampment of men, fury began to overcome her fear. She was much too young to die, she thought, and it wasn't fair! And now gentle Brenna was going to die and that would be Jenny's fault, too. She would have to face the good Lord with that deed on her conscience. And all because a bloodthirsty ogre was roaming the land, devouring everything in his path.

Her thundering heart doubled its beat as the horses

came to a jarring stop. All around her, metal clanked against metal as men moved about and then she heard the prisoners' voices—men's voices crying pathetically for mercy, "Have pity, Wolf—Pity, Wolf—" The awful chants were rising to a shout as she was unceremoniously yanked from her horse.

"Royce," her captor called out, "stay there—we've brought you something!"

Completely blinded by the cloak which had been thrown over her head, and her arms still bound by the rope, she was tossed over her captor's shoulder. Beside her, she heard Brenna scream her name as they were carried forward.

"Be brave, Brenna," Jenny cried, but her voice was muffled by the cloak, and she knew her terrified sister couldn't hear her.

Jenny was abruptly lowered to the ground and pushed forward. Her legs were numb and she stumbled, falling heavily to her knees. *Die like a Merrick. Die bravely. Die fighting,* the chant raged through her mind as she tried ineffectually to raise herself. Above her, the Wolf spoke for the first time and she knew the voice was his. The voice was gravelly, fiery—a voice straight from the bowels of hell. "What is this? Something to eat, I hope."

'Tis said he eats the flesh of those he kills . . . Young Thomas's words came back to her while rage blended with the sound of Brenna's scream and the calls for pity from the prisoners. The rope around her arms was suddenly jerked loose. Driven by the twin demons of fear and fury, Jenny surged clumsily to her feet, her arms flailing at the cloak, looking like an enraged ghost trying to fling off its shroud. And the moment it fell away, Jenny doubled up her fist and swung with all her might at the dark, demonic, shadowy giant before her, striking him on the jaw bone.

Brenna fainted.

"Monster!" Jenny shouted. *"Barbarian!"* and she swung again, but this time her fist was caught in a

painful viselike grip and held high above her head. *"Devil!"* she cried, squirming, and she landed a mighty kick at his shin. "Spawn of Satan! Despoiler of innoc—!"

"What the—!" Royce Westmoreland roared, and reaching out, he caught his assailant at the waist and jerked her off her feet, holding her at arm's length, high in the air. It was a mistake. Her booted foot struck out again, catching Royce squarely in the groin with an impact that nearly doubled him over.

"You little bitch!" he thundered, as surprise, pain, and fury made him drop her, then grasp her by the veil, catching a handful of hair beneath it, and jerking her head back. *"Be still!"* he roared.

Even nature seemed to obey him; prisoners stopped their keening cries, the sounds of clanging metal ceased and an awful, unearthly silence fell over the huge clearing. Her pulse racing and her scalp smarting, Jenny squeezed her eyes closed and waited for the blow from his mighty fist that would surely kill her.

But it didn't come.

Half in fear and half in morbid curiosity, she slowly opened her eyes and for the first time, she actually saw His Face. The demonic specter that towered before her nearly made her scream with terror: He was huge. Enormous. His hair was black and his black cloak was billowing out behind him, blowing eerily in the wind as if it had a life of its own. Firelight danced across his swarthy, hawklike features, casting shadows that made him look positively satanic; it blazed in his strange eyes, heating them until they glowed like molten silver coals in his bearded haggard face. His shoulders were massive and broad, his chest incredibly wide, his arms bulging with muscle. One look at him and Jenny knew that he was capable of every vile thing he'd been accused of doing.

Die bravely! Die swiftly!

She turned her head and sank her teeth into his thick wrist.

She saw his blazing eyes widen a split second before his hand raised, then crashed against her cheek with a force that snapped her head sideways and sent her sprawling to her knees. Instinctively, Jenny quickly curled herself into a protective ball, and waited, eyes clenched shut, for the deathblow to befall her, while terror screamed through every pore of her quaking body.

The voice of the giant spoke above her, only this time it was more terrible because it was so tautly controlled that it hissed with muted fury: "What in the *hell* have you done?" Royce raged at his younger brother. "Haven't we problems enough without this! The men are exhausted and hungry, and you bring in two women to further fire their discontent."

Before his brother could speak, Royce turned to issue a sharp command to the other man to leave them, then his gaze slashed to the two prone female figures lying at his feet, one of them in a dead faint, the other curled into a ball, trembling so violently that her body shook as if in the throes of convulsions. For some reason the quaking girl enraged him more than her unconscious counterpart. "Get up!" he snapped at Jenny, nudging her with the toe of his boot. "You were brave enough a minute ago, now *get up!*"

Jenny uncurled slowly and, bracing her hand against the ground beneath her, she staggered awkwardly to her feet, swaying unsteadily while Royce rounded on his brother again. "I'm waiting for an answer, Stefan!"

"And I'll give you one if you'll cease roaring at me. These women are—"

"Nuns!" Royce bit out, his gaze suddenly riveting on the heavy crucifix hanging from a black cord around Jenny's neck, then lifting to the soiled wimple and askew veil. For a moment his discovery left him nearly dumbstruck. "God's teeth, you brought *nuns* here to be used as whores?"

"Nuns!" Stefan gasped, astounded.

"Whores!" croaked Jenny, outraged. Surely he couldn't be so steeped in godlessness that he'd actually give them to his men to be used as whores.

"I could kill you for this folly, Stefan, so help me—"

"You'll feel differently when I tell you who they are," Stefan said, yanking his horrified gaze from Jenny's gray habit and crucifix. "Standing before you, dear brother," he announced with renewed delight, "is the Lady Jennifer, beloved eldest child of Lord Merrick."

Royce stared at his younger brother, the hands at his sides unclenching as he turned to contemptuously survey Jenny's dirty face. "Either you've been fooled, Stefan, or the land rings with false rumors, for 'tis said Merrick's daughter is the rarest beauty in the land."

"Nay, I wasn't fooled. She is truly his, I heard it from her own lips."

Catching Jenny's trembling chin between his thumb and forefinger, Royce stared hard at her smudged face, studying it by the firelight while his brows drew together and his lips twisted into a mirthless smile. "How could anyone possibly call you a beauty?" he said with deliberate, insulting sarcasm. "The jewel of Scotland?"

He saw the flare of anger his words brought to her face as she jerked it out of his grasp, but instead of being touched by her courage, he was angered by it. Everything about the name Merrick infuriated him, making vengeance boil up inside him, and he grasped her pale, smudged face and jerked it back to his. "Answer me!" he demanded in an awful voice.

In her state of near hysteria, it seemed to Brenna that Jenny was somehow accepting blame that was rightfully Brenna's and, groping at Jenny's gown, using it for leverage, she hauled herself to an unsteady, standing position, then she molded her body to Jenny's entire right side, like twins fused together at birth.

"They don't call Jenny that!" she croaked when it seemed as if Jenny's continued silence would surely bring terrible retribution from the terrifying giant before them. "They—they call me that."

"Who the hell are *you?*" he demanded furiously.

"She is no one!" Jenny burst out, discarding the eighth commandment in hopes that Brenna might be freed if she were believed to be a nun, rather than a Merrick. "She is merely Sister Brenna of Belkirk Abbey!"

"Is that true?" Royce demanded of Brenna.

"Yes!" Jenny cried.

"No," Brenna whispered meekly.

Clenching his hands into fists at his sides, Royce Westmoreland briefly closed his eyes. It was like a nightmare, he thought. An incredible nightmare. After a forced march, he was out of food, out of shelter, and out of patience. And now this. *Now,* he couldn't even manage to get a sensible, honest answer out of two terrified women. He was tired, he realized, exhausted from three days and nights without sleep. He turned his haggard face and blazing eyes on Brenna. "If you have any hope of surviving another hour," he informed her, correctly recognizing her as the most easily intimidated of the pair and, therefore, the least likely one to invent a lie, "you'll answer me now and with the truth." His rapier gaze stabbed into Brenna's fear-widened hazel eyes, imprisoning them. "Are you, or are you not, the daughter of Lord Merrick?"

Brenna swallowed and tried to speak but couldn't push a word past her trembling lips. Drooping with defeat, she bowed her head and meekly nodded. Satisfied, Royce shot a murderous glance at the hellcat in gentle nun's garb, then he turned to issue a curt order to his brother: "Tie them up and put them in a tent. Have Arik stand guard to protect them from the men. I want them both alive tomorrow for questioning."

I want them alive tomorrow for questioning . . . the words reverberated in Jenny's tortured mind as she lay in a tent on the ground beside poor Brenna, her wrists and feet bound with leather thongs, looking up at the cloudless, starlit sky through a hole in the top of the tent. What sort of questioning did the Wolf have in mind, she wondered as exhaustion finally overtook her fear. What means of torture would he use to exact answers from them, and what answers could he possibly want? Tomorrow, Jenny was certain, would mark the end of their lives.

"Jenny?" Brenna whispered shakily. "You don't think he means to kill us tomorrow, do you?"

"No," Jenny lied reassuringly.

Chapter Three

The Wolf's camp seemed to stir to life before the last stars faded from the sky, but Jenny had not slept more than an hour all night. Shivering beneath the thin covering of her light mantle, she stared up at the inky blue heavens, alternately apologizing to God for her many follies and begging Him to spare poor Brenna from the inevitable consequences of Jenny's foolish decision to walk up the hill at dusk yesterday.

"Brenna," she whispered when the movements of the men grew louder outside, indicating the camp was coming fully to life, "are you awake?"

"Yes."

"When the Wolf questions us, let me give the answers."

"Yes," she said again, her voice quaking.

"I'm not certain what he'll want to know, but it's bound to be something we shouldn't tell him. Perhaps I'll be able to guess why he asks a question and so know when to mislead him."

Dawn had scarcely streaked the sky with pink before two men came to untie them and to allow them both only a few minutes of privacy in the bushes in the woods on the edge of the wide clearing before they retied Jenny and led Brenna off to meet the Wolf. "Wait," Jenny gasped when she realized their intentions, "take me, please. My sister is . . . er . . . unwell."

One of them, a towering giant over seven feet tall who could only be the legendary colossus called Arik, gave her a blood-chilling look and walked off. The other guard continued leading poor Brenna away and, through the open flap of the tent, Jenny saw the lascivious looks the men in the camp were giving her as she walked through their midst, her wrists bound behind her.

The half hour Brenna was gone seemed like an eternity to Jenny, but to her enormous relief, Brenna didn't show any signs of having suffered any physical cruelty when she returned.

"Are you all right?" Jenny asked anxiously when the guard had walked away. "He didn't harm you, did he."

Brenna swallowed, shook her head, and promptly burst into tears. "No—" she cried hysterically, "although he grew very angry because I—I couldn't stop w-weeping. I was so very scared, Jenny, and he's so huge, and so fierce, and I couldn't s-stop crying, which only p-pro-provoked him more."

"Don't cry," Jenny soothed. "It's all over now," she lied. Lying, she thought sadly, was beginning to come very easily to her.

Stefan threw back the flap of Royce's tent and walked inside. "My God, she's a beauty," he said, referring to Brenna, who had just departed. "Too bad she's a nun."

"She's not," Royce snapped irritably. "She managed, between bouts of weeping, to explain she's a 'novice.'"

"What's that?"

Royce Westmoreland was a battle-hardened warrior whose firsthand knowledge of religious rights was virtually nonexistent. His entire world, since he was a boy, had been military, and so he translated Brenna's tearful explanation into military terms he understood: "Apparently, a novice is a volunteer who hasn't completed his training or sworn fealty to his liege lord yet."

"Do you believe she tells the truth about that?"

Royce grimaced and swallowed more of his ale. "She's too frightened to lie. For that matter, she's too frightened to talk."

Stefan's eyes narrowed in what might have been jealousy over the girl or merely annoyance at his brother's failure to learn more of value. "And too beautiful to question too harshly?"

Royce sent him a sardonic look, but his mind was on the matter at hand. "I want to know how well fortified Merrick castle is, as well as the lay of its land—anything we can learn that will be of help. Otherwise, you'll have to make that trip to Merrick you started on yesterday." He set the tankard down with a resolute thud upon the trestle table. "Have the sister brought to me," he said with deathly finality.

Brenna scooted backward in terror when the giant, Arik, entered their tent, the earth seeming to tremble with each of his footsteps. *"Nay, please,"* she whispered desperately. "Don't take me back before him."

Ignoring Brenna completely, he stalked over to Jenny, clenched her arm in his enormous fist and hauled her to her feet. Legend, Jenny realized a little hysterically, had not exaggerated the size of Arik's war axe: its handle *was* as thick as a stout tree limb.

The Wolf was pacing restlessly within the confines of his large tent, but he stopped abruptly when Jenny was thrust inside, his silver eyes raking over her as she stood proudly erect, her hands bound behind her. Although her face was carefully expressionless, Royce was amazed to see veiled contempt in the blue eyes staring defiantly into his. Contempt—and not a trace of tears. Suddenly he recalled what he'd heard of Merrick's eldest girl. The younger was called the "Jewel of Scotland," but legend had it that this one was a cold, proud heiress with a dowry so rich, and bloodlines so noble, that no man was above her touch. Not only that, she was purported to be a plain girl who'd scorned the only offer of marriage she was likely to receive and had then been sent to a nunnery by her father. With her face streaked all over with dirt, it was impossible to tell how "plain" she was, but she certainly didn't possess her sister's angelic beauty and temperament. The other girl had wept piteously—this one was glaring at him. "God's teeth, are you truly sisters?"

Her chin lifted higher. "Yes."

"Amazing," he said in a derisive voice. "Are you *full* sisters?" he asked suddenly as if puzzled. "Answer me!" he snapped when she remained stubbornly silent.

Jenny, who was far more terrified than she showed, suddenly doubted he meant to torture her or put her to death at the end of an interview which began with innocuous questions about her genealogy. "She is my stepsister," she admitted, and then a spurt of defiant courage overcame her terror. "I find it difficult to concentrate on anything when my wrists are bound behind me. It's painful and unnecessary,"

"You're right," he remarked with deliberate crudity, recalling she'd kicked him in the groin. "It's your *feet* that should be bound."

He sounded so disgruntled that amused satisfaction made her lips twitch. Royce saw it and could not believe his eyes. Grown men, warriors, quailed in his presence, but this young girl with the haughty stance and stubborn chin was actually enjoying defying him. His curiosity and his patience abruptly evaporated. "Enough polite trivialities," he said sharply, advancing slowly on her.

Jenny's amusement vanished and she retreated a

step, then she stopped and made herself hold her ground.

"I want answers to some questions. How many men-at-arms does your father keep at Merrick castle?"

"I don't know," Jenny said flatly, then she spoiled the effect of her bravado by taking another cautious step backward.

"Does your father think I mean to march on him?"

"I don't know."

"You're trying my patience," he warned in a silky, ominous voice. "Would you prefer I ask these questions of your tender little sister instead?"

That threat had the desired effect; her defiant expression turned desperate. "Why wouldn't he think you're going to attack him? For years, there have been rumors that you're going to do it. Now, you have an excuse! Not that you *need* one." Jennifer cried, frightened past all reason when he began advancing on her again. "You're an animal! You *enjoy* killing innocent people!" When he didn't deny that he enjoyed it, Jenny felt her insides cringe.

"Now that you know that much," he said in a dangerously soft voice, "suppose you tell me how many men-at-arms your father has?"

Jenny hastily calculated that there must be at least 500 left. "Two hundred," she said.

"You stupid, reckless little fool!" Royce hissed, grabbing her arms and giving her a hard shake. "I could break you in half with my bare hands, yet you still lie to me?"

"What do you expect me to do?" Jenny cried, quaking all over, but still stubborn. "Betray my own father to you?"

"Before you leave this tent," he promised, "you'll tell me what you know of his plans—willingly or with some help from me you won't enjoy."

"I don't know how many men he's gathered," Jenny cried helplessly. "It's true," she flung out. "Until yesterday, my father hadn't seen me in two years, and before that he rarely spoke to me!"

That answer so took Royce by surprise that he stared at her. "Why not?"

"I—I displeased him," she admitted.

"I can understand why," he said bluntly, thinking her to be the most unbiddable female he'd ever had the misfortune to encounter. She also, he noticed with a start, had the softest, most inviting mouth he'd ever seen and, very possibly, the bluest eyes.

"He hasn't spoken to you, or paid the slightest heed to you in years, and yet you risk your very life to protect him from me?"

"Yes."

"Why?"

There were several, truthful and safer, answers Jenny could have given, but anger and pain were numbing her brain. "Because," she said flatly, "I despise you, and I despise everything you represent."

Royce stared at her, caught somewhere between fury, amazement, and admiration for her defiant courage. Short of murdering her, which would not give him the answers he sought, he was at a loss as to how to deal with her, and although strangling her held a certain appeal at the moment, it was out of the question. In any case, with Merrick's daughters his captives, it was possible Merrick might surrender without putting up a struggle. "Get out," he said shortly.

Needing no further urging to leave his hated presence, Jenny turned to flee from the tent, but the flap was down and she stopped.

"I said, get out!" Royce warned ominously, and she swung around.

"There's nothing I'd like better, however, I can't very well walk through canvas."

Wordlessly, he reached out and lifted the flap, then to her surprise he bent low in an insulting mockery of a bow. "Your servant ma'am. If there's anything at all

I can do to help make your stay with us more pleasant, I hope you won't hesitate to call it to my attention."

"Untie my wrists then," Jenny demanded to his utter disbelief.

"No," Royce snapped. The flap dropped down, smacking her in the backside, and Jenny bolted forward in angry surprise, then let out a stifled scream when an unseen hand shot out and caught her arm, but it was merely one of the dozen guards who were posted just outside the Wolf's tent.

By the time Jenny returned to their tent, Brenna was ashen with fright at being left alone. "I'm perfectly all right, I promise," Jenny reassured her as she awkwardly lowered herself to the ground.

Chapter Four

Fires burned at periodic intervals in the valley where the Wolf's men were still encamped that night. Standing in the open doorway of the tent, her wrists bound behind her, Jenny thoughtfully studied the activity going on all about them. "If we're going to escape, Brenna—" she began.

"Escape?" her sister repeated, gaping. "How in the name of the Blessed Mother can we possibly do that, Jenny?"

"I'm not certain, but however we do it, we shall have to do it very soon. I heard some of the men talking outside, and they think we'll be used to force Father to surrender."

"Will he do that?"

Jenny bit her lip. "I don't know. There was a time—before Alexander came to Merrick—when my kinsmen would have laid down their weapons rather than see me harmed. Now I don't matter to them."

Brenna heard the catch in her sister's voice, and though she longed to comfort Jenny, she knew Alexander had so alienated clan Merrick from their young mistress that they *didn't* care about her any more.

"They do love you, however, so it's hard to know what they'll decide or how much influence Father will have on them. However, if we can escape soon, we could reach Merrick before any decision is made, which is what we must do."

Of all the obstacles in their way, the one that worried Jenny most was the actual trip back to Merrick, which she estimated to be a two-day journey on horseback from here. Every hour they would be required to spend on the road was risky; bandits roamed everywhere, and two women alone were considered fair game even by honest men. The roads simply were not safe. Neither were the inns. The only safe lodgings were to be found at abbeys and priories, which was where all honest, respectable travelers chose to stay.

"The problem is, we don't stand a chance of escaping with our hands bound," Jenny continued aloud, as she gazed out at the busy camp. "Which means we either have to convince them to untie our wrists, or else manage to escape into the woods during mealtime when we're not bound. But if we do that, our absence will be discovered as soon as they come to collect our trays before we're very far away. Still, if that's the only chance that presents itself during the next day or two, we shall very likely have to take it," she announced cheerfully.

"Once we slip into the woods, what will we do?" Brenna asked, bravely quelling her inner terror at the thought of being alone in the woods at night.

"I'm not certain—hide somewhere, I suppose, until they give up looking for us. Or else we might be able to fool them into thinking we went east instead of north. If we could steal two of their horses, that would increase our chances of outrunning them, even if it made it more difficult to hide. The trick is to find some way to do both. We need to be able to hide *and* outrun them."

"How can we do that?" Brenna asked, her forehead knotted deeply in futile thought.

"I don't know, but we have to try something." Lost in contemplation, she stared unseeing past the tall, bearded man who had stopped talking to one of his knights and was studying her intently.

The fires had dwindled and their guard had collected their trays and retied their wrists, but still neither girl had come up with an acceptable scheme, even though they'd discussed several outlandish ones. "We *can't* just remain here like willing pawns to be used to his advantage," Jenny burst out when they were lying side by side that night. "We must escape."

"Jenny, has it occurred to you what he might do to us when—if," she amended quickly, "he catches us?"

"I *don't* think he'd kill us," Jenny reassured her after a moment's contemplation. "We wouldn't be any use to him as hostages if we were dead. Father would insist on seeing us before agreeing to surrender, and the earl will have to produce us—alive and breathing —or else Father will tear him to shreds," Jenny said, deciding it was better, less frightening, to think of him as the earl of Claymore, rather than the Wolf.

"You're right," Brenna agreed and promptly fell asleep.

But it was several hours before Jenny could relax enough to do the same, for despite her outward show of bravery and confidence, she was more frightened than she'd ever been in her life. She was frightened for Brenna, for herself, and for her clan, and she hadn't the vaguest notion how to escape. She only knew they had to try.

As to their captor not murdering them if he caught them, that much was likely true; however, there were other—unthinkable—male alternatives to outright murder that he had at hand to retaliate against them. Her mind conjured up an image of his dark face all but hidden by at least a fortnight's growth of thick, black beard, and she shivered at the memory of those strange silver eyes as they'd looked last night with the leaping flames from the fires reflected in them. Today his eyes had been the angry gray of a stormy sky—but there had been a moment, when his eyes had shifted to her mouth, that the expression in their depths had changed—and that indefinable change had made him seem more threatening than ever before. It was his black beard, she told herself bracingly, that made him seem so frightening, for it hid his features. Without that dark beard, he'd doubtless look like any other elderly man of . . . thirty-five? Forty? She'd heard the legend of him since she was a child of three or four, so he must be very old indeed! She felt better, realizing he was old. 'Twas only his beard that made him seem alarming, she reassured herself. His beard, and his daunting height and build, and his strange, silver eyes.

Morning came and still she'd come up with no truly feasible plan that would satisfy their need to make all speed as well as hide and to avoid being set upon by bandits, or worse. "If only we had some men's clothing," Jenny said, not for the first time, "then we'd have a much better chance, both to escape and to reach our destination."

"We can't very well just ask our guard to lend us his," Brenna said a little desperately, as fear overwhelmed even her placid disposition. "I *wish* I had my sewing," she added with a ragged sigh. "I'm so jumpy I can hardly sit still. Besides, I always think most clearly when I've my needle in my hand. Do you suppose our guard would secure a needle for me if I asked him very nicely to do it?"

"Hardly," Jenny replied absently, plucking at the hem of her habit as she gazed out at the men tramping about in war-torn clothes. If anyone needed a needle and thread, it was those men. "Besides, what would you sew with the—" Jenny's voice dropped but her spirits soared, and it was all she could do to smooth the joyous smile from her face as she turned slowly to Brenna. "Brenna," she said in a carefully offhand voice, "you're quite right to ask the guard to secure you a needle and thread. He seems nice enough, and I know he finds you lovely. Why don't you call him over and ask him to get us *two* needles."

Jenny waited, laughing inwardly as Brenna went to the flap of the tent and motioned to the guard. Soon she would tell Brenna the plan, but not yet; Brenna's face would give her away if she tried to lie.

"It's a different guard—I don't know this one at all," Brenna whispered in disappointment as the man came toward her. "Shall I send him to fetch the nice guard?"

"By all means," Jenny said, grinning.

Sir Eustace was with Royce and Stefan looking over some maps when he was informed by the guard that the ladies were asking for him. "Is there no end to her arrogance!" Royce bit out, referring to Jenny. "She even sends her guards on errands, and what's more, they run to do her bidding." Checking his tirade, he said shortly, "I assume it was the blue-eyed one with the dirty face who sent you?"

Sir Lionel chuckled and shook his head. "I saw two *clean* faces, Royce, but the one who talked to me had greenish eyes, not blue."

"Ah, I see," Royce said sarcastically, "it wasn't Arrogance that sent you trotting away from your post, it was Beauty. What does she want?"

"She wouldn't tell me. Wants to see Eustace, she said."

"Get back to your post and stay there. Tell her to wait," he snapped.

"Royce, they're no more than two helpless females," the knight reminded him, "and small ones at that. What's more, you won't trust anyone to guard them except Arik or one of us," he said, referring to the knights who made up Royce's elite personal guard and were also trusted friends. "You're keeping them bound and under guard like they were dangerous men, able to overpower us and escape."

"I can't trust anyone else with the women," Royce said, absently rubbing the back of his neck. Abruptly, he lurched out of his chair. "I'm tired of the inside of this tent. I'll go with you and see what they want."

"So will I," Stefan said.

Jenny saw the earl coming, his long effortless strides bringing him swiftly toward their tent, two guards on his right and his brother on the left.

"Well?" Royce said, stepping into their tent with the three men. "What is it this time?" he demanded of Jenny.

Brenna whirled around in panic, her hand over her heart, her face a picture of flustered innocence as she hastened to take the blame for annoying him. "I—it was *I* who asked for him." She nodded in the direction of the guard. "For Sir Eustace."

With a sigh of impatience, Royce withdrew his gaze from Jenny and looked at her foolish sister. "Would you care to tell me *why* you did?"

"Yes."

It was actually all she was going to say, Royce realized. "Very well, then *tell* me."

"I . . . we"—she cast a look of sheer misery at Jenny, then plunged ahead—"we . . . would like very much to be given thread and needles."

Royce's gaze swung suspiciously to the person most likely to have conceived some way of using needles to his own physical discomfort, but today Lady Jennifer Merrick returned his gaze levelly, her face subdued, and he felt an odd sense of disappointment that her bravado had been depleted so quickly. "Needles?" he repeated, frowning at her.

"Yes," Jenny answered in a carefully modulated voice that was neither challenging nor submissive, but

43

calmly polite as if she'd quietly accepted her fate. "The days grow long and we have little to do. My sister, Brenna, suggested we spend the time sewing."

"Sewing?" Royce repeated, disgusted with himself for keeping them bound and under heavy guard. Lionel was right—Jenny was merely a small female. A young, reckless, headstrong girl with more bravado than sense. He'd overestimated her simply because no other prisoner brought before him had *dared* to strike him. "What do you think this is, the queen's drawing room?" he snapped. "We don't have any of those—" His brain stalled as he searched for the names of the contraptions which women at court spent hours of every day sewing upon with embroidery thread.

"Embroidery hoops?" Jenny provided helpfully.

His eyes raked over her in disgust. "I'm afraid not—no embroidery hoops."

"Perhaps a small quilting frame then?" she added, innocently widening her eyes as she held back her laughter.

"No!"

"There must be *something* we could use needle and thread on," Jenny added swiftly when he turned to leave. "We'll go quite mad with nothing to do, day after day. It doesn't matter *what* we sew. Surely you must have something that needs sewing—"

He swung around, looking startled and pleased and dubious. "You're volunteering to do *mending* for us?"

Brenna was a picture of innocent shock at his suggestion; Jenny tried to imitate her look. "I hadn't thought of mending exactly . . ."

"There's enough mending needed here to keep a hundred seamstresses busy for a year," Royce said decisively, deciding in that moment they ought to earn their bed and board—such as it was—and mending was exactly the right form of payment. Turning to Godfrey, he said, "See to it."

Brenna looked wonderfully stricken that her suggestion could have resulted in their practically joining forces with the enemy; Jenny made a serious effort to look balky, but the moment the four men were out of earshot, she threw her arms around her sister and hugged her exuberantly. "We've just overcome two of the three obstacles to our escape," she said. "Our hands will be unbound and we're to have access to *disguises,* Brenna."

"Disguises?" Brenna began, but before Jenny needed to answer, her eyes widened with comprehension and she enfolded her sister into a second hug, laughing softly. "Men's clothing," she giggled, "and *he* offered it to us."

Within an hour, their tent contained two miniature mountains of clothing and a third mountain of torn blankets and mantles belonging to the men-at-arms. One pile of clothing belonged exclusively to Royce and Stefan Westmoreland, the other to Royce's knights, two of whom Jenny was relieved to see were men of medium to small proportions.

Jenny and Brenna worked late into the night, their eyes straining in the flickering light. They'd already mended the items they'd chosen to wear for their escape and put them out of sight. Now they were diligently working on the pile of clothes belonging to Royce. "What time do you suppose it is?" Jenny asked as she carefully sewed the wrist of his shirt completely closed. Beside her were many other items of his clothing which had received equally creative alterations, including several pairs of hose which had been skillfully tightened at the knee to make it impossible for a leg to descend beyond that point.

"Ten o'clock, or so," Brenna answered as she bit off her thread. "You were right," she said smiling as she held up one of the earl's shirts which now had a skull and crossbones embroidered on the back in black. "He'll never notice when he puts it on." Jenny laughed, but Brenna was suddenly lost in thought. "I've been thinking about the MacPherson," Brenna said and Jenny paid attention, for when Brenna wasn't overwhelmed by fear, she was actually very clever. "I don't think you'll have to marry the Mac-Pherson, after all."

"Why do you say that?"

"Because Father will undoubtedly notify King James—maybe even the pope—that we were abducted from an abbey, and that may cause such an uproar that King James will send his forces to Merrick. An abbey is inviolable and we were under the protection of it. And so, if King James comes to our aid, we wouldn't need the MacPherson's clans, would we?"

A flame of hope ignited in Jenny's eyes, then wavered. "I don't think we were actually on the grounds of the abbey."

"Father won't know that, so he'll assume we were. So will everyone else, I think."

His brow furrowed in puzzlement, Royce stood outside his tent, his gaze turned on the smaller tent at the edge of the camp where his two female hostages were being kept. Eustace had just relieved Lionel and was standing guard.

The faint glow of candlelight seeping between the canvas and ground told Royce both women were still awake. Now in the relative peace of the moonlit night, he admitted to himself that part of the reason he'd gone to their tent earlier today was curiosity. As soon as he learned Jennifer's face was clean, he'd felt an undeniable curiosity to have a look at it. Now, he discovered he was ridiculously curious about the color of her hair. Judging by her winged brows, her hair was either auburn or brown, while her sister was definitely blond, but Brenna Merrick didn't interest him.

Jennifer did.

She was like a puzzle whose pieces he had to wait to see one at a time, and each piece was more surprising than the last.

She'd obviously heard the usual stories about his alleged atrocities, yet she was not half so afraid of him as most men were. That was the first and most intriguing piece of the puzzle—the entire girl. Her courage and lack of fear.

Then, there were her eyes—enormous, captivating eyes of a deep, rich blue that made him think of velvet. Amazing eyes. Candid and expressive with long russet eyelashes. Her eyes had made him want to see her face, and today when he had, he could scarce believe rumor called her plain.

She wasn't beautiful precisely, and "pretty" didn't quite suit her either, but when she'd looked up at him in the tent today he'd felt stunned. Her cheekbones were high and delicately molded, her skin was as smooth as alabaster, tinted with pale rose, her nose small. In contrast to these delicate features, her small chin had a decidedly stubborn bluntness to it, and yet when she smiled, he could have sworn he saw two tiny dimples.

Altogether it was an intriguing, alluring face, he decided. Definitely alluring. And that was *before* he allowed himself to remember her soft, generous lips.

Dragging his thoughts from Jennifer Merrick's lips, he lifted his head and looked inquiringly at Eustace. Understanding the unspoken question, Eustace turned slightly so the campfire would illuminate his features, and held up his right hand as if a needle was delicately poised between his two fingers, then he moved his arm, letting it rise and fall in the steady, undulating motion of sewing.

The girls were sewing. Royce found that notion rather difficult to comprehend, given the lateness of the hour. His own experience with wealthy women was that they sewed special items for their families and their homes, but they left mending for servants to do. He supposed, as he tried unsuccessfully to make out Jennifer's shadowed form against the canvas of the tent, that wealthy women might also sew to keep busy when they were bored. But not this late and by candlelight.

How very industrious the Merrick girls were, he thought with a tinge of sarcasm and disbelief. How nice of them to want to aid their captors by keeping their clothes in good repair. How generous.

How utterly unlikely.

Particularly in the case of Lady Jennifer Merrick, whose hostility he'd already experienced firsthand.

Shoving away from his tent, Royce strolled forward, wending his way past his exhausted, battle-scarred men sleeping on the ground, rolled up in their cloaks. As he neared the women's tent, the obvious answer to their sudden compulsion to have needles and shears suddenly struck him, and he stifled a curse as he quickened his pace. They were undoubtedly destroying the clothing they'd been given, he realized angrily!

Brenna stifled a scream of terrified surprise when the Wolf yanked the tent flap back and ducked inside, but Jenny merely started and then slowly rose to her feet, a suspiciously polite expression on her features.

"Let's see what you've been doing," Royce snapped, his gaze slashing from Brenna, whose hand rose protectively to her throat, to Jenny. "Show me!"

"Very well," Jenny said with sham innocence. "I was only now beginning to work on this shirt," she prevaricated as she carefully laid aside his shirt with the armholes she'd just sewn closed. Reaching to the pile of clothing she intended to wear, she held up a pair of thick woolen hose for his inspection and pointed to the neatly mended, two-inch rent down the front.

Completely baffled, Royce stared at the nearly invisible, tight seam she'd sewn. Proud, haughty, undisciplined, and headstrong she was, he admitted to himself, but she was also a damned expert seamstress.

"Does it pass your inspection, milord?" she prompted with a tinge of amusement. "May we keep our jobs, sire?"

If she'd been anyone else but his captive and the haughty daughter of his enemy, Royce would have been sorely tempted to lift her in his arms and kiss her soundly for her badly needed help. "You do excellent work," he admitted fairly. He started to leave, then he turned back, his arm holding the tent flap back. "My men would have been cold, their clothing torn and inadequate for the coming harsh weather. They'll be happy to know that what they have is at least wearable until the winter clothing arrives here."

Jenny had foreseen that he might realize how dangerous she and Brenna could be with a pair of shears, and that he might also arrive to inspect their work, hence she'd had the hose readily available to put him off the track. She had not, however, expected him to pay her an honest compliment, and she felt somehow uneasy and betrayed now that he'd shown he had at least one drop of humanity in his body.

When he left, both girls sank back down upon the rugs. "Oh dear," Brenna said apprehensively, her eyes on the pile of blankets in the corner that they had slashed to ribbons. "Somehow, I haven't thought of the men here as—people."

Jenny refused to admit she'd been thinking the same way. "They are our enemy," she reminded them both. "Our enemy, and papa's enemy, and King James's enemy." Despite that stated belief, Jenny's hand recoiled from the scissors when she reached out to touch them, but then she made herself pick them up and stoically hacked away at another cloak while she tried to decide the very best plan for their escape tomorrow morning.

Long after Brenna had fallen into an exhausted slumber, Jenny lay awake, considering all the things that could go right—and wrong.

Chapter Five

Frost lay sparkling on the grass, lit by the first rays of the rising sun, and Jenny arose silently, careful not to awaken poor Brenna any sooner than was necessary. After systematically reviewing all the alternatives, she'd arrived at the best possible plan, and she felt almost optimistic about their chances to make good an escape.

"Is it time?" Brenna whispered, her voice choked with fright as she rolled onto her back and saw Jenny already wearing the thick woolen hose, man's shirt, and jerkin that they'd each be wearing beneath their habits when their guard escorted them into the woods where they were allowed a few minutes' privacy to tend to their personal needs each morning.

"It's time," Jenny said with an encouraging smile.

Brenna paled, but she arose and with shaking hands, she began to dress. "I wish I weren't such a coward," Brenna whispered, her hand clutched over her pounding heart as she reached with her free hand for the leather jerkin.

"You're not a coward," Jenny assured her, keeping her voice low, "you simply worry to great excess—

and well in advance—about the possible consequences of anything you do. In fact," she added, as she helpfully tied the strings at the throat of Brenna's borrowed shirt, "you're actually braver than I. For if I was as frightened of consequences as you are, I'd never have the courage to dare the slightest thing."

Brenna's wavery smile was silent appreciation for the compliment, but she said nothing.

"Do you have your cap?"

When Brenna nodded, Jenny picked up the black cap she herself would soon put on to hide her long hair, and she lifted up her gray habit, tucking the cap in the waist of her hose. The sun rose a little higher, turning the sky a watery gray as the girls waited for the moment when the giant would appear to escort them to the woods, their loose convent robes hiding the men's clothes they wore beneath.

The moment drew near, and Jenny lowered her voice to a hush as she reiterated their plan for the last time, afraid lest Brenna forget what she must do in the fright of the moment. "Remember," she said, "every second will count, but we must not appear to move too quickly or we'll draw notice. When you remove your habit, hide it well beneath the brush. Our best hope for escape lies in their looking for two nuns, not two boys. If they spot our habits, they'll catch us before we can leave the camp."

Brenna nodded and swallowed, and Jenny went on. "Once we're free of our habits, keep your eyes on me and move quietly through the brush. Don't listen to anything else or look at anything else. When they realize we're gone, they'll raise a shout, but it means nothing to us, Brenna. Don't be frightened of the uproar."

"I won't," Brenna said, her eyes already huge with fright.

"We'll stay in the woods and move around the south border of the camp to the pen where the horses are kept. The searchers won't expect us to head back toward the camp, they'll be looking for us in the opposite direction—moving into the woods.

"When we near the pen, you stay just inside the woods, and I'll bring the horses. With luck, whoever watches the mounts will be more interested in the search for us than he is the horses."

Brenna nodded silently and Jenny considered how best to phrase the rest of what she must say. She knew that if they were seen, it would be up to her to try to create a diversion so that Brenna could make good her own escape, but convincing Brenna to go on without her was not going to be easy. In a low, urgent voice, Jenny said finally, "Now then, in case we become separated—"

"Nay!" Brenna burst out. "We won't. We can't."

"Listen to me!" Jenny whispered so sternly that Brenna swallowed the rest of her protest. "If we become separated, you must know the rest of the plan so that I can—catch up with you later." When Brenna nodded reluctantly, Jenny took both her sister's clammy hands in her own and squeezed them tightly, trying to infuse some of her own courage into Brenna. "North is toward that high hill—the one behind the pen where the horses are kept. Do you know which one I mean?"

"Yes."

"Good. Once I've gotten the horses and we're mounted, we're going to stay in the woods, working our way to the north, till we've topped the hill. Once there, we'll angle west as we head down the hill, but we must remain in the woods. When we're in sight of a road, we'll ride parallel to it, but we'll need to stay in the woods. Claymore will probably send someone to watch the roads, but they'll be looking for two nuns from Belkirk Abbey, not two young men. If we're lucky, we'll meet up with some travelers and join their group, which will add to our disguise and increase our chances of success.

"Brenna, there's one thing more. If they recognize

us and give chase, you head as fast as you can in the direction I just told you, and I'll veer off in another direction and lead them away from you. If that happens, stay under cover as much as you can. It's no more than five or six hours to the abbey, but if I am caught, you must go on without me. I don't know where we are now. I assume we're across the border in England. Ride north by northwest and when you come to a village, ask for direction to Belkirk."

"I can't just leave you," Brenna cried softly.

"You must—so that you can bring father and our kinsmen to my rescue."

Brenna's face cleared slightly as she understood she'd be ultimately helping Jenny, not abandoning her, and Jenny gave her a bright smile. "I feel certain we'll be at Merrick keep together by Saturday."

"Merrick keep?" Brenna blurted. "Should we not remain at the abbey and send someone else to inform father of what has happened?"

"You can stay at the abbey if you wish, and I'll ask Mother Ambrose for an escort so I can continue on home sometime today or tonight. Father will surely think we're hostages here, so I must reach him at once, before he accepts their terms. Besides, he'll have questions to ask about how many men there are here, what arms they bear—things like that, which only we can answer."

Brenna nodded, but that was not the entire reason Jenny wished to go in person to Merrick keep, and they both knew it. More than anything, Jenny wanted to do something to make her father and her clan proud of her, and this was her golden opportunity. When and if she succeeded, she wanted to be there to see it in their eyes.

The guard's footsteps sounded outside, and Jenny stood up, a polite, even conciliatory, smile fixed on her face. Brenna stood up, looking like she was about to face certain death.

"Good morning," Jenny said as Sir Godfrey escorted them toward the woods. "I feel as if I haven't yet slept."

Sir Godfrey, a man of perhaps thirty, cast an odd look at her—undoubtedly, Jenny thought, because she'd never spoken a civil word to him; then she stiffened as his frowning gaze seemed to drift down her habit, padded now with men's clothes beneath it.

"You slept little," he said, evidently aware of their late-night efforts with a needle.

Their footsteps were muffled by damp grass, as Jenny walked on his left with Brenna stumbling along on her other side.

Feigning a yawn, she cast a sidelong glance at him. "My sister is feeling rather peaked this morn from our late hours. 'Twould be very nice for us if we were permitted a few extra minutes to refresh ourselves at the stream?"

His deeply creased, sun-bronzed face, turned to her, watching her with a mixture of suspicion and uncertainty, then he nodded agreeably.

"Fifteen minutes," he said and Jenny's spirits soared, "but I want to be able to see the head of at least one of you."

He stood sentinel at the edge of the woods, his profile turned to them, his eyes, Jenny knew, dropping no lower than the top of their heads. So far, none of their guards had exhibited a lustful desire to glimpse them in any state of partial undress, for which she was particularly grateful today. "Stay calm," Jenny urged, leading Brenna directly toward the stream. Once there, she walked along the bank of the stream, moving as far into the woods as she dared without giving Sir Godfrey cause to barge into the woods in pursuit, then she stopped beneath the low limb of a tree that hung above a stand of brush.

"The water looks cold, Brenna," Jenny called, raising her voice so the guard could hear and would hopefully feel no need to watch them too closely. As she spoke, Jenny stood beneath the branch of the tree and carefully loosened her veil and wimple, nodding to Brenna to do the same. When both short veils had been removed, Jenny carefully ducked down, holding the veil above her head as if her head were still in it, and gingerly hung it on the limb just above her. Satisfied, she crouched and moved swiftly to Brenna who was likewise holding her headpiece above her head, and took it from Brenna's shaking fingers, attaching it as best she could to the bush.

Two minutes later, both girls had shed their habits and were stuffing them beneath the brush, heaping leaves and twigs over the gray cloth to hide it from view. In a moment of inspiration, Jenny reached into the pile of clothing and twigs and snatched out her handkerchief. Pressing her finger to her lips, she winked at Brenna and bent low, scurrying in a crouch until she was about fifteen yards downstream, in the opposite direction they intended to go. Pausing only long enough to attach the white handkerchief to a thorny branch, as if she'd lost it in flight, she turned back and raced toward Brenna.

"That ought to mislead them and get us much more time," she said. Brenna nodded, looking doubtful and hopeful at the same time, and the two women looked at one another for a moment, each checking the other's appearance. Brenna reached up and pulled Jenny's cap lower over her ears and tucked in a stray wisp of red gold hair and nodded.

With a smile of appreciation and encouragement, Jenny grabbed Brenna's hand and led her swiftly into the woods, moving north, keeping to the perimeter of the camp, praying that Godfrey would give them the full fifteen minutes he promised, and perhaps more.

A few minutes later they had worked their way around behind the pen where the horses were cordoned off, and they were crouched low in the brush, catching their breath. "Stay here and don't move!" Jenny said, her gaze scanning the immediate vicinity for the guard she felt certain would have been stationed near the warhorses. She saw him then, fast asleep on the ground on the far side of the pen. "The guard's asleep at his post," she whispered jubilantly, turning to Brenna, then she added quietly, "If he awakens and catches me trying to take the horses, follow our plan on foot. Do you understand? Stay in the woods and head for that high hill behind us."

Without waiting for an answer, Jenny crawled forward. At the edge of the woods, she paused to look around. The camp was still partially asleep, lulled by the overcast gray morning into believing it was earlier than it was. The horses were nearly within arm's reach.

The guard stirred only once in his sleep as Jenny quietly caught two restive horses by their halters and led them toward the rope that formed the pen. Standing awkwardly on tiptoe, she lifted the rope high enough for the horses to walk beneath it, and in two short minutes, she had handed one of the animals to Brenna and they were quickly leading them deeper into the woods, their hooves silenced by the thick mulch of damp leaves provided by the dewy morning.

Jenny could scarcely suppress her smile of jubilation as they led the horses to a fallen tree and, using that for height, they climbed upon the huge steeds' backs. They were well on their way toward the high ridge when the dim sounds of an alarm being sounded went up behind them.

The din created by that negated the need for quiet, and at the sounds of the men's shouts, both girls simultaneously dug their heels into their steeds' flanks and sent them bounding forward, flying through the woods.

They were both expert horsewomen, and they both adapted easily to riding astride. The lack of a saddle was something of a hindrance, however, because without one it was necessary to grip tightly with the knees, which the destriers took as a signal for speed, which necessitated hanging onto the horse's halter for dear life. Ahead of them was the high ridge, and then eventually, on the other side, a road, the abbey, and, finally, Merrick keep. They stopped briefly so that Jennifer could try to get her bearings, but the forest obscured what little sunlight there was, and Jenny gave up, forced to go on instincts. "Brenna," she said, grinning as she patted the satiny, thick neck of the enormous black warhorse she rode. "Think back on the legends about the Wolf—about his horse. Is it not said his name is Thor and that he's the fastest destrier in the land? As well as the most agile?"

"Aye," Brenna answered, shivering a little in the cool dawn as the horses began picking their way through the dense forest.

"And," Jenny continued, "is it not said he's as black as sin with only a white star on his forehead for a marking?"

"Aye."

"And does this horse have such a star?"

Brenna looked round and then nodded.

"Brenna," Jenny said, laughing softly, "I've stolen the black Wolf's mighty Thor!"

The animal's ears flickered at the sound of his name, and Brenna forgot her worries and burst out laughing.

"That's undoubtedly why he was tied and kept separate from the others," Jenny added gaily, her gaze roaming appreciatively over the magnificent animal. "That also explains why, when we first rode away from camp, he was ever so much faster than the horse you're riding, and I kept having to hold him back." Leaning forward, she patted his neck again. "What a beauty you are," she whispered, harboring no ill will for the horse—only for his former owner.

"Royce—" Godfrey stood in Royce's tent, his deep voice gruff with chagrin, an embarrassed flush creeping up his thick, tanned neck. "The women have . . . er . . . escaped, about three-quarters of an hour ago——Arik, Eustace, and Lionel are searching the woods."

Royce paused in the act of reaching for a shirt, his face almost comical in its expression of disbelief as he stared at the most wily and fiercest of his knights. "They've *what?*" he said, an incredulous smile mixed with dawning annoyance sweeping across his face. "Do you mean to tell me," he jibed, angrily snatching the shirt from the pile of clothing the girls had mended last night, "that you let two naive girls outwit——" He rammed his arm into the sleeve, then stared in furious disbelief at a wrist opening that refused to part so his fist could pass through it. Swearing savagely under his breath, he snatched up another, checked the wrist to ascertain it was all right, and shoved his arm into it. The entire sleeve parted from the body of the shirt and fell away as if by magic. "I *swear to God,*" he bit out between his teeth, "when I get my hands on that blue-eyed witch, I'll——" Flinging that shirt aside, he stalked over to a chest and pulled out a fresh one, jerked it on, too infuriated to finish his sentence. Reaching automatically for his short sword, he buckled it on and stalked past Godfrey. "Show me where you last saw them," he snapped.

"It was here, in the woods," Godfrey said. "Royce——" he added, as he showed him to the place where two veils were hanging crazily from branches without heads underneath them. "It . . . er . . . won't be necessary for the other men to hear of this, will it?"

A brief smile flickered in Royce's eyes as he shot a wry look at the big man, understanding at once that Godfrey's pride had suffered a grievous blow and that he hoped it could remain a private one. "There's no need to sound an alarm," Royce said, his long legs carrying him along the bank of the stream, his gaze delving into the trees and searching the brush. "It'll be easy enough to find them."

An hour later, he wasn't so sure of that, and his

amusement had been replaced by anger. He needed those women as hostages. They were the key that would open the gates to Merrick keep, perhaps without bloodshed and the loss of valuable men.

Together the five men combed the woods, working eastward in the belief that one of the girls had lost her handkerchief in flight, but when no trail could be found leading away from the spot, Royce reached the conclusion that one of the girls—the blue-eyed wench, no doubt—might actually have had the presence of mind to place the white scrap of cloth there in a deliberate attempt to mislead them. It was incongruous—incredible. But, apparently, true.

With Godfrey on one side and a scornful Arik on the other, Royce stalked past the two gray veils and snatched them furiously off their branches. "Sound an alarm and form a party to search every inch of these woods," he snapped as he passed the girls' tent. "No doubt they're hiding in the thicket. These woods are so dense, we may have walked right past them."

Twoscore men formed a line the length of their combined, outstretched hands and began to comb the woods, starting at the edge of the stream and moving slowly forward, looking beneath every bush and fallen log. The minutes became one hour, and then two, until, finally, it was afternoon.

Standing at the bank of the stream where the girls had last been seen, Royce squinted at the densely wooded hills to the north, his expression becoming more harsh with each passing moment that his captives remained missing. The wind had picked up and the sky was leaden.

Stefan walked up to him, having just returned from the hunting expedition he'd taken out last night. "I hear the women escaped this morning," he said, worriedly following Royce's gaze to the highest hill to the north. "Do you think they actually made it to yon ridge?"

"They haven't had time to get there on foot," Royce

answered, his voice harsh with anger. "But in case they took the longer route around it, I sent men out to check the road. They questioned every traveler they encountered, but no one has seen two young women. A cottager saw two boys riding into the hills on horseback and that was all.

"Wherever they are, they're bound to lose their way if they head into those hills—there isn't enough sun to use as a compass. Secondly, they don't know where they are so they can't know which direction to go."

Stefan was silent, his eyes searching the distant hills, then he looked sharply at Royce. "When I rode into camp just now, I wondered if you'd decided to go hunting on your own last night."

"Why?" Royce said shortly.

Stefan hesitated, knowing that Royce prized the mighty black warhorse for his enormous courage and loyalty more than he valued many people. In fact, Thor's feats in the lists and on the battlefield were nearly as legendary as his owner's. One famous lady at court had once complained to her friends that if Royce Westmoreland showed her half the affection he showed his damned horse, she'd count herself lucky. And Royce had replied, with typical acid sarcasm, that if the lady had half the loyalty and heart of his horse, he'd have married her.

There wasn't a man in Henry's army who would have dared to take Royce's horse out of the pen for a gallop. Which meant someone else had.

"Royce . . ."

Royce turned at the hesitancy he heard in his brother's voice, but his gaze was suddenly drawn to the ground beside Stefan where leaves and twigs formed an unnaturally high mound at the base of a bush. Some sixth sense made him poke at the mound with the toe of his boot—and then he saw it—the unmistakable somber gray of a nun's habit. Bending, he reached out and snatched at the cloth, just as Stefan added, "Thor isn't in the pen with our other horses. The girls must have taken him without the guard noticing."

Royce straightened slowly, his jaw clenched as he looked at the discarded garments, his voice edged with fury. "We've been looking for two nuns on foot. We should have been looking for two short *men*, mounted on *my* horse." Swearing under his breath, Royce turned on his heel and stalked toward the pen where the horses were kept. As he passed the girls' tent, he hurtled the gray habits at the open tent flap in a sharp gesture of fury and disgust, then he broke into a run with Stefan following at his heels.

The guard standing sentry at the huge horse pen saluted his liege lord, then stepped back in alarm as the Wolf reached out and caught him by the front of his jerkin, lifting him off the ground. "Who was on guard at dawn this morning?"

"I—I, milord."

"Did you desert your post?"

"Nay! Milord, no!" he cried, knowing the penalty for that in the king's army was death.

Royce flung him aside in disgust. Within minutes, a party of twelve men, with Royce and Stefan in the lead, galloped down the road, heading north. When they came to the steep hills that lay between the camp and the north road, Royce reined in sharply, calling out instructions. Assuming the women hadn't met with some accident or lost their direction, Royce knew they would already have made their way down the far side and climbed the next ridge. Even so, he dispatched four men with instructions to comb these hills from one side to the other.

With Stefan and Arik and the remaining five men at his side, Royce dug his spurs into his mount and sent the gelding flying down the road at a run. Two hours later, they rounded the hill and came to the north road. One fork led northeast, the other angled northwest. Frowning in indecision, Royce signaled his men to stop as he considered which route the women might have taken. Had they not had the presence of mind to leave that damned handkerchief in the woods in order to mislead their captors into searching in the wrong direction, he'd have taken all his men up the northwest fork. As it was, he couldn't dismiss the possibility that they'd deliberately taken a road that would lead them a half day's journey out of their way. It would cost them time but gain them safety, Royce knew. Still, he doubted if they *knew* which direction led back to their home. He glanced at the sky; there were only about two more hours of daylight left. The northwest road appeared to climb into the hills in the distance. The shortest route was also the most difficult to traverse at night. Two women, frightened and vulnerable even though dressed as men, would surely take the safest, easiest road even though it was longer. His decision made, he sent Arik and the remaining men to search a twenty-mile stretch of that route.

On the other hand, Royce thought angrily as he swung his own mount toward the northwest route and signaled Stefan to follow him, that arrogant, conniving blue-eyed witch would brave the hills alone and at night. She'd dare *anything,* that one, he thought with increasing fury as he recalled how politely he'd thanked her for mending their clothes last night—and how sweetly genteel she'd been as she accepted his thanks. She knew no fear. Not yet. But when he got his hands on her, she would learn the meaning of it. She'd learn to fear *him*.

Humming gaily to herself, Jenny added more twigs to the cozy campfire she'd built using the flint she'd been given yesterday to light their sewing candles. Somewhere in the dense forest nearby, an animal howled eerily at the rising moon, and Jenny hummed more determinedly, hiding her instinctive shudder of apprehension behind a bright, encouraging smile designed to reassure poor Brenna. The threat of rain had passed, leaving a black, starlit sky lit by a round golden moon, and for that Jenny was profoundly grateful. Rain was the *last* thing she wanted now.

The animal howled again, and Brenna tugged her horse's blanket tighter around her shoulders. "Jenny," she whispered, her eyes fastened trustingly upon her older sister. "Was that sound what I think it was?" As if the word was too unspeakable to voice, she formed the word "wolf" with her pale lips.

Jenny was reasonably certain it was several wolves, not one wolf. "Do you mean that owl we just heard?" she prevaricated, smiling.

"It wasn't an owl," Brenna said, and Jenny winced with alarm as a spasm of ugly, shrill coughing seized her sister, leaving her gasping for breath. The lung ailment that had plagued Brenna almost constantly as a child was recurring tonight, aggravated by the damp cold and by her fear.

"Even if it wasn't an owl," Jenny said gently, "no predator will come near this fire—I know that for fact. Garrick Carmichael told me so one night when the three of us were on our way back from Aberdeen and the snow forced us to make camp. He built a fire and told Becky and me just that."

At the moment, the danger of building this fire concerned Jenny almost as much as the danger of wolves. A small fire, even in the forest, could be seen for a long distance and, although they were several hundred yards away from the road, she couldn't shake the feeling that their pursuers might still find them.

Trying to divert herself from her own worries, she drew her knees up to her chest, propped her chin on them and nodded toward Thor. "Have you ever in your life seen a more magnificent animal than that? At first, I thought he was going to toss me off this morning when I mounted him, but then he seemed to sense our urgency and he settled down. And all day today—it's the oddest thing—he seemed to *know* what I wanted him to do, without my ever having to urge him or guide him. Imagine papa's delight when we return, having not only escaped from the Wolf's very clutches, but with his horse, to boot!"

"You can't be certain it's his horse," Brenna said, looking like she was seized by second thoughts about the wisdom of having stolen a steed of great value and greater fame.

"Of course it is!" Jenny declared proudly. "He is exactly as the minstrels tell of him in their songs. Besides, he looks at me whenever I say his name." To illustrate, she called his name softly, and the horse raised his magnificent head, regarding her through eyes so intelligent they seemed human. "It *is* he!" Jenny said jubilantly, but Brenna seemed to cringe at the thought.

"Jenny," she whispered, her huge hazel eyes sad as they studied her sister's brave, determined smile. "Why do you suppose you have so much courage and I have so very little?"

"Because," Jenny said with a chuckle, "our Lord is a just God and, since *you* received all the beauty, He wanted to give *me* something for balance."

"Oh, but—" Brenna stopped abruptly as the great black horse suddenly lifted his head and whickered loudly into the night.

Leaping to her feet, Jenny rushed over to Thor, clamping her hand against his nose to keep him quiet. "Quickly—put the fire out, Brenna! Use the blanket." Her heart pounding in her ears, Jenny tipped her head, listening for the sounds of riders, feeling their presence even though she couldn't hear them. "Listen to me," she whispered frantically. "As soon as I mount Thor, cut your horse loose and send him crashing down into the woods in that direction, then run over here and hide beneath that fallen tree. Don't leave there or make a sound until I return."

As she spoke, Jenny was vaulting onto a log and hoisting herself up onto Thor's back. "I'm going to ride Thor out onto the road and race him up that rise. If that devil earl is out there, he'll chase me. And

Brenna," she added breathlessly, already turning Thor toward the road, "if he catches me and I don't return, take the road to the abbey and follow our plan—send papa to rescue me."

"But—" Brenna whispered, shaking in terror.

"Do it! Please!" Jenny implored and sent her horse charging through the woods toward the road, deliberately making as much noise as possible to draw any pursuers away from Brenna.

"There!" Royce shouted at Stefan, pointing to the dark speck racing toward the ridge high above, then they spurred their horses, sending them flying down the road in pursuit of the horse and rider. When they came to the spot in the road near where the girls had camped, the unmistakable smell of a newly doused fire made Royce and Stefan rein in abruptly. "Search the camp," Royce shouted, already spurring his horse to a gallop. "You'll probably find the younger girl there."

"Damn, but she can ride!" Royce breathed in near-admiration, his gaze fastened on the small figure bent low over Thor's neck as she tried unsuccessfully to stay three hundred yards ahead of him. He knew instinctively it was Jenny he was chasing, and not her timid sister—just as surely as he knew the horse was Thor. Thor was running with all his heart, but not even the gallant black stallion's speed could make up for the time he lost whenever Jennifer refused to let him jump a particularly high obstacle and made him go around it instead. Without a saddle, she was obviously in jeopardy of being unseated if she let him jump too high.

Royce had narrowed the distance to fifty yards and was closing fast when he saw Thor suddenly veer away from the path he was on and refuse to jump a fallen tree—a sure sign that he sensed danger and was trying to protect himself and his rider. A shout of alarm and terror tore from Royce's chest as he peered into the night and realized there was nothing but a steep drop and thin air beyond the fallen tree. "Jennifer, *don't!*" he shouted, but she didn't heed the warning.

Frightened to the point of hysteria, she brought the horse around again, backed him up and dug her heels into his glossy flanks, "Go!" she screamed, and after a moment's hesitation, the huge horse gathered his hindquarters beneath him and gave a mighty leap. A human scream split the night almost instantly as Jenny lost her balance and slid off the leaping horse, hanging for a suspended instant by his thick mane, before she fell with a crash into the limbs of the fallen tree. And then there was another sound—the sickening thud of a huge animal plunging down a steep incline and rolling to its death.

Jenny was climbing unsteadily from the tangle of tree limbs as Royce vaulted down from his horse and ran to the edge of the cliff. She shoved her hair out of her eyes and realized there was nothing but blackness a few feet beyond her, then she dragged her eyes to her captor, but he was staring down the steep slope, his clenched jaw as hard as granite. So unnerved and disoriented was she that she made no protest when he grabbed her arm in a painful grip and yanked her with him as he deliberately slid down the steep hill.

For a moment, Jenny couldn't imagine what he was about—and then her mind cleared a little. Thor! He was looking for his horse, she realized, her gaze flying wildly over the rugged terrain, praying somehow that the magnificent animal might not be harmed. She spotted him at the same time Royce did—the still, black form lying only a few yards away at the base of the boulder that had broken his fall, and his neck.

Royce flung her arm aside, and Jenny stayed where she stood, paralyzed with remorse and anguish as she gazed at the beautiful animal she'd inadvertently killed. As if in a dream, she watched England's fiercest warrior kneel on one knee beside his dead horse, slowly stroking the animal's glossy black coat, and speaking words she could not quite hear in a voice that was raw.

Tears blurred her eyes but when Royce stood up and swung around to face her, panic collided with her sorrow. Instinct warned her to run and she turned to flee, but she wasn't quick enough. He caught her by the hair and jerked her back, swinging her around to face him, his fingers digging cruelly into her scalp. "God *damn* you!" he bit out savagely, his glittering eyes alive with rage. "That horse you just killed had more *courage* and more *loyalty* than most men! He had so damned much of both that he *let* you send him to his death." Sorrow and terror were etched on Jenny's pale face, but they had no softening effect on her captor, who tightened his painful grip on her hair, forcing her head further back, "He knew there was nothing but thin air beyond that tree, and he *warned* you, and then he let you send him to his death!"

As if he couldn't trust himself any longer, he flung her away, caught her wrist and dragged her roughly in his wake to the top of the ridge. It dawned on Jenny that the reason he'd insisted on taking her down there was doubtlessly to prevent her from stealing his other horse. At the time, she'd been so overwrought it hadn't occurred to her to try, even if the opportunity had presented itself. Now, however, she was recovering her senses, and as he hoisted her onto the back of his horse, another opportunity did arrive. Just as the earl started to swing his leg over the horse's back, Jenny made a sudden lunge for the bridle reins, managing to snatch one out of his hand. The plan failed, for he hoisted himself effortlessly onto the running horse and then wrapped his arm around Jenny's waist in a grip that cut off her air. "Try one more trick," he whispered in her ear in a tone of such undiluted fury that she cringed, "do one more thing to annoy me," his arm tightened horribly, "and I'll make you regret it for as long as you live! Do you *understand* me?" He underlined the question by tightening his grip sharply.

"Yes!" Jenny gasped, and he slowly released the pressure against her rib cage.

Huddled beneath the fallen tree where Jenny had instructed her to remain, Brenna watched as Stefan Westmoreland rode back into the clearing, leading her horse. From her vantage point, she could see only the legs of the animals, the forest floor, and as he dismounted, the legs of the man himself. She should have run deeper into the woods, Brenna decided frantically, but if she had, she might have gotten lost. Besides, Jenny had told her to remain where she was, and in all matters such as this, Brenna faithfully and impeccably followed Jenny's instructions.

The man's legs brought him nearer. He stopped at the fire, nudging the dying embers with the toe of his boot, and Brenna sensed instinctively that his eyes were probing the dark recess of the bushes where she was hidden. He moved suddenly, walking toward her, and her chest rose and fell in frightened spasms as her lungs fought for air. Clamping her hand over her mouth, she tried to silence the coughing fit that was bursting within her while she stared in frozen terror at the tips of his boots only inches from her own.

"All right now," the deep voice boomed in the little clearing, "come out of there, milady. You've given us a merry chase, but the chase is over."

Hoping it was a trap and that he didn't actually *know* she was there, Brenna pressed further back into her hiding-hole. "Very well," he sighed, "I suppose I'll have to reach in there and fetch you." He crouched abruptly and an instant later a big hand thrust through the branches, groping around and finally closing on Brenna's breast.

A squeal of indignant horror stuck in her throat as his hand snapped open, then closed again slowly, as if he was trying to identify what he'd found. When he did identify it, he jerked his hand back in momentary shock, then thrust it forward, grabbed Brenna's arm, and hauled her out.

"Well, well, well," Stefan said, unsmiling. "It seems I've found a woodland fairy."

Brenna hadn't courage enough to strike him or bite him as Jenny had done to his brother, but she did manage to glower at him as he tossed her up onto her horse and mounted his own, holding her horse's reins in his hand.

When they emerged from the woods onto the road, Brenna breathed a prayer that Jenny had escaped, then steeled herself to look up the road to the ridge. Her heart plummeted when she saw Jenny coming toward her, mounted in front of the black Wolf on his horse. Stefan guided his horse into step beside his brother's. "Where's Thor?" he asked, but the murderous expression on Royce's face answered the question before his voice did. "Dead."

Royce rode in tight-lipped silence, growing angrier with each passing minute. Besides the deep loss he felt because of Thor, he was also tired, hungry, and thoroughly enraged because one young girl (he rightly held Brenna blameless) with *red* hair (he knew that now) had managed to dupe a wily, experienced guard, throw half an army into an uproar, and force him to spend an entire day and night recapturing her. But what infuriated him most was her unbending will, her stiff spine, and defiant manner. She was like a spoiled child who'd not admit she was wrong by breaking down and crying.

When they rode into camp, heads turned to watch them and faces relaxed, but none of the men were foolish enough to cheer. That two captives had been permitted to escape in the first place was a cause for embarrassment, not rejoicing, but that those captives were women was unthinkable. It was humiliating.

Royce and Stefan rode toward the pen and Royce dismounted, then unceremoniously hauled Jenny down. She turned to start toward her tent, then stifled a cry of pain and surprise when Royce jerked her back. "I want to know how you got the horses out of the pen without the guard seeing you."

Every man within hearing distance seemed to tense in unison and turn toward Jenny, waiting for her to answer. Until then, they'd behaved as if she was invisible, but now she squirmed under their swift, intense stares.

"Answer me!"

"I didn't have to sneak them out," Jenny said with as much dignity and contempt as she could manage. "Your guard was asleep."

A look of pained disbelief flickered in Royce's angry eyes, but his face was otherwise blank as he nodded curtly at Arik. The blond giant, his war axe in hand, walked forward through the men, heading for the recalcitrant guard. Jenny watched the unfolding tableau, wondering what was going to happen to the poor man. No doubt he'd be punished for being derelict in his duty, she knew, but the punishment wouldn't be truly terrible. Or would it? She didn't know because Royce snatched her arm and began pulling her with him.

As Royce marched her through the camp, Jenny could feel the hostile rage blazing at her from every soldier and knight she passed. She had made fools of them all by escaping and by eluding them. They hated her for that now, and their hatred was so virulent it made her skin burn. Even the earl seemed angrier at her than he'd been before, Jenny thought, as she quickened her pace to a near-run, trying to keep up with him before he pulled her arm out of its socket.

Her concern over his anger was suddenly overwhelmed by a more immediate calamity—Royce Westmoreland was taking her to his tent, not to her own.

"I won't go in there!" she cried, jerking backward. Swearing under his breath, the earl reached out and tossed her over his shoulder like a sack of flour, her buttocks pointing skyward, her long hair falling to his calves. Lewd laughter and cheers rang out all over the clearing as the men witnessed her public humiliation, and Jenny almost gagged on her fury and mortification.

Inside the tent, he dumped her onto the heap of fur rugs on the ground, then stood watching her as Jenny scrambled to a sitting position, and then to her feet, watching him like a small, cornered animal. "If you defile me, I'll kill you, I swear it," she cried, mentally recoiling from the fury that turned his face to steel and his eyes to glittery silver shards.

"Defile you?" he repeated with scathing contempt. "The last thing you awaken in me right now is lust. You're going to stay in this tent because it's already heavily guarded, and I don't have to waste more of my men's time watching yours. Furthermore, you're in the center of the camp, and if you decide to make a run for it, my men will cut you down. Is that clear?"

She glowered at him but remained stonily silent, and her arrogant refusal to submit to his will enraged Royce yet more. His fists clenched at his sides, he fought down his rage and continued, "If you do one more thing to inconvenience me or anyone else in this camp, I will personally make your life a living hell. Do you understand me?"

Looking into that harsh, sinister face, Jenny fully believed he could, and would, do it.

"Answer me!" he ordered murderously.

Realizing that he was already pushed past reason, Jenny swallowed and nodded.

"And—" he began, then broke off abruptly as if he couldn't trust himself to say more. Turning, he snatched up a flagon of wine from the table and was about to drink from it when his squire, Gawin, entered the tent. In Gawin's arms were the blankets he'd fetched earlier from the ladies' tent—blankets which he'd been handing out to the men before he realized they'd been slashed, not mended. The boy's face was a study of anger and disbelief.

"What the hell is wrong with you?" Royce snapped, the flagon arrested halfway to his lips.

Gawin raised his young, indignant face to his master. "The blankets, sire," he said, turning his accusing gaze on Jenny, "she slashed them, 'stead of mending them. The men would have been cold enough with only these blankets for protection, but now . . ."

Jenny's heart began to pound in genuine terror as the earl very slowly, very carefully, lowered the flagon and put it on the table. He spoke and his voice was a raw whisper, rasping with rage. "Come here."

Shaking her head, Jenny retreated a step.

"You're making it worse on yourself," he warned as she retreated another step. "I said, *come here.*"

Jenny would have sooner jumped off a cliff. The tent flap was up, but there was no way to escape; men had been gathering out there since Royce had carried her into the tent, waiting no doubt to hear her whimper or scream for mercy.

Royce spoke to his squire, but his dagger gaze remained on Jenny. "Gawin, bring needle and thread."

"Aye, milord," Gawin agreed and scurried over to the corner, retrieving both. He put them on the table beside Royce, then stood back and watched in surprise as Royce merely lifted up the scraps that had once been blankets and held them out to the redhaired witch who'd destroyed them.

"You're going to mend every one of them," he told Jenny in an unnaturally quiet voice.

The tension left her body and she stared at her captor with a mixture of bafflement and relief. After causing him to spend a day and night chasing her, after killing his beautiful horse and destroying his

73

clothes, the only punishment he meant to exact from her was to make her mend the blankets she'd ruined. That was making her life a living hell?

"You'll not sleep with a blanket until every one of these are repaired, do you understand?" he added, his voice as smooth and hard as polished steel. "Until my men are warm, you'll be cold."

"I—I understand," Jenny said in a wavering voice. So restrained was his manner—so *parental*—that it did not occur to her that he meant to do anything further to her. In fact, as she walked forward and reached a shaking hand toward the tattered strips of cloth he held, the thought flashed across her mind that rumor had grossly exaggerated his ruthlessness—a thought that was shattered an instant later: "Ouch!" she cried as his big hand shot out like a striking snake and locked around her outstretched wrist, yanking her forward with a force that knocked the air from her lungs and snapped her head back. "You spoiled little bitch," he bit out. "Someone should have beat that pride out of you when you were still a child. However, since they didn't, *I* will—"

His hand lifted and Jenny threw up an arm to cover her head, thinking that he meant to strike her in the face, but the huge hand she'd expected to hit her yanked her arm down. "I'd snap your neck in two if I hit you like that. I have another target in mind—"

Before Jenny could react, he sat down and in one fluid motion yanked her across his lap. "Nay!" she gasped, wriggling in furious, frightened earnest, horribly aware of the men who were gathered outside the tent, trying to hear. "Don't you dare!" she cried, as she threw all her weight toward the floor. He clamped his leg over both of hers, imprisoning them between his thighs, and lifted his hand. "This," he said, as his hand crashed down against her backside, "is for my horse." Jenny counted through waves of pain, biting her lip until it bled in an effort to strangle her sobbing cries, as his hand rose and fell with relentless pain, again and again and again. "This is for your destructiveness . . . your stupid escape . . . the blankets you ruined . . ."

Intending to thrash her until she sobbed and pleaded with him to stop, Royce continued until his hand ached, but even though she squirmed frantically to avoid his hand, she never made a sound. In fact, if her whole body hadn't jerked spasmodically each time his hand struck her bottom, he'd have doubted that she was feeling anything at all.

Royce lifted his hand again and then hesitated. Her buttocks tightened, anticipating the strike of his hand, her body tensed, but still she did not cry out. Disgusted with himself and deprived of the satisfaction of making her weep and plead for mercy, he shoved her off his lap and stood up, glaring down at her and breathing fast.

Even now, her stubborn, unyielding pride refused to permit her to stay collapsed at his feet. Putting her hand to the ground, she rose slowly, unsteadily, until she was standing before him, clutching her breeches to her waist. Her head was bent forward, hiding her face from his view, but as he watched, she shuddered, trying to square her trembling shoulders. She looked so small and vulnerable that he felt a twinge of conscience. "Jennifer—" he bit out.

Her head lifted, and Royce froze in surprise and reluctant admiration for the amazing sight he beheld. Standing there like a wild enraged gypsy, her hair tumbling all about her like golden flames and her huge blue eyes alive with hatred and unshed tears, she slowly raised her hand . . . a hand which was holding a dagger which she'd obviously managed to snatch from his boot as he spanked her.

And in that unlikely moment, as she held his dagger poised high, ready to strike, Royce Westmoreland thought she was the most magnificent creature he'd ever beheld; a wild, beautiful, enraged angel of retribution, her chest rising and falling with fury as she courageously confronted an enemy who towered over her. He'd hurt her and humiliated her, Royce realized, but he hadn't broken that indomitable spirit of hers. Suddenly Royce wasn't certain he wanted her broken. Softly and without emphasis, he held out his hand. "Give me the dagger, Jennifer."

She raised it higher—aimed, Royce realized, straight at his heart.

"I'll not harm you again," he continued, talking calmly as young Gawin moved stealthily behind her, his face murderous as he prepared to defend his lord's life. "Nor," Royce added with the emphasis of a command aimed at Gawin, "will my overzealous squire, who is at this moment standing behind you, ready to slit your throat if you try."

In her fury, Jenny had forgotten the squire was in the tent—that the boy had witnessed her humiliation! The knowledge erupted inside her like a volcano.

"Give me the dagger," Royce said, extending his hand to her, confident now that she would give it to him. She did. The dagger slashed through the air with the speed of light, aimed straight at his heart. Only his swift reflexes enabled him to deflect it with his arm, then twist the blade free of her death grip, and even with that, as he jerked her against him and threw his arm around her, imprisoning her against his body, bright red blood was already seeping from the gash she'd managed to carve along his cheek near his ear.

"You bloodthirsty little wench!" he said in a savage underbreath, all his former admiration for her courage instantly demolished as he felt the blood begin to pour from his face. "If you were a man, I'd kill you for this!"

Gawin was staring at his lord's wound with a fury that outmeasured Royce's, and when the boy looked at Jenny, there was murder in his eye. "I'll fetch the guard," he said with a final loathsome look at her.

"Don't be a fool!" Royce snapped. "Would you have word spread throughout the camp and then the land that I was wounded by a nun? 'Tis fear of me, of my *legend,* that defeats our enemies before they ever raise their weapons against me!"

"I beg pardon, milord," Gawin said. "But how will you stop her from telling it once you let her loose?"

"Let me loose?" Jenny said, roused from her fear-induced trance as she stared at the blood she'd drawn. "You intend to let us *loose?"*

"Eventually, if I don't murder you first," the Wolf snapped, shoving her away from him with a force that sent her sprawling amidst the heap of rugs in the corner of his tent. He snatched up the flagon of wine, keeping a wary eye on her, and took a long swallow, then he glanced at the large needle on the table beside the thread. "Find a smaller needle," he ordered his squire.

Jenny sat where she was, bewildered by his words and actions. Now that her reason was returning, she could scarce believe he hadn't murdered her on the spot for trying to kill him. His words ran through her mind, *" 'Tis fear of me, of my legend, that defeats our enemies before they ever raise their weapons against me."* Somewhere in the dim recesses of her mind, she'd already arrived at the conclusion that the Wolf was not near so bad as legend had him—were he half as bad as they said, she'd already have been tortured and molested. Instead, he evidently intended to let Brenna and her go.

By the time Gawin returned with a smaller needle, Jenny was feeling almost charitable toward the man she'd tried to kill but minutes before. She could not and would not forgive him for physically abusing her, but she counted matters fairly even between them, now that she'd wounded both his body and his pride as he'd wounded hers. As she sat there watching him drink from the flagon, she decided that the wisest and best course, henceforth, would be to try her best not to provoke him into changing his mind about returning them to the abbey.

"I'll have to shave your beard, sire," Gawin said, "else I can't see the wound in order to stitch it."

"Shave it off then," Royce muttered. "you're not much good with that needle even when you can see what you're doing. I've scars all over me to prove it."

"A pity 'tis your face she cut," Gawin agreed, and Jenny had the feeling she'd ceased to exist for the moment. "'Tis scarred enough already," he added as he set out a sharp knife and a cup of water for shaving.

The boy's body blocked the Wolf from Jenny's view as he went about his task, and as the minutes slowly ticked by, she found herself leaning slightly to one side, then the other, intensely curious to see what sort of ferocious face had been concealed by his thick, black beard. Or did it hide a weak chin? she wondered, leaning further to the left, trying to see. No doubt it hid a weak chin, she decided, leaning so far to the right that she nearly lost her balance as she tried to peer around the squire.

Royce had not forgotten her presence, nor did he trust her, now that she'd showed herself bold enough to try to end his life. Watching her from the corner of his eye, he saw her leaning from one side to the other, and he mockingly told his squire, "Move aside, Gawin, so she can see my face before she topples like an overturned bottle, trying to see around you."

Jenny, who had leaned far to the right, trying to see, could not recover her balance quickly enough to pretend she hadn't been doing exactly that. Color washed up her cheeks and she jerked her gaze from Royce Westmoreland's face, but not before she'd gotten the startling impression that the Wolf was considerably younger than she'd thought. Moreover, he did not have a weak chin. It was a strong, square chin with a curious little dent in the center of it. More than that, she hadn't been able to tell.

"Come, come, don't be shy," Royce prodded sarcastically, but the strong wine he'd been drinking was doing much to soothe his temper. Besides, he found her swift, startling change from daring assassin to curious young girl both baffling and amusing. "Take a good look at the face you just tried to carve your initial into," he urged, watching her prim profile.

"I need to stitch that wound, milord," Gawin said, frowning. "It's deep and swelling and 'twill be ugly enough as it is."

"Try not to render me hideous to Lady Jennifer," Royce said sardonically.

"I'm your squire, milord, not a seamstress," Gawin replied, the needle and thread poised above the deep gash that began near his lord's temple and followed his jawline.

The word "seamstress" suddenly reminded Royce of the neat, nearly invisible stitches Jenny had sewn into a pair of woolen hose, and he waved Gawin aside, turning his speculative gaze on his captive. "Come here," he told Jenny in a calm voice that nevertheless rang with authority.

No longer eager to provoke him, lest he change his mind about releasing them, Jenny arose and warily obeyed, relieved to take the pressure off her throbbing backside.

"Come closer," he bade her when she paused just out of his reach. "It seems only fitting that you should have to mend *everything* you have rent. Stitch up my face."

In the light from the pair of candles, Jenny saw the gash she'd made in his face and the sight of that torn flesh, added to the thought of piercing it with a needle, made her feel like swooning. She swallowed the bile rising in her throat and whispered through parched lips, "I—I can't."

"You can and you will," Royce stated implacably. A second ago, he'd started to doubt the wisdom of letting her near him with a needle, but as he witnessed her horror at the sight of what she'd done, he felt reassured. In fact, he thought, forcing her to continue to look at it—to touch it—was just retribution!

With visible reluctance, Gawin handed her the needle and thread, and Jenny held it in her shaking hand, poised above Royce's face, but just when she was about to touch him, he stayed her hand with his and said in a cold, warning voice, "I hope you aren't foolish enough to entertain any thought of making this ordeal unnecessarily painful?"

"No, I wasn't. I won't," Jenny said weakly.

Satisfied, Royce held out the flagon of wine to her, "Here, drink some of this first. 'Twill steady your nerves." If he'd offered her poison at that moment, and told her it would steady her nerves, Jenny would have taken it, so distraught was she at the prospect of what she had to do. She lifted the flagon and took three long swallows, choked, then lifted it and drank some more. She would have had yet more, had the earl not firmly removed the flagon from her clenched hand. "Too much of it will cloud your vision and make you clumsy," he said dryly. "I don't want you trying to stitch my ear closed. Now, get on with it." Turning his head, he calmly offered his torn face for her ministrations while Gawin stood at Jenny's elbow, watching to make certain she did no harm.

Never had Jenny ever pierced human flesh with her needle, and as she forced the point through the earl's swollen skin, she couldn't completely suppress her moan of sick protest. Watching her from the corner of his eye, Royce tried not to wince for fear she'd see it and faint dead away. "For an assassin, you have an amazingly weak stomach," he remarked, trying to divert *his* mind from the pain, and *her* mind from her gory task.

Biting her lip, Jenny dug the needle into his flesh again. The color drained from her face, and Royce tried again to divert her with conversation. "Whatever made you think you had a calling to be a nun?"

"I—I didn't," she gasped.

"Then what were you doing at the abbey in Belkirk?"

"My father sent me there." she said, swallowing down the sickness at her gruesome task.

"Because *he* thinks you're meant to be a nun?" Royce demanded in disbelief, watching her out of the corners of his eyes. "He must see a different side of your nature than you've shown to me."

That almost made her laugh, he noted, watching her bite her lip as the color returned to her cheeks. "Actually," she admitted slowly, her soft voice amazingly lyrical when she wasn't angry or guarded, "I suppose you could say he sent me there *because* he'd seen the same side of my nature that you have."

"Really?" Royce inquired conversationally. "What reason had you to try to kill *him?*"

He sounded so genuinely disgruntled, that Jenny couldn't completely suppress a smile. Besides, she'd eaten nothing since yesterday and the heady wine was surging through her bloodstream, relaxing and warming her all the way to her toes.

"Well?" Royce prompted, studying the tiny dimple that peeked from the corner of her mouth.

"I did not try to kill my father," she said firmly, taking another stitch.

"What did you do then, that he banished you to a convent?"

"Among other things, I refused to wed someone— in a way."

"Really?" Royce said, genuinely surprised as he recalled what he'd heard of Merrick's eldest daughter when he was last at Henry's court. Rumor had it that Merrick's eldest was a plain, prim, cold woman and a dedicated spinster. He racked his brain, trying to remember who had actually described her to him in such terms. Edward Balder, he remembered now— the earl of Lochlordon, an emissary from King James's court, had said that of her. But then, so had

81

everyone else on those rare occasions he'd heard her mentioned at all. *A plain, prim, cold spinster,* they had said, but there had been more, though he couldn't recall it at the moment. "How old are you?" he asked abruptly.

The question startled her and seemed to embarrass her. "Seventeen years," she admitted, rather reluctantly, Royce thought, "and two weeks."

"That old?" he said, his lips twitching with a mixture of amusement and compassion. Seventeen was hardly ancient, although most girls married between fourteen and sixteen years of age. He supposed she was loosely qualified for the term spinster. "A spinster by choice then?"

Embarrassment and denial flickered in her deep blue eyes, and he tried to recall what else they said of her at court. He could remember nothing—except that they said her sister, Brenna, eclipsed her completely. Brenna, according to rumor, had a face whose beauty outshone the sun and stars. Idly, Royce wondered why any man would prefer a meek, pale blond to this fiery young temptress, and then he recalled that he himself had generally preferred the comforts of an angelic blond—one in particular. *"Are* you a spinster by choice?" he demanded, wisely waiting until she'd taken another stitch before using the word that made her flinch.

Jenny took another tiny stitch, and then another, and another, trying to stave off her sudden unaccustomed awareness of him as a handsome, virile male. And he was handsome, she realized fairly, astonishingly so. Clean-shaven, he possessed a rugged, thoroughly male sort of beauty that had taken her completely by surprise. His jaw was square, the chin clefted, his cheekbones high and wide. But what was so completely disarming was her latest discovery: The earl of Claymore, whose very name struck terror in the hearts of his enemy—had the thickest eyelashes she'd ever seen in her life! A smile danced in her eyes as she imagined how intrigued everyone would be at home when she imparted *that* piece of information. *"Are* you a spinster by choice?" Royce repeated a trifle impatiently.

"I suppose I am, since my father warned me he'd send me to the convent if I spoiled the only eminently suitable offer of marriage I was likely ever to receive."

"Who offered for you?" Royce asked, intrigued.

"Edward Balder, Earl of Lochlordon. Hold still!" she commanded with outrageous temerity when he jumped in surprise. "I'll not be blamed for making a poor job of this if you mean to leap about beneath the needle."

That sharply worded chastisement from a mere slip of a girl who was, moreover, his prisoner nearly made Royce laugh aloud. "How many damned stitches do you mean to take?" he countered irritably. "Twas only a small gash, anyway."

Offended that he apparently considered her daring attack nothing more than a slight inconvenience, Jenny drew back and glared at him. "'Tis a huge, nasty gash and nothing less!"

He opened his mouth to argue with her but his gaze was drawn to her breasts where they strained impudently against the fabric of the shirt she wore. Odd that he hadn't noticed until just now how amply endowed she was, or how tiny her waist, or how gently rounded her hips. On second thought, not odd at all, Royce reminded himself, since she'd been wearing shapeless nun's robes until a few hours ago, and until a few minutes ago, he'd been too furious to notice what she was wearing at all. And now that he'd noticed, he wished he hadn't. Having noticed all that, he remembered full well how delightfully rounded her bottom had been. Desire leapt inside him, and he shifted uncomfortably in his chair. "Finish your task," he said brusquely.

Jenny noted his sudden gruffness, but she put it down to his moodiness—the same moodiness that caused him to seem like an evil monster one moment and almost like a brother in the next. For her part, her body was almost as unpredictable as his moods. A few minutes ago she'd been cold, despite the fire burning in the tent. Now she felt over-warm in her shirt! Still, she rather wanted to restore the almost friendly companionship they'd shared for the last few moments, not because she desired him for a friend, but simply because it made her less afraid of him. Tentatively, she said, "You seemed surprised when I mentioned the earl of Lochlordon."

"I was," Royce said, keeping his expression non-committal.

"Why?"

He did not want to tell her that Edward Balder was probably responsible for the somewhat unjust rumors circulating all over London about her. Considering that Balder was a vain peacock, it wasn't entirely surprising that he reacted to being a rejected suitor by blackening the name of the woman who rejected him. "Because he's an old man," Royce hedged finally.

"He's also ugly."

"That, too." Try as he might, Royce could not imagine a loving father actually trying to marry his daughter off to that old lecher. For that matter, Royce couldn't believe her father actually intended to keep her locked away in a convent, either. No doubt the earl of Merrick had merely sent her there for a few weeks to teach her obedience. "How long have you been at Belkirk Abbey?"

"Two years."

His mouth dropped open, then he caught himself and closed it. His face was hurting like hell and his disposition was taking a sudden turn for the worse. "Evidently, your father finds you as unmanageable, headstrong, willful, and unreasonable as I do," he said irritably, wishing for another long draught of wine.

"If I were your daughter, how would you feel?" Jenny demanded indignantly.

"Cursed," he said bluntly, ignoring her wounded look. "In two days, you've shown me more resistance than I encountered at the last two castles I took by force."

"I meant," Jenny said, her eyes filled with ire, plunking her hands on her slim hips, "if I were *your* daughter, and your sworn enemy kidnapped me, how would *you* want me to behave?"

Momentarily dumbstruck, Royce stared at her as he considered what she said. She had not simpered nor pled for mercy. She had, instead, tried her damnedest to outwit him, to escape from him, and to kill him, in that order. She had not shed so much as one tear, even during the sound thrashing he'd given her. Afterward, when he'd thought she was crying, she'd been planning to stab him. It crossed his mind again that she must be incapable of tears, but for the moment he was absorbed in envisioning how he would feel, were she his daughter—an innocent captured from the safety of an abbey.

"Sheathe your claws, Jennifer," he said curtly. "You've made your point."

She accepted her victory with a gracious nod—in fact, with far more grace than Royce had conceded it.

It was the first time Royce had seen her really *smile,* and the effect on her face was more than startling. The smile came slowly, dawning in her eyes until they positively sparkled, then drifting to her generous lips, softening them at the corners until they parted, allowing a glimpse of perfect white teeth, and a pair of dimples that peeked at him from the corners of her soft mouth.

Royce might have grinned at her, but at that moment he caught the disdainful look on Gawin's face, and it dawned on him that he was behaving like a besotted gallant to his prisoner—more importantly, to the daughter of his enemy. Most of all, to the woman whose destructiveness meant that many of his men would shiver in the unseasonable cold tonight, without blankets to offer them any warmth. He nodded curtly at the pile of rugs. "Go to sleep. Tomorrow, you can start repairing the damage you did to the blankets."

His brusqueness banished the smile from her face, and she stepped back.

"I meant what I said," he added, angrier with himself than he was with her. "Until you've repaired the damage to the blankets, you sleep without them."

Her chin came up in the arrogant pose he'd grown used to from her, and she turned to walk toward the rugs that served as his bed. She moved, Royce noted grimly, with the provocative grace of a courtesan, *not* a nun.

Jenny lay down atop the furs while he blew out the candles; a few moments later, the earl stretched beside her, pulling the furs over him for warmth. Suddenly the comforting glow from the wine began to desert her, and her exhausted mind started replaying each nerve-shattering hour of the endless day, from early dawn when Brenna and she planned their escape, until a few hours ago, when the man beside her had recaptured her.

Staring up into the darkness, she relived the most shattering scene of all—the one she'd been trying to forget all night. Before her eyes she saw Thor in all his magnificent splendor, prancing effortlessly through the woods, racing along the ridge, jumping obstacle after obstacle, and then she saw him lying dead against the boulder, his glossy coat shining in the moonlight.

Tears gathered in her eyes; she drew a shattered breath and then another, trying to hold them back, but the anguish she felt for the courageous animal would not go away.

Royce, who was afraid to fall asleep until she did, heard the ragged texture of her breathing, and then a slight, suspicious sniff. Positive she was feigning tears in hopes he would relent and let her beneath the furs, he rolled onto his side and in one smooth motion caught her face and turned it toward him. Her eyes were glittering with unshed tears. "You're so cold, you're fighting back tears?" he uttered in disbelief, trying to see her face with only the dying embers of the little fire in the center of the tent for illumination.

"No," she said hoarsely.

"Then why?" he demanded, completely at a loss as to what could have finally battered down her stubborn pride and made her cry. "The thrashing I gave you?"

"No," she whispered achingly, her eyes locked with his. "Your horse."

Of all the things she could have said, that answer was the one he least expected and most wanted to hear. Somehow knowing that she regretted the senseless loss of his horse made it seem somehow less painful.

"He was the most beautiful animal I've ever seen," she added hoarsely. "If I'd known that taking him this morning might have led to his death, I'd have stayed here until I could—could find some other way."

Staring up into the earl's hooded eyes, Jenny saw him wince as he pulled his hand away from her face. "It's a miracle you fell off or you'd both have died," he said gruffly.

Turning onto her side she buried her face in the furs. "I didn't fall," she whispered brokenly, "he *threw* me. I'd ridden him over higher obstacles all day. I knew we could clear that tree with ease, but when he jumped, he reared up at the same time, for no reason at all, and I fell backward. He *shook* me off before he jumped.

"Thor sired two sons, Jennifer," Royce said with rough gentleness, "in his exact likeness. One of them is here, the other at Claymore being trained. He isn't completely lost to me."

His captive drew a shattered breath, and in the darkness, she said simply, "Thank you."

A biting wind howled through the moonlit valley,

taking sleeping soldiers in its frigid embrace until their teeth chattered convulsively, as fall made an ungraceful and early debut, masquerading as winter. In his tent, Royce rolled over beneath the warm furs and felt the unfamiliar brush of an icy hand against his arm.

He opened an eye and saw Jennifer shivering atop the furs, her slim body curled into a tight ball, her knees drawn up against her chest, as she tried to keep warm. In truth Royce was not so drugged with sleep that he knew not what he was doing, nor had he forgotten that he'd forbade her the warmth of blankets until she righted the damage she'd done to his men's. And, to be completely honest, as he wearily considered her shivering form, it did occur to him that his loyal men were shivering far more outdoors, without a tent. And so there was absolutely no justification for what Royce did next: Leaning up on his elbow he reached far across Jennifer and grasped the edge of the thick pile of furs, then he pulled them up and over her, rolling her into them until they made a warm bunting around her.

He lay back again and closed his eyes without remorse. After all, his men were conditioned to hardship and the elements. Jennifer Merrick was not.

She moved, snuggling deeper into the furs, and somehow her bottom came to rest against Royce's updrawn knee. Despite the insulating barrier of furs, his mind instantly began reminding him of all the delectable female attributes that lay just within his easy reach. And just as persistently, Royce shoved the thoughts aside. She had the peculiar ability to be at one and the same moment an innocent, untried girl and a golden-haired goddess—a child who could snap his temper as easily as a twig, and a woman who could soothe even pain with a whispered, "I'm sorry." But child or woman, he dared not touch her, for one way or another, he would have to let her go, or else relinquish all his carefully laid plans for a future that would be his in less than a month. Whether Jennifer's father yielded or no, it was actually no concern of Royce's. In a week, two at the most, he would either hand her over to her father, if he surrendered on terms that were agreeable to Henry, or to Henry himself if her father refused. She was Henry's property now, not Royce's, and he did not want the complications that would come from every direction if he bedded her.

The earl of Merrick paced before the fire in the center of the hall, his face contorted with wrath as he listened to suggestions from his two sons and the four men whom he counted as his closest friends and kinsmen.

"There's naught to be done," Garrick Carmichael put in wearily, "until King James sends us the reinforcements you asked for when you told him the Wolf has the girls."

"*Then* we can attack the bastard and demolish him," his youngest son, Malcolm, spat. "He's close to our borders now—there's no long march to Cornwall to weary us before we go to battle this time."

"I don't see what difference it makes how close he is or how many men we have," William, the eldest son, quietly said. "'Twould be folly to attack him unless we've freed Brenna and Jenny first."

"And how in God's name are we supposed to do that?" Malcolm snapped. "The girls are as good as dead as it is," he said flatly. "There's naught to do now but seek revenge."

Far smaller in stature than his brother and his stepfather—and far calmer of temperament—William brushed his auburn hair off his forehead and leaned forward in his chair, looking about him. "Even if King James sends us enough men to trample the Wolf, we'll not get the girls free. They'd be killed in the fighting—or murdered as soon as it began."

"Stop arguing with every plan unless you have a better one!" the earl snapped.

"I think I do," William quietly replied and all heads turned to him. "We can't get the girls out by force, but stealth might do the trick. Instead of sending an army out to challenge him, let me take a few men with me. We'll dress as merchants, or friars, or something, and we'll follow the Wolf's army until we can get close to the girls. Jenny," he said fondly, "may well realize what I say is true. If so, she'll be watching for us."

"I say we attack!" Malcolm burst out, his desire to pit himself against the Wolf again overwhelming his reason, as well as what little concern he had for his sisters.

Both young men turned to their father for an opinion. "Malcolm," the earl said fondly, " 'tis like you to want to take a man's approach—to exact revenge and damn the consequences. You'll have your chance to attack when Jamie sends us reinforcements. For now"—he glanced at William with a glimmer of new respect—"your brother's plan is the best we have."

Chapter Six

During the next five days, Jenny began to recognize the routine followed by the resting army. In the morning, shortly after dawn, the men arose and practiced with their weapons for several hours, making the fields and valley ring with the ceaseless, discordant clanging of sword against shield, broadsword against broadsword. The Wolf's archers, whose skill was legendary, practiced daily also, adding the twang of their bows to the clanking of metal on metal. Even the horses were taken out each day and drilled, their riders galloping them at breakneck speed in mock charges against imaginary foes, until the sounds of warfare continued to drum and echo in her ears long after the men ceased for the midday meal.

Sitting just inside Royce's tent, her fingers busily sewing at the blankets, Jenny listened to the endless clamor, trying unsuccessfully to keep her worries under control. She couldn't imagine how her father's army would survive when pitted against the finely honed "war machine" the Wolf had made of his men, nor could she help worrying that Merrick keep would be unprepared for the sort of assault it was bound to receive. Then her worries shifted to Brenna.

She hadn't had more than a brief glimpse of her sister since the night of their ill-fated escape. Stefan, the earl's younger brother, was evidently responsible for keeping Brenna prisoner in his tent, just as the earl of Claymore had assumed responsibility for Jenny; however, the earl had forbidden the girls to be together. Jenny questioned him repeatedly about Brenna's safety and he'd replied with seeming honesty that Brenna was perfectly safe and being treated as a guest by his brother.

Putting her sewing aside, Jenny stood up and went to the open flap of the tent, longing to walk about. The weather was lovely for early September—warm during the day, though cold at night. The Wolf's elite guard—fifteen men whose sole responsibility was to Royce, not the army—were practicing on horseback at the far side of the field, and though she longed to walk outside in the sunshine, even that was forbidden to her by her captor, whose attitude toward her seemed to harden more each day. The knights, especially Sir Godfrey and Sir Eustace, who'd been almost polite before, now treated her like an enemy whose presence they were forced to endure. Brenna and she had duped them, and none of them were likely ever to forget or overlook it.

That night, after she'd eaten, Jenny again brought up the subject most on her mind. "I wish to see my sister," she said to the earl, trying to match his cool mood.

"Then try *asking* me," he said shortly "not *telling* me."

Jenny stiffened at his tone, paused to assess her predicament and the importance of achieving her goal, and after a meaningful hesitation, she conceded with a nod, and sweetly said, "Very well, then. May I see my sister, my lord?"

"No."

"Why in God's name not?" Jenny exploded, momentarily forgetting her meek pose.

His eyes sparked with laughter. "Because," Royce commented, enjoying sparring with her even though he'd decided to keep her at arm's length physically and mentally. "As I've already told you, you are a bad influence on your sister. On her own, without you, she'd never have imagination or courage enough to plan an escape. And without her, you *can't* consider leaving."

Jenny would have dearly loved to call him names that would have scorched his ears, but to do that would only defeat her purpose. "I don't suppose you'd believe me if I give you my word not to try to escape."

"Are you willing to do that?"

"Yes. Now may I see my sister?"

"No," he rejoined politely, "I'm afraid not."

"I find it amazing," she announced with magnificent, regal disdain as she slowly arose, "that you aren't certain an entire English army can confine two mere females. Or is it *cruelty* that makes you refuse me?"

His mouth tightened, but he said nothing, and immediately after supper he left and did not return until long after Jennifer had gone to sleep.

The following morning, Jenny was astonished to see Brenna being led toward the tent. The gray habits they'd buried near the stream were too filthy to wear and, like Jenny, Brenna was now garbed in tunic, hose, and high soft boots obviously borrowed from one of the pages.

After embracing warmly, Jenny pulled her sister down beside her and was about to launch into a discussion of possible means of escape, when her gaze fell upon a pair of men's boots that were visible between the base of the tent and the ground. Boots with the golden spurs that were forbidden to any but a knight.

"How have you fared, sister?" Brenna asked worriedly.

"Very well," Jenny answered, wondering which of

the knights was out there and if whoever it was had been *ordered* to listen to what the girls said. A sudden, thoughtful look crossed Jenny's face and she added slowly, "In fact, had I known how well treated we would be amongst them, I'd not have attempted our foolhardy escape."

"What?" Brenna gasped, her face agog.

Jenny signaled her to keep silent, then she cupped Brenna's face between her hands and physically directed her gaze to the black boots just outside the tent. In the barest whisper, she said, "If we can convince them we no longer wish to escape, we'll stand a much better chance of getting an opportunity to do it. We have to leave, Brenna, before Father surrenders. If he does that, 'twill be too late."

Brenna nodded her understanding and Jenny continued, "I know 'tis not at all the way I felt when first we were captured, but to tell you truly, I was badly frightened alone in those hills the night we attempted to escape. And when I heard that wolf howl—"

"Wolf!" Brenna cried. "You said it was an owl."

"No, I'm almost certain as I reflect on it, that 'twas a horrible wolf! But the point is, we're safe here— we'll not be murdered or molested as I originally thought, so there's no reason for us to risk trying to escape and find our way home on our own. Soon enough, one way or another, Papa will gain our release."

"Oh, yes!" Brenna chimed in, when Jenny pantomimed for her to agree aloud. "I agree perfectly!"

As Jennifer hoped, Stefan Westmoreland, who'd been standing outside the tent, reported what he'd overheard. Royce listened with considerable surprise, but the logic behind Jennifer's apparent willingness to quietly resign herself to captivity was undeniable. Moreover, Jennifer's apparent willingness to quietly wait out her captivity was sensible, and so were the reasons she'd given her sister for her decision.

And so, albeit with some instinctive misgivings, Royce ordered the guard around his tent reduced from four to one, and that guard was Arik, who was there solely to ensure the captives' safety. No sooner had Royce given the order than he found himself stopping, wherever he might be in the camp, to look at his tent—always expecting to see a tousled mass of red-gold hair trying to creep from beneath it. When two days passed and she remained obediently within the tent, he reversed his other edict and told Jennifer she would be permitted to be with her sister an hour each day. And then he doubted the wisdom of that decision, too.

Jennifer, who knew full well the reason for these changes, vowed to watch for any further opportunity to strengthen the earl's ill-founded trust and thus lull him into further relaxing his guard.

The following night, fate handed her the ultimate chance, and Jenny took full advantage of it: She had just stepped outside with Brenna, intending to tell Arik they wished to stroll about the perimeter of the tent—the area they were now restricted to for exercise—when two things simultaneously occurred to Jenny: The first was that Arik and the Black Wolf's guards were more than twenty-five yards away, momentarily occupied with some sort of fight which had broken out among the men; the second was that, far off on her left, the earl had turned and was watching Jennifer and Brenna closely.

Had Jenny not known he was watching, she might well have attempted to flee into the woods with Brenna, but since she instantly realized he'd apprehend them within minutes if they tried, she did something much better: Careful to appear as if she had no idea they were being watched, Jenny linked her arm with Brenna's, and pointed toward the absent Arik, then she deliberately strolled away from the woods, obediently keeping to the perimeter of the tent as they had been told to do. In doing so, Jenny skillfully made it appear to Royce that, even without guards, she could be trusted not to try to escape.

The ploy worked magnificently. That night, Royce, Stefan, Arik, and the Black Guard gathered to discuss the plan to break camp the next day and begin marching thirty miles northeast to Hardin castle, where the army would rest while awaiting fresh reinforcements from London. During the discussion and the meal that followed it, Royce Westmoreland's behavior to Jenny verged on gallant! And when everyone had left the tent, he turned to her and quietly said, "There will no longer be any restrictions whatever on your visits with your sister."

Jenny, who'd been about to sit down amidst the pile of fur rugs, stopped in mid-motion at the unfamiliar gentleness in his voice and stared at him. Uneasiness coursed through her, inexplicable but tangible as she gazed at his proud, aristocratic face. It was as if he had stopped thinking of her as his enemy and was asking her to do the same, and she knew not how to react.

As she gazed into those fathomless silver eyes, some instinct warned her his offer of a truce could make him more dangerous to her than he had been as her foe, yet her mind rejected that notion, for it made no sense to her. Surely she could only benefit from a surface friendship between them, and, in truth, she'd rather enjoyed their lighthearted banter as she stitched his wound the other night.

She opened her mouth to thank him for his offer, then stopped. It seemed a betrayal to *thank* her kidnapper for his leniency, to pretend that all was forgiven and that they were—well—friends. Furthermore, although she was relieved that she had apparently made him trust her, she felt ashamed for the trickery and deceit she'd used to accomplish it. Even as a little girl, Jenny had been forthright and open— an attitude which had oft landed her in disfavor with her father and which ultimately led her to challenge her unscrupulous stepbrother to a duel of honor, rather than trying to beat him at his own game of deceit. Openness and honesty had gotten her banished to the abbey. Here, however, she'd been forced to resort to trickery, and although all her efforts were being rewarded, and her cause was worthy, she felt somehow ashamed of what she was doing. Pride and honesty and desperation were waging a war inside of her, and her conscience was being assaulted in the fray.

She tried to think what Mother Ambrose would do in this situation, but she simply could not imagine anyone daring to abduct the dignified abbess in the first place, let alone toss her over the back of a horse like a sack of grain, and all the other things Jenny had endured since coming here.

But one thing was certain, Mother Ambrose dealt justly with everyone, no matter how provoking the circumstance.

The earl was offering Jenny trust—even a sort of friendship—she could see it in the warmth of his eyes; hear it in the gentleness of his deep baritone voice. She could not, *dared* not turn his trust aside.

The future of her clan depended on her being able to escape—or else being easy to rescue, for they'd surely at least try that before they surrendered. For that, Jenny needed freedom of the camp—as much as possible. Shameful or no, she could not be righteous and scorn his trust. Nor could she refuse his gesture of friendship without jeopardizing his trust at the same time, but at least she could try to return his friendship with a degree of sincerity and honesty.

Having decided that after a prolonged period of silence, Jenny looked at the earl and lifted her chin and with an unintentionally cool nod, she accepted his offer of a truce.

More entertained than annoyed by what he misinterpreted as her "regal" acceptance of his leniency, Royce crossed his arms over his chest and leaned his hip against the table, one brow arched in speculative amusement. "Tell me something, Jennifer," he said as she sat down among the furs and curled her shapely legs beneath her, "when you were in the nunnery, were you not warned to avoid the seven vices?"

"Yes, of course."

"Including pride?" he murmured, distracted by the candlelight glinting in the golden threads of her hair as it cascaded over her shoulders.

"I'm truly not proud," she said with a bewitching smile, well aware that he was undoubtedly referring to her tardy, rather ungracious acceptance of his truce. "I'm willful, I suppose. Stubborn, too. And head-strong. But not, I think, proud."

"Rumor, and my own experience with you, would lead me to think otherwise."

His wry tone made Jenny burst out laughing, and Royce found himself captivated by the infectious joy, the beauty, of it. He'd never heard the music of her laughter before, nor seen it glowing in her magnificent eyes. Seated on a pile of lush furs, laughing up at him, Jennifer Merrick was unforgettable. He realized it as clearly as he realized that if he walked over and sat down beside her, there was every chance he was going to find her irresistible as well. He hesitated, watching her, silently recounting all the reasons he ought to remain right where he was—and then with carefully concealed purpose, he did the oppo-site.

Reaching out he picked up two tankards and the flagon of wine from the table beside his hip, then he carried all three over to the pile of furs. Pouring wine into the tankards, he handed her one. "You're called Jennifer the proud, did you know that?" he asked, grinning down at her enchanting face.

Unaware that she was plunging lightning-fast into dangerous, uncharted territory, Jenny shrugged, her eyes dancing merrily. " 'Tis merely rumor, the result of my one meeting with Lord Balder, I suspect. *You're* called the Scourge of Scotland, and 'tis said *you* murder babes and drink their blood."

"Really?" Royce said with an exaggerated shudder, as he sat down beside her. Half-jokingly he added, "No wonder I'm persona non grata in the better castles of England."

"Are you really that?" she asked, puzzled and fighting down a sudden absurd surge of sympathy. He might be Scotland's enemy, but he fought for England, and it seemed grossly unfair if his own people rejected him.

Raising her tankard, Jenny took several sips to steady her nerves, then she lowered the heavy vessel, studying him in the glow of light from the tallow candles on the table across the tent. Young Gawin was at the opposite end, seemingly engrossed in the endless task of polishing his lord's armor with sand and vinegar.

The English nobility, she decided, must be very odd indeed, for in Scotland, the man beside her would have been judged an exceedingly handsome hero and welcomed into any castle where there was an unwed daughter! True, there was a certain dark arrogance about him; the hard, rugged contours of his jaw and chin were stamped with granite determination and implacable authority, but, when taken altogether, it was a boldly masculine, handsome face. It was impossible to guess his age; a life spent in the wind and sun had etched lines at the corners of his eyes and grooves beside his mouth. She supposed he must be much older than he actually looked, since she could never remember a time when she didn't know the tales of the Wolf's exploits. Suddenly it occurred to her that it was very odd indeed that he had spent his life in conquest, yet he sought not to wed and have heirs to inherit all the wealth he must certainly have amassed.

"Why did you decide not to marry?" she blurted suddenly, and then could not believe she'd actually asked such a question.

Astonishment registered in Royce's expression as he realized that, at twenty-nine, she evidently regarded him as being long past the age of eligibility for marriage. Recovering his composure he asked in amusement, "Why do *you* think I haven't?"

"Because no suitable lady has asked you?" she ventured daringly with an impertinent sideways smile that Royce found utterly bewitching.

Despite the fact that many such marital overtures had been made to him, he merely grinned. "I gather you think it's too late for me?"

She nodded, smiling. "'Twould seem we're both destined to be spinsters."

"Ah, but you're a spinster by choice, and therein lies the difference." Enjoying himself enormously, Royce leaned back on an elbow, watching her cheeks pinken from the heady wine she was drinking. "Where have *I* erred, do you think?"

"I couldn't know that, of course. But I suppose," she continued after a moment's consideration, "that one hasn't an opportunity to meet very many suitable ladies on the battlefield."

"True. I've spent most of my life fighting to bring peace."

"The only reason there's no *peace* is because *you* keep disrupting it with your evil sieges and interminable battles," she informed him darkly. "The English cannot get along with anyone."

"Is that right?" he inquired dryly, enjoying her spirit as much as he'd enjoyed her laughter a moment before.

"Certainly. Why, you and your army have only just returned from fighting with us in Cornwall—"

"I was fighting in Cornwall, on *English* soil," Royce reminded her mildly, "because *your* beloved King James—who happens to have a weak chin, by the way—invaded *us* in an attempt to put his cousin's husband on the throne."

"Well," Jenny shot back indignantly, "Perkin Warbeck happens to be the rightful king of England and King James knows it! Perkin Warbeck is the long-lost son of Edward IV."

"Perkin Warbeck," Royce contradicted flatly, "is the long-lost son of a Flemish *boatman.*"

"That is merely *your* opinion."

When he seemed disinclined to argue the issue, she stole a look at his ruggedly chiseled face, "Does King James truly have a weak chin?" she blurted.

"He does," Royce averred, grinning at her.

"Well, we weren't discussing his looks in the first place," she said primly as she digested this information about her king, who was said to be as handsome as a god. "We were discussing your ceaseless wars. Before us, you were fighting with the Irish, and then you were in—"

"I fought the Irish," Royce interrupted with a mocking smile, "because *they* crowned Lambert Simnel king and then invaded *us* in an attempt to put him on the throne in Henry's place."

Somehow he made it sound as if Scotland and Ireland had been in the wrong, and Jenny simply didn't feel well enough informed to debate the matter adequately. With a sigh, she said, "I don't suppose there's any doubt about why you're here, now, so near our borders. You're waiting for more men to arrive, then Henry means to send you into Scotland to wage your bloody battles against us. Everyone in the camp knows that."

Determined to guide the conversation back to its former, lighthearted topic, Royce said, "As I recall, we were discussing my inability to find a suitable wife on the battlefield, not the outcome of my battles themselves."

Glad for the change of subject, Jenny deliberately turned her attention back to that problem. After a minute she said, "You must have been to Henry's court and met ladies there?"

"I have."

In thoughtful silence, she sipped her wine, while contemplating the tall man reclining beside her, his leg drawn up, his hand resting casually atop his knee, completely at ease in a tent on a battlefield. Everything about him bespoke the warrior. Even now, at rest, his body exuded predatory power; his shoulders were incredibly broad, his arms and chest bulged with muscle beneath his dark blue woolen tunic, and the muscles in his legs and thighs were clearly outlined by the heavy, black woolen hose above his high boots. Years of wearing armor and wielding a broadsword had hardened and toughened him for battle, but Jenny couldn't imagine that such a life could possibly benefit him when he went to court, or even prepare him to fit in with the people there. Although she'd never been to court herself, she'd heard all sorts of stories about the opulence there and the sophistication of its inhabitants. Suddenly she realized how horridly out of place this warrior must look and feel in such a place. "You—you don't feel at ease with the people at court?" she ventured hesitantly.

"Not particularly," Royce said, distracted by the myriad emotions playing in her expressive eyes.

His admission struck her tender heart and made it ache a little, for Jenny knew better than most how humiliating and painful it is to feel out of place amidst those very people one most wants to be accepted by. It seemed wrong, unfair, that this man who daily risked his life for England was shunned by his own people. "I'm certain the fault is not with you," she said charitably.

"Then where do you suppose the fault lies?" he asked, a faint smile playing at the corners of his chiseled lips. "Why do I not feel comfortable at court?"

"Are we talking about your feelings when you're with the ladies, or with the gentlemen?" she asked, feeling a sudden determined urge to help him that was the result of one part pity, one part strong wine, and one part reaction to his unwavering gray gaze. "If it's with the ladies, I might be able to help," she volunteered. "W-would you like some advice?"

"Please, by all means." Suppressing his grin, Royce smoothed his expression into an admirable imitation of earnest gravity. "Tell me how to treat the ladies so that when next I go to court, I'll be such a success that one of them may agree to have me as a husband."

"Oh, I can't promise they'll want to *wed* you," she burst out without thinking.

Royce choked on his wine and wiped the drops from the corner of his mouth. "If your intention was to build my confidence," he said, his voice still strangled with laughter, "you are making a bad job of it, my lady."

"I didn't mean—" Jenny faltered miserably. "Truly, I—"

"Perhaps we ought to *exchange* advice," he continued mirthfully. "You tell me how a highborn lady desires to be treated, and I'll warn you about the perils of demolishing a man's confidence. Here, have more wine," he added smoothly, reaching behind him for the flagon and pouring some into her tankard. He glanced over his shoulder at Gawin and a moment later the squire laid aside the shield he was polishing and left the tent.

"Do go on with your advice, I'm all eager attention," Royce said when she'd taken another sip of her wine. "Let's assume I'm at court and I've just walked into the queen's withdrawing room. Gathered around are several beautiful ladies, and I decide to make one of them my wife—"

Shock widened her eyes. "You aren't the least bit *particular,* are you?"

Royce threw back his head and gave a shout of laughter, and the unfamiliar sound brought three guards running into the tent to investigate the cause. Curtly waving them away, he looked at her pert nose, which was still wrinkled with disapproval, and he realized he'd just sunk to an unprecedented low in her estimation. Swallowing down a fresh surge of mirth, he said with sham contrition, "I did specify the ladies were all beautiful, did I not?"

Her expression cleared and she smiled, nodding. "That's true, you did. I'd forgotten that beauty is what matters most to a man."

"At *first* 'tis what matters most," Royce corrected. "All right, then. What do I do, now that I've, er— singled out the object of my matrimonial intentions?"

"What would you normally do?"

"What do *you* think I'd do?"

Her delicate brows drew together and amusement teased the corners of her generous mouth as she surveyed him, considering her answer. "Based on what *I* know of you, I can only assume you'd toss her over your lap and attempt to beat her into submission."

"You mean," Royce said straight-faced, "that *isn't* the way to handle the matter?"

Jenny saw the humor lurking in his eyes; she burst out laughing, and to Royce it seemed as if his tent were filled with music. "Ladies . . . that is, *wellborn* ladies," she clarified a minute later with a look that clearly implied his past experience had probably been with females of quite another sort, "have very definite ideas of the way they wish to be treated by the man who wins their heart."

"Just how does a *wellborn* lady dream of being treated?"

"Well, chivalrously, of course. But there's more to it than that," she added, a wistful light shining in her sapphire eyes. "A lady wants to think that when her knight enters a crowded room, he has eyes for no one but her. He's blind to everything but her beauty."

"In that case, he's in imminent danger of tripping

over his sword," Royce pointed out before he realized Jennifer was talking about her own dreams.

She sent him an admonishing look. *"And,"* she said emphatically, "she likes to think he's of a *romantic* nature—which you obviously are not!"

"Not if being romantic means I have to grope my way into rooms like a blind man," he teased. "But go on—what else do ladies like?"

"Loyalty and devotion. And words—especially words."

"What sort of words?"

"Words of love and tender admiration," Jenny said dreamily. "A lady wants to hear that her knight loves her above all else and that to him, she is beautiful. She wants him to tell her that her eyes remind him of the sea or the sky, and her lips remind him of rose petals . . ."

Royce studied her in appalled surprise. *"You* actually dream of a man saying such things to you?"

She paled as if he'd struck her, but then she seemed to dismiss the entire matter. "Even plain girls have dreams, milord," she pointed out with a smile.

"Jennifer," he said sharply, filled with remorse and amazement, "you are not plain. You're—" More attracted to her by the moment, he studied her, wondering about her allure, but it was more than just her face or her body that attracted him; Jennifer Merrick had a glowing gentleness that warmed him, a fiery spirit that challenged him—and a radiance that kept drawing him toward her with increasing power. "You're not plain."

She chuckled without rancor and shook her head. "Do not, under any circumstances, attempt to dazzle your lady fair with your glib flattery, milord, for you haven't a prayer of success!"

"If I cannot beat the lady into submission, nor cajole her with words," Royce answered, preoccupied with her rosy mouth, "I suppose I shall have to rely on my only other skill . . ."

He let the last word hang meaningfully in the air until Jenny, beguiled, could endure her fascinated curiosity no longer. "What skill do you mean?"

His eyes flicked to hers and he said with a wicked grin, "Modesty forbids me to name it."

"Don't be coy," Jenny chastised, so curious that she scarcely noticed his hand lifting to her shoulder. "What is it you do so very well that a lady would wish to *marry* you for it?"

"I believe I am quite good at"—his hand curved round her shoulder—"kissing."

"K-kissing!" she sputtered, laughing and simultaneously rearing back, dislodging his hand. "'Tis beyond belief that you would boast of such things to me!"

"'Twas not boasting," Royce countered, looking stung. "I've been given to believe I am quite good at it."

Jenny tried desperately to look sternly disapproving and failed miserably; her lips trembled with laughter at the idea of the "Scourge of Scotland" priding himself, not on his skill with lance or sword, but kissing!

"I gather you find that notion laughable?" Royce observed dryly.

She shook her head so emphatically that her hair came tumbling over her shoulder, but her eyes were dancing with merriment. "It—it is merely," she said on a suffocated laugh, "that I cannot quite reconcile such—such an *image* of you in my mind."

Without warning, his hand lifted and curved round her arm, drawing her firmly toward him. "Why don't you judge me on it then?" he suggested softly.

Jenny tried to rear back. "Don't be silly! I couldn't—I can't!" Suddenly, she could not tear her gaze from his lips. "I'll gladly take your word on it. Gladly!"

"Nay, I feel I must prove it."

"There's no need," she cried desperately. "How

could I possibly judge your skill when I've never been kissed in all my life?"

That admission only made her more desirable to Royce, who was accustomed to women whose experience in bed rivaled his own. His lips curved in a smile, but his hand tightened on her arm, drawing her inexorably closer, while his other hand lifted to her shoulder.

"Nay!" Jenny said, trying ineffectually to draw away.

"I insist."

Jenny braced herself for some unknown sort of physical assault; a whimper of terror lodged in her throat, but the next moment she realized there was nothing to fear. His lips were cool on hers and surprisingly smooth as they brushed lightly against her closed mouth. Stunned into quiescence, with her hands braced on either side of his shoulders, holding her rigid body away from his, she remained utterly immobile while her pulse began to race and she tried desperately to savor what it was like to be kissed and still keep her head.

Royce released the pressure of his hands just enough to let her lift her compressed lips from his. "Perhaps I'm not as good as I once thought," he said, keeping his amusement carefully hidden. "I could have sworn your mind was working the whole time."

Unnerved, alarmed, and thoroughly confused, Jenny nevertheless strove desperately not to struggle or do anything to upset the fragile balance of their tentative friendship. "W-what do you mean?" she demanded, acutely aware that his powerful body was now stretched out practically beneath and beside her in the most wanton fashion, his head upon the furs.

"I mean, would you say our kiss was the sort that wellborn ladies 'dream' about?"

"Please let go of me."

"I thought you were going to help me comport

107

myself to the pleasure of wellbred ladies, such as yourself."

"You kiss very well! Exactly how ladies dream of being kissed!" Jenny cried desperately, but he merely regarded her with a dubious expression, refusing to let her go.

"I just don't feel *confident,*" he teased, watching the little sparks of anger igniting in her incredibly blue eyes.

"Then practice on someone else!"

"Unfortunately, Arik does not appeal to me," Royce said, and before she could voice another objection, he swiftly switched tactics. "However," he said pleasantly, "I can see that, although threats of physical retribution have no effect on you, I've finally discovered what does."

"What," she demanded, suspicious, "do you mean?"

"I mean that, in future, when I want to bend you to my will, I'll simply kiss you into compliance. You're terrified of it."

Visions of being kissed—no doubt in front of his men—whenever she balked, rose to alarming prominence in her mind. Hoping that by speaking in a calm, reasonable voice, rather than heatedly protesting his statement, she could dissuade him from making her prove her claim, she said, "'Tis not fear I feel, but merely lack of interest."

With a mixture of amusement and admiration, Royce noted her ploy, but it only added to his inexplicable determination to taste her response to him.

"Really?" he breathed softly, his heavy-lidded gaze fixed on her lips. As he spoke, his hand curved round her head, pressing inexorably downward, inch by slow inch, until his warm breath was mingling with hers, and then his gaze lifted, locking with hers. Insistent, knowing gray eyes captured frightened, beguiling blue ones, imprisoning them as he brought her lips down against his. A jolt slammed through Jenny's entire nervous system, her eyes closed, and his lips began to move on hers, thoroughly and possessively exploring each tender curve and trembling contour.

Royce felt her lips soften involuntarily, felt her shaking arms give way, her breasts coming to rest against his chest, the wild pounding of her heart. His hand, which had been holding her mouth pressed against his, lightened its pressure at the same time his lips increased theirs. Rolling her onto her back, he leaned over her, deepening his kisses, his hand shifting soothingly over her side and hip. He slid the tip of his tongue along the crease of her lips, seeking entrance, insisting that they part, and when finally they did, his tongue plunged into the sweetness of her mouth and slowly withdrew, then plunged again in blatant imitation of the act he was beginning to crave with dangerous determination. Jenny gasped beneath him, stiffening, and then suddenly all the tension flowed out of her as a shattering explosion of delight poured through her. Totally innocent of the sort of heated passion he was deliberately, skillfully, arousing in her, she was intoxicated by it, seduced into forgetting he was her captor. He was lover now—ardent, persuasive, gentle, wanting. Tenderness overwhelmed her and, with a silent moan of helpless surrender, she curved her hand around his neck, her lips moving on his with awakening ardor.

Royce's mouth became more demanding, his tongue seeking, stroking, while his hand slid restlessly up her midriff, caressing her breast, then down again, swiftly unfastening her belt and gliding beneath her tunic. Jenny felt the firm, sliding stroke of his callused hand against her bare breast at the same instant her lips were seized in a devouring kiss.

She moaned beneath the sensual onslaught, and desire exploded in Royce as he felt her flesh swelling beneath his palm, her nipple rising up proudly against it. He brushed his fingers lightly back and forth against the impudent tip, then he caught it between his fingers, rolling it between them. He felt her gasp of shocked delight against his mouth as her fingers dug convulsively into his shoulders, and she kissed him deeply, as if trying to return the pleasure he was giving her.

Startled by the tormenting sweetness of her response, Royce lifted his mouth from hers, gazing down at her flushed, intoxicating face while he continued to caress her breast, telling himself that in a moment he would let her go.

The women he had bedded never wanted to be seduced or handled gently. They wanted the leashed violence, the power and stamina that were part of his legend. They wanted to be conquered, subdued, taken roughly, used—by the Wolf. The number of women who had implored "Hurt me" in bed with him were too numerous to count. The role of sexual conqueror had been thrust on him, and he'd accepted it for years, but with increasingly frequent bouts of boredom and, lately, disgust.

Slowly, Royce took his hand from her swollen breast, commanding himself to release her, to stop what he had begun and stop it *now*. Tomorrow, he was undoubtedly going to regret having taken things this far, he knew. On the other hand, if he *was* going to have regrets, he might as well have something substantial to regret, he decided. And with some half-formed idea of allowing them both a little more of the pleasure they seemed to be finding together tonight, Royce bent his head and kissed her, while he spread her tunic open. His gaze drifted downward, riveting on the enticing banquet bared before him. Exquisite breasts, round and full, tipped with pink nipples hardened into tight buds of desire, quivered beneath his gaze; her skin was as smooth as cream, glowing in the firelight, as untouched as new-fallen snow.

Drawing a steadying breath, he dragged his gaze from her breasts to her lips and then to her mesmerizing eyes, while his hand unfastened his tunic, pulling it out of the way so that he could feel those soft white mounds pressed against his bare chest.

Already seduced into near insensibility by the heat of his kisses, his gaze, and his wine, Jenny gazed dazedly at the firm sensual line of his lips, watching as they descended purposefully to hers. Her eyes closed and the world began to spin as his mouth seized hers with raw hunger, parting her lips as his tongue drove into her mouth. She moaned with delight as his hand cupped her breast, forcing it upward, holding it high, while he slowly lowered his bare, hair-roughened chest against it, and then his weight came down on her. His body half covering hers, he trailed sensuous kisses from her mouth to her ear, his tongue flicking into the sensitive crevice, then exquisitely exploring it until Jenny was writhing against him.

He shifted his mouth across her cheek to her lips, and his mouth began a slow, erotic seduction that soon had Jenny moaning low in her throat. His parted lips covered hers, forcing them to open wider until he captured her tongue, drawing it delicately into his mouth as if to sip from its sweetness, and then he gave her his until Jenny instinctively matched his movements and when she did the kiss went wild. His tongue tangled with hers, his hands shoved into her hair, and Jenny twined her arms around his neck, lost in the earth-shattering kiss.

His lower body lifted, his legs nudging hers apart, and he eased himself between them, forcing her into vibrant awareness of his rigid hardness pressing meaningfully between her thighs. Devastated by the raw hunger of his passion, she clung to him, stifling a cry of disappointment when he pulled his mouth from hers, then gasping with surprise as he lowered his mouth to her breasts. His lips closed on her nipple, tugging gently, then tightening, drawing hard on it until her back arched and shock waves of pure pleasure burst through every part of her being. And just when she thought she could bear no more, he tugged harder, wringing a low moan from her. The instant he heard it he stopped, turning his face to lavish the other breast with the same attention, while she ran her fingers through his thick dark hair, mindlessly holding his head pressed to her.

When she felt as if she would surely die of the pleasure, he suddenly braced his weight on his hands, lifting his chest away from her. Cold air against her heated skin, combined with the absence of his flesh against hers, pulled her partly from the mindless euphoria where he had taken her. Jenny dragged her eyes open and saw him hovering above her, his eyes hotly caressing her swollen breasts, their nipples proud and erect from his tongue and lips and teeth.

Panic—belated, lethargic—finally hit Jenny as the force of his demanding thighs sent desire spiraling up through her. He started to bend his head to her and, terrified that she had waited too long, she shook her head frantically. "Please," she gasped. But he was already lifting up, his body tensing, alert. A split second later, a guard called from outside the tent. "Your pardon, milord; the men have returned."

Without a word, Royce rolled to his feet, swiftly adjusted his clothing, and stalked out of the tent. In a daze of suspended yearning and confusion, Jenny watched him go, and then sanity slowly returned. Shame raged through her as she looked down at her disarranged clothing and tugged it back into place, running a shaking hand through her wildly disordered hair. It would have been bad enough had he forced her to yield to him, but he hadn't. As if some spell had been cast over her, she had wantonly, willingly joined in her own seduction. The shock of what she had done—*nearly* done—made her body tremble, and when she tried to blame him, her conscience refused to let her.

Frantically she began to think of things she could say, or do, when he returned, for as naive as she was, she knew instinctively that he would want to take up where they had left off, and her heart began to pound in fear—not of him, but of herself.

The minutes passed and became an hour, and her fear turned to surprise, and finally—blessedly—to exhaustion. Curled up in the furs, her eyes drifted closed, then snapped open what must have been hours later to find him standing over her.

Warily, she searched his hard, implacable features, her sleep-drugged mind registering that the "lover" who had left the tent, looked no more eager to continue his seduction than she was to have it begin again.

"It was a mistake," he said flatly, "for both of us. It won't happen again."

It was the very last thing she'd expected him to say, and as he turned and walked swiftly out of the tent into the night, she assumed that must be his form of curt apology for what had happened. Her lips parted in silent surprise, then she hastily closed her eyes as Gawin entered the tent and lay down upon his pallet near the entrance.

Chapter Seven

At sunrise the tents were dismantled and the sound of continuous, rolling thunder filled the air as five thousand mounted knights, mercenaries, and squires moved out of the valley, followed by heavy wagons groaning beneath the weight of bombards, mortars, battering rams, catapults, and all the equipment and supplies necessary for a siege.

To Jenny, who was riding beside Brenna, heavily guarded on both sides by armed knights, the world became an unreal blur of noise and dust and inner confusion. She didn't know where she was going, or where she was, or even *who* she was. It was as if the whole world was in upheaval and everyone had changed somehow. Now it was Brenna who cast reassuring smiles at Jenny, while Jenny, who had thought herself reasonably intelligent, found herself watching—*hoping* for a glimpse of Royce Westmoreland!

She saw him several times as he rode past her, and it was as if he, too, was a stranger. Mounted on a huge black destrier, and clad in sinister black from his tall boots to the mantle that draped his powerful shoulders and billowed out behind him, he was the most frighteningly overpowering figure that Jenny had ever beheld—a deadly stranger bent on destroying her family, her clan, and everything she held dear.

That night as she lay beside Brenna, staring up at the stars, she tried not to think of the ugly siege tower that cast its ominous shadow across the meadow— the tower that would soon be moved into place against Merrick keep's ancient walls. Before, in the valley, she'd glimpsed it among the trees, but she'd never been certain what it was. Or perhaps she simply hadn't wanted her fears confirmed.

Now, she could think of little else, and she found herself clinging desperately to Brenna's prediction that King James might send forces to help her clan in the battle. And all the while, some tiny part of her refused to believe there was going to *be* a battle. Perhaps it was because she could not quite believe that the man who'd kissed and touched her with such passionate tenderness could actually mean to turn around and, coldly and unemotionally, slay her family and her clan. In some gentle, naive part of her heart, Jenny could not believe the man who teased and laughed with her last night could be capable of that.

But then, she could not entirely believe last night had ever happened. Last night he had been a tender, persuasive, insistent lover. Today he was a stranger who was capable of forgetting she existed.

Royce had not forgotten she existed—not even on the second day of their journey. Memories of the way she'd felt in his arms, the heady sweetness of her kisses and tentative caresses, had kept him awake for two consecutive nights. All day yesterday, as he'd ridden past the columns of his men, he'd found himself watching for a glimpse of her.

Even now, as he rode at the head of his army and squinted at the sun, trying to gauge the time, her musical laughter tinkled like bells on the fringes of his mind. He shook his head, **as** if to clear it, and suddenly she was looking at him with that jaunty sideways smile of hers . . .

Why do you think I decided not to marry? he'd said.

Because no suitable lady has asked you? she'd teased.

He heard her muffled chuckle as she tried to look reproving: *Do not ever attempt to dazzle your lady fair with your glib flattery, milord, for you haven't a prayer of success . . .*

Based on what I know of you, I can only assume you'd toss the lady over your lap and attempt to beat her into submission . . .

He could not believe that one naive Scottish girl could possess so much spirit and courage. Royce tried to tell himself this growing fascination, this *obsession* with his captive was merely the result of the lust she'd fired in him two nights ago, but he knew it was more than lust that held him enthralled: Unlike most of her sex, Jennifer Merrick was neither repelled nor titillated by the thought of being handled and bedded by a man whose very name was associated with danger and death. The shy, passionate response he'd awakened in her two nights ago owed nothing to fear; it had been born of tenderness and then desire. Knowing all the rumors about him as she obviously did, she had still offered herself up to his caresses with innocent sweetness. And *that* was why he couldn't drag her from his mind. Or perhaps, he thought grimly, she had simply deluded herself into thinking that despite his reputation, he was actually like the virtuous, unsullied, gallant knight of her dreams. That possibility—that her tenderness and passion had been the result of some girlish, naive self-delusion—was so distasteful Royce angrily put all thoughts of her aside and firmly resolved to forget her.

At midday, just as Jennifer sank down onto the grass beside Brenna, about to partake of the usual fare of stringy fowl and a slab of stale bread, she looked up and saw Arik stalking toward them. He stopped directly in front of her, his booted feet planted at least a yard apart, and said, "Come."

Already accustomed to the blond giant's apparent unwillingness to utter more words than were absolutely necessary, Jenny stood up. Brenna started to do likewise, but Arik held up his arm. "Not you."

With his hand locked around Jenny's upper arm, he marched her forward past hundreds of men who'd also settled onto the grass to eat their Spartan fare, then he drew her toward the woods beside the road, stopping at a place where Royce's knights seemed to be standing guard beneath the trees.

Sir Godfrey and Sir Eustace stepped aside, their normally pleasant faces stony, and Arik propelled her forward with a light shove that sent her stumbling into a little clearing.

Her captor was seated on the ground, his broad shoulders propped against a tree trunk, his knee drawn up, studying her in silence. In the warmth of the day, he'd removed his mantle and was clad in a simple brown tunic with full sleeves, thick brown hose, and boots. He did not look nearly as much like the specter of death and destruction he'd appeared to be yesterday, and Jenny felt an absurd spurt of happiness that he'd evidently not forgotten her existence.

Pride prevented her from displaying any such emotion, however. Since she was completely uncertain about how she ought to act or feel, Jenny stayed where she was and even managed to return his steady gaze, until his speculative silence finally unnerved her. Trying to keep her tone politely noncommittal, she said, "I gather you want me?"

For some reason her question brought a mocking gleam to his eyes. "You're right."

Flustered by his odd, mocking tone, she waited and then said, "Why?"

"Now *there's* a question."

"Are—are we having a conversation?" Jenny demanded darkly, and to her complete confusion, he threw back his head and shouted with laughter, the rich, throaty sound echoing in the clearing.

Her face was a mirror of lovely confusion, and Royce sobered, taking pity on the innocence that made him laugh at the same time it made him want her more than he had two nights ago. He gestured toward the white cloth spread out upon the ground. On it were some pieces of the same fowl and bread that she'd been eating, along with some apples and a chunk of cheese. Quietly he said, "I enjoy your company. I also thought 'twould be more pleasant for you to eat here with me than to eat in an open field surrounded by thousands of soldiers. Was I wrong?"

If he hadn't said he enjoyed her company, Jenny might well have informed him that he was *quite* wrong, but she was not proof against that deep compelling voice telling her that, in essence, he had missed her. "No," she admitted, but in the interest of pride and prudence both, she did not sit down near him. Picking up a shiny red apple, she sat down on a fallen log, just beyond his reach, but after a few minutes of casual conversation, she began to feel perfectly relaxed in his company and oddly light-hearted. It never occurred to her that this strange phenomenon was the result of his deliberate efforts to make her feel safe from his advances, or to make her forget the abrupt and callous way he'd ended their preliminary lovemaking two nights ago, so that she wouldn't automatically rebuff his next attempt.

Royce knew exactly what he was doing, and why he was doing it, but he told himself that if by some holy miracle he were able to keep his hands off of her until he sent her either to her father or his king, then his efforts had not been wasted, for he was having a very pleasant and somewhat prolonged meal in a cozy clearing.

A few minutes later, in the midst of a perfectly

impersonal discussion of knights, Royce suddenly found himself thinking almost jealously of her former suitor. "Speaking of knights," he said abruptly, "what happened to yours?"

She bit into her apple, her expression quizzical. "My what?"

"Your knight," Royce clarified. "—Balder. If your father was in favor of the marriage, how did you dissuade old Balder from continuing to press you?"

The question seemed to discomfit her and, as if stalling for time in which to compose an answer, she drew her long shapely legs up against her chest and wrapped her arms around them, then she perched her chin upon her knees and raised brilliant blue, laughing eyes to his face. Perched upon that log, Royce thought she looked incredibly desirable—a charming wood nymph with long curly hair, clad in a boy's tunic and hose. A *wood nymph?* Next she would have him composing sonnets to her beauty—and wouldn't *that* delight her sire, not to mention enliven the gossip at court in two countries! "Was that question too difficult for you?" he said, his voice sharp with self-annoyance. "Shall I try to frame an easier one?"

"What an impatient nature you have!" she replied sternly, completely undaunted by his tone.

Her words were accompanied by such a wellbred, reproving look that Royce chuckled in spite of himself. "You're right," he admitted, grinning at the outrageous child-woman who dared to lecture him on his shortcomings. "Now, tell me why old Balder withdrew."

"Very well, but it's most unchivalrous of you to badger me so about matters which are of a most private nature—not to mention excruciatingly embarrassing."

"Embarrassing for whom?" Royce asked, ignoring her jibe. "For you, or for Balder?"

"*I* was embarrassed. Lord Balder was indignant.

119

You see," she clarified with smiling candor, "I'd never seen him until the night he came to Merrick to sign the betrothal contract. 'Twas an awful experience," she said, her expression as amused as it was horrified.

"What happened?" he prodded.

"If I tell you, you must promise to remember that I was much like any other girl of fourteen—filled with dreams of the wondrous young knight whose wife I would become. I knew in my mind just how he would look," she added, smiling ruefully as she thought back on it. "He would be fair-haired, and young, of course, his face wonderful to look upon. His eyes would be blue, and his bearing would be princely. He would be strong, too, strong enough to protect our holdings for the children we would someday have." She glanced at Royce, her expression wry. "Such was my secret hope, and in my own behalf, it must be said that neither my father nor my half-brothers said aught to make me think Lord Balder would be otherwise."

Royce frowned, a picture of the foppish, elderly Balder flashing across his mind.

"And so there I was, strolling into the great hall at Merrick after spending hours practicing my walking in my bed chamber."

"You'd *practiced* walking?" Royce uttered, his tone filled with a mixture of amusement and disbelief.

"But of course," Jennifer said gaily. "You see, I desired to present a *perfect* picture of myself for my future lord's benefit. And so, it would not do that I bolt into the hall and seem too eager, nor that I walk too slowly and thus give the impression that I was reluctant. It was an enormous dilemma—deciding just how to walk, not to mention what to wear. I was so desperate that I actually consulted my two step-brothers, Alexander and Malcolm, to get their male opinion. William, who is a darling, was away from home for the day with my stepmother."

"Surely they must have forewarned you about

Balder." The look in her eyes told him otherwise, but even so he was not prepared for the sharp stab of pity he felt as she shook her head.

"Quite the opposite. Alexander said he feared the gown my stepmother had chosen was not nearly fine enough. He urged me to wear the green one instead and dress it up with my mother's pearls. Which I did. Malcolm suggested I wear a jeweled dagger at my side so I'd not be overshadowed by my future husband's illustrious presence. Alex said my hair looked too common and carroty and must needs be caught up under a golden veil and laced with a rope of sapphires. Then, after I was attired to their satisfaction, they helped me practice walking . . ." As if loyalty prevented her from painting an unflattering image of her stepbrothers, she smiled brightly and said in a determinedly reassuring voice, "They were funning me, of course, as brothers will fun their sisters, but I was too filled with dreams to notice."

Royce saw beyond her words to the truth and recognized the heartless malice in their trick. He felt a sudden, overpowering desire to smash his fist into her brothers' faces—just for "fun."

"I was so concerned about every detail being just right," she was saying, her face perfectly cheerful now as if she were laughing at herself, "that I was quite late coming down to the hall to meet my betrothed. When I finally arrived I paraded across the hall at just the right speed, on legs that trembled not only with nervousness but with the *weight* of the pearls, rubies, sapphires, and gold chains at my throat and wrists and waist. You should have *seen* the look on my poor stepmother's face when she saw the way I was attired. It was quite a garish display, I can tell you," Jenny laughed, blithely unaware of the pent-up anger building in Royce as she continued.

"My stepmother later said I looked like a coffer of jewels with legs," she chuckled. "She did not say it

121

unkindly." Jennifer hastily added when she saw the black scowl on her captor's face. "She was quite sympathetic, actually."

When she fell silent, Royce prodded. "And your sister, Brenna? What had she to say?"

Jennifer's eyes lit with fondness. "Brenna will always find something good to say about me, no matter how shocking my mistakes or outrageous my conduct. She said I 'sparkled like the sun and moon and stars.'" A bubble of laughter escaped Jenny and she regarded Royce with eyes aglow with merriment. "Which of course I did—sparkle, I mean."

His voice harsh with feelings he could neither understand nor contain, Royce looked at her and said tightly, "Some women need no jewels to make them sparkle. You are one of them."

Jennifer's mouth dropped open in shock and she gaped at him. "Was that a *compliment?*"

Thoroughly annoyed that she'd actually reduced him to uttering gallantries, Royce shrugged curtly and said, "I'm a soldier, not a poet, Jennifer. It was merely a statement of fact. Go on with your story."

Abashed and confused, Jennifer hesitated and then dismissed his unaccountable mood change with a mental shrug. Helping herself to another bite of apple, she said cheerfully, "In any case, Lord Balder does not share *your* disinterest in jewels. In truth," she said, laughing, "his eyes nearly popped right out of his head—so *entranced* was he with my glitter. In fact, he was so bedazzled by my vulgar display that he passed only a cursory glance over my face before turning to my father and saying, 'I'll have her.'"

"And, just like that, you were betrothed?" Royce asked, frowning.

"No, 'just like that' I nearly fell into a dead swoon —so shocked was I by my first glimpse of my 'beloved's' countenance. William caught me before I fell to the floor and helped me onto the bench at the table, but even once I was seated and beginning to regain my senses, I could not tear my gaze from Lord Balder's features! Besides being older than my father, he was thin as a stick, and he was wearing—er—" Her voice trailed off and she hesitated uncertainly. "I ought not to tell you the rest."

"Tell me *all* of it," Royce commanded.

"All?" Jennifer echoed uncomfortably.

"Everything."

"Very well," she sighed, "but 'tis not a pretty story."

"What was Balder wearing?" Royce prodded, beginning to grin.

"Well, he was wearing . . ."—her shoulders rocked with mirth as she gasped—"he was wearing someone else's *hair!*"

Laughter, rich and deep echoed from Royce's chest, joining the lilting music of Jennifer's.

"I'd scarce recovered my senses from *that* when I next noted that he was eating the most peculiar-looking food I'd ever seen. Earlier, while my brothers had been helping me decide what to wear, I'd heard them joking between themselves about Lord Balder's desire to have artichokes at every meal. I realized at a glance that the peculiar-looking fried objects heaped upon Lord Balder's platter must be the food called the artichoke, and *that* was what led to my being banished from the hall and Balder crying off."

Royce, who already guessed why Balder had been eating the food which was purported to increase male potency, fought to keep his expression grave. "What happened?"

"Well, I was very nervous—stricken actually—at the prospect of wedding such a dreadful man. In truth he was a maiden's nightmare, not a maiden's dream, and as I studied him at table, I felt a most unladylike urge to shove my fists into my eyes and howl like a babe."

"But you didn't, of course," Royce guessed, smiling as he recalled her indomitable spirit.

"No, but 'twould have been better if I *had*," she admitted with a smile accompanied by a sigh. "What I *did* was much worse. I couldn't bear to look at *him*, so I concentrated upon the artichokes which I'd never seen before. I was watching him gobble the things up, wondering what they were and why he ate them. Malcolm noticed what I was looking at and so *he* told me why Lord Balder was eating them. And *that* was what made me begin to giggle . . ."

Her wide blue eyes swimming with mirth and her shoulders shaking helplessly, she said, "At first I managed to hide it, and then I snatched a handkerchief and pressed it to my lips, but I was so overwrought the giggles became a laugh. I laughed and I laughed and 'twas so contagious even poor Brenna began to laugh. We laughed ourselves into fits, until my father sent Brenna and me from the hall."

Raising her mirthful eyes to Royce's she gasped gaily, "Artichokes! Have you ever heard anything so absurd?"

With a supreme effort, Royce managed to look puzzled. "You don't believe artichokes are beneficial to a man's prowess?"

"I—er—" Jennifer blushed as she finally realized how inappropriate the topic was, but it was too late to turn back, and besides she was curious. "Do *you* believe it?"

"Certainly not," Royce said straight-faced. "Everyone knows 'tis *leeks and walnuts* that are beneficial in such matters."

"Leeks and —!" Jenny burst out in confusion, and then she saw the slight movement of his broad shoulders that betrayed his own laughter, and she shook her head in smiling reproof. "In any case, Lord Balder decided—quite rightly—that there weren't enough jewels on earth worth having *me* as his wife. Several months later, I committed another unforgivable folly," she said, looking more seriously at Royce, "and my father decided I was in want of a stronger guiding hand than my stepmother's."

"What 'unforgivable folly' did you commit that time?"

She sobered. "I openly challenged Alexander to either take back the things he was saying about me or else meet me on the field of honor—in a local tournament we had each year near Merrick."

"And he refused," Royce said with somber tenderness.

"Of course. 'Twould have been disgraceful for him to do otherwise. Besides my being a girl, I was only fourteen and he was twenty. I cared naught for his pride, however, for he was—not very nice," she finished mildly, but there was a wealth of pain in those three words.

"Did you ever avenge your honor?" Royce asked, an unfamiliar ache in his chest.

She nodded, a hint of a rueful smile touching her lips. "Despite Father's command that I not go near the tournament, I persuaded our armorer to lend me Malcolm's armor, and on the day of the joust, without anyone knowing who I was, I rode out onto the field and faced Alexander, who had distinguished himself often in the lists."

Royce felt his blood turn cold at the thought of her galloping down the field, charging toward a grown man wielding a lance. "You're lucky you were only unseated and not killed."

She chuckled. "'Twas Alexander who was unseated."

Royce stared at her in blank confusion. *"You* unseated *him?"*

"In a way," she grinned. "You see, just as he raised his lance to strike at me, I threw up my visor and stuck out my tongue."

In the shocked moment of silence that preceded Royce's explosion of laughter she added, "He *slid* off his horse."

Outside the little clearing, knights and squires, mercenaries and archers stopped what they were doing and stared at the woods where the earl of Claymore's laughter rose above the trees.

When at last he'd caught his breath, Royce regarded her with a tender smile filled with admiration. "Your strategy was brilliant. I'd have knighted you right there on the field."

"My father was not quite so enthusiastic," she said without rancor. "Alex's skill at the joust was the pride of our clan—something I'd failed to consider. Instead of knighting me on the field, my father gave me the thrashing I probably deserved. And then he sent me off to the abbey."

"Where he kept you for two full years," Royce summarized, his voice filled with gruff gentleness.

Jenny stared at him across the short distance separating them, while a startling discovery slowly revealed itself to her. The man who people called a ruthless, brutal barbarian was something quite different: he was, instead, a man who was capable of feeling acute sympathy for a foolish young girl—it was there in the softened lines of his face. Mesmerized, she watched him stand up, her eyes imprisoned by his hypnotic silver gaze, as he walked purposefully toward her. Without realizing what she was doing, Jenny slowly stood up, too. "I think," she whispered, her face turned up to his, "that legend plays you false. All the things they say you've done—they aren't true," she whispered softly, her beautiful eyes searching his face as if she could see into his soul.

"They're true," Royce contradicted shortly, as visions of the countless bloody battles he'd fought paraded across his mind in all their lurid ugliness, complete with battlefields littered with the corpses of his own men and those of his foes.

Jenny knew naught of his bleak memories, and her gentle heart rejected his self-proclaimed guilt. She knew only that the man standing before her was a man who had gazed upon his dead horse with pain and sorrow etched on his moonlit features; a man who had just now winced with sympathy at the silly story she'd told of dressing up to meet her elderly knight. "I don't believe it," she murmured.

"Believe it!" he warned. Part of the reason Royce wanted her was that she did not cast him in the role of bestial conqueror when he touched her, but he was equally unwilling to let her deceive herself by casting him in another role—that of her knight in virtuous, shining armor. "Most of it is true," he said flatly.

Dimly, Jenny was aware that he was reaching for her; she felt his hands close around her upper arms like velvet manacles, drawing her nearer, saw his mouth slowly descending to hers. And, as she gazed into those heavy-lidded, sensual eyes, some lambent protective instinct cried a warning that she was getting in too deep. Panicked, Jenny turned her face away a scant instant before his lips touched hers, her breath coming in rapid gasps as if she was running. Undaunted, Royce kissed her temple instead, trailing his warm lips over her cheek, pulling her nearer, brushing his lips down the sensitive column of her neck, while Jenny turned liquid inside. "Don't," she breathed shakily, turning her face further aside and, without realizing what she was doing, she clutched at the fabric of his tunic, clinging to him for support as the world began to reel. "Please," she whispered, as his arms tightened around her and his tongue slid up to her ear, sensuously, leisurely exploring each curve and crevice, making her shudder with longing while his hands shifted up and down her back. "Please, stop," she said achingly.

In response, his hand slid lower, splaying against her spine to force her body into intimate, thorough contact with his rigid thighs—an eloquent statement that he couldn't, and wouldn't, stop. His other hand slid to her nape, stroking sensuously, urging her to lift her head for his kiss. Drawing a shattered breath,

Jenny turned her face into his woolen tunic, refusing his tender persuasion. When she did, the hand at her nape tightened in an abrupt command. Helpless to deny either his urging or his command any longer, Jenny slowly lifted her face to receive his kiss.

His hand plunged into her thick hair, holding her captive while his mouth seized hers in a plundering, devouring kiss that sent her spiraling off into a hot darkness where nothing mattered except his seductive, urgent mouth and knowledgeable hands. Overwhelmed by her own tenderness and his raw, potent sexuality, Jenny fed his hunger, her parted lips welcoming the thrusting invasion of his tongue. She leaned into him and felt him gasp against her mouth the split second before his hands slid possessively over her back and sides and breasts, then swept down, pulling her tightly to his rigid arousal. Helplessly, Jenny melted against him, returning his endless drugging kisses, moaning in her throat as her breasts swelled to fill his palms. Fire trembled through her as his hand forced its way between the waist of her heavy hose, shoving downward, cupping her bare buttocks and moving her tighter against the thrusting hardness of his manhood, crushing her against him.

Between the wildly erotic sensation of his hand pressed against her bare skin and the bold evidence of his desire pressing insistently against her, Jenny was lost. Sliding her hands up his chest, she twined them around his neck and gave herself up to his pleasure, stimulating it, sharing it, glorying in the groan that tore from his chest.

When he finally dragged his mouth from hers, he held her clasped against his chest, his breathing harsh and rapid. Her eyes closed, her arms still twined around his neck, her ear pressed to the heavy beating of his heart, Jenny drifted between total peace and a strange, delirious joy. Twice he had made her feel wondrous, terrifying, exciting things. But today, he had made her feel something else: he had made her feel needed and cherished and wanted, and those last three things she'd longed to feel for as long as she could remember.

Lifting her face from his hard, muscled chest she tried to raise her head. Her cheek brushed against the soft brown fabric of his tunic, and even the simple touch of his clothing against her skin made her senses reel dizzily. Finally she managed to tip her head back and look at him. Passion was still smoldering in those smoky gray eyes. Quietly and without emphasis he stated, "I want you."

This time there was no doubt about his meaning, and her answer was whispered without thought, as if it had suddenly been born in her heart and not her mind: "Badly enough to give me your word not to attack Merrick?"

"No."

He said the word dispassionately, without hesitation, without regret or even annoyance; he refused as easily as he would have refused a meal he didn't want.

The single word hit her like a dousing of ice water; Jenny drew back and his hands fell away.

In a daze of shame and shock, she bit down hard on her trembling lower lip and turned aside, trying numbly to restore order to her hair and clothing, when what she longed to do was run from the woods—from everything that had happened here—before she choked on the tears that were nearly suffocating her. It wasn't so much that he had refused what she offered. Even now in all her misery, she realized that what she'd asked of him had been foolish—impossibly mad. What hurt so unbearably was the *callousness*, the *ease* with which he'd brushed aside all she'd tried to offer—her honor, her pride, her body, at the sacrifice of everything she'd been taught to believe in, to value.

She started to walk out of the woods, but his voice

stopped her in her tracks. "Jennifer," he said in that tone of implacable authority she was coming to loathe, "you'll ride beside me the rest of the way."

"I'd rather not," she said flatly, without turning. She would have drowned herself rather than let him see how much he'd hurt her, and so she added, haltingly, "It's your men—I've been sleeping in your tent, but Gawin has always been there. If I eat with you and *ride* beside you they'll . . . misinterpret . . . things."

"What my men think matters not," Royce replied, but that wasn't entirely true and he knew it. By openly treating Jenny as his "guest," he'd been rapidly losing face with the tired, loyal men who'd fought beside him. And not all his army obeyed him out of loyalty. Among the mercenaries, there were thieves and murderers, men who followed him because he kept bread in their bellies and because they feared the consequences should they dare to disobey. He ruled them with his strength. But whether they were loyal knights or common mercenaries, they all believed it was Royce's right, his *duty,* to throw her down and mount her, to use her body to humble her as the enemy deserved to be humbled.

"Of course it doesn't matter," Jenny said bitterly as the full force of her surrender in his arms hit her with all its humiliating clarity. "It isn't *your* reputation 'twill be slaughtered, 'tis *mine.*"

In a tone of calm finality he stated, "They'll think whatever it suits them to think. When you return to your horse, have your escort bring you forward."

Wordlessly, Jennifer cast a look of utter loathing at him, lifted her chin, and walked out of the clearing, her slender hips swaying with unconscious regal grace.

Despite the fact she'd only looked at him for a second before she'd walked out of the woods, Jenny had registered the odd light in his eyes and the indefinable smile lurking at the corner of his lips. She had no idea what was behind it, she only knew his smile increased her fury until it completely eclipsed her misery.

Had Stefan Westmoreland, or Sir Eustace, or Sir Godfrey been present to see that look, they could have told her what it presaged, and their explanation would have upset Jenny far more than she already was: Royce Westmoreland looked exactly as he did when he was about to storm a particularly challenging, desirable castle and claim it for his own. It meant that he would not be deterred by the odds or the opposition. It meant that he was already pleasantly contemplating victory.

Whether the men had somehow glimpsed their embrace through the trees, or whether it was because they'd heard her laughing with him, as Jenny walked stiffly back to her horse, she was subjected to leering gazes and knowing looks that surpassed anything she'd had to endure since her capture.

Unhurriedly, Royce strolled out of the woods and glanced at Arik. "She'll ride with us." He walked over to the horse Gawin was holding for him, and his knights automatically went to their horses, swinging into saddles with the ease of men who spent great portions of their lives on horseback. Behind them, the rest of the army followed suit, obeying an order before it was given.

His captive, however, chose to flagrantly disobey an order that *had* been given, and did not join him at the front of the column when it moved forward. Royce reacted to that piece of tempestuous rebellion with amused admiration for her courage, then he turned to Arik and said with a suppressed chuckle, "Go and get her."

Now that Royce had finally reached the decision to have her and was no longer waging an internal battle against desire, he was in excellent spirits. He found the prospect of soothing and winning her while they rode toward Hardin infinitely appealing. At Hardin, they would have the luxury of a soft bed and ample privacy; in the meantime, he would have the undeniable pleasure of her company for the rest of today and tonight.

It did not occur to him that the gentle, innocent temptress who'd surrendered in his arms both times he held her, who'd returned his passion with such intoxicating sweetness, might no longer be quite so easy to soothe. In battle he was undefeated, and the idea of being defeated now, by a girl whose desire for him was nearly as great as his for her, was beyond consideration. He wanted her, wanted her more than he would have believed possible, and he intended to have her. Not on her terms, of course, but he was willing to make concessions—*reasonable* concessions that, at the moment, seemed vaguely to call for splendid furs and jewels, as well as the respect she would be entitled to receive as his mistress from all who served him.

Jenny saw the giant riding purposefully toward the rear of the column at the same time she remembered the laughter she'd seen on Royce's face when she left him, and the wrath that burst inside of her made her head pound.

Swiveling his charger in a tight circle, Arik reined in sharply beside her and coolly raised his brows. He was, Jenny understood with infuriated clarity, silently ordering her to ride to the front with him. Jenny, however, was so overwrought she was beyond being intimidated. Feigning complete lack of knowledge as to the reason for his presence, she pointedly turned her head and began to speak to Brenna: "Have you observed—" she began and broke off with a start as Arik deftly reached out and grabbed the reins of Jenny's mare.

"Unhand my horse!" she snapped, jerking on the poor little mare's reins with enough force to pull the mare's nose to the sky. The horse swiveled and danced sideways in confusion, and Jenny turned her pent-up fury on the invulnerable emissary of her enemy.

Glowering at Arik, she hauled back on her left rein. "Take your hand away!"

Pale blue eyes regarded her with cold indifference, but he was, at least, forced to speak, and Jenny reveled in that tiny victory: "Come!"

Her rebellious eyes locked with his pale blue ones, Jenny hesitated, and then, because she knew he'd merely force her to do his bidding, she snapped, "Then kindly move out of my way!"

The mile ride to the front of the column was possibly the most humbling event of Jenny's young life. Until today, she'd been kept out of sight of most of the men or else flanked by knights. Now, male heads swiveled as she came abreast, and lewd eyes stayed riveted on her slender form as she continued past them. Comments were made upon her person, the general shape of her person, and the specific shapes of her shapes—comments of a nature so personal that she was sorely tempted to whip the little mare to a gallop.

When she reached Royce at the front of the column, he could not help smiling at the tempestuous young beauty who was regarding him with such blazing defiance; she looked exactly as she had the night she stabbed him with his own dagger. "It would seem," he teased, "that I've somehow fallen into disfavor."

"You," she replied, with every ounce of scorn she could put into her voice, "are unspeakable!"

He chuckled. "*That* bad?"

Chapter Eight

By the time they were nearing Hardin castle late the following day, Royce was no longer feeling quite so affable. Instead of enjoying her wit as he'd hoped to do, he found himself riding beside a young woman who responded to his teasing comments or serious observations with a blank, polite stare designed to make him feel like a court jester with bells on his hat. Today, she had changed her tactic. Now, instead of treating him to silence, she responded to any remark of his by asking him a question about things which he could not and would not discuss with her—such as the date he planned to attack Merrick, the number of men he intended to bring with him, and how long he meant to keep her prisoner.

If her intent was to illustrate to him in the clearest possible way that she was the victim of brute force, and that *he* was the brute, she'd achieved her goal. If her intent was to annoy him, she was beginning to succeed there, too.

Jennifer was not unaware that she'd managed to ruin the journey for him, but she was not as delighted with her success as Royce supposed. In fact, as she scanned the craggy hills for some sign of a castle, she felt little more than exhaustion from the strain of trying to understand the enigmatic male beside her, and her own reactions to him. The earl had told her he wanted her, and he obviously wanted her badly enough to tolerate two days of rudeness from her, which was somewhat soothing to her battered pride. On the other hand, he did not want her badly enough to spare her kinsmen or her home.

Mother Ambrose had cautioned her about the "effect" Jenny might have on men; evidently, Jenny decided, the wise abbess must have meant her "effect" would make them behave like hateful, tender, rude, unpredictable madmen—all in the space of one hour. With a sigh, Jenny gave up trying to understand any of it. She simply wanted to go home, or back to the abbey, where at least she knew what to expect from people. She stole a glance behind her and saw Brenna engaged in pleasant conversation with Stefan Westmoreland, who'd been acting as her escort ever since Jenny had been forced to ride at the front, with his brother. The fact that Brenna was safe and seemed content was the only bright spot in Jenny's dismal predicament.

Hardin castle came into view just before dusk. Situated high atop a bluff, it loomed like an immense fortress, sprawling in all directions, its mellowed stone walls lit by the sinking sun. Jenny's heart plummeted; it was five times larger than Merrick keep and it looked impregnable. Bright blue flags were flying from the castle's six round towers, proclaiming that the lord of the castle was expected to be in residence by eventide.

Their horses clattered across the drawbridge and into the bailey of the castle, and servants ran out into the courtyard to take hold of horses' bridles and make themselves useful to the new arrivals. The earl came around to lift Jenny down from her little mare, then he escorted her into the hall. A stooped, elderly man, who Jenny assumed must be the steward, approached, and Royce began issuing orders: "Have someone fetch refreshment for myself and my—" In the split second Royce took to decide on the right term to apply to Jennifer, the old steward took one look at the way she was dressed, and his contemptuous expression registered his own conclusion: *Slut.* "—my guest," Royce stated.

Being mistaken for one of the strumpets who traveled along with armies was the last and final indignity Jennifer could bear. Yanking her mortified gaze from the old man's scrutiny, she pretended to inspect the great hall while the earl continued issuing orders. He had told her that King Henry had only recently given him Hardin, and that he'd not been here before. As Jenny glanced about, her woman's eyes noticed at once that, although Hardin castle was huge, it was ill kept. The rushes on the floor had not been changed in years, cobwebs hung from the high, timbered ceiling like thick gray curtains, and the servants were slovenly.

"Would you like something to eat?" Royce asked, turning to her.

In a proud, angry effort to disabuse the old steward —and his entire staff of slatternly servants—that she was *not* what she appeared to be, Jennifer turned to the earl and coldly replied, "No, I would not. I would *like* to be shown to a chamber, preferably one somewhat cleaner than this hall, and I would like a bath and some clean clothing, if any of that is possible in this—this *pile* of *rocks.*"

Had Royce not seen the look the steward had given her, he would have reacted far more strongly to her words and her tone, but having seen it, he kept his temper under control. Turning to the steward he said, "Conduct *Countess* Merrick to the chamber next to mine." To Jennifer he said coolly, "Be down here for supper in two hours."

Any gratitude Jenny might have felt at his deliberate use of her title was obliterated by her turmoil at the location he'd chosen for her bedchamber. "I'll dine in my chamber, behind a *locked* door, or not at all," she informed him.

This wholly unacceptable piece of public defiance before fifty gaping serfs, added to the rest of her behavior for the last two days, finally convinced Royce that a sterner reprisal was in order, and he provided it unhesitatingly. "Jennifer," he said in a calm, uncompromising voice that completely belied the harshness of the punishment he was about to deliver, "until your disposition improves, your visits with your sister are over."

Jennifer paled, and Brenna, who was just being escorted into the hall by Stefan Westmoreland, sent a pleading look first to Jenny and then to the man beside her. To Jennifer's amazement, Stefan spoke up. "Royce, your edict is as much a punishment to Lady Brenna, who has done nothing—"

He broke off at the look of icy displeasure his brother sent him.

Freshly bathed and shaven, Royce sat at the table in the great hall with his knights and his brother. The servants had laid out trenchers filled with watery venison stew which was growing cool. Royce's attention, however, was not on the unappetizing food; he was watching the narrow steps that wound down from the bedchambers above, trying to decide whether or not to go up there and drag both women down, for, in an amazing show of spirit, Brenna had evidently chosen to join in her sister's rebellion and had ignored the servants' announcement that supper was being served below.

"They can go without eating," Royce decreed finally and picked up his eating dagger.

Long after the trestle tables had been dismantled and stacked against the walls, Royce remained sitting in the hall staring into the fire, his feet propped on a stool. His earlier intention of bedding Jennifer tonight had fallen by the wayside in the press of dozens of problems and decisions that had required his attention almost from the moment he'd started to sup. He considered going up to her chamber now, despite the lateness of the hour, but in the mood he was in, he was more likely to subdue her rebellion with brute force, rather than gently seducing her. After experiencing the exquisite pleasure of the way she felt in his arms when she was willing, he was reluctant to settle for anything less.

Godfrey and Eustace walked into the hall, relaxed and smiling after a night obviously spent with buxom castle wenches, and Royce's thoughts switched instantly to matters of a slightly different bent. Glancing at Godfrey, he said, "Instruct the sentries at the gate to detain anyone who seeks admittance and to notify me."

The knight nodded, but his handsome face was puzzled as he said, "If you're thinking of Merrick, he can't gather an army and get it here in less than a month."

"I'm not expecting an attack, I'm expecting some sort of trickery. If he attacks Hardin, he risks having his daughters slain in the battle, either accidentally by his own men or—he'll assume—by us. Since an attack is unthinkable under these circumstances, he'll have no choice but to try to get the women out. In order to do it, he'd have to get his people in here first. I've ordered the steward not to employ any additional servants unless they're specifically known to be from the village."

When both knights nodded, Royce abruptly stood up and started toward the stone steps at the end of the hall, then he turned back, his brows knitted into a slight frown. "Has Stefan said or done anything to give you the impression he's developing an . . . interest . . . in the younger girl?"

The two knights—both older than Stefan—looked

at each other and then at Royce, shaking their heads in the negative. "Why do you ask it?" Eustace asked.

"Because," Royce said wryly, "he leapt to her defense this afternoon when I ordered the women separated." Shrugging, he accepted his friends' opinion and headed up to his bedchamber.

Chapter Nine

Wrapped in a bedgown of soft cream wool, Jennifer gazed out the tiny window of her bedchamber the next morning, her eyes roving over the wooded hills just beyond the castle walls. Shifting her attention to the bailey below, she slowly scanned the thick walls surrounding it, looking for some sort of escape route . . . signs of a concealed door. There had to be one; Merrick had one inset into its wall, concealed behind an overgrowth of bushes; as far as she knew all castles had one which the residents could use for escape should an enemy penetrate the outer defenses. Despite her belief that such a door must exist, she could see no sign of it, or even a crack in the ten-foot-thick wall that she and Brenna might squeeze through. Raising her gaze, she watched the guards moving ceaselessly along the wall walk, their eyes trained on the road and surrounding hills. The domestic staff might be slovenly and slothful and sorely in need of training and direction, but the earl had not ignored the castle's defenses, she thought glumly. Every guard was alert, and they were posted at twenty-foot intervals.

The earl had told her that her father had been

notified that Brenna and she were his captives. That being the case, her father would have no trouble tracing an army of five thousand men to Hardin. If he meant to try to rescue them, then Hardin was no more than two days' hard ride—or a five-day march—from Merrick. But how on earth her father would be able to rescue her from such an incredibly well-fortified castle, she couldn't begin to imagine. Which brought her back to the same confounding problem she'd faced all along: It was up to her to think of some way to escape.

Her stomach growled, reminding her she'd had nothing to eat since before noon yesterday, and she turned away from the window in order to get dressed and go down to the hall. Starvation was no solution to her problem, she decided with a sigh as she walked over to the trunks of clothes that had been carried into her chamber this morning. Besides, if she didn't go down, she had no doubt that the earl would simply come fetch her, even if he had to break down her door.

She'd been able to soak in a wooden tub filled with hot water this morning, and at least she had the pleasure of feeling clean from her scalp to her toes. A dip in a freezing stream, she reflected, thinking back upon the last weeks, could not compare to warm water and a piece of soap.

The first trunk was filled with gowns belonging to the former lady of the castle and her daughters, many of which reminded Jenny of the lovely, whimsical style her Aunt Elinor preferred—the gowns ladies had worn with high conical headdresses and veils trailing to the floor. Although the gowns were no longer in fashion, no expense had been spared in the cloth, for there were rich satins and velvets and embroidered silks. Since all of them were too ornate for the occasion, and her position in this household, Jenny opened the next trunk. A gasp of sheer, feminine delight escaped her lips as she carefully removed a gown of softest cashmere.

She'd just finished smoothing her hair into place

when a servant rapped on her door and called in a shrill, panicky voice, "Milady, his lordship bade me tell you that if yer not down in the hall in five minutes to break yer fast, he'll come up here and bring you down hisself!"

Rather than let the earl think she was yielding from fear of that threat, Jenny called out, "You may tell his lordship that I *intended* to come down and that I'll be there in a few minutes."

Jenny waited what she deemed to be a "few" minutes, then she left the bedchamber. The stairway leading from the sleeping chambers above to the great hall below was steep and narrow, just like the one at Merrick, designed so that, in the event attackers gained entrance into the hall, they would have to fight their way upstairs with their sword arm blocked by the stone wall, while the defenders would not be nearly so hampered. Unlike the one at Merrick, however, this one was hung with spider webs. Shuddering as she imagined the leggy inhabitants of those webs, Jenny quickened her pace.

Lounging back in his chair, Royce watched the stairs, his jaw hardened with resolve, his mind mentally clicking off the passing minutes until her time ran out. The hall was mostly empty, save for a few of the knights who were lingering over their cups of ale, and the serfs who were clearing away the remnants of the morning meal.

Her time was up! he decided furiously and shoved back his chair with a force that made the legs screech against the flagstones. Then he stood stock still. Coming toward him in a soft, high-waisted gown the color of yellow sunlight was Jennifer Merrick. But not the charming nymph he'd become accustomed to seeing. In a transformation that both unnerved and enthralled him, the breathtaking young woman coming toward him was a countess fit to take her place in the most glittering courts in the land. Her hair was parted at the center, falling like a shimmering, red-gold waterfall, waving over her shoulders and down her back all the way to her waist, where it ended in thick curls.

The V-neck of her gown accented her full breasts, then it fell gently over her graceful hips in a long train; wide sleeves were turned back into cuffs at her wrists, then allowed to drape from her arms to her knees.

Royce had the odd sensation that she had become someone else, but when she drew near, there was no mistaking those brilliant blue eyes or that entrancing face.

She stopped in front of him, and his decision to have her, no matter how much trouble she put him to, now became an unshakable resolution. A slow, admiring smile drifted across his face as he said, "What a chameleon you are!"

Her eyes snapped with indignation. "Lizard?"

Royce bit back a laugh, trying to keep his eyes off the alluring display of smooth flesh exposed by the neckline of her gown, and to remember how justifiably annoyed with her he was. "I meant," he said levelly, "that you are changeable."

Jenny was not unaware of the odd, possessive gleam in his gray eyes as they roved over her, but she was momentarily distracted by the disquieting discovery of how handsome and elegant *he* looked in a deep blue tunic of the finest wool that set off the muscular width of his shoulders, its full sleeves drawn tightly at the wrists and trimmed with silver threads. A belt of flat silver disks rode low on his hips, from which hung a short sword with a large sapphire in its hilt. Below that, Jenny refused to look.

It finally dawned on her he was looking at her hair, and Jennifer belatedly realized that she was bareheaded. Reaching back, she caught up the wide yellow hood attached to her gown and pulled it up and forward, so that it framed her face and draped in graceful folds at her shoulders as it was meant to do.

"It's lovely," Royce said, watching her, "but I'd prefer to see your hair uncovered."

He was bent on charming her again today, she realized with a sinking feeling; she found it easier to deal with him when they were engaged in open hostilities than when he was being nice. Forcing herself to confront only one problem at a time, Jenny concentrated on his suggestion that she uncover her hair. "As you must surely know," she replied with cool civility as he pulled out a chair for her, " 'tis improper for any but young girls and brides to be bareheaded. A woman is required to conceal her—"

"Charms?" Royce provided, his appreciative gaze sliding over her hair and face and breasts.

"Yes."

"Because 'twas Eve who tempted Adam?" he speculated, stating what he knew was a religious belief.

Jenny reached for a trencher of porridge. "Yes."

"It has always seemed to me," he mockingly observed, "that what tempted him was an apple, in which case, 'twas gluttony that caused his downfall, not lust."

Knowing how she had twice fallen into his arms after just such lighthearted discourse as this, Jenny absolutely *refused* to be amused or shocked by that heresy, or even to venture any reply. Instead, she broached another topic in a carefully civil tone. "Would you be willing to reconsider your edict that my sister and I are to be separated?"

He quirked a speculative brow at her, "Has your disposition improved?"

His infuriating, unshakable calm, combined with his arrogance, nearly choked her. After a long moment, while she fought to dislodge the word from her throat, Jenny managed to say, "Yes."

Satisfied, Royce looked round at the serf hovering near his elbow and said, "Tell Lady Brenna her sister awaits her here." Then he turned back to Jennifer, pleasuring himself with the sight of her delicate profile. "Go ahead and eat."

"I was waiting for you to begin."

"I'm not hungry." An hour ago, he'd been ravenous, Royce thought wryly; now the only appetite he possessed was for her.

Famished from her self-imposed fast, Jenny did as he suggested and took a spoonful of porridge. Soon, however, his thoughtful gaze began to unnerve her. With a morsel of food partway to her lips, she slanted him a wary, sideways look. "Why are you watching me?"

Whatever answer he'd been about to give was interrupted by the serf who came rushing up to Jennifer and burst out in alarm, "It—it's your sister, milady. She wants you. She's coughin' in a way what makes me flesh crawl!"

Jenny's face drained of color. "Dear God, no!" she whispered, already bolting from her chair. "Not now —not here!"

"What do you mean?" Accustomed to dealing with every sort of emergency on a battlefield, Royce calmly put a restraining hand on her wrist.

"Brenna has an ailment of the chest—" Jenny explained desperately. "The attacks usually begin with coughing, and later she cannot breathe."

She tried to tug free of his grasp, but Royce stood up and accompanied her from the hall. "There must be some way to ease her."

"Not here!" Jenny said, so frightened her words were jumbled. "My Aunt Elinor mixes an aromatic— she knows more about herbs and cures than anyone in Scotland—there's some of it at the abbey."

"What's in it? Perhaps—"

"I don't know!" Jenny cried, almost pulling him up the steep steps. "All I know is the liquid has to be heated until steam comes from it, then Brenna breathes it, and it eases her."

Royce pushed open the door to Brenna's bedchamber, and Jenny raced to her bedside, her eyes frantically searching her sister's ashen face.

"Jenny?" Brenna whispered, clutching Jenny's hand, then she stopped, her body racked with violent spasms of coughing that lifted her spine clear off the bed. "I-I'm sick again," she gasped weakly.

"Don't worry," Jenny soothed, bending low and brushing the tangled blond curls from Brenna's forehead. "Don't worry——"

Brenna's anguished eyes shifted to the threatening figure of the earl looming in the doorway. "We have to go home," she told him, "I need the"——another siege of shrill, hacking coughing gripped her——"need the potion!"

Her heart hammering in mounting fear, Jenny looked over her shoulder at Royce. "Let her go home, *please!*"

"Nay, I think——"

Beside herself with fear, Jenny let go of Brenna's hand and hurried to the doorway motioning to Royce to follow her out of the chamber. Closing the door behind her, so her words wouldn't further distress Brenna, she faced her captor, her expression desperate. "Brenna can *die* from this without my aunt's aromatic. Her heart stopped beating the last time!"

Royce did not entirely believe the blond girl was actually in danger of death, but it was obvious Jennifer did believe it, and equally obvious that Brenna was not feigning that cough.

Jenny saw indecision flicker across his hard features and, thinking he was about to refuse, she tried to soften him by deliberately abasing herself. "You said I am too proud and I—I am," she said, laying her hand on his chest in supplication. "If you will let Brenna go, I'll do any humble task you give me. I'll scrub the floors. I'll wait upon you—I'll cook your food in the kitchen. I swear I'll repay you in a hundred ways."

Royce glanced down at the small, delicate hand laid upon his chest; heat was seeping through his tunic, desire already tightening his loins—and *that* with only her hand upon his chest. He didn't understand why she had such a volatile effect on him, but he understood that he wanted her—he wanted her willing and warm in his arms. And to accomplish that, he was prepared to do the first truly irrational thing in his life: he was prepared to let his most valuable hostage go—for despite Jennifer's belief that Lord Merrick was a loving—if stern—father, some of what she'd said made Royce doubt that the man had any deep feelings for his "troublesome" daughter.

Jenny's huge, fear-widened eyes were riveted to his face. "Please," she whispered, mistaking his silence for refusal. "I'll do *anything*. I'll *kneel* to you. Please, you have only to tell me what you want."

He finally spoke and Jenny tensed with hope, too overwrought to notice the odd, meaningful note in his voice as he said, "Anything?"

She nodded vigorously. "Anything—I'll have this castle set to rights and ready to receive a king within a few weeks, I'll say prayers for you each—"

" 'Tis not prayers I want," he interrupted.

Desperate to reach an agreement before he changed his mind, she said, "Then, tell me what it is you do want."

Implacably he stated, "You."

Jennifer's hand fell away from his tunic as he continued without emotion, "I do not want you on your knees, I want you in my bed. Willingly."

Her relief that he was willing to let Brenna leave was temporarily overwhelmed by blazing animosity at what he was demanding in return.

He was sacrificing nothing by releasing Brenna, for he would still have Jenny as hostage, yet he was requiring that she sacrifice everything. In willingly surrendering her honor to him, she would become a harlot; a disgrace to herself, her family, and all she held dear. True, she had offered herself to him once before—or nearly so—but what she had asked in return would have saved hundreds—mayhaps thousands—of lives. Lives of people she loved.

Moreover, when she'd made that offer, she'd been half-dazed from his passionate kisses and caresses. Now, however, she saw with cold clarity what the results of this bargain would be.

Behind her, Brenna's coughing rose to a terrible crescendo and Jenny shuddered with alarm; alarm for herself and her sister.

"Do we have a bargain?" he asked calmly.

Jenny lifted her small chin, looking like a proud young queen who'd just been stabbed by someone she trusted. "I was mistaken in you, my lord," she said bitterly. "I credited you with honor when you said me nay two days ago—for you could have promised me what I asked, taken what I offered, and then attacked Merrick anyway. Now I see 'twasn't honor, but arrogance. A *barbarian* has no honor."

Even when she knew she was vanquished, she was splendid, Royce thought, suppressing an admiring smile as he looked into her stormy blue eyes. "Is the bargain I offer you so loathsome?" he asked quietly, putting his hands on her stiff arms. "In truth, I have no need to bargain with you at all, Jennifer, and you know it. I could have taken you by force any time these past days."

Jennifer knew that and, although her resentment remained, she had to fight against falling under the spell of his deep voice as he continued, "I want you, and if that makes me a barbarian in your eyes, then so be it, but it doesn't have to be that way. If you let me, I'll make it good between us. There'll be no shame nor pain for you in my bed—except pain I must cause you the first time. After that, there will be only pleasure."

Coming from another knight, that speech might have been enough to sway the most sophisticated courtesan. Coming from England's most feared warrior to an unworldly, convent-bred Scottish girl, the effect was devastating. Jennifer felt blood rushing to her cheeks and a weak, trembling feeling from the pit of her stomach to her knees, as she was suddenly assaulted by memories of his heated kisses and caresses.

"Do we have a bargain?" Royce asked, his long fingers sliding up and down her arms in an unconscious caress. It occurred to him he'd just delivered the tenderest speech he'd ever spoken to a woman.

Jenny hesitated an endless moment, knowing she had no alternative, and then she felt herself nod imperceptibly.

"You'll keep your part of it?"

Jenny realized he was referring to the issue of her willingness, and this time her hesitation was longer. She wanted to hate him for this. She stood there, trying to do it, but some small, insistent voice reminded her sensibly that, at the hands of any other captor, she would undoubtedly have suffered a far worse fate already than the one he proposed. A brutal, unspeakable fate.

Staring up at his ruggedly chiseled face, she searched for some sign he might later relent, but instead of finding an answer, she suddenly became aware of how far back she had to tilt her head to look at him and how small she was in comparison to his height and breadth. Confronted with · his size, strength, and indomitable will, she had no choice, and she knew it. And realizing that made her defeat a little less painful, for she was completely outflanked and overpowered by a vastly superior force.

She met his gaze unflinchingly, proud even when she was surrendering. "I'll keep my part of the bargain."

"I'll have your word on it," he insisted when another siege of violent coughing drew her attention toward Brenna's chamber.

Jenny looked at him in surprise. The last time she'd

offered her word to him, he'd acted as if her word meant nothing, which wasn't surprising. Men, including her father, placed no value on the word of a mere woman. Evidently, Lord Westmoreland had changed his mind, and that amazed her. Feeling extremely uneasy and slightly proud at this, her first chance to have her pledge sought and honored, she whispered, "I give you my word."

He nodded, satisfied. "In that case, I'll go with you and you can tell your sister she's being taken back to the abbey. After that, you will not be permitted to be alone with her."

"Why ever not?" Jenny gasped.

"Because I doubt your sister has paid enough heed to Hardin's defenses to tell your father anything. *You,* however," he added in a voice of amused irony, "were calculating the thickness of its walls and counting my sentries as we rode across the drawbridge."

"No! Not without you!" Brenna cried when she heard she was being taken back to the abbey. "Jenny *must* come with me," she burst out, her gaze on Lord Westmoreland, "she *must!*" And for one astonishing moment, Jenny could have sworn Brenna looked more frustrated than frightened or sick.

An hour later, one hundred Westmoreland knights led by Stefan Westmoreland, were mounted and ready to leave the bailey. "Take care," Jennifer said, bending over Brenna, who was cozily ensconced in a cart atop a mound of bedding and pillows.

"I thought he would allow you to accompany me," Brenna coughed bitterly, her accusing glance sliding to the earl.

"Don't exhaust your strength with talking," Jenny said, reaching behind Brenna and trying to plump the feather pillows beneath her head and shoulders.

Turning, Royce gave the order, and heavy chains and weights were set in motion. Amidst a great clanking of metal and groaning of timbers, the spiked portcullis was raised and the drawbridge slowly fell forward. The knights spurred their mounts, Jennifer stepped back, and the caravan began moving across the drawbridge. Blue pennants emblazoned with the head of a snarling black wolf waved and snapped in the breeze, held by men at the front and the rear of the caravan, and Jenny's gaze clung to them. The insignia of the Wolf would protect Brenna until they reached the border; after that, if Lord Westmoreland's men were attacked, Brenna's name would needs be her protection.

The drawbridge was being raised again, blocking Jenny's view, and Lord Westmoreland put his hand on her elbow, turning her back toward the hall. Jenny followed, but her mind was on those sinister pennants with their deliberately malevolent image of a wolf with white fangs. Until today, the men had carried standards displaying the king of England's coat of arms—gold lions and trefoils.

"If you're worried that I mean to extract immediate payment on your part of the bargain," Royce said dryly, studying her frown, "then you may put your mind at ease. I have duties to occupy me until supper."

Jenny had no desire to *think* about her bargain, let alone discuss it, and she said quickly, "I—I was wondering why the knights who left just now were carrying your pennant, not your king's."

"Because they're my knights, not Henry's," he replied. "Their allegiance is to me."

Jenny drew up short in the middle of the bailey; Henry VII had reportedly made it illegal for his nobles to keep armies of their own. "But I thought 'twas illegal for English nobles to have their own army of knights."

"In my case, Henry decided to make an exception."

"Why?"

His brows lifted over sardonic gray eyes. "Perhaps because he trusts me?" Royce ventured, feeling no compunction to enlighten her beyond that.

Chapter Ten

Seated beside Jennifer after supper, Royce lounged back in his chair, his arm stretched across the back of hers, his expression thoughtful as he watched Jennifer deliberately charm and dazzle the four knights who'd remained seated at their table. It wasn't surprising to him that Eustace, Godfrey, and Lionel were lingering long after the meal was over: For one thing, Jennifer looked ravishing in a gown of sky blue velvet trimmed in cream satin. For another, midway through their meal, Jennifer had suddenly become lively and amiable and gay, and now they were seeing a side of her that even Royce had not seen. She told entertaining stories about her life at the abbey, and about the French abbess who'd insisted, among other things, that Jennifer and Brenna learn to speak without their Scots brogue.

She had deliberately set herself out to charm, and as Royce idly turned the stem of his silver wine goblet in his fingers, it was that effort which both amused and exasperated him.

She had made a glittering affair out of a rather tasteless meal that included roasted mutton, goose, and sparrow, as well as trenchers of greasy stew and pies filled with something that reminded Royce of brown gruel. The food at Hardin, he reflected with disgust, was little better than he'd had on the battlefield.

If Jennifer hadn't decided to make herself so delightful, his knights would undoubtedly have eaten just enough to fill their stomachs and then gone off without lingering—which was, Royce knew, *exactly* why she was doing this: she was trying to delay going upstairs with him.

Jennifer said something that made Godfrey, Lionel, and Eustace burst out laughing, and Royce casually glanced to his left where Arik was seated. Arik, Royce noted with amusement, was the only male at the table who'd not fallen under Jennifer's spell. With his chair tipped back on its hind legs, Arik was watching Jennifer with narrowed, suspicious eyes, his massive arms crossed over his chest in a disapproving posture which clearly indicated he wasn't fooled by her outward complaisance and didn't think she should be trusted for a second.

For the last hour, Royce had been willing to indulge her, using the time to enjoy her company and to savor the anticipation of what was to come. Now, however, he was no longer interested in anticipation.

"Royce—" Godfrey said, laughing heartily, "wasn't that an amusing tale Lady Jennifer just related?"

"Very," Royce agreed. Rather than rudely arising and putting an end to her socializing, Royce chose a subtler method: He gave Godfrey a look which clearly stated that supper was *over*.

Too occupied with her own worries to notice the subtle exchange of glances, Jenny turned to Royce with an overbright smile, thinking madly for some new topic to keep everyone lingering at the table. But before she could speak, there was a sudden scraping of chair legs and all the knights stood up, hastily bade her good night, and immediately took themselves off to the chairs near the fire.

"Did you not think that a trifle odd? Their abrupt leave-taking, I mean."

"I would have found it far more 'odd' had they remained."

"Why?"

"Because I told them to go." He stood up, too, and the moment Jenny had dreaded all day had arrived. It was there in his steady silver gaze as he held his hand out to her in an unmistakable indication that she should also arise. Her knees began to shake as she stood up; tentatively she reached for his hand, then snatched her hand away. "I—I didn't hear you tell them to go," she exclaimed.

"I was very discreet, Jennifer."

Upstairs, he paused at the chamber next to hers and shoved open the door so that Jenny could precede him.

Unlike Jenny's small, Spartan chamber, the sollar into which she stepped was spacious and lavish by comparison. In addition to his large four-poster bed, there were four comfortable chairs and several heavy trunks with ornate brass fittings. Tapestries hung on the wall, and there was even a thick mat in front of a hooded fireplace where a fire burned, warming and lighting the room. Moonlight spilled through a window across from the bed, and next to it was a door leading to what appeared to be a small parapet.

Behind her, she heard the heavy door latch fall into place, and her heart slammed into her ribs. Bent on doing anything to delay him from what he meant to do to her, Jenny fled to the chair furthest from the bed, sat down, and folded her hands in her lap. Fastening a bright, inquisitive smile upon her face, she seized on a subject sure to interest him, and began to bombard him with questions: "I've heard it said you've never been unhorsed in battle," she announced, leaning slightly forward in her chair in a posture of enraptured interest.

Instead of launching into a tale about his exploits as his knights had done at supper, the earl of Claymore sat down across from her, propped his booted foot atop the opposite knee, and leaned back in his chair, regarding her in complete silence.

From the moment she'd snatched her hand away from his as he helped her up from the table a few minutes ago, she'd had the uneasy feeling he knew she was hoping for some sort of miracle to save her from having to keep her bargain, and that he was not well pleased by her attitude. Widening her eyes, she redoubled her efforts to engage him in discourse. "Is it true?" she asked brightly.

"Is what true?" he replied with cool indifference.

"That you've never been unhorsed in battle?"

"No."

"It isn't?" she exclaimed. "Then . . . er . . . how many times has it happened?"

"Twice."

"Twice!" Twenty times would have been a minute number, she thought, feeling a tremor of panic for her clansmen who would soon face him. "I see. That's amazing, considering how many battles you must have fought in all these years. How many battles *have* you fought?"

"I don't count them, Jennifer."

"Perhaps you should. I have it! You could tell me about each one, and I could keep count," she suggested a little wildly, her tension compounded tenfold by his clipped answers. "Shall we do that now?"

"I don't think so."

Jenny swallowed, sensing that her time was up and that no angel of deliverance was going to swoop in through the window to save her from her fate. "What about—about the lists? Have you ever been unhorsed there?"

"I've never fought in the lists."

Startled into momentarily forgetting her own concerns, Jenny said with genuine surprise, "Why not? Don't many of your own countrymen wish to test their mettle against yours? Haven't they challenged you to a tilt?"

"Yes."

"But you don't accept?"

"I fight battles, not jousts. Jousts are games."

"Yes, but won't people . . . well . . . begin to think 'tis cowardice that makes you refuse? Or that— perhaps—you aren't quite so able a knight as rumor has it you are?"

"It's possible. Now I'll ask you a question," he interjected smoothly. "Can it be your sudden concern about my feats in battle and my reputation as a knight has to do with a bargain we made—one which you now hope to avoid keeping?"

Instead of lying to him, which Royce half expected her to do, she surprised him by saying in a helpless little whisper, "I'm frightened. More frightened than I've ever been in my life."

His brief spurt of annoyance at her attempts to manipulate him for the last few minutes abruptly dissolved, and as he looked at her seated primly in her chair, he realized he was expecting an entrancing innocent to accept what was going to happen between them as if she was one of the experienced courtesans he bedded at court.

Gentling his voice, he stood up, extending his hand to her. "Come here, Jennifer."

Her knees quaking violently, Jenny stood up and walked over to him, trying to tell her outraged conscience that the act she was about to commit wasn't sinful or traitorous; that in sacrificing herself to save her sister, she was actually doing something noble, even virtuous. She was, in a way, like Joan of Arc, accepting martyrdom.

Hesitantly, she placed her cold hand in his warm palm, watching as his long, tanned fingers closed around hers, finding a strange reassurance in the warmth of his grip and the compelling look in his eyes.

And when his arms encircled her, drawing her against his hard, muscular length, and his parted lips touched hers, her conscience abruptly went silent. It was a kiss like none of his others, for he knew where it would end—a kiss of exquisite restraint, of pagan hunger. His tongue slid across her lips, urging them to part, insisting, and the moment they did, it plunged into her mouth. His hands glided restlessly, possessively, up and down her back, her breasts, sliding across her spine, pressing her tightly to his hardened thighs, and Jennifer felt herself falling slowly into a dizzying abyss of sensuality and awakening passion. With a silent moan of helpless surrender, she wound her arms around his neck, clinging to him for support.

In some distant part of her mind, she felt her gown falling away, and then the brush of his palms against her swollen breasts, the sudden increase in ardor in each of his searing kisses. Arms like bands of steel surrounded her, lifting her, cradling her, and then she was being carried to the bed and gently laid down upon cool sheets. Suddenly the warmth, the security of his arms and body and mouth withdrew.

Surfacing slowly from the dreamlike daze where she had deliberately sought refuge from the reality of what was going to happen, Jenny felt cool air touch her skin and, against her will, her eyelids opened. He was standing beside the bed, removing his clothing, and a tremor of alarmed admiration quaked through her. In the glow of firelight, his skin was like oiled bronze, the heavy muscles in his arms and shoulders and thighs rippling as his fingers went to the waistband of his chausses. He was splendid, she realized, magnificent. Swallowing a knot of fear and embarrassed admiration, she swiftly turned her head away, her fingers clutching the edge of a sheet, using it to partially cover herself as he removed that last piece of concealing clothing.

The bed sank beneath his weight, and she waited, her face turned away, her eyes tightly shut, wanting him to hold her and take her swiftly, before more cold reality returned to her.

Royce had no such haste in mind. Stretching out on his side, he brushed a light kiss against her ear, and gently but inexorably pushed aside the sheet. His breath caught as he beheld her in all her naked splendor. A blush stained her satiny skin from her hair to her toes as he gazed upon the exquisite perfection of her lush, rosy-tipped breasts, tiny waist, gently rounded hips, and long shapely legs. Without thinking, he voiced his thoughts aloud. "Have you any idea how beautiful you are?" he whispered huskily, his gaze sweeping slowly upward to her enchanting face, roving over the tawny red-gold hair spread luxuriantly across his pillows, "or how much I want you?"

When Jenny kept her face averted, her eyes tightly closed, his fingers gently grasped her chin, turning her face toward his. In a voice like rough velvet, filled with desire and the trace of a languorous smile, he whispered, "Open your eyes, little one."

Reluctantly, Jenny obeyed and found herself staring into seductive silver eyes that held hers imprisoned while his hand slid from her cheek to her throat and then to her breast, cupping its fullness. "Don't be afraid," he ordered softly as his caressing fingers slid to her nipple, grazing it lightly, back and forth. The deep, husky timbre of his voice, combined with the tantalizing exploration of his skillful fingers, was already working its magic on Jenny as he added, "You've never feared me before. Don't begin now."

His flattened hand slid lightly upward from her breast, curving over her shoulder, and his finely molded mouth began a purposeful descent to hers. The first light, stroking touch of his lips sent pleasure streaking through Jenny's entire body, momentarily paralyzing her. His tongue slid over her lips, coaxing them to part, teasing with tormenting gentleness. And then his mouth opened on hers, hot and insistent in an endless kiss of deep, raw hunger. "Kiss me, Jenny," he ordered thickly.

And Jenny did. Curving her hand around his nape, she offered him her parted lips, moving them against his, kissing him as erotically as he was kissing her. He groaned with pleasure and deepened the kiss, his hand splaying across her spine turning her into his arms, bringing her into vibrant contact with his rigid erection. Kissed into insensibility, Jenny's hands slid up the bunched muscles of his chest and shoulders, then glided round his neck, sliding into the crisp curly hair at his nape.

When at last Royce lifted his mouth from hers, his breathing was harsh and rapid, and Jenny felt as if she would surely melt from the molten tenderness and desire pulsing through her veins with each thundering beat of her heart. Gazing into his scorching eyes, she lifted her trembling fingers, touching his face as he had touched hers, tracing his cheek and the groove beside his mouth with her fingertip, following it to his smooth lips, while inside her, an emotion sweetly unfolded, then burst into wild, vibrant bloom with a fierceness that made her tremble. Her chest aching with it, she slid her fingertips along his hard jaw, wincing as she touched the reddened scar she'd put there. Overwhelmed with guilt, she raised her eyes to his and whispered achingly, "I'm sorry."

Royce gazed down into her intoxicating blue eyes, his raging desire increased a hundred times by her touch and her voice, and still he held back, mesmerized by the incredible sweetness of her as she trailed her fingertips down his chest and saw the maze of long scars there. He watched her, knowing instinctively that, unlike the other women he'd bedded, she would not shudder with revulsion at those scars or, worse, shiver with sordid excitement at this visible evidence of the danger he lived in, the danger he represented.

He expected something different of the wanton angel in his arms, but he was not prepared for what happened, or for his own turbulent reaction to it: Her fingers touched his scars, sliding slowly toward the one closest to his heart, making his muscles leap reflexively as he fought to keep himself from taking her. When at last she raised her eyes to his, they were bright with unshed tears, and her beautiful face was pale with torment. In a fierce, tortured moan, she whispered, "Dear *God,* how they've *hurt* you—" And before he could imagine what she meant to do, she bent her head, her lips softly touching each scar as if trying to heal it, her arms sliding tightly, *protectively,* around him, and Royce lost control.

Shoving his fingers into her heavy, silken hair, he rolled her onto her back. "Jenny," he groaned hoarsely, kissing her eyes, her cheek, her forehead, her lips. "Jenny . . ." he whispered again and again. And the sound of that word, the hoarseness of his deep voice, affected Jenny as vibrantly as the things he began doing to her. His mouth went to her breast, teasing the taut peak, then closing tightly around it, drawing hard, until Jenny was gasping, arching her back, clasping his head to her breasts. His hands shifted, gliding down her midriff to her waist, then lower to her thighs.

Reflexively, she clamped her legs together, and a muffled, groaning laugh escaped him as his lips returned to plunder hers with searing passion. "Don't, sweetheart," he whispered hotly, his fingers delicately probing amidst the curly triangle between her thighs, seeking entrance. "It won't hurt."

Shivers of delight and fear were racing through Jenny's body, but she responded to neither of those; she responded instead to the need she heard in his voice. With a conscious effort, she forced the muscles in her legs to relax, and the moment she did, his knowledgeable fingers parted her, slipping deep inside her wet warmth, tenderly and skillfully pleasuring her, preparing the way for his passionate invasion.

Clutching him to her, her face buried against his corded neck, Jenny felt as if her body were on fire, melting and flowing, and a sob of startled pleasure escaped her. Just when she thought she would surely explode from the feelings building inside her, Royce's knee parted her thighs and he moved into position over her. Jenny opened her eyes and saw him poised above her—the warrior whose name made men tremble, the same man who had touched and kissed her with such violent tenderness. His face was hard and dark with passion and a pulse was throbbing in his temple as he fought to hold himself back.

His hands went beneath her, lifting her hips to receive him; she felt his hot hardness probing, poised at the entrance, and she met her fate as bravely as she'd met it each time at his hands. Closing her eyes, she wrapped her arms tightly around the same man she knew was going to hurt her. The poignancy of the gesture was shattering to Royce. A shudder shook him as she surrendered in his arms and he inched his throbbing shaft into her incredible warmth, uncertain how much pain he was going to cause her and desperate to lessen it. The time he had taken with her had eased his passage, and he felt her silken warmth tightly sheathing him, expanding to encase him. Twisted into knots of desire, his heart beating painfully, he eased himself into her until he finally encountered the fragile barrier.

He withdrew by inches, and shifted forward again, and then withdrew, poised to breach the barrier, desperate to bury himself within her, hating the pain he was going to cause her. Wrapping his arms tightly around her as if he could absorb the pain into himself, he spoke against her lips, his voice hoarse: "Jenny—

I'm sorry." And he drove full-length into her, hearing her gasp of pain as her arms tightened spasmodically.

He waited for her pain to subside, and then he began moving inside of her, gently sliding upward and withdrawing, entering deeper each time, withdrawing further, his body fully aroused and desperate, his will straining for control. Delicately he circled his hips against hers, his passion tripled by her soft moan of delight and her hands gliding to his hips, clasping him to her. Switching to deep, rhythmic thrusts, he plunged into her and felt her body begin moving with his. He could not believe the pleasure she was giving him, the way her body felt clasped around his swollen shaft, sheathing him, or the sweet torture of her instinctive movements.

Quick, piercing stabs of desire were rhythmically jarring Jenny's body and she moved with him, mindlessly seeking something she sensed he was trying to give her, and coming closer to it and closer to it as he quickened his driving, insistent strokes. The pulsing deep inside of her suddenly exploded in a wild burst of piercing pleasure that racked her body with wave after wave of sensation. Her spasms clasped him, clenching and pulling against his engorged manhood. Royce wrapped his arms tightly around her, holding perfectly still, to increase her pleasure, his breath coming in fast, deep pants against her cheek. He waited until they subsided, his heart thundering against his ribs, and then he drove into her, no longer able to control the force of his thrusts, his whole frame jerking convulsively again and again as his warmth spurted into her.

Floating in a sea of mindless pleasure, her body still joined with his, Jenny felt Royce move onto his side and bring her with him, and she drifted slowly back to consciousness. Her eyelids flickered open, the shadows in the bedchamber slowly took form and shape; a log crashed onto the stones, and sparks flickered brightly. The realization of all that had passed between them came flooding back to her and there, held securely in his arms, she knew a feeling of loneliness and terror beyond anything. What she had just done was not martyrdom, not even noble sacrifice—not when she'd found such pagan pleasure in it, such . . . heaven. Beneath her cheek, she heard the heavy, rhythmic beating of his heart, and she swallowed a lump of painful emotion. She had found something else here, something forbidden and dangerous to her, a feeling that shouldn't, *couldn't* exist.

And despite all her fear and guilt for what she felt, all she wanted at that moment was for him to call her "Jenny" again in that same rough, tender tone. Or to say, in *any* tone, "I love you."

As if her need to hear his voice communicated itself to him, he spoke, but what he said was not what she wanted to hear, nor was his tone the one her heart yearned for. Quietly, and without emotion, he asked, "Did I hurt you badly?"

She shook her head and, after two attempts, managed to whisper, "No."

"I'm sorry if I did."

"You didn't."

"It would have hurt, no matter who took you the first time."

Tears leapt to her eyes, clogging her throat, and she rolled onto her opposite side, trying to pull out of his arms, but he held her fast, her back and legs pressed to his chest and thighs. *No matter who took you,* Jenny thought miserably, was a very far thing from "I love you."

Royce knew it. He knew it as surely as he knew that it was folly to think the words, let alone say them. Not now, not yet . . . not *ever,* he corrected himself, as the vision of the woman he was supposed to marry floated across his mind. He felt no guilt at having made love to Jennifer; among other things, he was not yet betrothed—unless Henry had gotten impatient and arranged the matter with Lady Mary Hammel himself.

It occurred to Royce at that moment that, even if he were betrothed, he probably wouldn't feel any guilt. A vision of Mary Hammel's face, lovely and fair, framed by a cloud of silvery blond hair, crossed his mind. Mary was passionate and uninhibited in bed, trembling with excitement in his arms, and her reasons were no secret between them, for she had said them herself, smiling into his eyes, her voice husky and low: "*You, my lord, are Power and Violence and Might— and to most women, those are the most potent aphrodisiacs of all.*"

Staring into the firelight, Royce wondered idly whether Henry would have proceeded with the betrothal without waiting for his return at the end of the month. For a strong sovereign who'd seized the throne by conquest, Henry had immediately developed what Royce felt to be a rather distasteful habit of solving political problems, whenever possible, through the expedient measure of arranging marriages between the two hostile entities—beginning with Henry's own marriage to Elizabeth of York, daughter of the very king from whom Henry had seized the throne of England one year before, in a battle that ended in the other's death. Moreover, Henry had said more than once that if his daughter were old enough, he'd marry her to James of Scotland and end the interminable strife between the countries that way. Such a solution might satisfy Henry, but Royce wanted no such unfriendly alliance for himself. He wanted a compliant, biddable wife to warm his bed and grace his hall; he'd already had too much strife in his life to voluntarily subject himself to more of it in his own domain.

Jennifer stirred in his arms, trying to pull away. "May I return to my own chamber now?" she asked in a muffled voice.

"Nay," he said flatly, "our bargain is a long way

from met." And then, to prove he meant it, and to soften what he knew was an arbitrary order, he rolled her onto her back and buried his lips in hers, kissing her into mindless insensibility until she was clinging to him and returning his kisses with sweet, unbridled passion.

Chapter Eleven

Moonlight spilled through the window, and in his sleep Royce rolled onto his stomach, reaching out with his arm for Jennifer. His hand encountered cool sheets, not warm flesh. A lifetime spent with danger as his usual bed partner brought him from deep, sated sleep to sharp awareness in the space of seconds. His eyes snapped open as he rolled onto his back, his gaze scanning the room, sweeping over the furnishings that loomed like ghostly shadows in the pale moonlight.

Swinging his legs over the side of the bed, he stood up and rapidly began to dress, cursing his own stupidity for having failed to post a guard at the bottom of the steps. Out of habit, he grabbed his dagger as he stalked toward the door, furious with himself for falling asleep in the comfortable belief Jennifer could not cuddle up against him like that and then stay awake and coldly plot an escape. Jennifer Merrick was capable of that and more. All things considered, he was lucky she hadn't tried to slit his throat before she left! His hand hit the latch and he jerked the door open, almost stepping on his startled squire, who was sleeping on a pallet in front of the doorway. "What's amiss, milord?" Gawin asked anxiously, sitting upright, ready to scramble to his feet.

Some imperceptible movement—something blowing across the window from outside on the parapet— caught Royce's eye and his head jerked toward it.

"What's amiss, milord?"

The door slammed in Gawin's startled face.

Telling himself that he was simply relieved that she had spared him the unwanted task of another nocturnal pursuit, Royce silently opened the door and stepped outside. Jenny was standing on the parapet, her long hair blowing in the night breeze, her arms wrapped around herself, staring off into the distance. With narrowed eyes, Royce studied her expression, and a second wave of relief washed over him. She did not appear to be contemplating flinging herself from the parapet, nor was she weeping for the loss of her maidenhead. More than distraught or angry, she looked merely lost in thought.

Jenny was, in fact, so immersed in her own reflections that she had no idea she was no longer alone. The soothing caress of the unseasonably balmy night air had helped restore her spirits, but even so, she felt as if the whole world had turned upside down this night, and Brenna was part of the reason for it: Brenna and a feather pillow had been the reason for Jenny's "noble" sacrifice of her maidenhood. The awful realization had hit her just as she began to drift off to sleep tonight.

She had been mumbling a sleepy prayer for Brenna's recovery and safe journey, when a quill from her own pillow protruded through the linen case, jarring her memory of the moment she'd smoothed the pillows beneath Brenna's head as she lay in the cart. Feathers near Brenna's face or body made her cough horribly, and no one was more careful than she to avoid them. Evidently, Jenny decided, Brenna must have fallen asleep in her chamber and woken up coughing, but instead of removing the offending pillows, she'd become daring and inventive at last: Believing the earl would release them both, Brenna had probably lain upon them until she was coughing as if death was imminent.

Absolutely ingenious, Jenny thought—worthy of any scheme she herself might have devised—and just as ill-fated, she decided glumly.

Her thoughts left Brenna and shifted to the future she had once dreamed of having, a future that now, more than ever before, was lost to her.

"Jennifer—" Royce said behind her.

Jenny whirled around, making a stern effort to hide her treacherous heart's reaction to the deep timbre of his voice. Why, she wondered desperately, could she still feel his hands upon her skin, and why did the mere sight of his face call to mind the tender roughness of his kisses. "I—why are you dressed?" she asked, relieved that her voice sounded calm.

"I was about to go looking for you," he replied, stepping out of the shadows.

With a wry glance at the gleaming dagger in his hand, she asked, "What did you intend to do when you found me?"

"I'd forgotten about this parapet." Slipping the dagger into his belt he added, "I thought you'd managed to slip from the room."

"Isn't your squire sleeping just beyond the door?"

"Good point," Royce said sardonically.

"He generally makes a habit of stretching out to block the entrance to wherever you are," she pointed out.

"Right again," he said dryly, wondering at his unprecedented lack of forethought in dashing for his own door without checking every other alternative.

Now that he'd found her, Jenny sorely wished he'd go away; his presence wreaked havoc on the serenity she so desperately sought. Turning away from him in an unmistakable hint that he should leave, she gazed out across the moonlit landscape.

Royce hesitated, knowing she wished to be left alone, yet reluctant to leave her. He told himself it was merely concern over her strange mood, and not the pleasure he derived from her company or her profile, that kept him from leaving. Sensing she would not welcome his touch, he stopped within reach of her and leaned his shoulder against the wall surrounding the parapet. She remained lost in thought, and Royce's brows drew together into a slight frown as he reconsidered his earlier conclusion that she wasn't contemplating something as stupid as taking her own life. "What were you thinking of a few minutes ago, when I came out here?"

Jenny stiffened slightly at the question. She'd been thinking of only two things, and she certainly could not discuss one of them, which had been Brenna's ingenious ploy. " 'Twas nothing of great importance," she evaded.

"Tell me anyway," he insisted.

She glanced sideways, her heart giving a traitorous leap at the sight of his broad shoulders so close to hers and his sternly handsome face etched with moonlight. Ready, *willing,* to discuss anything to distract herself from her awareness of him, she gazed out across the hills and said with a sigh of capitulation, "I was recalling the times I used to stand on a parapet at Merrick and look out across the moors, thinking of a kingdom."

"A kingdom?" Royce repeated, surprised and relieved at the nonviolent nature of her thoughts. She nodded, her heavy hair sliding up and down her back, and he sternly repressed the urge to wrap his hand in the silken mass and gently turn her face up to his. "Which kingdom?"

"My own kingdom." She sighed, feeling foolish and sorely tried that he meant to pursue the issue. "I used to plan a kingdom of my own."

169

"Poor James," he teased, referring to the Scottish king. "Which of his kingdoms did you mean to seize?"

She sent him a rueful smile, but her voice was oddly tinged with sadness. "It wasn't a real kingdom with land and castles; it was a kingdom of dreams——a place where things would be just the way I wanted them to be."

A long-forgotten memory flickered across Royce's mind, and turning toward the wall, he leaned his forearms atop it, his fingers linked loosely together. Gazing out across the hills in the same direction Jennifer was looking, he admitted quietly, "There was a time, long ago, when I, too, used to imagine a kingdom of my own design. What was yours like?"

"There's little to tell," she said. "In my kingdom, there was prosperity and peace. Occasionally, of course, a crofter fell violently ill, or there was a dire threat to our safety."

"You had illness and strife in your dream kingdom?" Royce interrupted in surprise.

"Of course!" Jenny admitted with a rueful, sideways smile. "There had to be some of both, so that *I* could race to the rescue and save the day. *That* was the very reason I invented my kingdom."

"You wanted to be a heroine to your people," Royce concluded, smiling at a motivation he could readily understand.

She shook her head, the wistful yearning in her soft voice banishing his smile. "Nay. I wanted only to be loved by those whom I love; to be looked upon and not found wanting by those who know me."

"And that's all you wanted?"

She nodded, her beautiful profile solemn. "And so I invented a kingdom of dreams where I could accomplish great and daring deeds to make it happen."

Not far away, on the hill nearest the castle, the figure of a man was momentarily illuminated by a shaft of moonlight emerging from the clouds. At any other time, that brief glimpse would have caused Royce to dispatch men to investigate. Now, however, sated with lovemaking, knowing more of it was yet to come with the winsome beauty beside him, his brain paid no heed to what his eyes had noted. It was a night filled with warmth and rare confidences, far too soft and lovely a night to contemplate the unlikely threat of silent danger lurking so close to his own demesne.

Royce frowned, thinking of Jenny's puzzling words. The Scots, even the lowlanders who lived by feudal laws more than clan laws, were a fiercely loyal lot. And whether her clan called Jennifer's father "earl" or "the Merrick," he, and all his family, would still command clan Merrick's complete devotion and loyalty. They would not look upon Jennifer and find her wanting, and she would undoubtedly be loved by those whom she loved—ergo, she should not need to dream up a kingdom of her own. "You're a brave and beautiful young woman," he said finally, "and a countess in your own right. Your clan undoubtedly feels about you as you would wish them to feel—and probably more so."

She tore her gaze from his and seemed to become absorbed in the view again. "Actually," she replied in a carefully emotionless voice, "they think me some sort of—of changeling."

"Why would they think anything so absurd?" he demanded, dumbfounded.

To his surprise she leapt to their defense: "What else could they possibly think, given the things my stepbrother convinced them I've done?"

"What sort of things?"

She shivered, wrapping her arms around herself again, looking much as he had seen her when he first came out onto the parapet. "Unspeakable things," she whispered.

Royce watched her, silently insisting on an explanation, and she drew an unsteady breath and reluctantly complied: "There were many things, but most of all there was Rebecca's drowning. Becky and I were distant cousins and the best of friends. We were both thirteen," she added with a sad little smile. "Her father—Garrick Carmichael—was a widower and she his only child. He doted on her, as nearly all of us did. She was so sweet, you see, and so incredibly fair—fairer even than Brenna—that you couldn't help but love her. The thing was, her father loved her so much that he'd not let her do anything, for fear she'd come to harm. She wasn't even allowed to go near the river, because her father feared she'd drown. Becky decided to learn how to swim—to prove to him she'd be safe—and early each morning, we would sneak off to the river, so I could teach her how."

"The day before she drowned, we'd been at a fair, and we quarreled because I told her one of the jugglers had been looking at her in an unseemly way. My stepbrothers, Alexander and Malcolm, overheard us —as did several people—and Alexander accused me of being jealous because I'd had eyes for the juggler, which was silly in the extreme. Becky was so angry, embarrassed, I mean, that when we parted, she told me not to bother coming to the river in the morning because she no longer needed my assistance. I knew she didn't really mean it, and she couldn't swim at all well yet, and so naturally, I went there the next morning."

Jennifer's voice dropped to a whisper. "When I got there she was still angry; she called to me that she wanted to be alone. I was already at the top of the hill, walking away, when I heard a splash and she screamed to me to help her. I turned and started running down the hill, but I couldn't *see* her. When I was halfway there, she managed to get her head above the water— I know, because I saw her hair on the surface. Then I heard her scream to me to help her ..." Jenny shivered, absently rubbing her arms, "but the current was carrying her away. I dove in, and I tried to find her. I dove under again and again and again,"

Jenny whispered brokenly "but I—I couldn't find her to help her. The next day Becky was found several miles away, washed up on the banks."

Royce lifted his hand, then dropped it, sensing that she was fighting for control and would not welcome any gesture of comfort that might make her lose it. "It was an accident," he said gently.

She drew a long steadying breath. "Not according to Alexander. He must have been nearby, because he told everyone he heard Becky scream my name, which was true. But then he told them we were quarreling, and that I pushed her in."

"How did he explain your own wet clothing?" Royce said tersely.

"He said," Jenny answered with a ragged sigh, "that after I pushed her in, I must have waited and *then* tried to save her. Alexander," she added, "had already been told that he, not I, would succeed my father as laird. But it wasn't enough for him—he wanted me disgraced and far away. After that, it was easy for him."

"Easy in what way?"

Her slim shoulders lifted in a slight shrug. "A few more evil lies and twisted truths—a crofter's cottage that suddenly caught fire the night after I challenged with the weight of a sack of grain he brought to the keep. Things such as that."

Slowly she raised tear-brightened blue eyes to his and to Royce's surprise she tried to smile. "Do you see my hair?" she asked. Royce glanced needlessly at the golden red tresses he'd admired for weeks and nodded.

In a suffocated voice, Jenny said, "My hair used to be an awful color. Now, it's the color of Becky's hair. Becky knew . . . how much I . . . admired her hair," she whispered brokenly, "and . . . and I like to think she gave it to me. To show me she knows—I tried to save her."

The painful, unfamiliar constriction in Royce's

chest made his hand tremble as he started to lift it to lay against her cheek, but she pulled back, and although her huge eyes were shining with unshed tears, she did not break down and weep. *Now,* at last, he understood why this lovely young girl had not wept since her capture, not even during the sound thrashing he'd given her. Jennifer Merrick had stored all her tears inside her, and her pride and courage would never permit her to break down and shed them. Compared to what she'd already endured, a mere thrashing at his hands must have been as nothing to her.

For lack of knowing what else to do, Royce went into the bedchamber, poured wine from a flagon into a goblet, and brought it out to her. "Drink this," he said flatly.

With relief, he saw that she'd already gotten control of her sorrow, and a winsome smile touched her soft lips at his unintentionally abrupt tone. "It seems to me, milord," she replied, "that you are forever putting spirits into my hand."

"Usually for my own nefarious reasons," he admitted drolly, and she chuckled.

Taking a sip, she put the goblet aside, then she crossed her arms on the low wall, gazing out into the distance again as she leaned against it. Royce studied her in silence, unable to get her revelations out of his mind, feeling the need to say something encouraging about her plight. "I doubt you'd have liked having the responsibility for your clan, in any case."

She shook her head and quietly said, "I would have *loved* it. There were so many things I saw that might have been done differently—things a woman would notice that a man does not. Things I learned from Mother Abbess, too. There are new looms—yours are much better than ours—new ways of growing crops—hundreds of other things to be done differently and better."

Unable to argue the relative merits of one kind of

loom or crop over another, Royce tried a different argument. "You cannot live your life trying to prove yourself to your clan."

"*I can,*" she said in a low, fierce voice. "I would do *anything* to make them see me as one of them again. They are my people—their blood flows in my veins, and mine in theirs."

"You'd best forget it," Royce urged. " 'Twould seem you've embarked on a quest where victory is unlikely at best."

"For a while, these past few days, 'twasn't as unlikely as you think," she said, her beautiful profile somber. "William will be earl someday, and he's a kind, wonderful boy—well, man—since he is twenty. He isn't strong like Alexander was, or Malcolm is, but he is intelligent and wise and loyal. He feels for my plight with our clan, and once he became lord, he would have tried to set matters aright. But tonight, that became an impossibility."

"What has tonight to do with it?"

Jenny raised her eyes to his, the expression in them reminding him of a wounded doe, despite the calm, matter-of-fact tone she used. "Tonight, I became the consort of my family's worst enemy—the mistress of my people's foe. In the past, they despised me for things I *hadn't* done. Now, they have good reason to despise me for what I have, just as I have reason to despise myself. This time, I've done the unforgivable. Even God won't forgive me . . ."

The undeniable truth of her accusation about becoming his consort hit Royce with more force than he wanted to acknowledge, but his guilt was lessened by the knowledge that the life that was lost to her now was not much life at all. Reaching out, he took her firmly by the shoulders and turned her around, then he tipped her chin up, forcing her to meet his gaze. And even as he began to speak, in the midst of his concern and sympathy, his loins were already hardening in demanding response to her nearness. "Jennifer," he said with quiet firmness, "I didn't know how things stood between you and your people, but I've bedded you, and nothing can change that now."

"And if you could change it," she said, looking mutinous, "would you?"

Royce gazed down at the incredibly desirable young woman who was setting his body on fire at that very moment. Calmly and honestly, he said, "No."

"Then do not bother looking regretful," she snapped.

His lips quirked in a mirthless smile, his hand sliding along her cheek to her nape. "Do I look regretful? I'm not. I regret causing you humiliation, but I do not regret the fact that I had you an hour ago, nor will I regret having you again in a few minutes, which I mean to do." She glared at the arrogance of his statement, but Royce forged ahead with what he'd intended to say: "I do not believe in your God, nor any other, but I'm told by those who do, that your God is supposedly a just God. If so," he continued in a calm, philosophical tone, "He will surely hold you blameless in all this. After all, you only agreed to my bargain out of fear for your sister's life. 'Twas not your will, 'twas mine. And what passed between us in that bed was against your will, too. Wasn't it?"

As soon as he asked the question, Royce regretted it—regretted it so sharply that it confused him. And then he realized that, while he wanted her to assure him that he hadn't damned her in the eyes of her God, he did *not* want her to deny that she'd felt all the things he had in their mating, or that she had wanted him almost as much as he had wanted her. As if he suddenly needed to test her honesty and his instincts, he persisted, "Isn't that right? He will hold you blameless in all this because you merely submitted to me in bed against your will?"

"No!" The word burst out of her, filled with shame and helplessness, and a thousand other feelings Royce couldn't identify.

"No?" he repeated, while a heady sensation of relief burst within him. "Where am I wrong?" he asked, his voice low, but insistent. "Tell me where I'm wrong."

It was not the tone of command in his voice that made her answer. It was, instead, her sudden memories of the way he had made love to her; memories of his incredible gentleness and restraint; of his pained regret when he hurt her as he broke her maidenhead; of his whispered words of praise; of his labored breathing as he fought to hold back his passion. Added to all that was the memory of her own urgent desire to be filled with him, and to give him back the exquisite sensations he was making her feel. She opened her mouth, wanting to hurt him as he had hurt all her chances for happiness, but her conscience strangled the words in her throat. She had found glory, not shame in their mating, and she could not make herself lie to him and say otherwise. "'Twas not my will to come to your bed," she answered in a muffled whisper. Dragging her mortified gaze from his smoky gray one, she turned her head away and added, "but once there, 'twas not my will to leave it either."

She had looked away, so Jenny didn't see the new tenderness in his slow smile, but she felt it in the way his arms encircled her, his hand splaying against her spine, clasping her against his hardened length as his mouth took possession of hers, robbing her of speech, and then of breath.

Chapter Twelve

We have visitors," Godfrey announced, stalking into the hall, a frown upon his face as he looked at the knights seated at the table partaking of the midday meal. Twelve pairs of hands paused, their faces alert. "A large group carrying the king's standard and riding this way. A very large group," Godfrey amplified, "too many to be the usual messengers. Lionel got a glimpse of them from the road. He said he thought he recognized Graverley." His frown deepening, he glanced toward the gallery above. "Where's Royce?"

"He's gone out strolling with our hostage," Eustace answered, frowning. "I'm not certain where."

"I know," Arik said, his voice booming. "I'll go." Turning on his heel, Arik left the hall, his long, ground-eating strides solid and assured, but the look of stony, aloof calm that normally characterized his craggy face was marred by a worried look that deepened the grooves between his pale blue eyes.

Jenny's musical laughter pealed like bells startled by a sudden wind, and Royce grinned at her as she slumped helplessly against the tree trunk beside him, her shoulders shaking with mirth, her cheeks tinted the same pale pink as the fetching gown she wore. "I—I don't believe you," she gasped, wiping tears of hilarity from her eyes. "'Tis a gross falsehood which you invented just now."

"It's possible," he agreed, stretching his long legs out in front of him and grinning because her smile was infectious. This morning, she'd wakened in his bed when servants trooped into their bedchamber, and her distress at being found like that with him was almost painful to see. She had become his mistress and she was positive the entire castle would be gossiping about it, which, of course, was true. After considering the alternative of lying to her about it, or trying to seduce her into forgetting her woes, Royce had decided the best course was to take her away from the castle for a few hours so that she could relax a little. It had been a wise choice, he decided, looking at her sparkling eyes and glowing complexion.

"You must think me brainless to be fooled into believing such a falsehood," she said, trying to look stern and failing.

Royce smiled, but he shook his head in denial of both her accusations. "Nay, madam, you're wrong on all counts."

"All?" Jenny repeated quizzically. "What do you mean?"

Royce's smile widened as he explained, "'Twas no falsehood I told you, nor, I think, could you be easily fooled by anyone." He paused, waiting for her to respond and when she didn't, he said, smiling, "That was a compliment to your good sense."

"Oh," Jenny said, startled. "Thank you," she added uncertainly.

"Secondly, far from mistaking you for brainless, I find you to be a female of extraordinary intelligence."

"Thank you!" Jenny replied promptly.

"That was *not* a compliment," Royce corrected.

Jenny shot him a look of curious displeasure that silently demanded an explanation for his remark, and

Royce answered as he reached out and touched her cheek with his forefinger, tracing its smooth, delicate texture. "Were you less intelligent, you'd not spend so much time considering all the possible consequences of belonging to me, and you'd simply accept your situation, along with all the benefits attached to it." His gaze shifted meaningfully to the strand of pearls he'd insisted on placing around her neck this morning after giving her the entire cache of jewels.

Jenny's eyes widened with indignation, but Royce continued with imperturbable masculine logic. "Were you a woman of ordinary intelligence, you'd be concerned only with matters of normal interest to a woman, such as fashions, and the running of a household, and the rearing of children. You'd not be torturing yourself about subjects like loyalty, patriotism, and such."

Jenny stared at him in angry disbelief. "Accept my 'situation'?" she repeated. "I am not in a 'situation,' as you so nicely phrased it, my lord. I am living in sin with a man, in defiance of my family's wishes, my country's wishes, and God Almighty's wishes. And furthermore," she added, working herself into a fine temper, "it's all well and good for you to recommend that I think only of womanly matters, such as the running of a household, and the rearing of children, but 'tis *you* who have stolen from me the right to those things. Your wife will have the running of your households and she'll no doubt make my life a living hell if she can, and—"

"Jennifer," Royce interrupted, biting back a smile, "as you well know, I don't have a wife." He realized much of what she was saying was true, but she looked so damned pretty with her flashing liquid sapphire eyes and kissable mouth that he found it hard to concentrate; all he really wanted to do was to snatch her into his arms and cuddle her like an angry kitten.

"You don't have a wife *now*," Jenny argued bitterly,

"but you'll choose one someday soon—an Englishwoman!" she spat. "An Englishwoman with ice water for blood, and hair the color of mouse fur, and a sharp little nose that is forever red on the end and in danger of dripping—"

His shoulders shaking with silent, helpless laughter, Royce held up a hand in a mocking gesture of defense. "Hair the color of *mouse fur?*" he repeated. "Is that the best I can do? Until recently, I thought I fancied a blond wife, with big green eyes and—"

"And big pink lips and big—" So angry was she that Jenny actually raised her hands toward her breasts before she realized what she was about to say.

"Yes," Royce prompted, teasing. "Big what?"

"Ears!" she burst out furiously, "But whatever she looks like, the point is, she'll make my life a living hell."

Unable to restrain himself another moment, Royce leaned down and nuzzled her neck. "I'll strike a bargain with you," he whispered, kissing her ear. "We'll pick out a wife we *both* like." And in that unlikely instant, he suddenly realized that his obsession with Jennifer was clouding his thinking. He could not possibly marry and still keep Jennifer with him, he knew. Despite his teasing, he was not callous enough to wed Mary Hammel or anyone else and then force Jennifer to suffer the indignity of remaining his mistress. Yesterday, he might have considered it, but not now, not after last night, when he came to realize how much suffering she'd already endured in her brief young life.

Even now, his mind shied away from the thought of how she would be treated by her "beloved" clansmen when she went back to them after sharing the bed of their enemy.

The alternative of his remaining unmarried, and of going without children and heirs, was unappealing and unacceptable.

The only remaining alternative—that of marrying Jennifer—was out of the question. To wed her—and in so doing acquire sworn enemies as in-laws, as well as a wife with loyalties weighted heavily in favor of those enemies—was untenable. Such a marriage would only bring the battlefield into his own hall when what he sought there was peace and harmony. Simply because her innocent passion and selfless giving in bed brought him exquisite pleasure was no reason to subject himself to a life of continual strife. On the other hand, she was the only woman who made love with *him,* not with the *legend* he was. And she made him laugh as no other woman ever had; she had courage and wisdom and a face that bewitched and beguiled. Last, but far from least, she had a directness, an honesty about her that disarmed him completely.

Even now, he could not forget the feeling in his chest last night when she'd chosen honesty over pride and admitted that once in his bed, she'd not wanted to leave it. Honesty such as that, especially in a woman, was a rare thing indeed. It meant her word could be trusted.

Of course, all those things weren't reason enough to let all his carefully laid plans for his future be destroyed.

On the other hand, they weren't exactly strong incentives to give her up, either.

Royce glanced up as the guards on the castle wall sounded a single, long blast on their trumpets, signaling the approach of nonhostile visitors.

"What does that mean?" Jenny asked, startled.

"Couriers from Henry, I imagine," Royce replied, leaning back on his forearms and squinting up at the sun. If they were, he thought idly, they were here much sooner than he'd expected. "Whoever they are, they're friendly."

"Does your king know I'm your hostage?"

"Yes." Although he disliked the turn of the conversation, he understood her concern for her fate, and he added, "I sent word to him a few days after you were brought to my camp, along with my regular monthly dispatches."

"Am I"—she drew a shaky breath—"am I to be sent someplace—a dungeon, or—"

"No," Royce said quickly. "You'll remain under my protection. For the time being," he added vaguely.

"But suppose he commands otherwise?"

"He won't," Royce said flatly, glancing at her over his shoulder. "Henry cares naught how I win his victories for him, so long as I win them. If your father lays down his arms and surrenders because you're my hostage, then this victory will be the best kind—a bloodless one." Seeing that the subject was making her tense, he diverted her with a question that had been niggling at the back of his mind all morning. "When your stepbrothers began to turn your clan against you," he asked, "why did you not bring the problem to your father's attention, instead of trying to escape from it by building dream kingdoms in your mind? Your father is a powerful lord, he could have solved your problem the same way I would have."

"And how would you have solved it?" she asked with that unconsciously provocative, sideways smile that always made him long to drag her into his arms and kiss it off her lips.

More sharply than he intended, Royce said, "I would have commanded them to desist in their suspicions of you."

"Spoken like a warrior, not a lord," she commented lightly. "You cannot 'command' people's thoughts, you can merely terrify them into keeping them to themselves."

"What did your *father* do?" he asked in a cool voice that challenged her observation.

"At the time Becky drowned," she replied, "my father was off fighting *you* in some battle, as I recall."

"And when he returned—from fighting with me—" Royce added with a wry smile, "what did he do then?"

"By then, there were all sorts of stories circulating about me, but Father thought I was exaggerating, and that they would die away shortly. You see," she added when Royce frowned disapprovingly, "my father does not place a great deal of importance on what he calls 'women's matters.' He loves me very much," she stated with what Royce considered to be more loyalty than sense—given Merrick's choice of Balder as a husband for Jennifer, "but to him, women are . . . well . . . not quite so important to the world as men. He married my stepmother because we are distant kin and she had three healthy sons."

"He preferred to see his title handed over to distant kin," Royce summarized with ill-concealed distaste, "rather than handed down to you and, hopefully, his grandsons?"

"The clan means everything to him, and that is as it should be," Jennifer said, her loyalty driving her to speak with more force. "He did not feel I, as a woman, would have been able to hold their loyalty or guide them—even if King James had permitted my father's title to pass to me—which might have been a problem."

"Did he bother to petition James about it?"

"Well, no. But, as I said, 'twas not me, as a person, Father doubted, 'twas merely that I am a woman and therefore destined for other things."

Or other uses, Royce thought with anger on her behalf.

"You cannot understand my father, but 'tis because you do not know him. He is a great man and everyone feels as I do about him. We—all of us—would lay down our lives for him if he . . ." For a moment, Jenny thought she was either going quite mad or going quite blind—for standing just inside the woods, looking at her, his finger pressed to his lips in the signal for silence—was William. ". . . if he asked it," she breathed, but Royce didn't notice her sudden change in tone. He was occupied with fighting down a surge of irrational jealousy because her father could inspire such blind, total devotion in her.

Closing her eyes tightly, Jenny opened them again and stared harder. William had slipped back into the shadows of the trees, but she could still see the edge of his green jerkin. William was here! He'd come to take her back, she realized as joy and relief exploded in her breast.

"Jennifer—" Royce Westmoreland's quiet voice was edged with gravity, and Jenny tore her gaze from the place where William had vanished.

"Y-yes," she stammered, half expecting her father's entire army to leap from the woods at any instant and slaughter Royce where he sat. *Slaughter* him! The thought made bile rise up in her throat, and Jenny shot to her feet, obsessed with the simultaneous need to get him away from the woods and still manage to get into them herself.

Royce frowned at her pale face. "What's wrong—you seem—"

"Restless!" Jenny burst out. "I feel the need to stroll just a bit. I—"

Royce rolled to his feet and was about to ask the reason for her restlessness when he saw Arik walking up the hill. "Before Arik reaches us," he began, "I would like to tell you something."

Jenny swung around, her gaze freezing on the mighty Arik while crazy relief surged through her: With Arik here, at least Royce wouldn't die without someone to fight at his side. But if there was fighting, then her father or William or one of the clan might be killed.

"Jennifer—" Royce said, his tone reflecting his exasperation at her flagging attention.

Somehow, Jenny made herself turn to him and look attentive. "Yes?" If her father's men were going to attack Royce, surely they'd have moved from the woods by now; he'd never be more vulnerable than he was at this moment. Which meant, Jenny thought wildly, William must be alone and he'd seen Arik. If that was true, and she hoped at the moment it was, then she had only to stay calm and find some way to return to the woods as soon as possible.

"No one is going to lock you in a dungeon," he said with gentle firmness.

Gazing up into his compelling gray eyes, it suddenly dawned on Jenny that she'd be leaving him soon— perhaps within the hour, and the realization pierced her with unexpected poignancy. True, he had condoned her abduction, but he had never subjected her to the atrocities any other captor would have forced upon her. Moreover, he was the only man who'd admired her courage instead of condemning her headstrong conduct; she'd caused the death of his horse, and stabbed him, and made a fool of him by escaping. All things considered, she realized with an awful ache behind her eyes, he'd treated her with more gallantry —his own style of gallantry—than any courtier might have done. In fact, if things were different between their families and their countries, Royce Westmoreland and she would have been friends. Friends? He was more than that already. He was her lover.

"I—I'm sorry," Jenny said in a suffocated voice, "my mind has gone abegging. What did you say just now?"

"I said," he repeated with a slight worried frown at her panicked expression, "I don't want you imagining you're in any sort of peril. Until the time comes to send you home, you will remain under my protection."

Jenny nodded and swallowed. "Yes. Thank you," she whispered, her voice flooded with emotion.

Misinterpreting her tone for one of gratitude, Royce smiled lazily. "Would you care to express your gratitude with a kiss?" To his amazed delight, Jenny needed no strong persuasion at all. Reaching her arms around his neck, she kissed him with desperate ardor, crushing her lips to his in a kiss that was part farewell and part fear, her hands roving over the bunched muscles of his back, unconsciously memorizing the contours of it, clasping him to her tightly.

When he finally lifted his head, Royce gazed down at her, his arms still wrapped tightly around her. "My God," he whispered. He started to lower his head again, then stopped, his gaze on Arik. "Damn, here's Arik." He took her arm and guided her toward the knight, but when they reached Arik, he instantly drew Royce aside, speaking swiftly.

Royce turned back to Jennifer, preoccupied with the unpleasant news of Graverley's arrival. "We'll have to go back," he began, but the look of misery on her face tugged at his heart. This morning, she had lit up like a candle when he'd offered to take her out of the castle. "I've been confined to a tent or else under guard for so long," she'd told him, "that the thought of sitting on a hillside makes me feel reborn!"

Obviously, the time out here had done her a world of good, Royce thought wryly, recalling the ardor of her kiss, and wondering if he would be insane to offer her the right to remain here alone. She was on foot, with no way to get a horse, and she was intelligent enough to know that if she tried to escape on foot, the five thousand men camped all around the castle would be able to find her within an hour. Moreover, he could instruct the guards on the wall to keep an eye on her.

With the taste of her kiss still on his lips, and the memory of her decision not to try to escape from camp several nights ago still fresh in his mind, he walked over to her. "Jennifer," he said, his reservations about the wisdom of what he was doing making his voice sound stern, "if I allow you to remain out here, can I trust you to stay in this spot?"

The look of joyous disbelief on her face was reward enough for his generosity.

"Yes!" she exclaimed, unable to believe this boon from fate.

The lazy smile that wafted across his bronzed features made him look very handsome and almost boyish. "I won't be long," he promised.

She watched him walk away with Arik, unconsciously memorizing the way he looked, his broad shoulders encased in a tan jerkin, a brown belt drawn loosely around his narrow waist, and thick hose outlining the heavy muscles of his thighs above his high boots. Partway down the hill, he stopped and turned. Raising his head, Royce scanned the trees, his black brows drawn into a frown, as if he sensed the threat to him lurking in the woods. Terrified that he'd seen or heard something and meant to come back, Jenny did the first thing that came to mind: Raising her hand in a slight wave, she drew his attention and smiled at him, then she touched her fingers to her lips. The gesture had been unintended, a forestalled impulse to cover her mouth and stifle a cry of panic. To Royce, it appeared that she was blowing him a kiss. With a grin that bespoke his surprised gratification, he lifted his hand in a gesture of farewell to Jennifer. Beside him, Arik spoke sharply, and he pulled his attention from Jennifer and the woods. Turning, he walked swiftly down the steep hill beside Arik, his mind pleasurably occupied with the enthusiastic ardor of Jennifer's kiss and his body's equally enthusiastic response to it.

"Jennifer!" William's low, urgent voice from the woods behind her made Jenny's entire body tense for her impending flight, but she was careful not to make a move for the woods—not until the earl had disappeared through the hidden doorway cut into the thick stone wall surrounding Hardin castle. Then she whirled, almost stumbling in her haste, as she raced up the short incline and bolted into the woods, her gaze searching madly for her rescuers. "William, where—" she began, then stifled a scream as strong, wiry arms caught her at the waist from behind, lifting her clear off the ground, hauling her into the deeper seclusion of the ancient oaks.

"Jennifer!" William whispered hoarsely, his beloved face only inches from hers. Regret and anxiety were etched into his worried frown. "My poor girl—" he began, his eyes searching her face, and then, obviously recalling the kisses he'd witnessed, he said bleakly, "He forced you to become his mistress, didn't he?"

"I—I'll explain later. We must make haste," she implored, obsessed with the remembered urgency to persuade her clansmen to leave without bloodshed. "Brenna's already on her way home. Where is Father and our people?" she began.

"Father is at Merrick, and there's only six of us here."

"Six!" Jenny exclaimed, stumbling as her slipper caught in a vine and then recovering, running beside him.

He nodded. "I thought we'd have a better chance of freeing you if we used stealth rather than might."

When Royce walked into the hall, Graverley was standing in the center of the room, his narrow face slowly surveying the interior of Hardin castle, his thin nose pinched with resentment and ill-concealed greed. As privy councillor to the king and the most influential member of the powerful Court of the Star Chamber, Graverley enjoyed tremendous influence, but his very position denied him the hope of a title and the estates that he so obviously coveted.

From the time Henry seized the throne, he had begun taking steps to avoid meeting the same fate as his predecessors—defeat at the hands of powerful nobles who swore allegiance to their king and then rose up when discontented and overthrew that same sovereign. To prevent such an occurrence, he had reinstated the Court of the Star Chamber which he then filled with councillors and ministers *outside* the peerage, men like Graverley, who then sat in judgment on the nobles fining them heavily, for any misdeed, an action which simultaneously fattened Henry's coffers and deprived said nobles of the wealth necessary for revolt.

Of all the privy councillors, Graverley was the most influential and most vindictive; with Henry's full trust and authority behind him, Graverley had successfully impoverished or completely broken nearly every powerful noble in Britain . . . with the exception of the earl of Claymore who, to his unconcealed fury, had continued to prosper, growing more powerful and more wealthy with each battle he won for his king.

Graverley's hatred for Royce Westmoreland was known to everyone at court, and was equalled by Royce's contempt for him.

Royce's features were perfectly bland as he crossed the one hundred-foot distance separating him from his foe, but he was registering all the subtle indications that an unusually unpleasant confrontation was evidently about to occur over some issue. For one thing, there was the smirk of satisfaction on Graverley's face; for another, positioned behind Graverley were thirty-five of Henry's men-at-arms, who were standing with military rigidity, their faces set and grim. Royce's own men, headed by Godfrey and Eustace, were formed into two lines at the end of the hall near the dais, their faces watchful, alert, tense—as if they, too, sensed something seriously amiss in this unexpected and unprecedented visit from Graverley. As Royce strode past the last pair of his men, they fell into step behind him in a formal honor guard.

"Well, Graverley," Royce said, stopping in front of his adversary, "what brings you out from your hiding place behind Henry's throne?"

Rage burned in Graverley's eyes, but his voice was

equally bland, and the words he spoke scored a hit every bit as deep as Royce's had done: "Fortunately for civilization, Claymore, the majority of us do not share your pleasure in the sight of blood and the stench of rotting bodies."

"Now that we've exchanged civilities," Royce clipped, "What do you want?"

"Your hostages."

In frigid silence, Royce listened to the rest of Graverley's scathing tirade, but it seemed to his benumbed mind that the words were coming from somewhere very far away: "The king heeded my advice," Graverley was saying, "and has been trying to negotiate a peace with King James. In the midst of those delicate negotiations, *you* seized the daughters of one of the most powerful lords in Scotland and, by your actions, may have rendered such a peace all but impossible." His voice rang with authority as he finished, "Assuming you haven't already butchered your prisoners in your usual barbarous fashion, you are hereby commanded by our Sovereign King to release Lady Jennifer Merrick and her sister into my custody at once, whereupon they will be returned to their family."

"No." The single icy word, which constituted a treasonous refusal to obey a royal edict, escaped from Royce without volition, and it hit the room with the explosive force of a giant boulder hurtled into the hall by an invisible catapult. The king's men automatically tightened their grips on their swords and stared ominously at Royce, while his own men stiffened in amazed alarm and also stared at Royce. Only Arik betrayed no emotion whatsoever, his stony gaze riveted unflinchingly on Graverley.

Even Graverley was too shocked to conceal it. Staring at Royce through narrowed eyes, he said in a tone of utter disbelief, "Do you challenge the accuracy with which I deliver the king's message, or do you actually dare to refuse the command itself?"

"I challenge," Royce improvised coldly, "your accusation of butchery."

"I'd no idea you were so sensitive on the subject, Claymore," Graverley lied.

Automatically stalling for time, Royce said, "Prisoners, as you above all should know, are taken before Henry's ministers and their fate decided there."

"Enough dissembling," Graverley snapped. "Will you or will you not comply with the king's command?"

In the space of the few moments alloted to him by perverse fate and an unpredictable king, Royce rapidly considered all the myriad reasons he would be insane to wed Jennifer Merrick, and the several compelling reasons why he was going to do it.

After years of victories on battlefields all over the continent, he had evidently ridden to defeat in his own bed atop a winsome seventeen-year-old with more courage and wit than any ten women he had ever known. Try though he might, he could not make himself send her home.

She had fought him like a tigress, but she surrendered like an angel. She had tried to stab him—but she had kissed his scars; she had slashed his blankets and sewn his shirts closed—but she had kissed him a few minutes ago with a sweet, desperate ardor that had twisted him into knots of desire; she had a smile that lit up the dark recesses of his heart, a laugh so infectious it made him grin. She had honesty, too, and he prized that above all.

Those things were in the back of his mind, but he refused to concentrate on them or even consider the word "love." To do so would have meant that he was more than physically involved with her, and *that* he refused to accept. With the same impartial, lightning logic he used to make decisions in battle, Royce considered instead that, given the way her father and clan Merrick already felt about her, if she returned to them, they would treat her as a traitor, not a victim. She had lain with their enemy and, whether she was already with child or not, she'd spend the rest of her life locked away in some nunnery, building dream kingdoms where she was accepted and loved, kingdoms that would never be.

These facts, added to the knowledge that she suited him in bed more than any other, were the only facts Royce permitted himself to consider in making his decision. And having arrived at it, he acted with typical speed and resolve. Knowing that he was going to need a few minutes alone with Jennifer in order to make her see reason before she leapt blindly at Graverley's offer, he forced a dry smile to his face and said to his foe, "While my man is fetching Lady Jennifer to the hall, shall we lay down the gauntlet long enough to partake of a light repast?" With a wave of his arm, he gestured toward the table where servants were trooping into the hall carrying trays laden with whatever cold fare they'd been able to assemble on such short notice.

Graverley's brows pulled together into a suspicious frown, and Royce glanced at Henry's men-at-arms, some of whom had fought beside him in past battles, wondering if they'd soon be locked in mortal combat against each other. Turning back to Graverley, he snapped, "Well?" Then, because he knew that, even after Jennifer agreed to stay with him, he was still going to have to dissuade Graverley from *forcing* her to leave, Royce injected a note of pleasantness into his voice. "Lady Brenna is already on her way home with my brother's escort." Hoping to appeal to Graverley's innate weakness for gossip, Royce added almost cordially, " 'Tis a story which you'll undoubtedly enjoy hearing while we eat . . ."

Graverley's curiosity won out over his suspicion. After a split second's hesitation, he nodded and headed for the table. Royce made a show of starting to escort him partway there, then he excused himself for a moment. "Let me send someone for Lady Jennifer," he said, already turning to Arik.

In a low, swift voice, he told Arik, "Take Godfrey with you and find her, then bring her here."

The giant nodded as Royce added, "Tell her not to trust Graverley's offer nor accept it until she's heard me out in private. Make that clear to her."

The possibility that Jennifer might listen to his own offer and still insist on leaving was beyond the bounds of feasibility in Royce's estimation. Although he rejected the notion that his decision to wed her might be motivated by anything more than lust or compassion, he always made it a point in every battle to be aware of the strength of his opponent's motivation to oppose him. In this case, he was well aware that Jennifer's feelings for him were deeper than even she knew. She could not have given herself to him so completely in bed, or honestly admitted that she'd wanted to stay there, if that weren't so. And she certainly could not have kissed him the way she had on the hill a few minutes ago. She was too sweet, too honest, and innocent to feign those emotions.

Comfortable with the conviction that victory—after a minor skirmish first with Jennifer and then Graverley—was in his grasp, Royce strode to the table where Graverley had just seated himself.

"So," Graverley said, many long minutes later, after Royce had relayed the tale of Brenna's leaving, and added every possible inconsequential detail he could think of in order to stall for time, "you let the beautiful girl leave and kept the proud one? Forgive me if I find that difficult to fathom," Graverley said, daintily chewing on a hunk of bread.

Royce scarcely heard this; he was reviewing his alternatives in the event Graverley refused to accept Jennifer's decision to remain at Hardin. Having alternatives—and being ready to choose the best one in any volatile situation—was what had kept him

194

alive and victorious in battle. Therefore, Royce decided, in the likely event that Graverley refused to accept Jennifer's decision to remain with Royce, Royce would then demand the right to hear Henry's edict from Henry himself.

Refusing to "believe" Graverley was not exactly treason, and Henry, although he would undoubtedly be angry, was unlikely to order Royce hanged for it. Once Henry heard Jennifer say, with her own soft lips, that she wished to wed Royce, there was a strong possibility Henry would like the notion. After all, Henry liked settling potentially dangerous political situations with expedient marriages, including his own.

That pleasant image of Henry benignly accepting Royce's defiance of a command and then promptly blessing their marriage was not very likely to become a reality, but Royce preferred to dwell on it rather than consider the remaining possibilities—such as the gallows, being drawn and quartered, or being stripped of the lands and estates he'd won at the repeated risk of his life. There were dozens of other equally unpleasant possibilities—and combinations of them—and, sitting at the table across from his foe, Royce considered them all. All except the possibility that Jennifer might have kissed him with her lips and heart and body, while she meant to escape the moment his back was turned.

"Why did you let her go if she was such a beauty?"

"I told you," Royce said shortly, "she was sick." Trying to avoid talking further to Graverley, Royce made a great show of being hungry. Reaching forward, he pulled his own trencher of bread toward him and took a large bite. His stomach lurched in protest to the bread, which was covered with rancid goose and soaked with its grease.

Twenty-five minutes later, it was taking a physical effort for Royce to keep his growing tension from showing. Arik and Godfrey must have given Jennifer

Royce's message and she was evidently balking; as a result they must be trying to reason with her and delaying bringing her into the hall. But would she balk? And if she did, what would Arik do? For a horrible moment, Royce imagined his loyal knight using physical force on Jennifer to make her acquiesce. Arik could snap Jennifer's arm in two with no more effort than it would take another man to break a tiny dry twig between his fingers. The thought made Royce's hand shake with alarm.

Across the distance of the rough-hewn planks that formed the makeshift table, Graverley was looking about him, his suspicion of trickery growing. Suddenly he leapt to his feet. "Enough of waiting!" he said sharply, glowering at Royce, who was slowly coming to his feet. "You're playing me for a fool, Westmoreland. I can sense it. You've not sent your men for her. If she is here, she's being hidden, and if that's the case, you're a greater *fool* than I thought." Pointing to Royce, he turned to his sergeant-at-arms and ordered, "Seize this man and then begin searching the castle for the Merrick woman. Tear this place apart, stone by stone if necessary, but find her! Unless I miss my guess, both women were murdered days ago. Question his men, use the sword if necessary. Do it!"

Two of Henry's knights stepped forward, under the apparent misapprehension that, as the king's men, they would be permitted to reach Royce without opposition. The moment they moved, Royce's men instantly closed ranks, their hands on the hilts of their swords, forming a human barrier between Henry's men and Royce.

A clash between Henry's men and his was the last thing on earth Royce wanted to happen, particularly now. "Hold!" he thundered, well aware that every one of his knights was committing a treasonous act merely by obstructing the king's men. All ninety of the men in the hall froze at the bellowed command, turning their faces to their respective leaders, awaiting the next command.

Royce's gaze slashed over Graverley, shocking the older man with its blazing contempt. "You above all dislike being made to look absurd, and that's what you're doing. The lady who you think I've murdered and hidden, has been taking a pleasant stroll—without a guard—on the hill behind the castle. Furthermore, far from being a prisoner here, Lady Jennifer enjoys complete freedom and has been accorded every comfort. In fact, when you see her, you'll find she's lavishly garbed in the clothes belonging to the former chatelaine of this castle, and around her throat is a strand of rather priceless pearls—also owned by the former chatelaine here."

Graverley's mouth fell open. "*You* gave jewels to *her?* The ruthless Black Wolf—the 'Scourge of Scotland'—has been lavishing his ill-gotten gains on his own prisoner?"

"A coffer full of them," Royce drawled blandly.

The look of amazement on Graverley's face at that revelation was so comical that Royce was torn between the urge to laugh and the more appealing urge to smash his fist into the other man's face. However, at that moment, his chief concern was to prevent an outbreak between the opposing forces in the hall and avert the unthinkable repercussions of such an act. To achieve that goal he was willing to say anything, confess to any folly, until Arik appeared with Jennifer in tow. "Furthermore," he continued, leaning his hip upon the table and affecting an attitude of complete confidence, "if you're expecting Lady Jennifer to fall at your feet and weep with joy that you've come to her 'rescue,' you're in for a disappointment. She will want to stay with me—"

"Why should she?" Graverley demanded, but far from being enraged, he was, for the moment, evidently finding the situation highly diverting. Like Royce

Westmoreland, Graverley knew the value of alternatives, and *if* all this rubbish about Lady Jennifer Merrick's willingness should prove to be true—and *if* Royce could persuade Henry to hold him blameless—then all this diverting information about Westmoreland's tender treatment of his captive would still provide enough hilarious gossip to keep the English court laughing for years. "I gather from your proprietary air that Lady Jennifer has been cavorting in your bed. Evidently, because she has, you think she'll now be willing to betray her family and her country because of it. It sounds to me," Graverley finished with open amusement, "that you've begun to believe all the court gossip over your supposed prowess in bed. Or was she so good to lie with that you've lost your wits? If so, I'll have to invite her for a tumble with me. You won't mind will you?"

Royce's voice was like icicles. "Inasmuch as I intend to wed her, 'twill give me an excuse to cut your tongue out—something I'll look forward to with considerable relish!" Royce was about to say more, but Graverley's gaze suddenly shifted to a point beyond Royce's shoulder.

"Here's the faithful Arik," he drawled with amused insolence, "but where's your eager bride?"

Royce swiveled around, his gaze riveting on Arik's harsh, craggy face. "Where is she?" he demanded.

"She's escaped."

In the frozen silence that followed that announcement, Godfrey added, "Judging by the looks of the tracks in the woods, there were six men and seven horses; she left with no signs of a struggle. One of the men was waiting in the woods only a few yards from where you sat with her today." *Only a few yards from where she kissed him as if she never wanted to leave him,* Royce thought furiously. *Only a few yards from where she used her lips and body and smile to lull him into leaving her there alone . . .*

Graverley, however, was not caught in the grip of paralyzing disbelief. Swinging around, he began snapping orders, the first aimed at Godfrey. "Show my men where you claim this happened." Turning to one of his own men, he added, "Go with Sir Godfrey and if it looks as if an escape actually happened the way he described it, take twelve men and overtake the Merrick clan. When you catch up with them, do not draw arms—any of you. Extend greetings from Henry of England and escort them to the Scottish border. Is that clear?"

Without waiting for an answer, Graverley turned to Royce, his voice tolling ominously in the cavernous hall: "Royce Westmoreland, by the authority of Henry, King of England, I hereby order you to accompany me to London where you will be called upon to answer for the abduction of the Merrick women. You will also answer for deliberately attempting to obstruct me in carrying out my sovereign's commands today regarding the Merrick women—which can and will be considered a treasonous act. Will you place yourself into our custody or must we take you by force?"

Royce's men, who outnumbered Graverley's, tensed—their loyalties understandably torn between their vows of fealty to Royce, their liege lord, and their vows to their king. Somewhere in the inferno of fury that was his mind, Royce noted their plight, and with a curt jerk of his head, he ordered them to lay down their arms.

Seeing that there was to be no resistance, one of Graverley's men, who had moved into position near Royce, caught both Royce's arms, yanked them behind him, and swiftly bound his wrists with stout leather thongs. The thongs were tight, cutting into Royce's wrists, but Royce scarcely noticed: a white hot fury unlike anything he'd ever experienced had consumed him, turning his mind into a fiery volcano of boiling rage. Parading before his eyes were visions of a bewitching Scottish girl: Jennifer lying in his arms . . . Jennifer laughing up at him . . . Jennifer blowing him a kiss . . .

For his stupidity in trusting her, he would face charges of treason. At best, he would forfeit all his lands and titles; at worst, he'd forfeit his life.

At that moment, he was too infuriated to care.

Chapter Thirteen

Royce stood at the window of the small but well-appointed bedchamber that had been his "cell" since his arrival, two weeks ago, at the Tower of London, Henry's royal residence. His expression was impassive as he stared out across the London rooftops, lost in impatient contemplation, his legs braced wide apart. His hands were behind his back, but they were not bound, nor had they been since that first day when his fury at Jennifer Merrick—and at his own gullibility—had temporarily robbed him of his ability to react. He had permitted it then, partly to prevent his men from endangering their own necks by fighting for him, and partly because, at the time, he was too incensed to care.

By that night, however, his fury had been reduced to a dangerous calm. When Graverley had attempted to retie his wrists after Royce finished eating, Graverley had found himself jerked to the ground with the leather thong wrapped taut around his throat, Royce's face, dark with rage, only inches from his own. "Attempt to bind me again," Royce had bit out between his teeth, "and I'll slit your throat within five minutes after my interview with Henry."

Writhing in surprise and fear, Graverley had nevertheless managed to gasp, "Five minutes after your interview with the king . . . you'll be on your way . . . to the gallows!"

Without thinking, Royce had tightened his hand, the subtle twist of his wrist effectively cutting off his adversary's air. Not until his victim's face had begun to change color did Royce realize what he was doing, and then he released him with a contemptuous shove. Graverley staggered unsteadily to his feet, his eyes blazing with hatred, but he gave no order to Henry's men to seize Royce and bind him. At the time, Royce had attributed that to the likelihood that Graverley had realized he could be treading on dangerous ground by deliberately abusing the rights of Henry's favorite noble.

Now, however, after waiting weeks for a summons from the king, Royce was beginning to wonder if Henry was actually in complete accord with the privy councillor. From his position at the window, Royce stared out at the dark night that was scented with the usual malodorous smells of London—sewage, garbage, and excrement—trying to find a reason for Henry's obvious reluctance to see him and discuss the reason Royce was being encarcerated.

He had known Henry for twelve years; he had fought beside him at the Battle of Bosworth Field, had watched as Henry was proclaimed king and crowned on that same battlefield. In recognition of Royce's deeds during that battle, Henry had knighted him that same day, despite the fact that Royce was only seventeen. It was, in fact, his first official act as king. In the years that followed, Henry's trust and reliance on Royce had grown apace with his mistrust of his other nobles.

Royce fought his battles for him and each flamboyant victory made it easier for Henry to exact—without bloodshed—concessions from England's enemies and Henry's personal ones. As a result, Royce had been rewarded with fourteen estates and riches enough to make him one of the wealthiest men in England. Equally important, Henry trusted him—trusted him enough to permit Royce to fortify his castle at Claymore and to keep a private, liveried army of his own men. Although, in this instance, there was strategy behind Henry's leniency: the Black Wolf was a threat to all Henry's enemies; the sight of pennants with a snarling wolf pictured on them often crushed hostility before it had a chance to bloom into opposition.

In addition to trust and gratitude, Henry had also given Royce the privilege of speaking his mind freely and without the interference of Graverley and the other members of the powerful Star Chamber. And that was what was niggling at Royce now—this long period of refusal to give Royce an audience in order to defend himself was not indicative of the sort of relationship he'd enjoyed with Henry in the past. Nor did it bode well for the outcome of the audience itself.

The sound of a key being inserted in his door made Royce glance up, but hope shriveled when he saw it was only a guard bearing a tray with his meal. "Mutton, my lord," the guard provided helpfully in answer to Royce's unspoken inquiry.

"God's teeth!" he exploded, his impatience with everything coming to a rolling boil.

"Don't like mutton much myself, my lord," the guard agreed, but he knew the food had nothing to do with the Black Wolf's outburst. After putting the tray down, the man straightened respectfully. Confined or not, the Black Wolf was a dangerous man and, more importantly, a great hero to every male who fancied himself a true man. "Do you wish for anything else, my lord?"

"News!" Royce bit out, his expression so harsh, so threatening, that the guard backed away a step, before he nodded obediently. The Wolf always inquired about news—usually in a friendly man-to-man way—

and tonight the guard was happy to be privy to some gossip. Still, 'twas not exactly gossip the Wolf would likely be happy to hear.

"There is some news, my lord. Gossip it be, but reliable-like, heert from those what are in a position to know."

Royce was instantly alert. "What 'gossip'?"

"'Tis said yer brother was called afore the king last night."

"My brother is here in London?"

The guard nodded. "Came here yesterday, demandin' to see yer and practically threatnin' to lay siege to the place if'n he didn't."

An awful feeling of foreboding crept over Royce. "Where is he now?"

The guard tipped his head to the left. "One floor above ye and a few rooms to the west, I heert. Under guard."

Royce expelled his breath in a rush of frustrated alarm. Stefan's coming here was reckless in the extreme. When Henry was angered, the best tack was to stay out of his way until he got control of his royal temper. "Thank you," Royce said, trying to recall the guard's name, "er . . . ?"

"Larraby, my—" They both broke off and glanced toward the door as it swung open. Graverley stood in the doorway, grinning evilly.

"Our sovereign has bade me bring you to him."

Relief mixed with concern for Stefan ran through Royce, as he stalked past Graverley, shouldering him aside. "Where is the king?" Royce demanded.

"In the throne room."

Royce, who'd been a guest here at the Tower several times in the past, knew it well. Leaving Graverley to follow and try to keep pace, he strode swiftly down the long hall to the steps which wound down two stories and then led through a maze of chambers.

As he passed through the gallery with his escort/guard following behind, Royce noted that everyone was turning to stare. Judging from the derision on many of their faces, the fact that he'd been confined here and was out of favor with Henry was a fact known to all.

Lord and Lady Ellington, attired in full court dress, bowed to Royce as he passed, and again Royce witnessed their strange expressions. He was accustomed to some fear and mistrust when he was at court; but tonight he could have sworn they were hiding amused smiles, and he discovered that he vastly preferred being mistrusted to being laughed at.

Graverley gleefully provided the answer for the odd looks: "The story of Lady Jennifer's escape from the notorious Black Wolf has been cause for much hilarity here."

Royce clamped his jaws together and increased his pace, but Graverley quickened his to match. In a confiding voice ringing with mockery, he added, "So has the story of our famous hero's infatuation with a plain Scottish girl who ran away, wearing a fortune in pearls he'd given her, rather than wed him."

Royce swung around on his heel, fully intending to smash his fist into Graverley's grinning face, but behind him the liveried footmen were already pulling open the tall doors to the throne room. Restraining himself with the knowledge that Stefan's future, as well as his own, would not be improved by murdering Henry's most valued councillor, Royce turned away and strode through the doors the footmen were holding open for him.

Henry was sitting at the far end of the room, garbed in formal robes of state, his fingers tapping impatiently on the arms of his throne. "Leave us!" he ordered Graverley, and then he turned his cold, distant gaze on Royce. Silence followed Royce's polite greeting— an unusual, icy silence that did not bode well for the outcome of the interview. After several endless minutes of it, Royce said with cool politeness, "I understood you wished to see me, Sire."

"Silence!" Henry snapped furiously. "You'll speak to me when I give you leave to do it!" But now that the dam of silence had been breached, Henry's own anger could no longer be held in check, and his words issued forth like lashes from a whip. "Graverley claims you had your men turn their weapons on my men. He further charges that you deliberately disobeyed my instructions and impeded his efforts to free the Merrick women. How plead you to this accusation of treason, Royce Westmoreland?" Before Royce could reply, his enraged sovereign shoved himself from his chair and continued. "You condoned the seizure of the Merrick women—an act which has become an affair of state threatening the peace of my realm. And having done so, you let two women—two *Scottish* women—escape from your clutches, thus turning an affair of state into a joke that has swept all England! How plead you?" he said in a low roar. *"Well?"* he roared again without taking a breath. "Well? Well?"

"Which accusation do you desire me to address first, Sire?" Royce replied with courtesy. "The accusation of treason? Or the rest, which constitutes stupidity?"

Disbelief, anger, and a twinge of reluctant amusement widened Henry's eyes. "You *arrogant pup!* I could have you whipped! Hung! Pilloried!"

"Aye," Royce quietly agreed. "But tell me first for which offense. I have taken hostages many times in the last decade, and on more than one occasion you've commended it as a more peaceful means of scoring a win than outright battle. When the Merrick women were taken, I could not have guessed you'd suddenly decided to seek peace with James—particularly not when we were defeating him in Cornwall. Before I left for Cornwall, we spoke in this very chamber and agreed that, as soon as the Scots were subdued enough for me to leave Cornwall, I was to take command of a fresh army near the Scottish border and install it at Hardin, where our strength would be very visible to the enemy. At that time, it was clearly agreed between us that I would then—"

"Yes, yes," Henry interrupted angrily, not wanting to hear again what Royce intended to do next. "Explain to me," he ordered irritably, unwilling to admit aloud that Royce's reasoning in taking the two hostages had been valid, "what happened in the hall at Hardin. Graverley claims your men tried to attack mine on your order when he placed you under arrest. I've no doubt," he said with a grimace, "your version will vary from his. He detests you, you know."

Ignoring the last part of that, Royce replied with calm, indisputable logic, "My men outnumbered yours almost two to one. Had they attacked your men, none of them would have survived to take me into custody—yet they all returned here without so much as a scratch."

Henry relaxed slightly. With a curt nod, he said, "Which is exactly what Jordeaux pointed out in the privy council when Graverley told us his tale."

"Jordeaux?" Royce repeated. "I wasn't aware I had an ally in Jordeaux."

"You don't. He hates you, too, but he hates Graverley more because he wants Graverley's position, not yours, which he knows he cannot have." Darkly he said, "I'm entirely surrounded by men whose brilliance is only exceeded by their malice and ambition."

Royce stiffened at the unintended insult. "Not entirely surrounded, Sire," he said coolly.

In no mood to agree, even though he knew his earl spoke the truth, the king sighed irritably and motioned to a table on which reposed a tray with several jewelled goblets and some wine. In the closest thing to a conciliatory gesture he was willing to make in his present mood, Henry said, "Pour us something to drink." Rubbing the joints of his hands, he added absently, "I hate this place in the winter. The cold dampness makes my joints ache incessantly. Were it not for this tempest you've created, I'd be in a warm house in the country."

Royce complied, carrying the first goblet of wine to the king and then pouring one for himself and returning to the foot of the steps which led up to the dais. Standing in silence, he sipped the wine, waiting for Henry to emerge from his brooding reflections.

"Some good has come of this, in any case," the king finally admitted, glancing at Royce. "I'll confess I've had many second thoughts about letting you fortify Claymore and keep your own liveried retainers. However, when you let yourself be taken into custody on charges of treason by my men, who were obviously outnumbered by your retainers, you gave me proof that you will not turn against me, no matter how tempting it might be to do so." In a lightening-swift change of topic, designed to trap the relaxed and unwary, Henry said smoothly, "Yet, despite all your loyalty to me, you didn't intend to release Lady Jennifer Merrick into Graverley's custody so that she could be escorted home, did you?"

Anger raged through Royce at this reminder of his utter stupidity. Lowering his goblet he said icily, "I believed at the time that she herself would refuse to go and would explain that to Graverley."

Henry gaped at him, open-mouthed, the goblet in his fingers tipping precariously. "So Graverley spoke the truth about that. *Both* women duped you."

"Both?" Royce repeated.

"Aye, my boy," Henry said with a mixture of amusement and annoyance. "Standing outside the doors to this chamber are two emissaries from King James. Through them I have been in constant contact with James, and he has been in contact with the earl of Merrick, and everyone else involved in this mess. Based on what James has somewhat gleefully reported to me, it appears to me that the younger girl—who you believed to be hovering at death's door—had actually put her face into a pillow filled with feathers, which made her cough. Then she convinced you it was actually a recurrence of an ailment of the lungs, thus duping you into sending her home. The older one— Lady Jennifer—obviously went along with the ploy, stayed behind for one day, then duped you into leaving her alone so that *she* could escape with her stepbrother, who'd undoubtedly managed to get word to her where to meet him."

Henry's voice hardened. " 'Tis the joke of Scotland that my own champion was duped by a pair of young maids. 'Tis also a story that's been well told and embellished in my own court. The next time you confront an adversary, Claymore, you may find he laughs in your face instead of trembling with fear."

A moment ago, Royce didn't think he could be angrier than he'd been that day at Hardin when Jennifer escaped. However, the realization that Brenna Merrick, who cried at the sight of her own shadow, had actually duped him was enough to make him grind his teeth. And that was *before* the rest of Henry's words sank in: Jennifer's tears and pleading for her sister's life had been false! She had feigned all that. No doubt when she offered her virginity for her sister's "life," she expected to be rescued before nightfall!

Henry abruptly stood up and walked down the steps, beginning to pace slowly. "You've not heard the lot of it! There has been an outcry over all this, an outcry that has surpassed even my expectations when you first sent me word about the identity of your hostages. I did not grant you an audience until now because I was waiting for your reckless brother to turn up, so that I could question him in person as to the exact location whence he snatched the girls. It seems," King Henry said in an explosive breath, "that there is every possibility he snatched them from the grounds of the abbey where they were staying, exactly as their father is claiming.

"As a result, Rome has been demanding reparation

from me in every conceivable form! Then, besides the protests from Rome and all Catholic Scotland over the girls' abduction from a holy abbey, there's the MacPherson, who's threatening to lead every clan in the highlands into war against us because *you* despoiled his affianced wife!"

"*His what!*" Royce hissed.

Henry glanced at him in disgruntled annoyance. "You were not aware that the young woman whom you deflowered, and then lavished your jewels upon, was already betrothed to the most powerful chieftain in Scotland?"

Rage exploded in a red mist before Royce's eyes, and in that moment he was absolutely convinced that Jennifer Merrick was the most consummate liar on earth. He could still see her, her *innocent* smiling eyes never leaving his as she talked about being sent to the abbey—leading him to believe that she'd been sent to remain, possibly for the rest of her life. She had failed to mention that she was on the brink of marriage. And *then* he remembered her poignant little story about planning a dream kingdom, and the fury inside him was almost past bearing. He had no doubt that she had invented it all . . . everything. She had played upon his sympathies as skillfully as a harpist plays upon the strings of his instrument.

"You are spoiling the shape of that goblet, Claymore," Henry pointed out with wry irritability, watching as Royce's clenched hand forced the silver rim of the goblet into an oval. "By the way, since you haven't denied it, I assume you did bed the Merrick woman?"

His jaw clenched tight with rage, Royce inclined his head in the barest sign of a nod.

"Enough discussion," the monarch snapped abruptly, all casual friendliness banished from his voice. Putting his goblet down on a richly carved table of gilded oak, he ascended the steps to the throne, saying, "James cannot agree to a treaty when his subjects are in an uproar over our violation of one of their abbeys. Nor will Rome be satisfied with a mere gift to their coffers. Therefore, James and I have agreed there is only one solution, and we are in complete accord for once."

Switching to the royal plural for emphasis, the king announced in ringing tones that brooked no objection, "It is Our decision that you will proceed to Scotland at once, whereupon you will wed Lady Jennifer Merrick in the presence of diplomatic emissaries from both courts, and in full view of her kinsmen. Several members from Our own court will accompany you on your journey, their presence at the nuptials to represent the English nobility's full acceptance of your wife as an equal in rank."

Having spoken, Henry kept his ominous gaze leveled on the tall man who was standing before him, white-faced with fury, a nerve jerking in his dark cheek. When he could finally trust himself to speak, Royce's voice erupted like hissing steam. "You ask the *impossible.*"

"I've asked it of you before—in battle—and you've not refused me. You've no reason, and no *right* to do so now, Claymore. Moreover," he continued, reverting back to the royal plural while his tone grew more dire, "We did not *ask,* We commanded. Furthermore, for not yielding to Our emissary at once when he conveyed Our orders to release your hostage, We hereby fine you the estate of Grand Oak together with all income derived therefrom during this past year."

So consumed with fury was Royce over the thought of wedding that scheming, deceitful red-haired witch, he scarcely heard the rest of what Henry was saying.

"However," said the royal voice, gentling somewhat, now that its owner could see that the earl of Claymore was apparently not going to voice foolish—and intolerable—objections. "In order that the estate of Grand Oak will not be entirely lost to you, I shall grant it to your bride as a wedding gift." Ever mindful of the need to continue fattening his coffers, the king added politely, "You shall, however, forfeit the income derived from it for the full year past."

With his hand he gestured toward the rolled parchment resting on the table at the foot of the dais beside his discarded wine goblet. "That parchment will leave here within an hour in the hands of James's emissaries, who will deliver it directly to him. It sets forth all I've told you—everything that James and I have already agreed upon—and I've set my hand and seal to it. As soon as he receives it, James will send his emissaries to Merrick, who will then inform the earl of the marriage that is to take place at once between his daughter and you at Merrick keep, a fortnight hence."

Having said all that, King Henry paused, waiting for polite words of acceptance and a promise of obedience from his subject.

His subject, however, spoke in the same infuriated hiss he'd spoken in before. "Is that *all,* Sire?"

Henry's brows snapped together, his tolerance at an end. "I'll have your word to obey. Make your choice," he growled. "The gallows, Claymore, or else your word to marry the Merrick woman with all haste."

"With all haste," Royce bit out between his teeth.

"Excellent!" Henry decreed, slapping his knee, his good will completely restored now that all was settled. "To tell you truly, my friend, I thought for a moment you actually meant to choose death over a wedding."

"I've little doubt I'll oft regret I didn't," Royce snapped.

Henry chuckled and motioned with a beringed finger to his discarded wine goblet. "We shall drink a toast to your marriage, Claymore. I can see," he continued a minute later, watching Royce toss down a fresh goblet of wine in an obvious attempt to calm his ire, "that you regard this forced marriage as poor reward for your years of faithful service, yet I have never forgotten that you fought beside me long before there was much hope for gain."

"What I hoped to gain was peace for England, Sire," Royce said bitterly. "Peace and a strong king with better ideas for keeping that peace than the old methods, with battle axe and battering ram. I did not know at the time, however," Royce added with poorly concealed sarcasm, "that one of your methods would be to wed the hostile parties to each other. If I had," he finished acidly, "I might well have thrown my lot in with Richard instead."

That outrageous piece of treason made Henry throw back his head and roar with laughter. "My friend, you've always known I deem marriage an excellent compromise. Did we not sit up late one night by a campfire at Bosworth Field, just the two of us? If you think back on the occasion, you'll recollect I told you then I'd offer my own sister to James if I thought 'twould bring peace."

"You don't have a sister," Royce pointed out shortly.

"Nay, but I have *you* instead," he quietly replied. It was the highest of royal compliments, and even Royce was not proof against it. With an irritated sigh, he put his chalice down and absently raked his right hand through the side of his hair.

"Truces and tournaments—that's the way to peace," Henry added, well pleased with himself. "Truces for restraint and tournaments to work off hostilities. I've invited James to send anyone he likes to the tournament near Claymore later in the fall. We'll let the clans fight us on the field of honor— harmless. Quite enjoyable, actually," he announced, reversing his earlier opinion on the subject. "Naturally, you needn't participate."

When Henry fell silent, Royce said, "Have you more to say to me, Sire, or may I beg your leave to retire?"

"Certainly," Henry replied good-naturedly. "Come to see me in the morn, and we'll talk more. Don't be too hard on your brother—he volunteered to marry the sister in order to spare you. Seemed not at all reluctant to do it, in fact. Unfortunately, that won't do. Oh, and Claymore, you needn't worry about telling Lady Hammel of your broken betrothal. I've done that already. Poor lovely thing—she was quite overset. I've sent her off to the country in hopes the change of scene will help restore her spirits."

The knowledge that Henry had proceeded with the betrothal, and that Mary had undoubtedly been subjected to tremendous humiliation as a result of Royce's notorious behavior with Jennifer, was the last piece of ill news he could tolerate in one night. With a brief bow, he turned on his heel and the footmen opened the doors. A few steps away, however, Henry called his name.

Wondering what impossible demand he was about to make now, Royce reluctantly turned to face him.

"Your future bride is a countess," Henry said, an odd smile lingering at his lips. "It is a title inherited by her through her mother—a title far older than your own, by the by. Did you know that?"

"If she were queen of Scotland," Royce replied bluntly, "I wouldn't want her. Therefore, her present title is scarcely an inducement."

"I quite agree. In fact, I regard it as a likely hindrance to marital harmony." When Royce merely looked at him, Henry explained with a widening smile, "Inasmuch as the young countess has already duped my most fierce and brilliant warrior, I think 'twould be a tactical mistake to have her *outrank* him as well. Therefore, Royce Westmoreland, I hereby confer upon you the title of duke . . ."

When Royce emerged from the throne room, the antechamber was filled with staring nobles, all of them visibly eager to have a look at him and thus assess how his interview with the king had gone. The answer came from a footman who rushed out of the throne room and loudly said, "Your grace?"

Royce turned to hear that King Henry bade him convey his personal regards to his future wife, but the nobles in the antechamber heard only two things: "your grace," which meant that Royce Westmoreland was now a duke, the holder of the most exalted title in the land, and that he was evidently about to be married. It was, Royce realized grimly, Henry's way of announcing both events to those in the antechamber.

Lady Amelia Wildale and her husband were the first to recover from the shock. "So," said Lord Wildale, bowing to Royce, "'twould appear congratulations are in order."

"I disagree," Royce snapped.

"Who is the lucky lady?" Lord Avery called good-naturedly. "Obviously, it is not Lady Hammel."

Royce stiffened and slowly turned while tension and expectation crackled in the air, but before he could reply, Henry's voice boomed from the doorway: "Lady Jennifer Merrick."

The stunned silence that followed was broken first by a loud laugh that was abruptly stifled, and then giggles, and then a deafening babble of denials and amazed exclamations.

"Jennifer Merrick?" Lady Elizabeth repeated, looking at Royce, her sultry eyes silently reminding Royce of the intimacies they had once shared. "Not the beautiful one? The plain one then?"

His mind bent only on getting out of there, Royce nodded distantly and started to turn.

"She's quite *old*, isn't she?" Lady Elizabeth persisted.

"Not too old to snatch up her skirts and run away from the Black Wolf," Graverley put in smoothly, strolling out from the midst of the crowd. "No doubt you'll have to *beat* her into submission, won't you? A little *torture*, a little pain, and then mayhaps she'll *stay* in your bed?"

Royce's hands clenched against the urge to strangle the bastard.

Someone laughed to diffuse the tension and joked, *"It's England against Scotland,* Claymore, except the battles will take place in the bedchamber. My purse is on you."

"Mine, too," someone else called.

"Mine is on the woman," Graverley proclaimed.

Further back in the crowd an elderly gentleman cupped his hand to his ear and called to a friend who was closer to the duke, "Eh? What's all this about? What's happened to Claymore?"

"He has to marry the Merrick slut," his friend replied, raising his voice to be heard over the increasing hubbub.

"What did he say?" called a lady far back in the crowd, craning her neck.

"Claymore has to marry the Merrick *slut!"* the elderly gentleman obligingly called out.

In the uproar that followed, only two nobles in the antechamber remained still and silent—Lord MacLeash and Lord Dugal, the emissaries from King James, who were waiting for the signed marriage agreement which they were to take to Scotland tonight.

Within two hours, word had passed from noble to servant to guards outside, and then to passersby: "Claymore has to marry the Merrick slut."

Chapter Fourteen

In answer to her father's summons, Jenny dragged her thoughts from the memories of the handsome, gray-eyed man who still haunted her days and nights. Laying down her embroidery, she gave Brenna a puzzled look, then she pulled her dark green mantle closer about her shoulders and left the solar. Male voices raised in debate made her pause on the gallery and glance down into the hall. At least two dozen men—kinsmen and nobles from surrounding demesnes—were gathered around the fire, their rough-hewn faces grim as death. Friar Benedict was there, too, and the sight of his stern, icy face made Jenny cringe with a combination of alarm and shame.

Even now, she could recall every word of his blistering tirade when she confessed to him the sin she had committed with Royce Westmoreland: *"You shamed your father, your country, and your God with your uncontrollable desires for this man. Were you not guilty of the sin of lust, you'd have surrendered your life before your honor!"* Instead of feeling cleansed, which she normally did after confessing her sins, Jenny had felt dirtied and almost beyond salvation.

Now, in retrospect, she thought it a little odd that he had placed God in the last position of importance when he listed those she had shamed. And despite her lingering guilt at having actually enjoyed the things Lord Westmoreland had done to her, she refused to believe *her* God would blame her for making the original bargain. In the first place, Lord Westmoreland had not *wanted* her life, he had wanted her body. And although she'd been wrong to enjoy lying with a man who was not her husband, the actual bargain had been nobly made for the sake of sparing Brenna's life—or so she'd thought.

The God whom Friar Benedict spoke of in such frightening terms of fiery vengeance and righteousness, was not the same God to whom Jenny frequently poured out her heart. *Her* God was reasonable, kind, and only somewhat stern. Hopefully, He even understood why she could not seem to permanently blot out of her mind the exquisite sweetness of the night she'd spent in Royce Westmoreland's arms. The memory of his passionate kisses, of his whispered words of praise and passion, kept coming back to torment her, and she couldn't prevent it. Sometimes, she didn't want to try . . . several times, she'd dreamed of him, of the way he looked when that lazy white smile swept across his tanned face, or . . .

Jenny jerked her mind from such thoughts and stepped into the hall, her reluctance to face the men assembled around the fireplace growing with each step she took. Until now, she'd remained virtually secluded within Merrick, needing somehow the security of its ancient, familiar walls around her. Despite her self-imposed seclusion, she had no doubt the men in the hall knew what she had done. Her father had demanded a full accounting of her abduction, and partway through Jenny's explanation, he had interrupted her to bluntly demand to know if the Wolf had forced her to lie with him. Jenny's face had given away the answer, and despite her efforts to ease his fury by explaining about the bargain and assuring him that her captor had not been brutal, his rage was uncontainable. His shouted curses had rung to the rafters, and the reason for it had not been kept secret. Although, whether the men in the hall viewed her as a helpless victim or a common slut, she had no way of knowing.

Her father was standing at the fireplace, his rigid back to his guests. "You wished to see me, Father?"

Without turning he spoke, and the ominous tone of his voice made alarm tingle up her spine. "Sit down, daughter," he said, and her cousin, Angus, quickly stood up to offer Jenny his chair. The swiftness, the *eagerness* of the polite gesture took Jenny by surprise.

"How are you feeling, Jenny?" Garrick Carmichael asked, and Jenny stared at him in amazement, a lump of emotion filling her throat. It was the first time since Becky's drowning that Becky's father had spoken to her.

"I—I'm very well," she whispered, looking at him with her heart in her eyes. "And I—I thank you for asking, Garrick Carmichael."

"Yer a brave lass," another of her kinsmen spoke up, and Jenny's heart began to soar.

"Aye," said another. "Yer a true Merrick."

A fleeting thought passed her delighted mind that, despite her father's inexplicably black look, this was beginning to feel like the best day of her life.

Hollis Fergusson spoke up, his voice gruff as he issued an apology on behalf of everyone for their past behavior: "William has told us all about what happened while you were in the clutches of the Barbarian —about how you escaped on his own horse, and attacked him with his sword, and slashed their blankets. You've made him a laughingstock with your escape. A lass with courage like yours would no' sneak about doin' the sorts o' vile things Alexander accused you o' doin. William has made us see that. Alexander was mistaken in you."

Jenny's gaze flew to her stepbrother's face, and there was a world of love and gratitude in her eyes.

"I only told the truth," he said, his smile gentle and inexplicably sad as he returned her gaze—as if his pleasure in what he'd accomplished was being dimmed by something else weighing heavily on him.

"Yer a Merrick," Hollis Fergusson put in proudly. "A Merrick through and through. Not one 'o us has ever given the Wolf a taste of our blades, but *you* did, small though you are, and a lass, at that."

"Thank you, Hollis," Jenny said softly.

Only Malcolm, Jenny's youngest stepbrother, continued to regard her as he had in the past, his face filled with cold malice.

Her father turned abruptly, and the expression on his face banished some of Jenny's delight. "Has something . . . bad happened?" she asked hesitantly.

"Aye," he said bitterly. "Our fates have been decided by our meddling monarch, not ourselves." Clasping his hands behind his back, he began to pace slowly back and forth while he explained in a harsh monotone: "When you and your sister were taken, I petitioned King James for two thousand armed men to join with ours so that we could pursue the Barbarian into England. James sent word back, commanding me to take no action until he had time to demand your release, as well as reparation for this outrage, from Henry. He had just agreed on a truce with the English, he said.

"I should *no'* have told James what I wanted to do. That was my mistake," he gritted, beginning to pace. "We'd no' have needed his help! The sanctity of one of our abbeys had been violated when you were taken from its grounds. Within days, all Catholic Scotland was ready—*anxious*—to take arms and march with us! But James," he finished angrily, "wants peace. Peace at the cost of Merrick pride—peace at any cost! He promised me revenge. He promised all Scotland that he would make the Barbarian pay for this outrage. Well," Lord Merrick spat furiously, "he's made him *pay,* all right! He's gotten his *'reparation'* from the English."

For a sick moment, Jenny wondered if Royce Westmoreland had been imprisoned or worse, but judging by her father's furious look, neither of those punishments—which he would see as fitting—had been meted out. "What did James accept in the form of reparation?" she asked when her father seemed unable to continue.

Across from her, William flinched and the other men began to look at their hands.

"Marriage," her father gritted.

"Whose?"

"Yours."

For a moment Jenny's mind went completely blank. "My—my marriage to whom?"

"To the Spawn of Satan. To the murderer of my brother and my son. To the Black Wolf!"

Jenny gripped the arms of her chair so tightly her knuckles whitened. *"Whaat!"*

Her father jerked his head in a nod, but his voice and expression took on an odd note of triumph as he came to stand directly in front of her. "You are supposed to be the instrument of peace, daughter," he said, "but later, you will be the instrument of *victory* for the Merricks and for all Scotland!"

Very slowly Jenny shook her head, staring at him in confused shock. The remainder of her color drained from her face as her father continued, "Without realizing it, James has given me the means to destroy the Barbarian, not on the battlefield, by putting an end to his life, as I'd hoped to do, but instead in his own castle, by ruining what is *left* of his misbegotten life. In fact," he finished with a sly, proud smile, "you've already begun."

"What—what do you mean?" Jenny whispered hoarsely.

"All England is laughing at him because of you. The stories of your two escapes, your wounding him with his own dagger, all of it, have been circulating from Scotland to England. His brutality has gained him enemies in his own country, and those enemies are busy spreading those same stories everywhere. You've made a laughingstock of Henry's champion, my dear. You've ruined his reputation, but his wealth remains, along with his titles—wealth and titles he accumulated by crushing Scotland beneath his heel. 'Tis up to you to see he never enjoys those gains—and you *can*, by denying him an heir. By denying him your favors, by—"

Shock and fear combined to send Jenny surging to her feet. "This is madness! Tell King James I wish for no 'reparation.'"

"'Tis of no consequence what *we* want! Rome wants reparation. Scotland wants it. Claymore is on his way here even as we speak. The betrothal contract will be signed and the wedding is to follow immediately. James has left us no alternative."

Jenny shook her head slowly, in silent, desperate denial, while her voice slid to a frightened whisper. "Nay, Papa, you don't understand. You see—I—he trusted me not to try to escape, and I did. And if I've truly made him a laughingstock, he'll never forgive me for that . . ."

Anger turned her father's face a terrible shade of red. "You do not want his *forgiveness*. We want his *defeat* in every way—large and small—that we can have it! Every Merrick, every *Scot*, will depend on you to deliver it. You have the courage to do it, Jennifer. You proved that while you were his captive . . ."

Jenny no longer heard him. She had humiliated Royce Westmoreland, and now he was coming here; she trembled at the realization of how much he must loathe her and how angry he must be: her mind promptly presented her with frightening visions of the times she had seen him angry; she saw him as he had looked the night she'd been dumped at his feet, his black mantle billowing eerily, the orange flames of the fire giving his face a satanic look. She saw the expression on his face when his horse was dead because of her; the fury that blackened his features when she cut his face. But none of that had been breaking his trust. Or, worse, making a *fool* of him.

"He must be deprived of an heir as he deprived me of mine!" her father's voice slashed through her thoughts. "He must! God has granted me this revenge when all other paths were closed to me. I have other heirs, but he will have none. Never. Your marriage will be my revenge."

Reeling with anguish, Jenny cried, "Papa, please, don't ask me to do this. I'll do anything else. I'll go back to the abbey, or to my Aunt Elinor, or anywhere you say."

"Nay! He would only marry another of *his* choice and beget his heirs on her."

"I *won't* do it," Jenny insisted wildly, voicing the first logical arguments that tumbled to mind. "I can't! It's wrong. It's impossible! If—if the Black Wolf wants me—wants an heir," she corrected with a shamed, blushing glance at the other men, "how can I prevent it? His strength is five times mine. Although, after all that's passed between us, I don't think he'll want me in the same castle with him, let alone in his"—she tried desperately to think of a word to substitute, but there was none—"bed," she finished weakly, her gaze shying away from their guests.

"Would you were right, my child, but you're wrong. There is about you the same quality your mother possessed, the quality that stirs lust in a man when he looks upon you. The Wolf will want you whether he *likes* you or no." Suddenly he paused for emphasis, a slow smile on his face, "however, 'tis possible he'll no' be able to do much about it if I send your Aunt Elinor with you."

"Aunt Elinor," Jenny repeated blankly. "Papa, I

know naught of what you mean, but all of this is wrong!" Her hands clutching helplessly at her woolen skirts, she looked with desperate appeal at the men surrounding her, while in her mind she saw another Royce Westmoreland than the one they knew—the man who had teased her in the glade, and talked with her on the parapet; the man who bargained her into his bed and treated her gently, when another captor would have raped her and given her to his men.

"Please," she said, looking around at all of them and then at her father. "Try to understand. 'Tis not disloyalty, 'tis reason that makes me say this: I know how many of our people have died in battle with the Wolf, but such is the way of all battles. He cannot be blamed for Alexander's death or—"

"You dare to exonerate him?" her father breathed, looking at her as if she was changing into a serpent before his eyes. "Or can it be that your loyalty is to him, not us?"

Jenny felt as if he had slapped her, yet in some tiny part of her she realized her feelings for her former captor were a strange enigma, even to her. "I only seek peace—for all of us—"

" 'Tis obvious, Jennifer," her father said bitterly, "you cannot be spared the humiliation of hearing what your affianced husband thinks of this 'peaceful' union, and of *you*. Within hearing of everyone at Henry's court, he said he wouldn't want you if you were the *queen* of Scotland. When he refused to have you as his wife, his king threatened to deprive him of all he possessed and *still* he refused. It took the threat of death to finally make him agree! Afterward, he called you the Merrick *slut;* he boasted he would *beat* you into submission. His friends began placing wagers on him, laughing because he means to bring you to heel as he has brought *Scotland* to heel. *That* is what he thinks of you and this marriage! As for the rest of them—they've given you the title he conferred on you: The Merrick *Slut!"*

Each word her father spoke struck Jenny's heart like a lash, making her cringe with a shame and hurt that was almost past bearing. When he was finished, she stood there while a blessed, cold numbness came over her, until she felt nothing at all. When she finally lifted her head and looked about at the tired, valiant Scots her voice was brittle and hard. "I hope they wagered *all* their wealth on it!"

Chapter Fifteen

Jenny stood alone on the parapet looking out across the moors, the wind playfully tossing her hair about her shoulders, her hands clutching the stone ledge in front of her. The hope that her "bridegroom" might not arrive for his wedding, which was to take place in two hours, had been snatched from her a few minutes ago when a castle guard had called out that riders were approaching. A hundred and fifty mounted knights were riding toward the drawbridge, the light from the setting sun glinting on their polished shields, turning them to shining gold. The figure of a snarling wolf danced ominously before her eyes, undulating on blue pennants, and waving on the horses' trappings and knights' surcoats.

With the same unemotional detachment she'd felt for five days, she stood where she was, watching as the large group neared the castle gates. Now she could see there were women among them and a few standards bearing markings other than the Wolf. She had been told some English nobles would be present tonight, but she had not expected any women. Her gaze shifted reluctantly to the broad-shouldered man riding at the front of the party, bareheaded and without shield or sword, mounted atop a great black destrier with flowing mane and tail that could have been sired only by Thor. Beside Royce rode Arik, also bareheaded and without armor, which Jenny assumed was their way of illustrating their utter contempt for any puny attempt clan Merrick might make to slay them.

Jenny couldn't see Royce Westmoreland's face at all from this distance, but as he waited for the drawbridge to be lowered, she could almost feel his impatience.

As if he sensed that he was being watched, he lifted his head abruptly, his gaze sweeping over the roofline of the castle, and without meaning to, Jenny pressed back against the wall, hiding herself from view. Fear. The first emotion she'd felt in five days, she realized with disgust, had been fear. Squaring her shoulders, she turned and reentered the castle.

Two hours later, Jenny glanced at herself in the mirror. The feeling of pleasant numbness that had vanished on the parapet had deserted her for good, leaving her a mass of quaking emotion, but the face in the mirror was a pale, emotionless mask.

"It won't be nearly so terrible as you think, Jenny," Brenna said, trying with all her heart to cheer her as she helped two maids straighten the train of Jenny's gown. "'Twill all be over in less than an hour."

"If only the marriage could be as short as the wedding," Jenny said miserably.

"Sir Stefan is down in the hall. I saw him myself. He'll not let the duke do anything to disgrace you down there. He's an honorable, strong knight."

Jenny turned, the brush in her hand forgotten, studying her sister's face with a wan, puzzled smile. "Brenna, are we discussing the same 'honorable knight' who kidnapped us in the first place?"

227

"Well," said Brenna defensively, "unlike his wicked brother, at least *he* didn't attempt to make any immoral bargains with me afterward!"

"That's quite true," Jenny said, completely distracted for the moment from her own woes. "However, I wouldn't count on his good will tonight. I've little doubt he'll be longing to wring your neck when he sets eyes on you, because now he knows *you* tricked him."

"Oh, but he doesn't feel that way at all!" Brenna burst out. "He told me it was a very daring and brave thing I did." Ruefully, she added. "*Then* he said he could wring my neck for it. And besides, 'twasn't him I tricked, 'twas his wretched brother!"

"You've already spoken to Sir Stefan?" Jenny said, dumbfounded. Brenna had never shown the slightest interest in any of the young swains who'd been pursuing her for the last three years, yet now she was evidently meeting in secret with the last man in the world her father would permit her to wed.

"I managed to have a few words with him in the hall, when I went to ask William a question," Brenna confessed, her cheeks stained hot pink, then she suddenly became absorbed in straightening the sleeve of her red velvet gown. "Jenny," she said softly, her head bent, "now that there's to be peace between our countries, I was thinking I should be able to send you messages often. And if I included one for Sir Stefan, would you see that he receives it?"

Jenny felt as if the world were turning upside down. "If you're certain you want to do that, I will. And," she continued, hiding a laugh that was part hysteria and part dismay for her sister's hopeless attachment, "will I also be including messages from Sir Stefan with mine to you?"

"Sir Stefan," Brenna replied, lifting her smiling eyes to Jenny's, "suggested just that."

"I—" Jenny began, but she broke off as the door to her chamber was swung open and a tiny, elderly woman rushed forward, then stopped in her tracks.

Dressed in an outdated, but lovely gown of dove gray satin lined with rabbit, an old-fashioned, gauzy white wimple completely swathing her neck and part of her chin, and a silvery veil trailing down her shoulders, Aunt Elinor looked from one girl to the other in confusion. "I know *you're* little Brenna," Aunt Elinor said, beaming at Brenna, and then at Jenny, "but can this beautiful creature be my plain little Jenny?"

She stared in stunned admiration at the bride, who was standing before her clad in a cream velvet and satin gown with a low, square-cut bodice, high waist, and wide full sleeves heavily encrusted in pearls and sprinkled with rubies and diamonds from elbow to wrist. A magnificent satin cape lined in velvet was also bordered in pearls, attached at Jenny's shoulders with a pair of magnificent gold brooches set with pearls, rubies, and diamonds. Her hair spilled over her shoulders and back, glinting like the gold and rubies she wore.

"Cream velvet—" said Aunt Elinor smiling and opening her arms. "So very impractical, my love, but so very beautiful! Almost as beautiful as you—"

Jenny raced into her embrace. "Oh, Aunt Elinor, I'm so very happy to see you. I was afraid you weren't coming—"

Brenna answered a knock on the door, and then she turned to Jenny, her words abruptly choking Jenny's outpouring of delighted greeting: "Jenny, Papa desires you to come downstairs now. The documents are ready to be signed."

A terror that was almost uncontrollable swept over Jenny, twisting her stomach into sick knots and draining the color from her face. Aunt Elinor tucked her arm in Jenny's and, in an obvious effort to distract her from concentrating on what awaited her, she gently drew Jennifer toward the door, while chatting about the scene that awaited her downstairs.

"You shan't believe your eyes when you see how full the hall is," she jabbered in the mistaken belief that a crowd would lessen Jenny's fear of a confrontation with her future husband. "Your papa has one hundred of your men standing at arms at one side of the hall, and *he*"—the faint sniff of superiority in her voice made it clear "he" was the Black Wolf—"has at least that many of his own knights standing directly across the room, watching *your* men."

Jenny walked woodenly down the long hall, each slow step feeling like her last one. "It sounds," she said tautly, "like the setting for a battle, not a betrothal."

"Well, yes, but it isn't. Not exactly. There are more nobles than knights down there. King James must have sent half of his court here to witness the ceremony, and the heads of the nearby clans are here, too."

Jenny took another wooden step down the long dark hallway. "I saw them arrive this morning."

"Yes, well, King Henry must have wanted this to seem a special occasion for celebration, for there are all sorts of English nobles here, too, and a few of them brought their wives. It's very wondrous to behold— the Scots and the English in their velvets and satins all gathered together . . ."

Jenny turned and started the short, steep descent down the winding stone steps to the hall. "It's very quiet down there—" she said shakily, her ears picking up the muted sounds of male voices raised in forced joviality, a few coughs, a woman's nervous laughter . . . and nothing else. "What are they all doing?

"Why, they're either exchanging cold looks," Aunt Elinor cheerfully replied, "or pretending they don't know the other half of the room is present."

Jenny was rounding the last turn near the bottom of the stairs. Pausing to steady herself, she bit her trembling lip, then with a defiant toss of her head, she lifted her chin high and walked forward.

An ominous hush slowly swept over the hall as Jennifer came into view, and the spectacle that greeted her eyes was as foreboding as the silence. Torches burned brightly in stands mounted on the stone walls, casting their light on the staring, hostile spectators. Men-at-arms stood stiff and straight beneath the torches; ladies and lords stood side by side—the English on one side of the hall and the Scots on the opposite—exactly as Aunt Elinor had said.

But it was not the guests who made Jenny's knees begin to shake uncontrollably, it was the tall, powerfully built figure who stood aloof in the center of the hall, watching her with hard, glittering eyes. Like an evil specter, he loomed before her in a wine-colored cloak lined with sable, emanating wrath so forceful that even his own countrymen were standing well away from him.

Jennifer's father came forward to take Jennifer's hand, a guard on each side of him, but the Wolf stood alone. Omnipotent and contemptuous of his paltry enemy, he openly scorned the need for protection from them. Her father tucked her hand through his arm as he guided her forward, and the wide path through the great hall that divided the Scots from the English widened yet more as they approached. On her right stood the Scots, their proud, stern faces turned toward her with anger and sympathy; on her left were the haughty English, staring at her with cold hostility. And straight ahead, blocking her way, was the sinister figure of her future husband, his cloak thrown back over his wide shoulders, his feet planted slightly apart, his arms crossed over his chest, inspecting her as if she were some repulsive creature crawling across the floor.

Unable to endure his gaze, Jenny focused her eyes on a point just above his left shoulder, and wondered a little wildly if he meant to stand aside and let them pass. Her heart thundering like a battering ram in her chest, she clutched her father's arm, but still the devil refused to budge, deliberately forcing Jenny and her father to walk around him. It was, Jenny realized hysterically, only the first act of contempt and humiliation to which he would treat her publicly and privately for the rest of her life.

Fortunately, there was little time to dwell on that, because another horror awaited her directly ahead—the signing of her betrothal contract, which was spread open upon a table. Two men stood beside it, one of them the emissary from King James's court, the other the emissary from King Henry's court, both of whom were here to witness the proceedings.

At the table, Jennifer's father stopped and released her clammy hand from the comfort of his grip. "The Barbarian," he enunciated clearly and audibly, "has already signed it."

The hostility in the room seemed to escalate to frighteningly tangible proportions at his words, crackling through the air like a million daggers hurtling back and forth from the Scots side of the hall to the English. In frozen, mute rebellion, Jenny stared at the long parchment containing all the words that set out her dowry and condemned her irrevocably to a life, and all eternity, as the wife and chattel of a man she loathed, and who loathed her. At the bottom of the parchment, the duke of Claymore had scrawled his signature in a bold hand—the signature of her captor, and now her jailor.

On the table beside the parchment lay a quill and inkhorn and, though Jenny willed herself to touch the quill, her trembling fingers refused to obey. The emissary from King James moved forward, and Jenny looked up at him in helpless, angry misery. "My lady," he said with sympathetic courtesy and the obvious intention of showing the English in the hall that Lady Jennifer held the respect of King James himself, "our sovereign king, James of Scotland, has bade me to extend his greetings to you, and to further say that all of Scotland is indebted to you for this sacrifice you make on behalf of our beloved homeland. You are an honor to the great clan of Merrick and to Scotland as well."

Was there an emphasis on the word "sacrifice," Jenny wondered dazedly, but the emissary was already picking up the quill and pointedly handing it to her.

As if from afar, she watched her hand slowly reach for it, grasp it, and then sign the loathsome document, but when she straightened, she could not tear her eyes from it. Transfixed, she stared at her own name, written in the scholarly script Mother Ambrose had made her practice and perfect. The abbey! Suddenly, she could not, would not, believe God was actually letting this happen to her. Surely, during her long years at Belkirk abbey, God must have noticed her piety and obedience and devotion . . . well, at least her attempt to be obedient, pious, and devoted. *"Please God . . ."* she repeated wildly, over and over again. *"Don't let this happen to me."*

"Ladies and gentlemen—" Stefan Westmoreland's bold voice slashed through the hall, echoing off the stone walls. "A toast to the duke of Claymore and his new bride."

His new bride . . . the words reverberated dizzily in Jenny's brain, jarring her from her recollections of the past weeks. She looked around in a dazed panic, not certain whether her reverie had lasted seconds or minutes, and then she began to pray again:

"Please God, don't let this happen to me . . ." she cried in her heart one last time, but it was too late. Her widened eyes were riveted on the great oaken doors that opened into the hall to admit the priest for whom everyone was waiting.

"Friar Benedict," her father loudly proclaimed as he stood at the doors.

Jenny's breath stopped.

"Has sent us word he is unwell."

Her heart began to hammer.

"And the wedding cannot be performed until tomorrow."

"Thank you, God!"

Jenny tried to step back, away from the table, but the room was suddenly beginning to spin, and she couldn't move. She was going to faint, she realized with horror. And the person nearest to her was Royce Westmoreland.

Suddenly Aunt Elinor let out a cry of dismay as she recognized Jenny's plight, and she rushed forward, shamelessly jostling startled clansmen aside with her elbows. An instant later, Jenny found herself wrapped in a fierce hug, a parchment cheek pressed to hers, an achingly familiar voice bubbling in her ear. "Now, now, babe, take a deep breath, and you'll feel right as can be in a moment," the voice crooned. "Your Aunt Elinor is here now, and I'll take you upstairs."

The world tilted crazily, then suddenly righted itself. Joy and relief poured through Jenny as her father addressed the company in the hall:

"'Twill only be a day's delay," he boomed, his back turned to the English. "Friar Benedict is only mildly afflicted, and the good man promises to leave his pallet and come here on the morrow to perform the ceremony, no matter how ill he may still be."

Jenny turned to leave the hall with her aunt, and she stole a quick glance at her "betrothed" to see his reaction to the delay. But the Black Wolf seemed not to know she was there. His narrowed gaze was trained on her father, and though his expression was as inscrutable as a sphinx, there was a cold, speculative look in his eyes. Outside, the storm that had been threatening all day suddenly whipped itself into a frenzy, and lightning split the sky, followed by the first ominous, primitive boom of thunder.

"However," her father continued, turning to address the entire hall without ever actually looking at the English on his right, "the feasting will take place as planned this eve. 'Tis my understanding from the emissary of King Henry that most of you wished to return to England at once on the morrow; however, I fear you may have to remain an extra day, since our roads aren't fit for English travel when the storms come."

A babble of voices burst out on both sides of the room. Ignoring the stares aimed at her, Jenny walked with her aunt through the crowded hall, straight to the stairs that led up two stories to her bedchamber. To sanity and solace. To a reprieve.

When the heavy oaken door of her bedchamber closed behind her, Jenny turned into Aunt Elinor's arms and wept unashamedly with relief.

"There, there now, my kitten," said her mother's elderly aunt, patting Jenny's back with her small hand, and talking in the eager, disjointed, determined way that was so much a part of her, "There's no doubt in my mind that when I didn't arrive yesterday or the day before, you gave up and thought I wasn't coming to be with you. 'Tis true, is it not?"

Swallowing back her tears, Jenny leaned back slightly in her aunt's fond embrace and nodded sheepishly. Ever since her father had suggested Aunt Elinor accompany Jenny to England, Jenny had been concentrating on that as the only joy on her gloomy, frightening horizon.

Cupping Jennifer's tear-streaked face in her palms, Aunt Elinor went on with bright determination. "But I am here now, and I've talked with your father this morn. I'm here and I'll be with you every day from now on. Won't that be nice? We'll have lovely times together. Even though you'll needs be married to that Englishman and reside with him, beast that he is, we'll forget him altogether and go about the way we used to do, before your father banished me to the dower house at Glencarin. Not that I blame him, for I do chatter so, but I fear it's worse now than ever, for I've been deprived so long of loved ones who I can talk with."

Jenny looked at her, a little dazed from her aunt's long, breathless speech. Smiling, she wrapped the small lady in a tight hug.

Seated at the long table on the dais, oblivious to the din of three hundred people dining and drinking around and below her, Jenny stared fixedly across the hall. Beside her, their elbows nearly touching, sat the man to whom the betrothal contract had bound her as irrevocably as the formal wedding ceremony which would follow tomorrow. For the last two hours that she'd been forced to sit beside him, she'd felt his icy gaze on her only thrice. It was as if he couldn't stand the sight of her and was only waiting to get her in his clutches so that he could begin making her life a hell.

A future of verbal attacks and physical beatings loomed before her, for even among the Scots it was not uncommon for a husband to beat his wife if he felt she was in need of discipline or encouragement. Knowing that, and knowing the temper and reputation of the angry, cold man beside her, Jenny was certain her life would be filled with misery. The tightness in her throat that had nearly choked her all day almost cut off her breath now, and she tried valiantly to think of something to look forward to in the life she'd be forced to lead. Aunt Elinor would be with her, she reminded herself. And someday— someday soon, considering her knowledge of her husband's lustful nature—she'd have children to love and care for. Children. She closed her eyes briefly and drew a painful breath, feeling the tightness slowly lessen. A baby to hold and cuddle would be something to look forward to. She'd cling to that thought, she decided.

Royce reached for his goblet of wine and she stole a glance at him from the corner of her eye. He was, she noted sourly, watching a particularly comely acrobat who was balancing on her hands on a bed of sharp swordpoints, her skirts tied to her knees to prevent them falling over her head—a necessity that allowed her shapely, stockinged legs to be exposed from knee to ankle. On the other side of the room, jesters wearing pointed hats with balls at the ends, cavorted before the table which ran the full length of the hall. The festive entertainment and lavish supper fare was her father's way of showing the hated English that the Merricks had pride and wealth.

Disgusted with Royce's open admiration for the acrobat with the pretty legs, Jenny reached for her goblet of wine, pretending to sip from it rather than face the malicious, scornful eyes of the English, who'd been watching her with derision all night. Based on some of the remarks she'd overheard, she had been judged and found completely lacking. "Look at that hair," one woman had sniggered. "I thought only horses had manes of that color." "Look at that haughty face," a man had said as Jennifer walked past him with her head high and her stomach in knots. "Royce won't abide that haughty attitude of hers. Once he has her at Claymore, he'll beat it out of her."

Turning her gaze from the jesters, Jenny looked at her father, who was seated on her left. Pride filled her as she studied his aristocratic, bearded profile. He had such dignity . . . such noble bearing. In fact, whenever she'd watching him sitting in judgment in the great hall, listening to disputes that periodically cropped up among his people, she couldn't help thinking that God must look just like him, sitting on His heavenly throne and passing judgment on each soul who came before Him.

Tonight, however, her father seemed to be in a very strange mood, particularly given the awful circumstances. All evening, while talking and drinking with the other heads of the various clans in the hall, he'd seemed preoccupied and edgy, and yet . . . oddly . . . pleased. Satisfied about something. Feeling Jennifer's gaze on him, Lord Merrick turned to her, his sympathetic blue eyes drifting over her pale face. Leaning so close to her that his beard tickled her cheek, he spoke in her ear, his voice raised slightly, but not enough to carry to anyone else. "Do not vex yourself, my child," he said. "Take heart," he added, "all will be well."

That remark seemed so absurd that Jenny didn't know whether to laugh or cry. Seeing the panic in her widened blue eyes, he reached out and covered Jenny's clammy hand, which was at that moment clutching the edge of the table as if she were holding onto it for her life. His big warm hand covered hers reassuringly, and Jenny managed a wobbly smile.

"Trust me," he said, "all will be well on the morrow."

Jenny's spirits plummeted. After the morrow, it would be too late. After the morrow, she'd be wed for eternity to the man whose wide shoulders beside her made her feel puny and insignificant. She stole a quick, worried look at her betrothed to belatedly make certain he hadn't somehow managed to overhear the hushed conversation she'd just had with her father. But his attention was elsewhere. No longer idly watching the comely acrobat, Royce was gazing straight ahead.

Curious, Jenny surreptitiously followed the direction of his gaze and saw Arik, who'd just reentered the hall. As Jenny watched, the blond, bearded giant slowly nodded once, then once more at Royce. From the corner of her eyes, Jenny saw Royce's jaw harden, then he inclined his head almost imperceptibly, before calmly and deliberately returning his attention to the acrobat. Arik waited a moment and then casually walked over to Stefan, who was ostensibly watching the pipers.

Jenny sensed that some sort of information had just been silently exchanged, and it made her intensely uneasy, particularly when her father's words were ringing through her mind. Something was happening, she knew it, though she knew not what. Some deadly serious game was being played and she wondered if her future was somehow hanging on the outcome.

Unable to endure the noise and suspense any more, Jenny decided to seek the peace of her bedchamber so that she could savor what little reason she had to be hopeful. "Papa," she said swiftly, turning to him, "I beg your leave to retire now. I would seek the peace of my bedchamber."

"Of course, my dear," he said at once. "You've had little peace in your short life, but 'tis just what you need, isn't it?"

Jenny hesitated a split second, feeling that there was some sort of double meaning in his words, but failing to understand it she nodded, and then she stood up.

The moment she moved, Royce's head turned toward her, though she could have sworn that he hadn't really known she was there all night. "Leaving?" he asked, his insolent gaze lifting to her bosom. Jenny froze at the inexplicable fury in his eyes when they finally lifted to hers. "Shall I accompany you to your chamber?"

With a physical effort, Jenny willed her body to move and straightened to a full standing position, giving herself the momentary pleasure of looking down on *him*. "Certainly not!" she snapped. "My aunt will accompany me."

"What a dreadful evening!" Aunt Elinor burst out the instant they reached Jenny's chamber. "Why, the way those English looked at you made me yearn to order them from the hall, which I swear I very nearly did. Lord Hastings, the Englishman from that odious Henry's court, was whispering to the fellow on his right throughout the meal, and ignoring me completely, which was more than rude of him, though I had no wish to talk to *him*. And, dear, I do not mean to add to your burdens, but I cannot like your husband at all."

Jenny, who'd forgotten her aunt's habit of running on like a little magpie, grinned affectionately at the disapproving Scotswoman, but her mind was on a different matter: "Papa seemed in a strange mood at supper."

"I always felt he did."

"Did what?"

"Have strange moods."

Jenny swallowed a hysterical, exhausted giggle and abandoned any further attempt to discuss the evening. Standing up, she turned around so her aunt could help unfasten her gown.

"Your father means to send me back to Glencarin," Aunt Elinor said.

Jenny's head jerked around and she stared at her aunt. "Why do you say such a thing?"

"Because he did."

Completely confused, Jenny turned and took her firmly by the shoulders. "Aunt Elinor, exactly what did papa say?"

"This eve when I arrived later than expected," she replied, her narrow shoulders drooping, "I expected him to be vexed, which would have been most unfair, for it wasn't my fault it was raining so hard to the west. You know how it is this time of year—"

"Aunt Elinor—" Jenny said in a dire, warning tone. "*What* did Papa say?"

"I'm most sorry, child. I've been so long without human company, storing up so much conversation for lack of anyone to speak to, that now that I have— someone to speak to, I mean—I cannot seem to stop. There were two pigeons who used to land on the window of my bedchamber at Glencarin, and we three conversed, though of course, pigeons have little to say—"

At this, the most ominous time of her life, Jenny's shoulders began to shake with helpless laughter, and she wrapped her arms around the startled little woman, while mirth exploded from her chest and tears of fear and exhaustion filled her eyes.

"Poor child," Aunt Elinor said, patting Jennifer's

back. "You are under such strain and I'm but adding to it. Now then," she paused, thinking, "your papa told me at supper tonight that I should not plan on accompanying you after all, but that I could stay to see you married if I wished." Her arms fell from Jennifer and she slumped dejectedly onto the bed, her elderly, sweet face filled with appeal. "I would do anything not to go back to Glencarin. It's so very lonely, you see."

Nodding, Jenny laid her hand atop her aunt's snowy hair and gently soothed the shining crown, remembering years past when her aunt had run her own huge household with bustling efficiency. It was grossly unjust that enforced solitude combined with advancing years had wrought such a change in the courageous woman. "I will appeal to him on the morrow to change his mind," she said with weary determination. Her emotions were battered from the long, trying day, and exhaustion was beginning to sweep over her in heavy, crushing waves. "Once he understands how much I want you with me," she said with a sigh, suddenly yearning for the comfort of her narrow cot, "he'll surely relent."

Chapter Sixteen

Nearly every foot of floor space, from the great hall to the kitchens, was covered with sleeping guests and exhausted servants, lying upon whatever they had, or could find, to cushion the hard stones. A chorus of snores rose and fell discordantly throughout the castle, clashing and ebbing like confused, tumultuous waves.

Unaccustomed to the peculiar sounds that disrupted the dark, moonless night, Jenny stirred fitfully in her sleep, then turned her face on the pillow and opened her eyes, startled into a somnambulant wakefulness by some unknown noise or movement in the room.

Her heart racing in confused fright, she blinked, trying to calm her rapid pulse and peer through the inky darkness of her bedchamber. On the low pallet beside Jenny's narrow bed, her aunt turned over. *Aunt Elinor,* Jenny realized with relief—no doubt Aunt Elinor's movements had awakened her. The poor thing suffered quite often from a stiffness in her joints that made sleeping on a hard pallet preferable to a soft bed, and even then she tossed and turned seeking comfort. Jenny's pulse returned to normal, she rolled onto her back, shivering from a sudden cold blast of air . . . A scream tore from her chest at the same instant a large hand clamped over her mouth, throttling it. While Jenny stared in paralyzed terror at the dark face only inches above her own, Royce Westmoreland whispered, "If you cry out, I'll knock you senseless." He paused, waiting for Jennifer to recover her wits. "Do you understand me?" he snapped.

Jenny hesitated, swallowed, then nodded jerkily.

"In that case," he began, loosening his grip very slightly. The moment he did, Jennifer sank her teeth into the fleshy part of his palm and flung herself to the left, trying to gain the window and shout to the guards in the bailey below. He grabbed her before her feet left the bed and threw her onto her back, his wounded hand clamping down on her nose and mouth so tightly that she couldn't breath. "That's the second time you've drawn my blood," he bit out between his teeth, his eyes alive with fury. "And 'twill be the *last.*"

He's going to suffocate me! Jenny thought wildly. She shook her head frantically, her eyes wide, her chest straining, heaving for air.

"That's better," he jeered, softly. " 'Tis wise for you to learn to fear me. Now listen to me very carefully, *Countess,"* he continued, ignoring her terrified struggles. "One way or another, I'm going to lower you out that window over there. If you give me one more instant of trouble, you'll be unconscious when I do it, which greatly reduces your chances of reaching the ground alive, since you won't be able to hang on."

He lightened the pressure of his hand just enough for her to drag air into her lungs, but even when she'd gulped down several heaving breaths, Jenny could not stop trembling. "The window!" she mumbled against his muffling hand. "Are you mad? It's more than eighty feet above the moat."

Ignoring that, he fired his most deadly weapon, the threat guaranteed to demolish her resistance. "Arik is holding your sister prisoner, not to be released until I give the signal. If you do anything to prevent me signaling him, I wouldn't like to think what he might do to her."

What little fight Jenny had left within her drained away. This was like reliving a nightmare, and trying to escape it was pointless. Tomorrow she'd have been wed to the devil anyway, so what difference was one more night in what was bound to be years of misery and confusion.

"Take your hand away," she said wearily. "I won't cry out. You can trust—"

The last sentence was a mistake; she knew it the instant the words escaped her lips and she saw his face tighten with furious contempt. "Get up!" he snapped, jerking her out of bed. Reaching out into the darkness, he snatched up the velvet wedding gown lying across a trunk at the foot of her bed and thrust it into her arms. Clutching the gown to her bosom, Jenny said shakily, "Turn your back."

"Shall I fetch you a dagger to use as well?" he jeered icily, and before she could reply, he snapped, "Get dressed!"

When she'd donned gown, slippers, and a dark blue mantle, he pulled her toward him, and before she realized what he meant to do, he was wrapping a black cloth around her mouth, gagging her. Finished, he spun her around and pushed her toward the window.

Jenny stared down in terror at the long smooth wall that dropped straight into a deep dark moat. It was like looking at her own death. Wildly she shook her head, but Royce shoved her forward, snatching the stout rope he'd left dangling over the window ledge and tying it tightly around her midriff.

"Hold onto the rope with your hands," he ordered mercilessly as he wrapped the other end of the rope around his wrist, "and use your feet to hold your body away from the wall." Without hesitation he lifted her off her feet and onto the sill.

Seeing the terror in her enormous eyes as she

244

clutched mindlessly at both sides of the window casing, Royce said curtly, "Don't look down. The rope is stout, and I've lowered far heavier burdens than you."

A moan rose in Jenny's throat as his hands grasped her waist, relentlessly forcing her outward. "Grab the rope," he snapped, and Jenny obeyed at the same moment he lifted her clear of the sill, holding her dangling in a moment of breathless terror high above the murky water below.

"Push away from the wall with your feet," he ordered sharply. Jennifer, who was already out the window, twisting and turning helplessly as a leaf in the wind, groped frantically for the wall with her feet and finally managed to stop herself from revolving. Bracing her feet against the rough stones with only her head and neck above the window opening, she stared at him, her breath coming in shallow, terrified gasps.

And in that most unlikely—and least desirable—of moments, hanging eighty feet above a deep moat with only a strong pair of hands and a stout rope to keep her from plunging to her death, Jenny was granted the rare opportunity to see the Black Wolf's face register total, blank shock as Aunt Elinor rose up from beside Jenny's bed like a ghostly apparition in white bedgown and demanded imperiously, "*What* do you think you are doing?"

Royce's head jerked toward her, his face a mask of almost comical disbelief as he realized the utter helplessness of his plight, for he could neither reach for his dagger to threaten her, nor dash across the room to silence her.

At any other time, Jenny would have relished seeing him at such a complete loss, but not now, not when he literally held her life in his hands. Her last view of him was of his profile staring at Aunt Elinor, and then the rope began to play out and she was lowered joltingly down the endless wall, left to dangle and to pray and to wonder what in God's holy name was happening in her bedchamber and *why* Aunt Elinor had revealed herself at all, let alone at *that* moment.

Royce was wondering the same thing as he stared through the darkness at the elderly woman who had, for some incomprehensible reason of her own, deliberately waited until this impossible moment to present herself. He glanced at the rope biting into his wrists, automatically testing the tension, and then he finally answered her question. "I'm abducting your niece."

"Just as I thought."

Royce peered at her closely, uncertain whether Jennifer's aunt was simple-minded or devious. "What do you intend to do about it?"

"I *could* open the door behind me and call for help," she said, "but since you have Brenna captive, I probably oughtn't do that."

"No," Royce agreed with hesitation. "Probably not."

For an endless moment their gazes locked as they assessed one another, and then she said, "Of course, you *could* be lying, which I cannot know."

"I could be," Royce agreed cautiously.

"Then again, you might not. How did you manage to scale the wall?"

"How do you think I did?" Royce replied, shifting his gaze to the rope and stalling for time. His shoulders straining, his lower body braced against the wall, he continued slowly letting out the rope, hand over hand.

"Perhaps one of your men came up here during supper, pretending he wished to use the garderobe, since there was a crowd outside the one in the hall. Then he slipped in here, anchored the rope to that chest beneath the window, and tossed the other end out the window."

Royce confirmed her completely accurate conclusion with a slight, mocking inclination of his head. Her next words brought him another jolt—this time of alarm. "On further reflection, I do *not* think you're holding Brenna captive, after all."

Royce, who had deliberately misled Jennifer into believing he did, now had urgent need of the old woman's silence. "What makes you think not?" he asked, bargaining for precious time as he continued to let out the rope.

"For one thing, my nephew was posting guards in the hall at the foot of the stairs when I retired this eve---undoubtedly to prevent something such as this. And so, in order to take Brenna, you'd have had to scale this wall once already this eve, which would be a great deal of needless trouble since your only need for Brenna was to ensure that Jennifer left quietly with you."

That summary was so concise and so correct that Royce's opinion of the old woman climbed another notch. "On the other hand," he drawled calmly, watching her closely, trying to judge Jennifer's distance from the moat below, "you can't be certain I'm not a very cautious man."

"That's quite true," she agreed.

Royce breathed an inward sigh of relief that turned into alarm as she added, "But I do not believe you have Brenna. Therefore, I shall strike a bargain with you."

His brows snapped together. "What sort of bargain?"

"In return for my not summoning the guards now, you will lower me out of that window and take me with you tonight."

If she'd invited him to join her in bed, Royce would not have been more stunned. Recovering his composure with an effort, he assessed her thin, frail body and the danger of having to carry her with him down the rope. "It's out of the question," he snapped.

"In that case," she said, turning and extending her hand to the door, "you leave me no choice, young man---"

Stifling an oath at his current helplessness, Royce continued letting the rope play out. "Why should you want to go with us?"

Her voice lost its imperious confidence and her shoulders drooped a little. "Because my nephew means to send me back into seclusion on the morrow, and I truly cannot bear the thought of it. However," she added with a trace of slyness, "'twould also be in your best interest to take me with you."

"Why?"

"Because," Aunt Elinor replied, "my niece, as you well know, can be a troublesome woman; however, she will do as *I* tell her."

A faint gleam of interest entered Royce's eyes as he considered the long journey ahead and the need for speed. A "cooperative" Jennifer could mean the difference between success and failure of his plan. However, as he considered Jennifer's rebelliousness, obstinacy, and cunning, he found it difficult to believe the red-haired she-devil would meekly acquiesce to her aunt. Even now he felt the imprint of her teeth in his bloodied palm. "Frankly, I find that difficult to believe."

The woman lifted her white-crowned head and looked at him down the length of her nose. "'Tis our way, Englishman. 'Tis why her father sent for me and meant to send me with her when she left with you on the morrow."

Royce recalculated the benefits of taking the old woman with him against the difficulties she'd create by slowing their pace. He had just decided against taking her, when her next words changed his mind. "If you leave me behind," she said piteously, "my nephew will surely kill me for letting you take her. His hatred for you surpasses his love for me—even for poor Jennifer. He'll never believe you could silence both of us. He'll think I put the rope there for you."

Mentally cursing all Scotswomen to perdition,

Royce hesitated and then jerked his head in a reluctant nod. "Get dressed," he gritted.

The rope biting painfully into her ribs, her arms and legs smarting from wide scrapes on her skin where it slid against the stone wall, Jenny swallowed and glanced downward. In the murky darkness of the moat she could just discern the figures of two men who appeared to be standing eerily on the surface of the water. Firmly stifling that hysterical notion, she squinted her eyes and saw the outline of a flat raft beneath them. A scant few moments later, hands that were huge and rough snatched her out of the air, grasping her at the waist, indifferently brushing her breasts, as Arik untied the rope that held her, then lowered her onto the rocking insecurity of the makeshift raft.

Reaching behind her head, Jenny started to untie the black cloth that gagged her, but Arik jerked her hands down and bound them roughly behind her, then he shoved her none too gently toward the other man standing on the rocking raft, who caught her. Still trembling from her ordeal, Jenny found herself staring at the expressionless face of Stefan Westmoreland, who coldly turned away from her and stared up into the darkness at the window high above.

Awkwardly, Jenny lowered herself to a sitting position on the raft, grateful for what little security it provided in a world that no longer made any sense to her.

A few minutes later the silence of the two men on the raft was broken by a low, startled whisper from Stefan Westmoreland. "What the hell—!" he breathed, staring up in disbelief at the castle wall Jennifer had just descended.

Her head lurched up, following the direction of their gazes, half in hopes of seeing Royce Westmoreland plunging helplessly toward the water. What she saw was the unmistakable figure of a man with a body thrown over his shoulder like a sack of wheat and tied to him at the waist.

Shock sent Jenny halfway to her feet when she realized it was poor Aunt Elinor he carried, but the raft pitched and Arik's head jerked toward her, his sharp gaze warning her to be still. In breathless tension, Jenny waited, watching the cumbersome outline moving with painful slowness down the ropes. Not until Arik and Stefan Westmoreland were reaching up and grasping their accomplice, helping lower him onto the raft, did Jenny draw a normal breath.

Royce was still disentangling himself from his "prisoner," when the raft began to move with effortless stealth to the far shore. Simultaneously Jenny noticed two things: Unlike herself, Aunt Elinor was not gagged to prevent her from screaming, and the raft was being guided to the opposite shore with ropes that were being hauled in by men stationed in the woods on the opposite bank.

Two bright flashes of lightning rent the sky with jagged blue light and Jenny glanced over her shoulder, praying a guard on the castle wall might turn this way and see the raft illuminated by the angry sky. On second thought, she decided wearily, there was no reason to pray they'd be seen, nor any reason for her to be gagged. One way or another, she'd have been leaving Merrick with Royce Westmoreland. She preferred leaving this way, she decided as her fear began to subside, rather than leaving as his *wife*.

Chapter Seventeen

The storm that had been gathering strength for two days blew in with a vengeance, causing the sky to remain almost black for two full hours past the normal time for dawn. Rain pounded down on their heads and lashed their faces, bending stout saplings almost in two, and still the band moved doggedly onward, keeping to the protection of the woods whenever possible.

With his shoulders hunched forward, Royce let the rain pelt his back, irritated that his posture was also providing a sheltering barrier against the rain for the exhausted woman who was responsible for all of this and who was now sleeping fitfully against his chest.

With the sun completely vanquished by the dark clouds overhead, it seemed as if they'd been riding through a perpetual dawn. Had it not been for the rain, they'd have come upon the place he sought hours ago. Idly, Royce patted Zeus's shiny neck, well pleased with Thor's son, who carried his double burden with the effortless ease of his sire. The slight movement of his gloved hand seemed to stir Jennifer from her slumber, and she snuggled closer against the warmth of Royce's body. Once, not long ago, that same slight movement would have made him want to cuddle her close against his chest, but not today. No longer. When he had need of her body, he would use it, but never again with care and gentleness. He would permit himself to feel lust for the scheming little slut, but nothing more. Never. Her youth, her big blue eyes, her touching lies had fooled him once, but never again.

As if suddenly realizing where she was and what she was doing, Jenny stirred in his arms, then she opened her eyes, looking about her as if trying to understand what had happened. "Where are we?" Her voice was deliciously husky with sleep as she spoke the first words she'd said since he lowered her down the castle wall; it reminded Royce of the way she'd sounded when he awakened her to make love to her again during that endless night of passion they'd spent together at Hardin.

His jaw hardened as he coldly rejected the memory, and he glanced down at her upturned face, noting the bewilderment that was currently replacing her normal hauteur.

When he remained silent, she persisted with a weary sigh, "Where are we *going?*"

"We're moving west by southwest," he replied uninformatively.

"Would it be too terribly inconvenient to tell me our *destination?*"

"Yes," he bit out between his teeth, "it would."

The last numbing traces of sleep vanished, and Jenny straightened as the full realization of his night's work descended upon her. Rain hit her in the face as she moved from the shelter of his big body, her gaze flying over the cloaked figures hunched over their horses, moving stealthily through the woods beside them. Stefan Westmoreland was riding on their left and Arik on their right. Aunt Elinor was wide awake, sitting erect in her saddle, peering at Jenny with a reassuring smile and an expression on her face which made it obvious she was pleased to be *anywhere* but the dower house. Last night on the raft she'd managed to whisper to Jenny that she'd tricked the duke into taking her along, but beyond that, Jenny knew nothing. In fact, her gag had not been removed until after she'd fallen asleep.

"Where is Brenna?" she gasped, her mind snapping into sudden focus. "Did you release her?"

Now, when Jenny least expected an informative answer, she received one. In a tone reeking with sarcasm, Royce Westmoreland replied, "I never had her."

"You *bastard!*" Jenny hissed furiously, then gasped in alarmed surprise as his arm coiled around her like a striking snake, squeezing the breath from her as he hauled her sharply against his chest. "Don't *ever,*" he said, enunciating in an awful voice, "use that tone or that word to me again!"

Royce was about to say more when he caught sight of a long stone building nestled against a hillside ahead. Turning to Stefan, he raised his voice to be heard above the slackening rain. "That looks like the place." As he spoke, he dug his spurs into the stallion, sending the animal into a ground-devouring gallop. Beside and behind him the band of fifty men followed suit, and a moment later they were all galloping down the rutted road with Aunt Elinor's protests about the jouncing she was receiving rising above the hoof beats.

He drew up before what was unmistakably a priory and dismounted, leaving Jenny to sit there and stare at his back in angry curiosity, longing to know her fate and trying to eavesdrop as he said to Stefan: "Arik will stay here with us. Leave us the spare horse."

"What about Lady Elinor? What if she can't withstand the ride?"

"If she can't, you'll have to find a cottage and leave her there."

"Royce," Stefan said with a worried frown, "don't

be more foolish than you have been. Merrick's people could be right behind you."

"He'll lose most of today trying to convince Hastings and Dugal he's innocent of the plot, then he'll have to guess our direction whenever he loses our tracks. That should cost him plenty of time. If not, our men know what to do. You ride for Claymore and make certain all is in readiness for a possible attack."

With a reluctant nod, Stefan reeled his horse around and rode off. "Plot?" Jenny demanded heatedly, glowering at her uninformative abductor. "What plot?"

"What a cunning little liar you are," Royce snapped, grabbing her by the waist and hauling her from the saddle. "You know what plot. You were a party to it." He caught her by the arm and began dragging her forward toward the door of the priory, heedless of the heavy weight of Jennifer's sodden mantle. "Although," he added bitingly, his strides long and angry, "I find it hard to imagine that a woman with your hot-blooded nature would actually commit herself to life in a cloister rather than marry a man—*any* man, including me."

"I do not know what you are talking about!" Jenny cried, wondering wildly what form of new terror a peaceful priory could possibly hold—particularly one which looked quite deserted.

"I am talking about the abbess from Lunduggan who arrived at the castle during our feast last night escorted by a small 'army' of her own, and you damned well know it," he snapped, lifting his fist and pounding imperatively on the heavy oaken door. "They were slowed by the rain, which was why your pious Friar Benedict was forced to pretend to an illness that would delay the ceremony."

Her chest heaving with indignation, Jenny turned on him, her eyes shooting sparks of ire. "In the first place, I've never *heard* of Lunduggan *or* an abbey there. Secondly, what difference would it make if an abbess arrived? Now," she ranted "you tell *me* something: Am I to understand that you dragged me out of my bed, flung me down a castle wall, hauled me across Scotland in a storm, and brought me here, because you didn't want to wait a day longer to *wed* me?"

His insolent gaze roved down her bare, wet bosom, making Jenny mentally cringe at his look of distaste. "You flatter yourself," he said bitingly. "It took nothing less than the threat of death, added to the threat of impoverishment to make me agree to have you in the first place."

Lifting his arm, he pounded with impatient vigor on the oaken panel, which swung open, revealing the polite face of a startled friar. Ignoring the friar for the moment, Royce glared contemptuously at his future bride. "We're here because two kings decided we were to wed with all haste, my sweet, and that's what we're going to do. You aren't worth starting a war over. We're also here because the prospect of being beheaded offends my sensibilities. But most of all, we're here because I find it irresistibly appealing to thwart your father's plans for me."

"You are mad!" she snapped, her chest heaving. "And you are a devil!"

"And you, my dear," Royce imperturbably replied, "are a bitch." With that, he turned to the horrified friar and unhesitatingly announced, "The lady and I wish to be wed."

A look of comical disbelief spread over the pious man who was garbed in the white robes and black mantle of a Dominican friar. He stepped back more from shock than courtesy, allowing them to enter the hushed priory. "I—I must have misheard you, my lord," he replied.

"No, you did not," Royce said, stalking inside, and hauling Jennifer with him by the elbow. He stopped, pausing to thoroughly inspect the beautiful stained-glass windows high above, then he lowered his gaze to the paralyzed friar and his brows snapped together impatiently. "Well?" he demanded.

Recovering from his earlier shock, the friar, who appeared to be about twenty-five, turned to Jennifer and said calmly, "I am Friar Gregory, my child. Would *you* care to tell me what this is all about?" Jenny, who responded automatically to the sanctity of her surroundings, dropped her voice to a more suitable hush than Royce's imperative baritone, and shakily and respectfully said, "Friar Gregory, you must help me. This man has abducted me from my home. I am Lady Jennifer Merrick, and my father is—"

"A treacherous, scheming bastard," Royce snapped, his fingers digging painfully into Jennifer's arm, warning her to be silent or risk having her bone broken.

"I—I see," Friar Gregory said with admirable composure. Lifting his brows he gazed expectantly at Royce. "Now that we've discovered the identity of the lady, and the supposedly tainted circumstances surrounding the birth of her sire, would it be too presumptuous of me to inquire as to *your* identity, my lord? If so, I believe I can hazard a guess—"

For a split second, a glimmer of amused respect replaced Royce's anger as he gazed at the undaunted young friar, whom he towered over, but who as yet showed no fear of him. "I am—" he began, but Jenny's angry voice cut him off. "He is the Black Wolf! The Scourge of Scotland. A beast and a madman!"

Friar Gregory's eyes widened at her outburst, but he remained outwardly calm. Nodding, he provided, "The duke of Claymore."

"Since we've all been properly introduced," Royce told the friar curtly, "say the words and have done with it."

With great dignity, Friar Gregory replied, "Normally there would be formalities to be met. However, from what I've heard at this priory and elsewhere, the Church and King James have already sanctioned it. Therefore there is no obstacle here." Jenny's spirits sank, then soared crazily as he turned to her and said, "However, it appears to me, my child, that it is not your *wish* to marry this man. Am I correct?"

"Yes!" Jenny cried.

With only a momentary hesitation to gather his courage, the young friar turned slowly to the powerful, implacable man beside her and said, "My Lord Westmoreland—your grace—I cannot possibly perform the marriage without the consent of the—" He broke off in confusion as the duke of Claymore continued to regard him in mocking silence, as if he was calmly waiting for Friar Gregory to recall something—something that would leave him no choice but to do as he'd been bidden.

With a start of dismay, the friar realized what he should have considered from the very first, and he turned back to Jennifer. "Lady Jennifer," he said gently, "I do not mean to distress you with what must be a most humiliating circumstance, however, it is known to all that you were . . . *with* . . . this man for several weeks, and that he—and you—"

"Not of my own will," Jenny cried softly, consumed again with guilt and shame.

"I know that," Friar Gregory soothed gently. "But before I refuse to perform the ceremony, I must ask you if you are certain you did not conceive as a result of that er . . . time you spent as his hostage? If you are not certain, then you must permit me to perform this marriage for the sake of any possible child. It is a *necessity.*"

Jennifer's face turned scarlet at this totally humiliating discussion, and her loathing for Royce Westmoreland escalated to unparalleled heights.

"No," she said hoarsely, "there is no chance."

"In that event," Friar Gregory said, courageously addressing the duke, "you must understand that I cannot—"

"I understand *perfectly*," Royce said in a silky, courteous voice, his grasp on Jenny's arm tightening painfully. "If you will excuse us, we'll return in about a quarter of an hour, and you can perform the ceremony *then*."

Panic exploded in Jenny, and she stared at him, rooted to the floor. "Where are you taking me?"

"To the hut I saw right behind this place," he replied with implacable calm.

"Why?" she cried, her voice rising with fear, trying again to free her arm from his grasp.

"In order to make wedding us a *necessity*."

Jenny had no doubt whatsoever that Royce Westmoreland could, and would, drag her to a hut, force himself upon her, and then haul her back in here so that the friar would have no choice but to marry them. Hope for reprieve died along with her resistance, and her shoulders drooped in defeat and shame. "I hate you," she said with deadly calm.

"A perfect basis for the perfect marriage," Royce replied sarcastically. Turning to face the friar he ordered curtly, "Do it. We've lost too much time here already."

A few minutes later, bound by unholy matrimony for all eternity, with hatred instead of love or affection as the basis for it, Jenny was hauled out of the priory and tossed up onto Royce's horse. Instead of climbing up onto the spare horse, Royce turned and spoke rapidly to Arik, who nodded. Jenny couldn't hear what orders Royce had given the giant, but she saw him turn and begin walking purposefully into the priory.

"Why is he going in there?" Jenny cried, remembering that Friar Gregory had said he was alone in the priory today. "He can be no threat to you. He said himself he was only stopping at the priory on a journey."

"Shut up," he snapped, and climbed up behind her.

The next hour was a blur, punctuated only by the pounding of the horse against Jenny's backside as they galloped headlong down the muddy road. As they neared a fork in the road, Royce suddenly reined the big horse into the woods and then stopped, as if waiting for something. A few minutes passed and then a few more, while Jenny peered down the road, wondering why they were waiting. And then she saw it: galloping toward them at a breakneck pace came Arik, his outstretched hand holding the reins of the spare horse, which was running beside him. And bouncing and jouncing upon the animal's back as if he'd never ridden before, hanging onto the pommel for his very life was—Friar Gregory.

Jenny gaped at the rather comic spectacle, unable to believe her own eyes until Friar Gregory was so close she could actually see the stricken expression on his face. Rounding on her husband, sputtering in her furious indignation, she burst out, "You—*you madman!* You've stolen a *priest* this time! You've actually done it! You've stolen a priest right out of a holy priory!"

Transferring his gaze from the riders to her, Royce regarded her in bland silence, his utter lack of concern only adding to her outrage. "They'll hang you for this!" Jenny prophesied with furious glee. "The pope himself will make sure of it! They'll behead you, they'll draw and quarter you, they'll hang your head from a pike and feed your entrails to—"

"Please," Royce drawled in exaggerated horror, "you will give me nightmares."

His ability to mock his fate and ignore his crime was more than Jenny could bear. Her voice dropped to a strangled whisper, and she stared over her shoulder at him as if he was some curious, inhuman being beyond her comprehension. "Is there no *limit* to what you will dare?"

"No," he said. "No limit whatsoever." Jerking on the reins he turned Zeus into the road and spurred him forward just as Arik and Friar Gregory galloped abreast. Tearing her eyes from Royce's granite features, Jenny clutched at Zeus's flying mane and glanced sympathetically at poor Friar Gregory, who bounced past, his fear-widened eyes clinging to her in mute appeal and terrified misery.

They kept up the breakneck pace until nightfall, stopping only long enough to rest the horses periodically and give them water. By the time Royce finally signaled Arik to stop, and a suitable camp had been found in a small glade deep within the protection of the forest, Jenny was limp with exhaustion. The rain had stopped earlier that morning, and a watery sun had put in its appearance, and then shone with a vengeance, causing steam to rise from the valleys and adding tenfold to Jenny's discomfort in her damp, heavy velvet gown.

With a tired grimace, she tramped out of the thicket she'd used to shield herself from the men so that she could attend to her personal needs. Raking her fingers through her hopelessly tangled hair, she trudged over to the fire and sent a murderous glance at Royce, who still looked rested and alert as he knelt on one knee, tossing logs onto the fire he'd built. "I must say," she told his broad back, "if this is the life you've led all these years past, it leaves *much* to be desired." Jenny expected no answer, nor did she receive one, and she began to understand why Aunt Elinor, who'd been deprived of human companionship for twenty years, had missed it so much that now she eagerly chattered away at anyone she could find to listen to her— willingly or no. After an entire night and day of Royce's silence, she was desperate to vent her ire on him.

Too exhausted to stand, Jenny sank down onto a pile of leaves a few paces from the fire, reveling in the opportunity to sit upon something soft, something that didn't lurch and bump and jar her teeth, even though it was damp. Drawing her legs up to her chest, she wrapped her arms around them. "On the other hand," she said, continuing her one-way conversation with his back, "perhaps you find much pleasure in galloping through the woods, ducking tree limbs, and fleeing for your life. And, when that becomes tedious, you can always divert yourself with a siege or a bloody battle, or an abduction of helpless, innocent people. 'Tis truly a perfect existence for a man like you!"

Over his shoulder, Royce glanced at her and saw her sitting with her chin perched upon her knees, her delicate brows raised in challenge, and could not believe her daring. After everything he'd put her through in the past twenty-four hours, Jennifer Merrick—no, he corrected himself, Jennifer Westmoreland—could still calmly sit on a pile of leaves and *mock* him.

Jenny would have said more, but just then poor Friar Gregory staggered out of the woods, saw her, and stumbled over to sink gingerly onto the leaves beside her. Once sitting, he shifted experimentally from one hip to the other, wincing. "I—" he began, and winced again—"have not ridden much," he admitted ruefully.

It dawned on Jenny that his entire body must be racked with aches and pains, and she managed to smile at him in helpless sympathy. Next it occurred to her that the poor friar was a prisoner of a man with a reputation for unspeakable brutality, and she sought to allay his inevitable fears as best she could, given her animosity for the man who'd captured them both. "I do not think he will murder you or torture you," she began, and the friar looked at her askance.

"I have already been tortured to the full limits, by that horse," he stated dryly, then he sobered. "However, I shouldn't think I'll be killed. 'Twould be foolhardy, and I don't think your husband is a fool. Reckless, yes. Foolish, no."

"Then you aren't concerned for your life?" Jenny asked, studying the friar with new respect as she recalled her own terror at her first sight of the Black Wolf.

Friar Gregory shook his head. "From the three words that blond giant over there allotted me, I gather that I'm to be taken with you to bear witness to the inevitable inquiry that is bound to take place on the matter of whether you are well and truly married. You see," he admitted ruefully, "As I explained to you at the priory, I was merely a visitor there; the prior himself and all the friars having gone into a nearby village to minister to the poor in spirit. Had I left on the morn, as I meant to do, there would have been no one to attest to the vows you spoke."

A brief flair of blazing anger pierced Jenny's weary mind. "If he"—she glanced furiously at her husband, who was near the fire, his knee bent as he tossed more logs onto the blaze—"wanted witnesses to the marriage, he had only to leave me in peace and wait until today when Friar Benedict would have married us."

"Yes, I know, and it seems odd he didn't do that. 'Tis known from England to Scotland that he was reluctant, no, violently *opposed,* to the idea of wedding you."

Shame made Jenny look away, feigning interest in the wet leaves beside her as she traced her finger on their veined surface. Beside her, Friar Gregory said gently, "I speak plainly to you, because I sensed from our first meeting at the priory that you are not fainthearted and would prefer to know the truth."

Jenny swallowed the lump of humiliation in her throat and nodded, cringing inside at the realization that everyone of importance in two countries evidently knew she was an unwanted bride. Moreover an unvirginal one. She felt unclean and humiliated beyond words—humbled and brought to her knees before the populace of two entire countries. Angrily she said, "I don't think his actions of the past two days will go unpunished. He snatched me from my bed and hauled me out a tower window and down a rope. Now he's snatched you! I think the MacPherson and all the other clans may well break the truce and attack him!" she said with morbid satisfaction.

"Oh, I doubt there'll be much in the way of *official* retaliation; 'tis said Henry commanded him to wed you posthaste. Lord Westmoreland—er—his grace, has certainly complied with that, although there's bound to be a bit of an outcry from James to Henry over the way he did it. However, at least in theory, the duke obeyed Henry to the letter, so perhaps Henry will be merely amused by all this.

Jenny looked at him in humiliated fury. "Amused!"

"Possibly," Friar Gregory said. "For, like the Wolf, Henry has technically fulfilled the agreement he made with James to the very letter. His vassal, the duke, has wed you, and wed you with all haste. And in the process, he evidently breached your castle, which was doubtlessly heavily guarded, and snatched you right from your family's midst. Yes," he continued more to himself than to her, as if impartially considering a question of dogmatic theory, "I can see that the English may find all this highly entertaining."

Bile surged in Jenny's throat, almost choking her as she recalled all that had happened last night in the hall, and realized the priest was right. The hated English had been wagering amongst themselves, actually *wagering* in the hall at Merrick, that her husband would soon bring her to her knees, while her kinsmen could do naught but look at her—look at her with their proud, set faces, as they bore her shame as their own. But they were hoping, depending upon her, to redeem herself and all of them by never yielding.

"Although," Friar Gregory said more to himself than to her, "I cannot ken why he would have put himself to such risk and trouble."

"He raves about some plot," Jenny said in a suffocated whisper. "How do you know so much about us—about everything that's been happening?"

"News of famous people flies from castle to castle often with surprising speed. As a friar of Saint Dominic, 'tis my duty and my privilege to go among our Lord's people *on foot,*" he emphasized wryly. "Whilst my time is spent among the poor, the poor live in villages. And where there are villages, there are *castles;* news filters down from lord's solar to villein's hut—*particularly* when that news concerns a man who is a legend, like the Wolf."

"So my shame is known to all," Jenny said chokily.

"'Tis not a secret," he admitted. "But neither is it *your* shame, to my thinking. You mustn't blame yourself for—" Friar Gregory saw her piteous expression and was instantly consumed with contrition. "My dear child, I beg your forgiveness. Instead of talking to you about forgiveness and peace, I'm discussing shame and causing bitterness."

"You've no need to apologize," Jenny said in a shaky voice. "After all, you, too have been taken captive by that—that monster—forced, dragged from your priory, as I was dragged from my bed, and—"

"Now, now," he soothed, sensing she was teetering between hysteria and exhaustion, "I wouldn't say I was taken captive. Not really. Nor dragged from the priory. It was more a matter that I was *invited* to come along by the most enormous man I've ever beheld, who also happens to carry a war axe in his belt with a handle nearly the size of a tree trunk. So when he graciously thundered, 'Come. No harm,' I accepted his invitation without delay."

"I hate *him,* too!" Jenny cried softly, watching Arik stroll out of the woods holding two plump rabbits he'd beheaded with a throw of his axe.

"Really?" Friar Gregory looked nonplused and fascinated. "'Tis hard to hate a man who doesn't speak. Is he always so stingy with words?"

"Yes!" Jenny said vengefully. "All he nee-needs to do"—the tears she was fighting to hold back clogged her voice—"is look at y-you with those freezing cold blue eyes of his and you j-just *know* what he wants you to do, and y-you d-do it, because he's a m-monster, too." Friar Gregory put his arm around her shoulders and Jenny, who was more accustomed to adversity than sympathy, especially of late, turned her face into his sleeve. "I hate him!" she cried brokenly, heedless of Friar Gregory's warning squeeze on her arm. "I hate him, I *hate* him!"

Fighting for control, she moved away from him. As she did so, her eyes riveted on the pair of black boots planted firmly in front of her, and she followed them the full distance up Royce's muscled legs and thighs, his narrow waist and wide chest, until she finally met his hooded gaze. "I hate you," she said straight to his face.

Royce studied her in impassive silence, then he transferred his contemptuous gaze to the friar. Sarcastically, he asked, "Tending to your flock, Friar? Preaching love and forgiveness?"

To Jenny's amazement, Friar Gregory took no offence at this biting criticism, but instead looked abashed. "I greatly fear," he admitted ruefully as he awkwardly and unsteadily came to his feet, "that I may be no better at that than I am at riding horses. The Lady Jennifer is one of my first 'flocks,' you see. I've only been about the Lord's work a short time."

"You're not very good at it," Royce stated flatly. "Is it not your goal to console rather than incite? Or is it to line your purse and grow fat on your patron's good graces? If the latter is the case, you'd be wise to counsel my wife to try to please me, rather than encourage her to tell me of her hatred."

At that moment, Jenny would have given her very life to have Friar Benedict standing here instead of Friar Gregory, for she would have relished seeing Royce Westmoreland receive the sort of thundering tirade that Friar Benedict would have launched at the insolent duke.

In that respect, however, she had misjudged the young friar again. Although he did not rise to the Black Wolf's verbal attack, neither did he retreat or cower before his daunting adversary. "I gather that you do not hold those of us who wear these robes in very high regard?"

"None whatsoever," Royce snapped.

In her mind, Jenny wistfully envisioned Friar Benedict in this clearing, his eyes bulging with fury as he advanced on Royce Westmoreland like the angel of death. But, regretfully, Friar Gregory merely looked interested and a little puzzled. "I see," he said politely. "May I ask why?"

Royce Westmoreland stared at him with biting scorn. "I despise hypocrisy, particularly when it is coated with holiness."

"May I ask for a specific example?"

"Fat priests," Royce replied, "with fat purses, who lecture starving peasants on the dangers of gluttony and the merits of poverty." Turning on his heel, he strode back to the fire where Arik was roasting the rabbits on a makeshift spit.

"Oh dear God!" Jenny whispered a minute later, without realizing she had started fearing for the immortal soul of the very same man she'd just wished to perdition. "He must be a heretic!"

Friar Gregory shot her an odd, thoughtful glance. "If he is, he is an honorable one." Turning, he stared at the Black Wolf, who was crouching near the fire beside the giant who guarded him. In that same preoccupied, almost amused voice, he said softly, "A very honorable one, I think."

Chapter Eighteen

All the next day, Jenny endured her husband's stony silence, while her mind whirled with questions that only he could answer, until in sheer desperation she finally broke down just before noon and spoke herself: "How long will this interminable journey to Claymore last, *assuming* that is our destination?"

"About three days, depending on how muddy the roads are."

Ten words. That was all he'd said in days! *No wonder he and Arik were so congenial,* Jenny thought furiously, vowing not to give him the satisfaction of speaking to him again. She concentrated on Brenna, instead, wondering how she was faring at Merrick.

Two days later, Jennifer broke down again. She knew they must be nearing Claymore and her fears of what awaited her there were escalating by the minute. The horses were three abreast, moving down a country lane at a walk, with Arik riding in the middle and slightly ahead. She considered talking to Friar Gregory, but his head was bowed slightly forward, suggesting he might be at prayer, which is how he'd spent most of their journey. Desperate to talk about anything to take her mind off the future, she glanced over her shoulder at the man behind her. "What happened to all your men—the ones who were with us until we reached the priory?" she asked.

She waited for some answer, but he remained coldly silent. Pushed past the boundary of reason and caution by his cruel refusal even to speak to her, Jenny shot him a mutinous look. "Was that question too difficult for you, your grace?"

Her jeering tone pricked the cold wall of reserve Royce had carefully erected around himself to guard against the inevitable result of having her body pressed intimately against his for three endless days. Slanting her a heavy-lidded look, he considered the foolhardiness of opening up any sort of conversation with her and decided against it.

When he couldn't even be *angered* into speaking to her, Jenny suddenly saw a rare opportunity to enjoy herself at his expense. With childlike delight and well-concealed animosity, she promptly launched into mocking conversation *without* his participation. "Yes, I can see the question about your men has baffled you, your grace," she began. "Very well, let me find a way to make it simpler."

Royce realized she was deliberately mocking him, but his momentary irritation soon gave way to reluctant amusement as she continued her charming, reckless, one-way conversation with him: " 'Tis obvious to me," she remarked, giving him a look of false sympathy beneath her long, curly lashes, "that 'tis not lack of intelligence which causes you to stare at me so blankly when I question you about your men, but rather that your memory is failing! Alas," she sighed, looking momentarily crestfallen on his behalf, "I fear your advanced years are already taking their toll on your mind. But fear not," she told him brightly, sending him an encouraging look over her shoulder, "I shall keep my questions very, very simple, and I shall try to help you recall where you've put your misplaced men. Now then, when we arrived at the priory—you *do* recall the priory do you not?" she prompted, looking at him. "The priory? You know——the big stone building where we first met Friar Gregory?" she prompted again.

Royce said nothing; he glanced at Arik, who was staring straight ahead, impervious to everything, and then at the friar, whose shoulders were beginning to shake suspiciously as Jenny continued with sad gravity: "You poor, *poor* man——you've forgotten who *Friar Gregory* is, haven't you?" Lifting her arm, she glanced brightly over her shoulder at Royce, pointing her long, tapered finger at the friar. "There he is!" she declared eagerly. "That man, right there, is *Friar Gregory!* Do you see him? Of *course* you do!" she answered, deliberately treating him like a backward child. "Now then, concentrate very, very hard, because the next question is more difficult: Do you remember the *men* who were with you when we arrived at the priory where Friar Gregory was?" Helpfully, she added, "There were about forty of them. *Forty,"* she emphasized with extreme courtesy, and to Royce's disbelief, she actually held up her small hand before his eyes, splayed out five fingers, and politely explained, "Forty is this many——"

Royce tore his gaze from her hand, swallowing back his laughter.

"And this many more," she daringly continued, holding up her other hand. "And this many more," she repeated thrice more, holding up ten fingers each time. Now!" she finished triumphantly, "can you remember where you *left* them?"

Silence.

"Or where you sent them?"

Silence.

"Oh dear, you're worse off than I thought," she sighed. "You've *lost* them completely, haven't you? Oh well," she said, turning away from him in frustration at his continued silence, as her momentary delight at mocking him was demolished by a burst of anger. "Don't worry overmuch! I'm certain you'll find other men to help you steal innocents from abbeys and slaughter children, and—"

Royce's arm tightened suddenly, jerking her back against his chest, and his warm breath in her ear sent unwanted tingles up and down Jenny's spine as he bent his head and said softly, "Jennifer, you merely try my patience with your mindless chatter, but you test my temper with your jibes, and *that* is a mistake." The horse beneath them responded instantly to the slackened pressure from his master's knees and instantly slowed his pace, letting the other horses move ahead.

But Jenny didn't notice; she was so deliriously relieved by the sound of a human voice, and conversely furious that he'd denied her even that for so long, that she could hardly contain her ire. "Good heavens, your grace, I shouldn't wish to rile your temper!" she said with deliberately exaggerated alarm. "Were I to do that, I might suffer a horrible fate at your hands. Let me think, now—what dire things could you do to me? I know! You might compromise my reputation. No," she continued as if considering the matter impartially, "you couldn't do that because you compromised it beyond recall when you forced me to stay with you at Hardin without my sister there. I have it!" she cried, inspired. "You might force me to lie with you! And then, you could arrange it so that everyone in two countries knows that I shared your bed! But no, you've already done those things—"

Each barbed word she spoke pricked Royce's conscience, making him feel like the barbarian he was oft called, and still she continued hammering at him with her words:

"I have it at last! Having done all that to me, there's only one thing left to do."

Unable to stop himself, Royce said with feigned unconcern, "And that is?"

"You could marry me!" she exclaimed in pretended

triumphant delight, but what had begun as a jibe directed at him, now seemed to Jenny like a painful joke on her, and her voice shook with bitterness and pain, despite her valiant effort to speak in the same bright, satirical vein as she continued: "You could marry me, and in so doing, take me away from my home and country and bind me to a life of public humiliation and scorn at your hands. Yes, that's it! It's *exactly* what I deserve, is it not, my lord, for committing the unspeakable crime of walking up a hill near an abbey and putting myself in the way of your marauding brother!" With sham disdain she said, "Why—considering the enormity of my crime— having me drawn and quartered is much too kind! It would end my shame and misery prematurely. It would—"

She gasped as Royce's hand suddenly swept up from her waist and gently cupped the side of her breast in a caressing gesture which shocked her into speechlessness. And before she could recover, he put his cheek against her temple, and spoke in her ear, his gruff whisper strangely gentle. "Cease, Jennifer. That's enough." His other arm went around her waist, drawing her back against his chest. Clasped against his body with his hand caressing her breast, surrounded by his reassuring strength, Jenny succumbed helplessly to the unexpected comfort he was offering her now, when she faced the terrors of an unknown, and unkind, future.

Numbly, she relaxed against him, and the moment she did, his arm tightened, drawing her nearer, while the hand that had been caressing her breast slid forward to softly cup the other one. His unshaven jaw rubbed lightly against her temple as he turned his head and touched his warm lips to her cheek, his hand sliding slowly, endlessly over her breasts and midriff, soothing and caressing, while the hand that curved around her waist clasped her tightly between his muscular thighs. Faced with a future that held nothing but misery and fright, Jenny closed her eyes, trying to hold her fears at bay, and gave in to the fleeting sweetness of the moment, to the poignant sensation of feeling safe again, of being surrounded by his body, protected by his strength.

Telling himself that he was doing no more than comforting and distracting a frightened child from her woes, Royce brushed the heavy hair from her nape and kissed her, then he trailed his lips lightly up her neck to her ear, nuzzling her there before he brushed his mouth against the creamy skin of her cheek. Without realizing what he was doing, his hand slid upward, over her breast to the warm flesh above her bodice, then it delved down to cup the sweet breast beneath. And that was his mistake—whether from protest or surprise, Jennifer squirmed against him, and the sliding pressure of her buttocks against his loins ignited the very desire he'd been fighting to control for three long days . . . three endless days of having her hips between his thighs and her breasts tantalizingly exposed to his view, within reach of his hand. Now those three days of suppressed desire erupted, raging through his veins like wildfire, nearly obliterating his reason.

With an effort of will that was almost painful, Royce dragged his hand away and lifted his lips from her cheek. But the moment he did, his hand, which seemed to have developed a will of its own, lifted to her face. Taking her chin between his thumb and forefinger, he turned her face and tipped it up to his, gazing down into the bluest eyes on earth—a child's eyes filled with confusion and bewilderment, while the gist of her words revolved around and around in his brain, stabbing at a conscience that would no longer keep silent. *I put myself in the way of your marauding brother by walking up a hill . . . and for that crime I deserve my fate . . . You compromised my reputation. You forced me to lie with you and then you humiliated me in the eyes of two countries. But I*

*deserve to be drawn and quartered—Why? Because I
put myself in the way of your marauding brother . . .
All because of that . . . only that.*

Without thinking what he was doing, Royce tenderly laid his fingers against her smooth cheek, knowing
he was going to kiss her, no longer certain he'd had
any right to berate her. *All because I put myself in the
way of your marauding brother . . .*

A plump quail ran out of the woods, dashing across
the road in front of the horse. Beside the road, the
bushes parted and a boy's round, freckled face peered
out, his eyes slowly scanning the brush on his right for
the quail he'd been illegally stalking through Claymore's woods. Puzzled, his gaze retraced the same
path, moving slowly to the left now . . . along the
road . . . directly in front of him . . . then a few feet
further. His brown eyes riveted in alarm on the
powerful legs of a great black warhorse just to his left.
His heart thumping with fear that he'd been caught
poaching, Tom Thornton reluctantly followed the legs
of the stallion upward, past its wide, satiny chest,
praying hard that when he looked at the rider's face
he'd not be staring into the cold eyes of the castle
bailiff—but no—this rider wore golden spurs, which
signified his knighthood. With relief, Tom also noted
the man's leg was very long and very muscular—not
fat like the bailiff's leg. Tom heaved a sigh of relief,
glanced up and almost screamed in terror as his eyes
riveted on the shield hanging beside the knight's
leg—a shield emblazoned with the dreaded symbol of
a snarling black wolf with white fangs bared.

Tom turned to flee, took a step, then checked the
motion, and cautiously turned back. 'Twas said the
Black Wolf's knights were coming to Claymore, and
the Wolf himself was going to reside in the great castle
there, he remembered suddenly. And if so, the knight
on the horse could possibly be . . . might actually
be . . .

With hands that shook from a combination of terror and excitement, Tom reached for the bush and hesitated, trying to recall every description he'd heard of the Wolf. Legend had it that he rode a huge stallion as black as sin, and that he was so tall men had to lean back to see his face—the warhorse in the road was *definitely* black, and the man who rode him had the long, powerful legs of a very tall man. It was also said, Tom remembered excitedly, that on his face, near his mouth, the Wolf bore a scar in the shape of a C—put there by a wolf he killed with his bare hands when he was but a boy of eight and the animal attacked him.

Excited at the thought of the envy he'd enjoy were he to be the first to actually set eyes on the Wolf, Tom parted the leaves and peered out and stared straight at the man's dark face. There, beneath the stubble, near the corner of his mouth—there was . . . a scar! In the shape of a C! His heart hammering wildly, he stared at the scar, then he remembered something else and tore his gaze from the Wolf's face. Glancing eagerly up and down the road, he searched expectantly for the fair-haired giant called Arik—the giant who was said to guard his master day and night, and who carried an axe with a handle thick as a tree trunk.

Failing to catch sight of the giant, Tom quickly turned his gaze back for a longer study of the entire, famous man, and this time he took in the entire picture before him—a picture that made his mouth drop open in shock and disbelief: The Black Wolf, the most fierce warrier in all England—in the *world*—was sitting atop his mighty warhorse, with a *girl* cradled in his arms—holding her as tenderly as a *babe!*

Lost in his own reflections, Royce paid no heed to the slight sounds beside him as the branches of a bush snapped together and something raced off in the direction of the village. He was gazing at the stubborn, rebellious child-woman who was now his wife. She was other things, too, like scheming and dishonest, but at the moment he didn't want to think about all that. Not when his mind was more pleasurably occupied with the kiss he was about to give her. Her eyes were nearly closed, her long curly lashes lying like russet fans, casting shadows on her creamy cheeks. His gaze dropped to her lips, soft and rosy, lips that beckoned to a man to kiss them. Generous, inviting lips.

Drowsy and relaxed as she lay against his chest, Jenny scarcely felt his hand tighten on her chin.

"Jennifer—"

Her eyes opened at the odd, husky note in his voice, and she found herself gazing into smoldering gray eyes, his finely chiseled lips poised just above her own. It hit her then what she'd let happen, and what was going to happen if she didn't stop it. She shook her head, trying to dig her elbow into his ribs and push away, but his arm held her fast. "No!" she burst out.

His hypnotic gray eyes held hers imprisoned as his lips formed a single, irrefutable command: *"Yes."*

A moan of angry protest lodged in her throat, stifled by a hard, possessive kiss that seemed to go on forever and only became more insistent the longer she resisted. His parted lips moved on hers, demanding that they part, and the moment they did, his tongue slipped between them and the kiss gentled. He kissed her long and lingeringly, forcing her to remember how it had been between them at Hardin, and Jenny's traitorous mind did exactly that. With an inner groan of surrender, she yielded and kissed him back, telling herself one kiss meant very little, but when it was over she was shaking.

Lifting his head, Royce stared down into her slumberous blue eyes, and Jenny saw the look of pure satisfaction mingled with puzzlement on his face—"Why is it when you yield, I feel like the one who has been conquered?"

Jenny flinched and turned her back on him, her slim

shoulders rigid. "'Twas no more than a minor skirmish I yielded, your grace; the *war* has yet to be fought."

The road to Claymore wound in a wide arc around the woods, a route that took them far out of their way but eliminated the need to force their way through the dense forest. Had he been alone, Royce would have taken the shorter route, for now that they were so close, he was anxious for a glimpse of it. Suddenly he wanted Jennifer to share in his eagerness. For want of anything better to say to reduce the friction between them, Royce answered the question she'd asked him before, about the whereabouts of the men who'd been with them at the priory. With a smile in his voice, he said, "In case you're still curious, the *fifty* men who were with us at the priory left there in groups of five. Each group then took a slightly different route so that pursuers from Merrick would have to split up into smaller groups in order to give chase." Teasingly he added, "Would you like to know the rest of what they did?"

Jenny gave her red-gold hair a disdainful toss. "I know the rest. After choosing an advantageous spot for an ambush, your men then hid themselves beneath bushes and rocks like serpents, waiting to strike my father's people from their backs."

He chuckled at her outrageous slur on his code of ethics. "A pity I didn't think of that," he teased.

Although Jennifer did not deign to reply, the stiffness went out of her shoulders, and Royce could sense her curiosity to know more. Willing now to satisfy that curiosity, he continued his explanation as they rounded the last bend in the road. "Until a few hours ago, my men were about ten miles behind us, fanned out across five miles in each direction. In the last few hours, they've been moving closer, and very soon they'll close ranks and move in directly behind us." Good-naturedly, he added, "They've been back there, *waiting* to be stabbed in the back by *your father's* men."

"Which," she pointedly replied, "would not be necessary had I not been taken from the abbey in the first place and brought to you—"

"Cease!" he said, irritated at her continued hostility. "You were not ill treated, all things considered."

"Not ill treated!" she burst out in disbelief. "Do you deem it a kindness, then, to force yourself upon a helpless maiden, destroy her honor along with her chances to wed a man of her choice?"

Royce opened his mouth to answer her, then closed it again, frustrated because he could no longer defend, nor completely condemn, his actions. From Jennifer's irate viewpoint, he had acted dishonorably in holding her captive. From his own point of view, his treatment of his captive had been downright chivalrous!

A moment later, they cantered round the last bend and all such unpleasant thoughts vanished from Royce's mind. His hand tightened reflexively on the reins, inadvertently jerking Zeus to an unnecessarily sharp halt that nearly pitched Jenny out of the saddle.

Recovering her balance, Jenny threw a dark look over her shoulder, but Royce was staring straight ahead at something in the distance, a faint smile playing about his lips. In an odd voice, he tipped his head in the direction he was staring and said softly, "Look."

Puzzled, she turned to see what he was gazing at, and her eyes widened with pleasure at the incredible beauty spread out before her. Directly in front of them, decked out in golden autumn splendor, lay a wide valley dotted with thatched cottages and neatly tended fields. Ahead, nestled into gently rolling hills, was a picturesque village. And higher yet, completely covering a wide plateau, stood a gigantic castle, with flags flying from its soaring turrets and stained-glass windows glinting like tiny jewels in the sun.

As the horse continued forward at a brisk walk, Jenny temporarily forgot her problems and admired the splendor and symmetry before her eyes. A high wall punctuated with twelve gracefully rounded towers completely enclosed the castle on all four sides.

As Jenny watched, the guards along the castle wall raised trumpets and blew a long, double blast, and a minute later, the drawbridge was let down. Soon liveried riders were clattering across it, their helmets shining in the sun, the pennants they carried undulating like small excited dots. Up ahead, along the road, Jenny saw peasants running from the fields and huts and pouring down from the village, hastening toward the road and lining up on both sides of it. Evidently, Jenny thought, the lofty personage who owned the place must be expecting them and had planned this lavish welcome.

"Well," Royce said behind her, "what do you think?"

Her eyes were alight with pleasure as she turned to look at him. "'Tis a wondrous place," she said softly. "I've naught seen the equal to it."

"How does it compare to your dream kingdom?" he teased, grinning, and she could tell he was inordinately pleased that she appreciated the splendor of the castle and the beauty of its setting.

His smile was almost irresistible, and Jenny hastily turned her head toward the castle, lest she start to weaken, but she was no test against the beauty spread out before her. Suddenly she became aware of the distant thunder of horses coming up from the rear, which she assumed must be Royce's men closing the gap that separated them from him. For the first time in days, Jenny felt acutely dismayed over her appearance. She was still wearing her wedding gown, which she'd worn the night Royce took her from Merrick, but it was soiled and torn from her unwilling descent down Merrick's wall and their breakneck rides through forests. Moreover, the rain had ruined the gown and her mantle, and the sun had dried it into a faded, splotchy, crushed mess.

Now they were obviously about to stop at the castle of someone of great importance, and although she told herself she didn't care a snap of her fingers what an English nobleman or his villeins and serfs thought of her, she hated the thought of disgracing herself, ergo her kinsmen, before them. She tried to console herself with the fact that she'd at least had an opportunity to wash her hair this morning in the icy creek that ran near the place where they'd camped for the night, but she was morbidly certain her hair, which was her only real asset, was a mass of tangles strewn with twigs and leaves.

Turning, she glanced a little apprehensively at Royce and asked, "Who is lord here? Who owns such a place as this?"

His gaze shifted from the castle on the hill, which seemed to fascinate him almost as much as it did Jennifer, and he looked down at her, his eyes glinting with mocking amusement. "I do."

"*You* do!" she exclaimed, "But you said 'twould be three days, not two, before we reached Claymore."

"The roads were drier than I expected."

Horrified that his vassals were going to have their first glimpse of her when she looked such a fright, Jenny's hand flew automatically to her tangled hair in the gesture that universally signified a woman's worry over her appearance.

The gesture was not lost on Royce, who politely halted the big destrier so that Jennifer could try to comb the tangles from her hair with her fingers. He watched her, amused by her concern over her appearance, for she looked adorable with her hair tousled and her creamy skin and vivid blue eyes glowing with health from her days in the sun and fresh air. In fact, he decided, his first official act as her husband was going to be to forbid her to hide that magnificent mass of golden red hair beneath the usual veils and hoods. He liked it down, falling about her shoulders in wild abandon, or better yet, spread across his pillow like thick, waving satin . . .

"You might have warned me!" Jenny said darkly, wriggling in the saddle and trying ineffectually to smooth the wrinkles from her ruined velvet gown, while she glanced anxiously toward the people lining the road up ahead. The liveried retainers riding toward them in the distance were obviously an honor guard coming to escort their lord home with appropriate fanfare. "I never imagined this was *your* demesne," she said nervously. "You've been looking at it as if you've not set eyes on it before."

"I haven't. At least not when it looked like this. Eight years ago, I commissioned architects to come here, and together we drew plans for the home I wanted when I was finished with battles. I kept meaning to come back here to see it, but Henry always had urgent need of me somewhere else. In a way, it's been for the best. I have amassed a large enough fortune now to ensure that my sons will never have to earn their gold with their own muscle and blood, as I have done."

Jenny stared at him in confusion. "Did you say you're *done* with battles?"

His eyes flicked to her face and he said with amused irony, "Had I attacked Merrick 'twould have been my last battle. As it is, I breached my last castle wall when I took you from there."

Jenny was so dazed by these startling revelations that she actually entertained the absurd thought that he might somehow have made this decision on her account, and before she could stop herself, she blurted, "When did you decide all this?"

"Four months ago," he stated, his voice harsh with resolve. "If I ever raise my arm in battle again, 'twill be because someone is laying siege to what is mine." He was silent after that, staring straight ahead, and then the tense muscles of his face slowly relaxed. When he finally pulled his gaze from the castle, he looked down at her with a wry smile and said, "Do you know what I'm looking forward to most in my new life—next to a soft bed to sleep in at night?"

"No," Jenny said, studying his chiseled profile, feeling as if she scarcely knew him at all. "What are you most looking forward to?"

"Food," he stated unequivocally, his spirits restored. "Good food. No—not just good, but *excellent*, and served three times a day. Delicate French food and spicy Spanish food and wholesome English food. I want it served on a plate, cooked to perfection—instead of hanging off a spit, raw or else charred. And then I want desserts—pastries and tarts and every kind of sweets." He shot her a look filled with amused self-mockery as he continued, "On the night before a battle begins, most men think of their homes and families. Do you know what *I* used to lie awake thinking of?"

"No," Jenny said, fighting back a smile.

"Food."

She lost the battle to remain aloof and burst out laughing at this incredible admission from the man the Scots called the son of Satan, but although Royce spared her a brief, answering smile, his attention had reverted to the view in the distance, his gaze roving over the land and its castle as if he was drinking in the sight of it. "The last time I was here," he explained "'twas eight years ago, when I worked with the architects. The castle had been under siege for six months, and the outer walls were in ruins. Part of the castle itself had been destroyed, and all these hills had been burned."

"Who laid siege to it?" Jenny asked suspiciously.

"I did."

A sarcastic reply sprang to her lips, but she was suddenly loath to spoil their pleasant mood. Instead, she said lightly, "'Tis little wonder the Scots and English must always be at odds, for there's naught in common in the way we think."

"Really," he said, grinning at her upturned face. "Why so?"

"Well, you will agree," she replied with polite superiority, "'tis a very queer custom the English have of razing your own castles—as you've done for centuries—when you could be fighting with Scot—with other enemies," she corrected hastily "and razing *their* castles."

"What an intriguing idea," he teased. "However, we do try to do both." While she chuckled at his answer, he continued, "However, if *my* knowledge of *Scottish* history serves me, it seems the clans have been battling with each other for centuries, and still managing to cross our borders and raid and burn, and generally 'annoy' us."

Deciding it was best to drop the subject, she glanced back at the enormous castle shining in the sun and asked curiously, "Is that why you laid siege to this place—because you wanted it for yourself?"

"I attacked it because the baron to whom it belonged had conspired with several other barons in a plot to have Henry murdered—a plot which nearly succeeded. This place was called Wilsely then—after the family to whom it belonged, but Henry gave it to me with the stipulation that I rename it."

"Why?"

Royce's glance was wry. "Because Henry was the one who raised Wilsely to baron and rewarded him with the place. Wilsely had been one of his few trusted nobles. I named it Claymore in honor of my mother's family and my father's," Royce added, as he spurred his horse, sending Zeus forward in a flashy trot.

The riders from the castle had wended down the hill and were bearing down on them from the front. Behind her the low, constant rumble that had been moving ever closer and louder became the distinct sound of galloping horses. Jenny glanced over her shoulder and saw all fifty men closing in on them from behind. "Do you always plan things with such precise timing?" she asked, her eyes twinkling with reluctant admiration.

His heavy-lidded glance was amused. "Always."

"Why?"

"Because," he explained obligingly, "timing is the key to leaving a battle on your horse, instead of stretched out on your shield."

"But you aren't fighting battles any more, so you don't need to think about timing and such."

His lazy smile was almost boyish. "True, but 'tis a habit, and one that will not be easy to break. The men behind us have fought beside me for years. They know how I think and what I want done almost without my saying it."

There was no more time to reply, for the castle guard was almost on top of them, with Arik in the lead. Just when Jenny was wondering if the guards meant to *stop,* all twenty-five of them suddenly executed a whirling turn with such precision that she felt like clapping. Arik moved into position directly in front of Royce, while, behind them, fifty knights formed into precise columns.

Jenny felt her spirits lift at the colorful procession of prancing horses and fluttering flags, and despite her determination not to care what his people thought of her when they saw her, she was suddenly filled with violent nervousness and uncontrollable hope. Whatever her feelings for her husband, these were going to be *her* people, she was going to live all her life among them, and the awful truth was that she couldn't help wanting them to like her. That realization was instantly followed by a fresh surge of terrible self-consciousness over her messy appearance and general physical shortcomings. Biting her lip, Jenny said a swift, impassioned prayer that God would make them like her, then she hastily considered how she ought best to comport herself in the next few minutes. Should she smile at the villagers? No, she thought hastily, it might not be appropriate under the circumstances. But neither did she want to appear too aloof, for then they might mistake her for being cold or haughty. She was a Scot, after all, and Scots were regarded by many as cold, proud people. And although she was proud to be a Scot, under no circumstances did she want these people—her people—to mistakenly think she was unapproachable.

They were within a few yards of the four hundred or so villagers lining the road, and Jenny decided it was better to smile just a little than to be mistaken for being cold or too proud. Fixing a small smile upon her mouth, she self-consciously smoothed her gown one last time, then she sat up very straight.

As their entourage began making its decorous way past the spectators, however, Jenny's inner excitement gave way to bafflement. In Scotland, when a lord, victorious or otherwise, returned home from battle, he was met with cheers and smiles, yet the peasants along this road were silent, watchful, uneasy. A few of their faces showed downright belligerence, while a great many more looked frightened as they beheld their new lord. Jenny saw it, felt it, and wondered why they would fear their own hero. Or was it her they somehow feared, she wondered nervously.

The answer came a scant second later, when a loud, belligerent male voice finally broke the taut silence: "Merrick slut!" he shouted. In an eager frenzy to demonstrate to their notorious master that they shared the duke's well-known feelings about this marriage, the crowd picked up the chant: "Merrick slut!" they shouted, jeering, *"Slut!* Merrick slut!" Everything happened so suddenly there was no time for Jenny to react, to *feel* anything, because directly beside them, a boy of about nine rashly snatched up a clump of dirt and threw it, striking Jenny squarely on her right cheek.

Jenny's cry of startled fright was muffled by Royce, who instantly threw himself forward, shielding her with his body from an attack he hadn't seen and hadn't anticipated. Arik, who had only glimpsed a raised arm throwing something that could as easily have been a dagger, let out a blood-chilling bellow of rage and hurtled out of his saddle, whipping his war axe out of his belt as he launched himself at the boy. In the mistaken belief that Royce had been the boy's target, Arik grabbed him by his thick hair, lifted him several feet off the ground, and while the screaming boy's legs were flailing wildly in the air, the giant raised his axe in a wide arc . . .

Jenny reacted without thinking. With a strength born of terror she reared back wildly, dislodging Royce, and drowning out whatever command he was about to give with one of her own: "No!—No, *don't!*" she screamed wildly, "DON'T!"

Arik's axe froze at the top of its arc, and the giant looked over his shoulder, not to Jennifer, but to Royce for a judgment. So did Jenny, who took one look at the cold rage on Royce's profile and instantly knew what he was about to tell Arik to do. "No!" she screamed hysterically, clutching Royce's arm. His head jerked to her and, if anything, he looked even more murderous than the moment before. Jenny saw the muscle jerking in his taut jaw, and in mindless terror she cried, "Would you murder a child for aping your own words—for trying to show you he supports you in everything, including your feelings about me! For the love of God, he's naught but a child! A foolish child—" Her voice broke as Royce coldly turned from her to Arik to issue his command: "Have him brought to me on the morrow," he snapped, then he dug his spurs into the black horse, sending him bolting forward; as if by some silent signal, the knights behind them shot forward, forming into a moving curtain on both sides of Royce and Jennifer.

No more shouts came from the crowd; in complete, utter stillness they watched the caravan gallop past. Even so, Jenny didn't draw an easy breath until they were clear of all of the villagers, and then she went limp. Drained. Slumping against Royce's unnaturally rigid body, she let the whole scene replay in her mind. In retrospect, it occurred to her that his rage at the child had been on her behalf, and that he acceded to her wishes by giving the boy a reprieve. Turning in the saddle she looked at him. When he continued staring straight ahead, she said hesitantly, "My lord, I would like to—to thank you for sparing—"

His gaze snapped to her face, and Jenny recoiled in shock from the scorching fury in his gray eyes. "If you ever," he warned savagely, "defy me in public again or dare to address me in that tone, I won't be responsible for the consequences, I swear to God!"

Before Royce's eyes, her expressive face went from gratitude, to shock, to fury, and then she coldly turned her back on him.

Royce stared at the back of her head, furious because she actually believed he would let a child be decapitated for a misdeed that deserved a less harsh punishment—furious because, by her actions, Jenny had led all his serfs and villeins to believe the same thing. But most of all, Royce was furious with himself for failing to anticipate that such a scene as the one with the villagers might occur, and for not taking steps to avert it.

Whenever he planned a siege or went into battle, he always considered everything that could possibly go wrong, but when it came to today, to Claymore, he'd foolishly trusted everything to chance, assuming it would all come out all right.

On the other hand, Royce decided with an irritated sigh, in a *battle* his smallest order was anticipated and carried out without question or argument. In a battle, he did *not* have Jennifer to contend with—Jennifer, who argued or questioned him about everything.

Blind to the beauty of the place he'd been yearning to see for eight long years, Royce wondered grimly how it was possible that he could intimidate knights, nobles, squires, and battle-hardened soldiers into doing his bidding with a single glance, and yet he could not seem to force one young, stubborn, defiant Scottish girl to behave. She was so damned unpredictable that she made it impossible to anticipate her reaction to anything. She was impulsive, headstrong, and completely lacking in wifely respect. As they rode across the drawbridge, he glanced down at her stiff shoulders, belatedly realizing how humiliating the scene in the valley must have been to her. With a twinge of pity and reluctant admiration, he admitted that she was also very young, very frightened, very brave, and extremely compassionate. Any other woman of her rank might well have demanded the boy's head, rather than pleading for his life as Jennifer had done.

The castle's huge courtyard was filled with the people who lived or worked within its walls—a veritable army of stable grooms, laundresses, scullions, carpenters, farriers, archers, serfs, and footmen, in addition to the castle's guards. The higher-ranking members of the castle staff—bailiffs, clerks, butler, pantler, and a host of others—were lined up formally on the steps leading into the hall. Now, however, as he looked about him, Royce did not fail to observe the cold hostility being directed at Jennifer by nearly everyone, nor did he intend to leave their reaction to her to chance. So that every single person in the crowded bailey would have a clear view of Jennifer and himself, Royce turned to the captain of the guard and nodded curtly toward the stables. Not until the last knight had disappeared into the crowd, leading their horses to the stable, did Royce dismount. Turning, he reached up and caught Jennifer by the waist and lifted her down, noting as he did so that her pretty face was stiff, and she was carefully avoiding meeting the eyes of anyone. She didn't try to smooth her hair, or straighten her gown, and his heart squeezed with pity because she'd obviously decided it didn't matter how she looked any more.

Aware of the unpleasant murmuring rising from the crowd in the bailey, Royce took her arm and led her to the foot of the steps, but when Jennifer started to walk up them, he drew her firmly back, then he turned.

Jenny surfaced from the pit of shame she felt and shot him a desperate glance, but Royce didn't see it. He was standing without moving a muscle, his face hard and implacable as he gazed steadily at the restless crowd in the bailey. Even in her state of numb misery, Jenny suddenly felt as if there was a strange power emanating from him now, a force that seemed to communicate itself to all. As if a spell were being cast over them, the crowd grew silent and slowly straightened, their eyes riveted on him. Then and only then did Royce speak. His deep voice rang out in the unnatural stillness of the bailey, carrying with it the power and force of a thunderclap.

"Behold your new mistress, my wife," he pronounced, "and know that when *she* bids you, *I* have bidden you. What service you render her, you are rendering me. What loyalty you give or *withhold* from her, you give or withhold from me!"

His harsh gaze slashed across them for one breath-stopping, threatening moment, and then he turned to Jennifer and offered her his arm.

Unshed tears of poignant gratitude and awed wonder shimmered in Jenny's blue eyes as she looked up at him and slowly, almost reverently placed her hand upon his arm.

Behind them, the armorer clapped his hands slowly —twice. The smith joined in. Then a dozen more serfs. By the time Royce had guided her up the wide steps leading to the hall doors where Stefan and Friar Gregory were waiting, the entire bailey was thundering with steady clapping—not the sort of uninhibited, spontaneous salute that marks heartfelt enthusiasm, but rather the rhythmic response of the spellbound who are awed by a power too potent to resist.

Stefan Westmoreland was the first to speak after they entered the great, cavernous hall. Clasping Royce's shoulder with warm affection, he joked, "Would that *I* could do that to a crowd, dear brother." Meaningfully, he added, "Can you grant us a few moments? We have something that needs discussing."

Royce turned to Jenny, excusing himself for a minute, and she watched the two men walk over to the fire where Sir Godfrey, Sir Eustace, and Sir Lionel were standing. Evidently they'd all come ahead to Claymore along with Stefan Westmoreland, Jenny realized.

Her mind still dazed by Royce's incredible thoughtfulness in making that speech, Jenny pulled her gaze from his broad shoulders and looked about her with dawning awe. The hall in which she stood was immense, with a soaring, timbered roof and smooth stone floor swept clean of rushes. Above, a wide gallery, supported by richly carved stone arches, wrapped around on three sides, instead of only one. On the fourth wall was a hearth so large a man could easily stand in it, its chimney heavily imbellished with scrollwork. Tapestries, depicting scenes of battles and hunts, hung upon the walls, and someone, she noted with horror, had actually placed two large tapestries on the *floor* near the hearth. At the far end of the hall, opposite where she stood, was a long table set upon a dais and cupboards displaying goblets, platters, and bowls of gleaming gold and silver, many of them encrusted with jewels. Although only a few torches were burning in wall holders, it was not nearly as dark and gloomy as the hall at Merrick. And the reason, Jenny noted with a gasp of admiration, was a huge round window of stained glass, set high in the wall beside the chimney.

Jenny's preoccupation with the stained glass window was abruptly cut off by a joyous semi-shriek from above:

"Jennifer!" Aunt Elinor cried, standing up on tiptoe in order to see over the shoulder-high wall that enclosed the gallery. "Jennifer! my poor, poor child!" she said, and disappeared from sight completely as she rushed along the gallery. Although Aunt Elinor could not be seen, the echo of her happy monologue could easily be heard as she headed for the steps leading down to the hall: "Jennifer, I'm so very glad to see you, poor child!"

Tipping her head back, scanning the gallery, Jenny started forward, following the sound of her aunt's voice as she continued: "I was so *worried* about you, child, I could scarcely eat or sleep. Not that I was in any condition to do either, for I've been bounced and jounced clear across England on the most uncomfortable horse I've ever had the *misfortune* to sit upon!"

Tilting her head and listening closely, Jenny slowly followed the voice toward the opposite end of the great hall, searching for the body that belonged to the sound.

"And the weather was perfectly abominable!" Aunt Elinor continued. "Just when I thought the rain would surely drown me, the sun came out and baked me alive! My head began to ache, my bones began to ache, and I surely would have caught my death, had Sir Stefan not finally agreed to let us stop for a short while so that I could gather curative herbs."

Aunt Elinor descended the last step and materialized before Jenny's eyes twenty-five yards away, walking toward her and still talking: "Which was a very good thing, for once I convinced him to swallow my secret tisane, which he was loathe to do at first, he did not get so much as a *snuffle.*" She glanced toward Stefan Westmoreland, who was about to lift a tankard of ale to his lips, and interrupted him to insist on confirmation of her words: "You did not get so much as a tiny *snuffle,* did you, dear boy?"

Stefan lowered his tankard of ale. Obediently, he replied, "No, ma'am," bowed slightly, then he lifted his tankard of ale to his lips, carefully averting his eyes from Royce's mocking, sidewise glance. Arik stalked into the hall and went over to the fire, and Aunt Elinor gave him a reproving look as she continued to Jenny, who was walking toward her: "Altogether, it was not such a very bad journey. At least it wasn't when I was not forced to ride with that fellow, Arik, as I was forced to do when we first left Merrick . . ."

The knights by the fire turned to stare, and Jenny broke into an alarmed run, heading for her aunt in a futile effort to stop her from treading into such dangerous territory as the axe-wielding giant.

Opening her arms wide to Jennifer, her face wreathed in a beaming smile, Aunt Elinor continued: "Arik returned here a full twenty minutes before you arrived, and would *not* answer my anxious inquiries about you." Anticipating that she might not have time to finish her thought before Jennifer got to her, Aunt Elinor doubled the speed of her words: "Although I do not think 'tis meanness that makes him look so sour. I think he has trouble with his—"

Jenny flung her arms around her aunt, wrapping her in a tight hug, but Aunt Elinor managed to wriggle free enough to finish triumphantly, *"bowel!"*

The split-second of taut silence that followed that slander was exploded by a loud guffaw that suddenly erupted from Sir Godfrey and was abruptly choked off by an icy glance from Arik. To Jenny's horror, helpless laughter welled up inside of her, too, brought on partly by the incredible stress of the last day, and by the sounds of stifled mirth at the fireplace. "Oh, Aunt

Elinor!" she giggled helplessly and buried her laughing face in her aunt's neck to hide it.

"Now, now, sweet little dove," Aunt Elinor soothed, but her attention was on the knights who'd laughed at her diagnosis. Over Jenny's shaking shoulders, she aimed a severe look at the fascinated audience of five knights and one lord. In her severest voice she informed them, "A bad bowel is *not* a laughing matter." Then she switched her focus to the glowering Arik and commiserated, "Just look at the sour expression on your face, poor man—an *unmistakable* sign that a purgative is called for. I shall fix one for you from my own secret recipe. In no time at all, you'll be smiling and cheerful again!"

Grabbing her aunt's hand, and scrupulously avoiding meeting the laughing gazes of the other knights, Jenny looked at her amused husband. "Your grace," she said, "my aunt and I have much to discuss, and I am wishful of a rest. If you would pardon us, we will retire to—to—" it occurred to her that the discussion of sleeping arrangements was not a subject she wanted to approach any sooner than absolutely necessary, and she hastily finished "—to—er—my aunt's chamber."

Her husband, with a tankard of ale arrested in his hand in exactly the same place it had been when Aunt Elinor had first said Arik's name, managed to keep his face straight and to gravely reply, "By all means, Jennifer."

"What a delightful idea, child," Aunt Elinor exclaimed at once. "You must be fatigued to death."

"However," Royce interjected, directing a calm, implacable look in Jennifer's direction, "have one of the maids upstairs show you to *your* chamber, which I'm certain you'll find more comfortable. There will be a celebration this evening, so ask her for whatever you need to prepare yourself when you awaken."

"Yes, well, er . . . thank you," she said lamely.

But as she guided her aunt toward the stairs at the

far end of the hall, she was acutely aware of the stark silence from the fireplace, and equally certain they were all waiting to hear whatever outrageous thing Aunt Elinor might say next. Aunt Elinor did not disappoint them.

A few steps beyond the fireplace, she drew back in order to point out to Jennifer some of the merits of Jennifer's new home—several of which Jennifer had already noted. "Look up there, my dear," said Aunt Elinor with pleasure, pointing to the stained-glass window. "Isn't it delightful? Stained-glass windows! You won't *believe* the size of the gallery above, nor the comforts in the solar. And the candlesticks are gold. The beds are hung with silk, and nearly all the goblets have jewels in them! In fact," she declared in a thoughtful voice, "after seeing this place as I have done, I'm *quite* convinced pillaging and plundering must be a very profitable thing—" With that, Aunt Elinor turned back to the fireplace and politely inquired of the "pillager and plunderer" who owned the castle, "Would you say there is great profit to be had from pillaging and plundering, your grace, or am I mistaken?"

Through her haze of mortification, Jenny saw that her husband's tankard of ale was now frozen in midair a few inches from his lips. He lowered it very slowly, causing Jenny to fear he was about to have Aunt Elinor pitched over the castle wall. Instead he inclined his head politely and said, straight-faced, "A very great profit indeed, madame, I recommend it highly as a profession."

"How *very* nice to hear," Aunt Elinor exclaimed, "that you speak French!"

Jenny caught her aunt's arm in an unbreakable grip and began marching her toward the steps as Aunt Elinor continued brightly, "We must speak to Sir Albert at once about finding you some suitable gowns to wear. There are trunks of things belonging to the former owners. Sir Albert is the steward here, and he is not a well man. He has worms, I believe. I made him a nice tisane yesterday and insisted he drink it. He's *dreadfully* ill today, but he'll be fit tomorrow, you'll see. And you ought to have a nap at once, you look pale and exhausted . . ."

Four knights turned to Royce in unison, their faces wreathed in helpless grins. In a laughter-tinged voice, Stefan said, "God's teeth! She was not quite that bad on the way here. But then she could scarcely talk when she was clinging to a horse for dear life. She must've been storing up her words all those days."

Royce quirked a sardonic brow in the direction Aunt Elinor had disappeared. "She's crafty as an old fox if your hands are tied. Where's Albert Prisham?" he said, suddenly anxious to see his steward and to discover first hand how Claymore was prospering.

"He's ill," Stefan replied, settling down in a chair by the fire, "as Lady Elinor said. But 'tis his heart, I think, judging from the short time I spoke with him when we arrived yesterday. He's arranged for the celebration tonight, but begs your leave not to join you until the morrow. Don't you want to have a look around the place?"

Royce put his tankard of ale down and wearily rubbed the back of his neck. "I'll do it later. For now, I need some sleep."

"So do I," Sir Godfrey said, yawning and stretching at the same time. "First I want to sleep, and then I want to stuff myself with good food and drink. And then, I want a warm, willing wench in my arms for the rest of the night. In that order," he added grinning, and the other knights nodded in agreement.

When they were gone, Stefan relaxed in his chair, eyeing his brother with mild concern as Royce frowned distractedly into the contents of his tankard. "What is it that makes you look so grim, brother? If it's thoughts of that messy scene in the valley, put them aside and do not let them spoil the celebration tonight."

Royce glanced up at him. "I was wondering if 'uninvited guests' were going to arrive in the middle of it."

Stefan understood instantly that Royce was referring to the arrival of a contingent from Merrick. "The two emissaries from James and Henry will naturally come here. They'll demand to see proof of the marriage with their own eyes, which the good friar can provide. But I doubt her people will ride all this way when they can do naught once they get here."

"They'll come," Royce said flatly. "And they'll come in sufficient numbers to show they have might."

"So what if they do?" Stefan said with a reckless grin. "They can do naught but shout at us over the castle walls. You've fortified this place to withstand the worst assault that *you* could give it."

Royce's expression turned hard and implacable. "I'm done with battles! I told you that and I told Henry that. I'm sick of it, all of it—the blood, the stench, the sounds." Oblivious to the fascinated serf who had come up behind him to refill his tankard, Royce finished harshly, "I've no stomach for it any more."

"Then what do you intend to do if Merrick does come here?"

One sardonic brow lifted over mocking gray eyes. "I intend to invite him in to join the celebration."

Stefan saw he was serious and stood up very slowly. "And then what?" he demanded.

"And then we'll hope he sees the futility of trying to fight me when he is vastly outnumbered."

"And if he doesn't?" Stefan prodded. "Or if he insists on fighting you alone, which is more likely, what will you do then?"

"What would you have me do—" Royce snapped in angry frustration. "Slay my own father-in-law? Shall I invite his daughter to watch? Or shall I send her upstairs until we've mopped up his blood from the floor where her children will play someday?"

It was Stefan's turn to look angry and frustrated. "Then what are you going to do?"

"Sleep," Royce replied, deliberately misunderstanding Stefan's question. "I'm going to meet briefly with my steward, and then I'm going to sleep for a few hours."

An hour later, after meeting with his steward and leaving instructions with a servant to see to a bath and clothes for him, Royce walked into his bedchamber and with great anticipation, he stretched out atop the huge four-poster bed, linking his hands behind his head. His gaze roved idly over the dark blue and gold canopy above the bed with its heavy, brocaded silk draperies pulled back and held with gold ropes, then he glanced at the wall across the room. Jennifer was on the other side of it, he knew. A servant had provided that information, along with the information that Jennifer had entered her bedchamber a few minutes ago, after requesting to be awakened in three hours and to have a bath and whatever clothing might be available for her to wear to the celebration.

Memories of the way Jennifer looked in sleep with her hair strewn about the pillow and her bare satiny skin exposed above the sheets made his body tighten in instant need. Ignoring it, Royce closed his eyes. It was wiser to wait to bed his reluctant bride until after the celebration, he decided. It was going to take some persuasion to make her agree to fulfill this part of her marriage vows, of that Royce had little doubt, and at the moment he was not in a fit state of mind to deal with her on the matter.

Tonight, when she was mellowed with wine and music, he would bring her to his bed. But willing or unwilling, he intended to make love to her tonight and any night hereafter that he pleased. If she would not come to him eagerly, she would come because he willed it, and it was as simple as that, he decided forcefully. But the last recollection he had as he drifted off to sleep was of his outrageously pretty, impertinent young bride holding up her fingers and informing him with saucy superiority, "Forty is this many—"

Chapter Nineteen

Jenny climbed out of the wooden tub, wrapped herself in the soft, light blue wrapper a serving maid handed her, and then parted the curtains that hid an alcove where the shoulder-high tub was kept. The voluminous wrapper, although very fine, had obviously belonged to someone much taller; the sleeves hung down six inches past her fingertips and the hem trailed a full yard behind her, but it was clean and warm, and after spending days in the same soiled gown, Jenny thought the wrapper heavenly. A cozy fire was burning to ward off the chill, and Jenny sat down upon her bed and began to dry her hair.

The serving maid came up behind her, a brush in her hand, and began wordlessly to brush the tangles from Jenny's heavy hair, while another maid appeared with an armful of shimmering, pale gold brocade that Jenny assumed must be a gown. Neither of the maids betrayed any sign of overt hostility, which was little wonder, Jenny thought, considering the warning their duke had delivered in the bailey.

The memory of that kept coming back to taunt Jenny like a riddle. Despite all the bitter feelings between them, Royce had publicly and deliberately endowed her with his own authority, before one and all. He had elevated her to his equal, and that seemed like a very odd thing for any man to do, particularly a man like him. In this instance he seemed to have acted out of kindness to her, and yet, she could not think of a single action he'd ever taken, including releasing Brenna, that he'd done without an ulterior motive that served his purpose.

To endow him with a virtue like kindness was to be a fool. She'd seen with her own eyes the full extent of the cruelty of which he was capable: to murder a child for throwing a—a piece of dirt was more than cruel, it was barbarous. On the other hand, perhaps he'd never intended to let the boy die; perhaps he'd simply reacted more slowly than Jenny had.

With a sigh, Jenny gave up trying to solve the riddle of her husband for the moment and turned to the maid called Agnes. At Merrick there was always chatter and gossip and confidences exchanged between maids and mistresses, and although it was impossible to imagine these servants ever laughing and gossiping with her, Jenny was determined that they should at least speak to her. "Agnes," she said in a carefully modulated tone of quiet courtesy, "is that the gown I'm to wear tonight?"

"Yes, my lady."

"It belonged to someone else, I gather?"

"Yes, my lady."

In the last two hours those were the only words the two maids had said to her, and Jenny felt frustrated and sad at the same time. "To whom did it belong?" she persisted politely.

"The daughter of the former lord, my lady." They both turned at the knock on the door, and a moment later, three stout serfs were placing large trunks upon the floor.

"What is in those?" she asked, puzzled. When neither maid seemed able to answer, Jenny climbed off the high bed and went to inspect the contents herself. Inside the trunks was the most breathtaking array of fabrics she'd ever seen: there were rich satins and brocaded velvets, embroidered silks, soft cashmeres, and linen so fine it was almost transparent. "How beautiful!" Jenny breathed, touching a length of emerald satin.

A voice from the doorway made all three of the women whirl around. "I gather you're pleased then?" Royce asked. He was standing in the doorway, his shoulder propped against the frame, clad in an under doublet of dark ruby silk with an over-doublet of pewter gray velvet. A narrow silver belt with rubies at the clasp circled his waist and from it hung a dress dagger with a huge, fiery ruby winking in its hilt.

"Pleased?" Jenny repeated, distracted by the way his gaze had drifted down her hair and stopped at the neckline of her wrapper. She looked down, trying to see what he was looking at, and snatched the gaping fabric together, clutching it with a fist.

A faint mocking smile touched his lips at her modest gesture, then he glanced at the two maids. "Leave us," he said flatly, and they did so with almost panicky haste, sidling past him as quickly as possible.

As Agnes slipped behind him, Jenny saw the woman hastily cross herself.

Alarm trickled down Jenny's spine as he closed the door behind him and looked at her across the room. Trying to take refuge in conversation, she said the first thing that came to mind: "You really oughtn't speak to serving maids so sharply. I think you frighten them."

"I haven't come to discuss servants," he said calmly, and started walking toward her. Acutely aware of her nakedness beneath the wrapper, Jenny took a cautious step back and inadvertently planted her foot on its trailing hem. Unable to move further, she watched him walk over to the open trunks. Reaching into one of them, he flipped through the assortment of fabrics. "Are you pleased?" he asked again.

"With what?" she said, clutching her wrapper so tightly at the throat and breasts that she could scarcely breathe.

"With these," he said dryly, gesturing to the trunks. "They're for you. Use them to make gowns and whatever else you need."

Jenny nodded, watching him warily as he lost interest in the trunks and started toward her.

"W-what do you want?" she said, hating the shaky sound of her voice.

He stopped within an arm's length of her, but instead of reaching for her he said quietly, "For one thing, I want you to loosen your grip on that gown you're wearing before you strangle yourself. I've seen men hung on ropes no tighter than that."

Jenny forced her stiff fingers to loosen a little. She waited for him to go on, and when he continued to study her in silence, she finally prompted, "Yes? And now what?"

"Now," he said calmly, "I would like to talk to you, so please sit down."

"You've come here to—to talk?" she repeated, and when he nodded, she was so relieved she obeyed without hesitation. Walking over to the bed, trailing a yard of blue wool behind her, she sat down. Reaching up, she raked her hair off her forehead with her fingers and gave it a hard shake to move it off her shoulders. Royce watched her as she tried to restore order to the lush waves tumbling over her shoulders and down her back.

She was, he thought wryly, the only woman alive who could manage to look provocative in a gown that nearly engulfed her. Satisfied with her hair, she faced him, her expression attentive. "What have you come to talk about?"

"About us. About tonight," he said, walking toward her.

She shot off the bed as if her little derrière was on

fire and backed two paces from him until her shoulders were pressed against the wall.

"Jennifer—"

"What?" she gasped nervously.

"There's a fire burning behind you."

"I'm cold," she said shakily.

"In another minute you're going to be on fire."

She eyed him suspiciously, glanced down at the hem of her long gown, then let out a cry of alarm as she snatched it from the ashes. Frantically brushing ashes from the hem, she said, "I'm sorry. 'Tis a lovely gown but perhaps a little—"

"I was referring to the celebration tonight," he interrupted firmly, "not what is going to happen afterward, between us. However, since we're on the subject," he continued, surveying her panicky expression, "suppose you tell me why the prospect of lying with me suddenly seems to frighten you so."

"I'm not frightened," she denied desperately, thinking it might be a mistake to admit to any form of weakness. "But having already done it—I simply feel no desire to do it again. I felt much the same about—about pomegranates. After I tried them, I just didn't *want* them any more. I'm like that sometimes."

His lips twitched, and he advanced on her until he was standing directly in front of her. "If lack of wanting is what alarms you, I think I can remedy it."

"Don't touch me!" she warned. "Or I'll—"

"Don't threaten me, Jennifer," he interrupted quietly. "'Tis a mistake you'll regret. I'll touch you, whenever and *however* I please."

"Now that you've destroyed any pleasure I might have taken in the forthcoming evening," Jenny said stonily, "may I be allowed to dress in private?"

Her insulting words didn't put so much as a scratch in his damnable composure, but his voice seemed to gentle. "'Twas not my intention to come in here and give you news that would cause you to dread the night, but 'tis kinder to tell you how things are going to be than to let you wonder. There are many other matters that need to be settled between us, but they can wait until later. However, to answer your original question, *this* was my real purpose in coming in here—"

Jenny missed the imperceptible movement of his arm and continued to watch his face in wary confusion, thinking he was going to try to kiss her. He must have guessed it, because his firm, sensual lips twisted with a smile, but he continued to look back at her face without moving toward it. After a long moment, he said softly, "Give me your hand, Jennifer."

Jenny glanced down at her hand and, in complete confusion, reluctantly pried her fingers from their grasp on the throat of her wrapper. "My hand?" she repeated blankly, holding it an inch or two toward him.

He took her fingers in his left hand, his warm grasp sending unwanted tingles up her arm; then and only then did she finally notice the magnificent ring resting in a small jewel-encrusted box in the outstretched palm of his right hand. Embedded in a heavy, wide circlet of gold were the most beautiful emeralds Jenny had ever beheld, fiery stones that glowed and winked at her in the candlelight as he slid the heavy ring onto her finger.

Perhaps it was the weight of the ring and all that it implied, or perhaps it was the odd combination of gentleness and solemnity in his gray eyes as they gazed into hers, but whatever the cause, Jenny's heart had doubled its pace. In a voice like rough velvet, he said, "We haven't done anything in its usual order, you and I. We consummated the marriage before the betrothal, and I've placed your ring on your finger long after we exchanged vows."

Mesmerized, Jenny stared into his fathomless silver eyes while his deep husky voice caressed her, pulling her further under his spell as he continued, "And although nothing else has been normal about our marriage thus far, I would ask a favor of you—"

Jenny scarcely recognized the breathy whisper that was her own voice. "What . . . favor?"

"Just for tonight," he said, reaching up and tracing the curve of her flushed cheek with his fingertips, "could we put aside our differences and behave like a normal, newly wedded couple at a normal marriage feast?"

Jenny had assumed tonight's feast was to be a celebration of his homecoming and his recent victory against *her* people, rather than their marriage. He saw her hesitation, and his lips quirked in a wry smile. "Since it evidently takes more than a simple request to soften your heart, I'll offer you a bargain to go with it."

Intensely aware of the effect of his fingertips brushing her cheek and the magnetism his big body was suddenly exuding, she whispered shakily, "What sort of bargain?"

"In return for giving me this night, I will give you one of your own at any time you name. No matter how you wish to spend it, I'll spend it with you doing whatever *you'd* like." When she still hesitated, he shook his head in amused exasperation. "'Tis fortunate I've never met such a stubborn adversary as you on the battlefield, for I fear I'd have gone down to defeat."

For some reason, that admission, made as it was with a tinge of admiration in his voice, did much damage to Jenny's resistance. What he said next demolished it yet more: "I do not ask this favor only for myself, little one, but for you as well. Don't you think, after all the turmoil that has preceded this night—and will probably follow it—that we both deserve one special, unsullied memory of our wedding to keep and hold for ourselves?"

A lump of nameless emotion constricted her throat, and although she had not forgotten all the valid grievances she had against him, the memory of the incredible speech he had delivered on her behalf to his people was still vibrantly fresh in her mind. Moreover, the prospect of pretending, for just a few hours —just this once—that she was a cherished bride and he an eager groom, seemed not only harmless but irresistibly, sweetly appealing. She nodded finally and softly said, "As you wish."

"Why is it," Royce murmured, gazing into her intoxicating eyes, "that every time you surrender willingly, like this, you make me feel like a king who has conquered. Yet when I conquer you against your will, you make me feel like a defeated beggar?"

Before Jenny could recover from that staggering admission, he had started to leave. "Wait," Jenny said, holding out the box to him. "You've left this."

"It's yours, along with the other two things that are in it. Go ahead and open it."

The box was gold and very ornate, and the top completely encrusted with sapphires, rubies, emeralds, and pearls. Inside was a gold ring—a lady's ring with a large ruby deeply embedded in it. Beside it was—Jenny's brow furrowed in surprise and she looked up at him. "A ribbon?" she asked, glancing down at the simple, narrow pink ribbon neatly folded, reposing in a box worthy of crown jewels.

"The two rings and the ribbon were my mother's. They're all that was left after the place Stefan and I were born in was razed during a siege." With that he left, telling her that he would await her downstairs.

Royce closed the door behind him and for a minute he was very still, almost as surprised by the things he'd said to her—and the way he'd said them—as Jennifer had obviously been. It still rankled him that she had twice tricked him at Hardin Castle, and that she had collaborated with her father in a scheme that would simultaneously have cheated him of a wife and of heirs. But Jennifer had one irrefutable defense in her favor, and no matter how he'd tried to ignore it, it *did* exonerate her:

All because I put myself in the way of your marauding brother by walking up a hill . . .

With a smile of anticipation, Royce crossed the gallery and headed down the winding oak steps to the great hall below where the revelry was already well under way. He was ready to forgive her past deeds; however, he would have to make her understand that he would not tolerate deceit in any form in the future.

For several minutes after he left, Jenny remained where she stood, oblivious to the increased sounds of revelry coming from the great hall. Staring down at the jewel-encrusted, velvet-lined box he'd pressed into her palm when he left, she tried to still the sudden outcry of her conscience over what she'd agreed to do. Turning, she walked slowly over to the foot of the bed, but she hesitated as she started to pick up the shining gold gown that lay across it. Surely, she argued with her conscience, she would not be betraying her family or her country or anyone else by putting aside all the animosity that lay between the duke and herself—just for a few short hours. Surely she was entitled to this small, single pleasure. It was so little to ask for out of the rest of her married life—just one brief period of a few hours to feel carefree, to feel like a bride.

The gold brocade was cool to the touch as she slowly picked up the gown and held it up against herself. Looking down at her toes, she noted with delight that the gown was the right length.

The maid called Agnes entered, and over her arm was a long overgown of blue green velvet and a matching velvet mantle lined in gold. The stern-faced woman stopped short and for a split second, confusion softened her stony expression, for the infamous red-haired daughter of the treacherous Merrick was standing in the center of the room, her bare toes peeping from beneath the hem of a long wrapper, while she clutched a hastily altered gold gown to herself, looking down at it with eyes that were shining with joy. "'Tis beautiful, isn't it?" she said in awe, raising glowing eyes to a startled Agnes.

"It—" Agnes faltered. "'Twas brought down along with whatever gowns could be found belonging to the old lord and his daughters," she said gruffly.

Instead of tossing the used gown aside with contempt, as Agnes half-expected her to do, the young duchess smiled with joy and said, "But look—it's going to *fit!*"

"'Twas—" Agnes faltered again as she tried to compare the reality of the ingenuous girl with the stories being told about her. The master himself had called her a slut, according to the serfs' gossip. "'Twas cut down and shorted while you slept, my lady," she managed, carefully laying down the overgown and mantle upon the bed.

"Really?" Jenny said, looking genuinely impressed as she glanced at the fine seams at the sides of the golden undergown. "Did you sew these seams?"

"Aye."

"And in only a few hours?"

"Aye," Agnes said shortly, disliking the confusion she was being forced to feel about the woman she was set to despise.

"They're very fine seams," Jenny said softly. "I could not have done so well."

"Do you want me to help you put your hair up?" Agnes said, coldly disregarding the compliment though she felt somehow that she was in the wrong for doing it. Walking around behind Jenny, Agnes picked up the brush.

"Oh no, I think not," her new mistress declared, smiling brightly over her shoulder at the dumbfounded maid. "Tonight, I'm going to be a bride for a few hours, and brides are allowed to wear their hair down."

Chapter Twenty

The noise that had been audible in her bedchamber became a deafening roar as Jenny neared the great hall, a cacophony of male laughter and music overlaying a sea of conversation. With her foot upon the last step, she hesitated before stepping into view of the revelers.

She knew, without needing to look, that the hall would be filled with men who knew all about her; men who'd undoubtedly been present in camp the night she'd been delivered to Royce like a trussed-up goose; other men who'd undoubtedly participated in her removal by force from Merrick; and still others who had witnessed her humiliating reception in the village today.

A half hour ago, when her husband had been talking in his deep, persuasive voice about memories to store, the prospect of a celebration had seemed wonderful; now, however, the reality of *how* she had come to be here was demolishing all the pleasure. She considered returning to her chamber, but her husband would only come up to fetch her. Besides, she told herself bracingly, she would have to face all these people some time, and a Merrick never cowered.

Drawing a long, steadying breath, Jenny walked down the last step and rounded the corner. The sight that greeted her in the torchlit hall made her blink in momentary confusion. Easily three hundred people were present, standing and talking, or sitting at long tables that had been set up along the length of one side of the hall. Still others were watching the entertainment—and of that, there seemed to be a dazzling variety: on the gallery above, a band of minstrels was playing, while other minstrels were strolling about the floor entertaining smaller groups; four jugglers in particolored costumes were tossing balls high into the air in the center of the room and exchanging them with each other; while at the far end of the hall three acrobats hurtled into the air. Behind the great table upon the dais, a lutist played upon his instrument, adding its sweet chords to the general chaotic gaiety of the hall.

There were women present, too, Jenny noted in some surprise, about thirty of them—wives of some of the knights, or else neighbors, Jenny decided. She spotted Royce easily, for with the exception of Arik, he was the tallest man in the great hall. He was standing not far away, talking to a group of men and women, a goblet in his hand, laughing at something one of them said. It hit her then that she'd never seen him like this—laughing and relaxed, the master of his own castle. Tonight, he did not resemble the predator for whom he was named; he looked like a powerful noble, and a dangerously handsome one, Jenny thought with a tiny tingle of pride as her gaze drifted over his tanned, chiseled features.

Alerted to Jenny's presence by the sudden dropping of the noise level in the hall, Royce put his goblet down, excused himself to his guests, turned, and stopped cold. A slow smile of admiration swept across his face as he beheld the regal young duchess who was walking toward him in a gown of blue-green velvet with a fitted bodice and a slashed skirt that parted at the front to reveal a shining gold undergown. A matching velvet mantle lined in gold was draped over her shoulders and held in place with a flat gold chain inset with aquamarines. At her tiny waist was a curving, stiffened belt of gold satin edged in blue-green and set with aquamarines. Her glorious hair, parted in the center, tumbled over her shoulders and back in luxurious waves and shining curls, a ravishing contrast to the rich blue-green of her gown.

Belatedly realizing that he was forcing his courageous young bride to come to him, he walked forward, meeting her partway. Taking her cold hands in both of his, he drew her close, grinning down at her with unconcealed admiration, "You are beautiful," he said softly. "Stay still for a moment so they can all look their fill."

"I was given to understand, my lord, that one of your many reasons for objecting to marrying me— even if I were the queen of Scotland—is because I am plain." Jenny saw the surprised bafflement in his gray eyes and knew instinctively that it was genuine.

"I'm sure I voiced many objections during that angry interview with Henry, but that was assuredly not one of them." Quietly he added, "I am many things, Jennifer, but I am not blind."

"In that case," she answered teasingly, "I yield to your excellent judgment on the matter of my appearance tonight."

There was a meaningful note in his deep voice as he said, "And will you yield to me on anything else?"

She inclined her head like a queen bestowing a regal favor upon a lesser mortal. "Everything—for as long as we remain down here."

"Stubborn wench," he said with sham severity, then his eyes took on a tender, intimate look as he added, "'Tis time for the bride and groom to join their guests." Tucking her hand into the crook of his elbow, he turned, and Jenny realized that while he'd been talking to her, his knights had formed into a line behind him—obviously by prearranged plan—in order to be formally presented to their new duchess. At the head of them stood Stefan Westmoreland, who'd scarcely glanced at her except to scowl at her in the hall at Merrick. Now, he pressed a light, brotherly kiss to her cheek. When he stepped back and grinned at her, Jenny was struck anew by how very much he resembled Royce, especially when he smiled. Stefan's hair was lighter and his features slightly less rugged; his eyes were blue not gray, but like his brother, he did not lack for charm when he cared to use it—as he did now. "An apology for the trouble I have caused you is not enough, my lady, but 'tis long overdue. I make it now, most sincerely, in hopes you will someday find it in your heart to forgive me."

The apology was made with such sincerity, and so prettily, that Jenny could not, in the spirit of the evening and the dictates of good manners, do anything but accept it, which she did. Her reward was an irrepressible grin from her new brother-in-law, who leaned forward and said, "Naturally, I needn't apologize to my brother, for 'twas a grand favor I did *him.*"

Jenny couldn't help it; that notion was so outrageous that she burst out laughing. Beside her, she felt Royce look down at her, and when she glanced at him, his gray eyes were warm with approval and something that looked very much like pride.

Arik was next, and the stone floor seemed to rumble as the terrifying giant strode forward, each step double the stride of an average man's. As Jenny expected, the granite-faced giant did not demean himself with an apology, let alone a gallant speech, or even so much as a bow. Instead, he stood before her, looking down his nose at her from his towering height and then, with his strange pale eyes looking into hers, he merely jerked his head in a curt nod. Turning, he stalked off, leaving Jenny feeling as if he had just accepted dominion over *her* instead of the reverse.

Seeing her startled discomfiture, Royce leaned

down and chuckled in her ear, "Don't be insulted—Arik has never condescended to actually swear fealty to *me* either."

Jenny looked into those smiling gray eyes and suddenly the whole evening seemed to stretch before her with all the promise and excitement of the first warm night of spring.

The knights who made up Royce's personal guard came next. Sir Godfrey, a tall, handsome man in his late twenties, was first and instantly became her favorite because, immediately after kissing her hand, he did something that completely dispelled the tension over their past association: Turning to all within hearing, he proclaimed her the only woman alive with wit and courage enough to dupe an entire army. Then he turned back to her and said with an irrepressible grin, "I trust, my lady, that if you ever decide to escape Claymore as you did our camp a few weeks ago, you'll spare our pride by leaving us a better trail to follow?"

Jenny, who was partaking of the goblet of wine Royce had pressed into her hand, replied with sham solemnity, "Should I ever try to escape from here, I shall contrive to do it very badly, to be sure," which made Sir Godfrey roar with laughter and kiss her cheek.

Sir Eustace, blond and handsome with merry brown eyes, gallantly announced that if her hair had been unbound when she escaped, they'd have spotted its golden flame and been able to find her no matter *where* she hid, which earned him a mild, quelling look from Royce. Undaunted, Sir Eustace leaned forward and teasingly told Jennifer, "He's jealous, you can see—of my superior looks and chivalrous conversation."

One at a time, they came to stand before her, skilled, deadly knights who once would have killed her at a word from their lord, but who were now bound to protect her, even at the cost of their own lives. Attired in fine velvets and wools, instead of chain mail and helmets, the older knights treated her with differential courtesy while a few of the younger ones actually exhibited an endearing embarrassment for something they had done: "I trust," young Sir Lionel said to Jennifer, "I didn't cause your grace any undue discomfort when I—when I—that is, er, grabbed your arm and drag—"

Jenny chuckled and raised her brows, "and *escorted* me to my tent that first night?"

"Yes, *escorted*," he said with a sigh of relief.

Gawin, Royce's young squire, was the last to be formally presented to her as his mistress. Obviously too young and idealistic to follow the older, more experienced knight's example and let bygones be bygones, he bowed to Jenny, kissed her hand, and then with ill-concealed rancor said, "I *suppose*, my lady, 'twas not your *true* intention to make us *freeze* when you slashed our blankets."

That remark earned him a hard cuff from Sir Eustace, who had lingered at Jenny's side, and who said to him with disgust, "If that's your idea of gallantry, no wonder young Lady Anne casts her eye at Roderick, not you."

The mention of Roderick and Lady Anne made the youth stiffen in umbrage and throw an irate look about the room. Issuing a hasty apology to Jennifer, Gawin hastened off in the direction of a pretty brunette who was talking to a man Jenny didn't recognize, looking more belligerent than gallant.

Royce watched him leave and glanced at Jennifer with a look of apologetic amusement. "Gawin has lost his head over that pretty maid over there, and evidently his sense as well." Offering her his arm, he added, "Come and meet the rest of our guests, my lady."

The fears Jenny had harbored about her reception from those who were not bound to Royce by pledges of fealty were completely allayed during the next two hours, as she was introduced to each. The unprecedented words Royce had spoken earlier on the castle steps had obviously been repeated far and wide—including to the guests who'd come from neighboring estates—and though Jenny occasionally encountered a hostile gaze, the owner of it was careful to hide it behind a polite smile.

When all the introductions had been made, Royce insisted that Jenny should dine, and at the table on the raised dais there was more conversation—all of it gay and pleasant, interrupted only by the blast of trumpets from the gallery that heralded the arrival of each new course from the kitchen.

Aunt Elinor was in her glory, with a captive audience of more than three hundred people to converse with, although the person she was most often seen near was none other than Arik! Jenny watched her, amused by the elderly lady's fascination with the one person who didn't want to talk to anyone at all.

"Does the food live up to your expectations, my lord?" Jenny asked, turning to Royce, who was helping himself to a second portion of roasted peacock and another of stuffed swan.

"It's adequate," he said with a mild frown. "But I'd expected better fare from kitchens under Prisham's supervision." At that moment, the steward himself materialized behind Royce, and Jenny had her first glimpse of Albert Prisham as he said in a cool, formal voice, "I fear I have little interest in food, your grace." He glanced at Jennifer and said, "A cup of mild broth, a lean joint of meat is enough to satisfy me. However, I feel certain your *wife* will take the kitchens in hand and create menus and recipes to better please you."

Jenny, who knew nothing whatever of recipes and menus, paid no heed to that remark, because she was trying to stifle a surge of instant dislike for the man. Wearing a gold chain about his waist and carrying a white staff, the insignias of his exalted position, he was thin to the point of emaciation. His jawbones protruded sharply beneath skin that was white and nearly transparent. But it wasn't that which made Jenny react so negatively to him, it was the coldness in his eyes when he looked about him. "I trust," he continued, showing more respect to Royce, but certainly no more warmth than he'd showed Jennifer, "that with the exception of the food, all else is to your satisfaction tonight?"

"Everything is fine," Royce replied, sliding his chair back as the dancing began at the far end of the hall. "If you're well enough tomorrow, I'd like to see the ledgers, and the following day, we should tour the estate."

"Certainly, your grace, but the day after tomorrow is the twenty-third, which is customarily Judgment Day. Do you desire me to postpone it?"

"No," Royce said without hesitation, his hand under Jennifer's elbow as he indicated she should rise. "I'd be interested to watch and see how it is done."

With a bow to Royce and a curt inclination of his head to Jennifer, Sir Albert withdrew. Leaning on his staff, he made his slow way to his own chambers.

When Jenny realized Royce meant to join the dancing, she drew back and shot him an apprehensive look. "I have danced little, your grace," she explained, watching the swirling, energetic dancers and trying to see what steps they were doing. "Perhaps we ought not to do it, just now, when there are so many—"

With a grin, Royce took her firmly in his arms. "Just hold on tightly," he said and began to whirl her expertly. He was, Jenny realized at once, an excellent dancer. Moreover, he was an excellent teacher—by the third dance she was twirling and skipping and leaping right along with the others. Those dances were followed immediately by a dozen more, as Stefan Westmoreland claimed his dance, and then Sir Godfrey and Sir Lionel and the rest of the knights claimed theirs.

Breathless and laughing, Jenny shook her head no

when Sir Godfrey tried to lead her into another dance. Royce, who'd danced with several of the other ladies present, had been standing on the sidelines for the last half hour talking with a group of guests. Now he materialized at Jennifer's side as if sensing her exhaustion. "Jennifer needs a rest, Godfrey." Nodding toward Gawin, who seemed to be having a belligerent conversation with the knight called Sir Roderick in the presence of Lady Anne, Royce added dryly, "I suggest you invite Lady Anne to dance instead— before Gawin does something foolish to win her admiration, like provoking a fight with Roderick and getting himself killed."

Sir Godfrey obligingly went off to solicit a dance from the lady in question, and Royce led Jenny over to a quiet corner in the hall. Handing her a goblet of wine, he blocked her from view by standing directly in front of her and bracing his hand on the wall near her head.

"Thank you," she said, happy and flushed, her chest heaving with exertion. "I truly needed a moment to rest." Royce's gaze drifted appreciatively to the rosy skin swelling above the square bodice of her gown, making Jenny feel strangely excited and nervous at the same time. "You're an excellent dancer," she said, and he reluctantly forced his gaze to hers. "You must have danced a great deal at court."

"And on the battlefield," he said with a disarming grin.

"On the battlefield?" she echoed, perplexed.

He nodded, his grin widening. "Watch any warrior who's trying to dodge arrows and lances and you'll see dance steps and footwork that would dazzle you."

His ability to laugh at himself warmed Jenny's heart, which was already liberally warmed by several cups of strong wine and a great deal of dancing. Self-conscious, she glanced sideways and saw Arik only a few yards away. Unlike everyone else who was laughing, eating, or dancing, Arik was standing with his arms crossed over his chest, his legs braced wide apart, staring straight ahead with an expression on his face that looked absolutely lethal. And at his side was Aunt Elinor, chattering up at him as if her very life depended on making him respond.

Royce followed the direction of Jennifer's gaze. "Your aunt," he teased, "would seem to enjoy courting danger."

Emboldened by the wine, Jenny returned his smile. "Does Arik ever talk—I mean in real sentences? Or laugh?"

"I've never seen him laugh. And he speaks as little as necessary."

Gazing up into his compelling eyes, Jenny felt strangely safe and sheltered, and yet uneasily aware that her husband was a virtual mystery to her. Sensing that in his approachable mood, he'd be willing to answer a question, she said softly, "How did you meet him?"

"We were never actually introduced," he teased. When she continued to regard him as if waiting for more information, he obliged by saying, "The first time I saw Arik 'twas eight years ago, in the thick of a battle that had been raging for over a sennight. He was trying to fend off six attackers who'd singled him out as a target and were pounding him with swords and arrows. I went to his aid, and between the two of us we managed to fell the attackers. When the skirmish was over, I was wounded, but Arik didn't give me so much as a thank you for my efforts. He just looked at me and then he rode off, plunging into the heat of battle again."

"And that was all there was to it?" Jenny asked, when Royce fell silent.

"Not quite. The next day, near nightfall, I was wounded again, and this time unhorsed as well. As I bent down to pick up my shield, I glanced up and there was a rider coming straight at me, his lance aimed at my heart. The next instant, the lancer was headless, and there was Arik, swooping down to pick up his bloodied axe and riding off. Again without a word.

"My wounds had rendered me virtually useless, and twice more that night Arik appeared—seemingly from nowhere—to fend off my attackers when I was outnumbered. The next day, we routed the enemy and gave chase. I looked over to see Arik riding beside me. He's been there ever since."

"So you gained his undying loyalty because you rescued him from six attackers?" Jenny summarized.

Royce shook his head. "I suspect I gained his *undying* loyalty a week after that when I killed a large snake that was trying to share Arik's blanket without his knowledge."

"You don't mean to tell me," Jenny giggled, "that giant of a man is afraid of *snakes.*"

Royce gave her a look of feigned affront. "Women are *afraid* of snakes," he explained unequivocally. "Men *hate* them." Then he spoiled the whole effect with a boyish grin. "It means the same thing, however."

Royce gazed down into her laughing blue eyes, longing to kiss her, and Jenny, carried away by this tender, joking, approachable side of him, suddenly blurted the question that had been haunting her. "Did you truly mean to let him murder that child today?"

He stiffened slightly, and then he quietly said, "I think it's time we go upstairs."

Uncertain just why he'd suddenly made that decision, or if talking was what he intended to do once they got there, Jenny hesitated suspiciously. "Why?"

"Because you want to talk," he stated levelly, "and I want to take you to bed. In which case, my chamber is better suited to both our purposes than this hall."

Short of making a scene which would only humiliate her, Jenny knew she had no choice but to leave the hall with him. A thought struck her before she took the first step, and the eyes she turned on him were imploring. "They aren't going to try to follow us—" she pleaded. "I mean, there'll be no bedding ritual, will there?"

"Even if there was, there's no harm in it," he said patiently. "'Tis an ancient custom. We can always talk *afterward,*" he said meaningfully.

"Please," Jenny said. "'Twould be a farce, for the world knows we've already—already done that, and a bedding will only make the talk start up again."

He didn't answer her, but as they passed Arik and Aunt Elinor, he stopped to speak to Arik.

The impending departure of the bride and groom was noted almost at once, however, and by the time they'd passed the table on the dais, Jenny's face was scarlet from the bawdy encouragement and advice being shouted at Royce. As they started up the stairs, she stole a frantic glance over her shoulder and to her relief she saw that Arik had positioned himself at the bottom of the steps, folded his arms across his chest, and had taken up a post—obviously at Royce's order —to prevent the revelers from following them.

By the time Royce opened the door to his bedchamber, Jenny was in a state of generalized terror and helplessness. In frozen silence, she watched him close the door, her startled eyes dazedly registering an extremely large and very luxurious room with a huge four-poster canopied bed with fine velvet hangings and a pair of massive chairs with carved arms placed before a large hooded fireplace. Three large, ornately carved chests were against the wall, one for clothes, Jenny knew without looking, and the others evidently containing coins and other riches, judging from the size of their massive locks. A pair of tall silver stands with candles burning in them flanked the bed, and another pair stood on either side of the fireplace. Tapestries hung on the walls and there was even a mat on the polished wood floor. But the most amazing thing about the room was the window—a large bay window with leaded glass that overlooked the bailey and would make the room cheerful and airy in the daylight.

A door to the left was ajar and opened into a solar; the door on the right evidently opened into the chamber Jenny occupied. Scrupulously avoiding looking at the bed, she stared at the two remaining doors, and the instant Royce moved, she jumped and said the first thing that came to mind: "Wh-where do those two doors lead?"

"One to a privy, the other to a closet," he answered, noting the way she was averting her gaze from the bed. In a calm voice that nevertheless carried an unmistakable thread of command, he said, "Would you mind explaining to me why you seem to find the prospect of lying with me even more alarming when we're married than you did before, when you had everything to lose?"

"I had no choice then," she said in nervous defense, turning to face him.

"You have none now," he pointed out reasonably.

Jenny's mouth went dry. She wrapped her arms around her middle as if she were very cold, her eyes desperate with confusion. "I don't understand you," she tried to explain, "I never know what to expect. Sometimes you seem almost kind and quite rational. And just when I think you're actually quite nice—I mean *normal*," she amended quickly, "you do mad things and you make insane accusations." She held out her hands as if asking him to understand. "I cannot be at ease with a man who is a stranger to me! A frightening, unpredictable stranger!"

He took a step forward and then another, and Jenny retreated step for step, until the backs of her legs bumped against the bed. Unable to go forward, and adamantly unwilling to move backward, she stood in mutinous silence. "Don't you dare touch me. I hate it when you touch me!" she warned shakily.

His dark brows pulled together, and he reached out and hooked his fingertip in the neck of her gown, looking straight into her eyes as he drew it downward until his fingertip was deep in the hollow between her breasts. It stayed there, moving up and down, stroking the sides of her breasts, while tiny flames began shooting through Jenny's body, making her breathing shallow and rapid. His hand forced its way between her bodice and her skin and closed on her full breast. "Now tell me you hate my touch," he invited her softly, his eyes holding hers imprisoned, his fingers teasing her hardening nipple.

Jenny felt her breast swelling to fill his hand and she turned her head aside, staring fixedly at the fire in the grate, drowning in shame at her inability to control her own treacherous body.

Abruptly he pulled his hand away. "I'm beginning to think you must enjoy baiting me, for you do it better than anyone I've ever known." Raking his hand through the side of his hair in angry self-disgust, Royce walked over to the flagon of mulled wine resting near the fire and poured some into a goblet. Turning, he studied her in silence. After a minute, he said in a quiet, almost apologetic tone that startled Jenny into looking at him, "The fault for what happened just now was mine and had little to do with your 'baiting' me. You merely gave me an excuse to do what I've longed to do since I first set eyes on you in this gown."

When she remained silent, watching him with wary suspicion, he said with an irritated sigh, "Jennifer, this marriage was not of our choosing, but the deed is done, and we will have to find a way to live in harmony with it. We have wronged each other, and nothing can change that. I'd hoped to bury the past, but perhaps it's best to let you talk about it as you seem determined to do. Very well," he said as if reaching a conclusion, "go ahead and itemize your grievances. What do you want to know?"

"Two things for a start," Jenny replied tartly. "When did you finally come to the realization that

I've been wronged? And how in God's holy name can you *possibly* say I've wronged you?"

"I'd prefer to leave the last question unanswered," he said evenly. "Before I came in to see you this evening, I spent two hours in this room, coming to grips with the things you have done, and I've decided to put all that behind me."

"How *very* virtuous of you," Jenny said derisively. "It so happens, my lord, that I have done nothing, *nothing* for which I require your forgiveness or for which I owe you explanations, for that matter. However," she amended tightly, "I will be happy to give any explanations you wish once you've made yours to me. Is that agreeable?"

His lips quirked in a reluctant grin as Royce contemplated the stormy beauty in aquamarine velvet who'd already abandoned fear in favor of anger. He found it acutely painful when she feared him. Making an effort to smooth the grin from his face, he nodded. "Perfectly agreeable. You may proceed."

Jenny needed no more encouragement. Studying his face, watching for any signs of deceit, she said abruptly, "Were you or were you not going to let Arik kill that boy in the village today?"

"No," he said flatly. "I was not."

Some of Jenny's hostility and fear began to dissolve. "Then why didn't you say anything?"

"I didn't need to. Arik does not act except on my orders. He stopped, not because you screamed, but because he was waiting for a decision from me."

"You—you aren't lying are you?" she asked, searching his inscrutable features.

"What do you think?"

Jenny bit her lip, feeling slightly churlish. "I apologize. That was needlessly rude."

Accepting her apology with a nod, he said civilly, "Go on. What's your next question?"

Jenny drew a deep breath and slowly expelled it,

knowing she was treading on dangerous ground now. "I would like to know why you felt compelled to humiliate my father and my family by proving you could breach Merrick's defenses and stealing me from my own bedchamber?" Ignoring the sudden angry gleam flaring in his eyes, she continued doggedly, "You've proved your skill and prowess in such things. Why, if you ever wanted us to live in harmony, did you need to prove it in such a petty, small-minded—"

"Jennifer," he interrupted in a cutting voice, "you've made a fool of me twice and caused me to make a fool of myself once. That's quite a record," he applauded sarcastically. "Now take your bow, and let the matter drop!"

Fortified with a considerable amount of wine and a good deal of natural stubbornness, Jenny searched his features. Despite his tone of sarcasm, there was a harshness in his gray eyes that told her whatever "plot" he was referring to did more than merely anger him, it cut him deeply enough to make him bitter. Trying to ignore the dangerous, magnetic tug that seemed to be pulling her toward him with each moment since he'd begun to answer her questions, she said lightly, "I shall happily take my bow, but first, I'd like to be absolutely certain what it is I've done to deserve such credit."

"You damn well know what I'm referring to."

"I'm not entirely—certain. I'd hate to take credit where it wasn't due," she said, raising her glass.

"You're amazing. You can lie and look me straight in the eye. Very well," he said, his voice reeking with irony. "Let's play your game to its distasteful end. First, there was the little ruse that your sister—who I'd have sworn didn't have sense enough to dress herself—pulled off with your help and the help of feather pillows . . ."

"You know about that?" she said, choking on her wine and trying to hide her smile.

"I wouldn't advise you to laugh," he warned.

"Why not?" Jenny said wryly. "'Twas as much a 'joke' on me as 'twas on you."

"I suppose you knew nothing about it?" he snapped, studying the telltale flush on her cheeks, wondering if it was due to the wine or lying.

"If I had," she said, turning serious, "do you think I'd have been so eager to trade my honor for *feathers?*"

"I don't know. Would you?"

She lowered her glass and said somberly, "I'm not certain. To help her escape, I suppose I might have— but not until I'd exhausted every other possibility. So I can't quite take credit for duping you in this instance. What are the other two?"

He slapped his goblet onto the table and started toward her.

"I gather you're referring to my escape with William?" she prompted uneasily, backing away a step from the ominous expression in his eyes. "I can't take credit for that either. He was standing in the woods, and I didn't notice him until you were about to leave with Arik."

"Right," he said icily, "and although you *are* aware of my remark about the queen of Scotland, you *aren't* aware that while *you* were escaping, *I* was telling Graverley, like a besotted fool, that I intended to marry you. And you *aren't* aware that you were leaving for a cloister immediately after our wedding at Merrick? Which would have neatly bound me to you for life at the same time it deprived me of heirs? And if you lie to me just one more time—" He took the goblet of wine from her and jerked her into his arms.

"You were doing *what?*" she whispered.

"Enough of this nonsense," he said shortly, bending his head and taking her lips in a hard, silencing kiss. To his surprise, she didn't fight him. In fact, she seemed not to know what he was doing to her. When he lifted his head she was staring at him with an expression in her blue eyes he'd not seen before.

"You were doing *what?*" she breathed again.

"You heard me," he said shortly.

An awful, treacherous warmth was seeping through every pore of Jenny's body as she gazed into his mesmerizing eyes. "Why?" she whispered. "Why did you tell him you intended to marry me?"

"I was insane at the time," he said coldly.

"About me?" she whispered, so carried away with what her heart was telling her that she spoke without thinking.

"About your delectable body," he said crudely, but somewhere in her heart, Jenny was accepting something else . . . another explanation so exquisite that she was afraid to think it. It explained everything.

"I didn't know," she said simply. "I never imagined you would want to marry me."

"And I suppose if you had, you'd have sent your stepbrother off and stayed at Hardin with me?" he jeered.

It was the greatest risk Jenny had ever taken in her life, because she told him the truth: "If I—I'd known how I was going to feel after I left, I might have." She saw his jaw harden, and without thinking, she lifted her hand and touched her fingertips to his taut cheek. "Please don't look at me like this," she whispered, her eyes gazing deeply into his. "I am not lying to you."

Trying without complete success to ignore the tender innocence of her touch and to stifle the sudden memory of the way she had kissed his scars, Royce said flatly, "And I suppose you knew nothing about your father's plot?"

"I was not going to any cloister, I was leaving with you in the morn," she said simply. "I would never have done anything so . . . so low."

In sheer frustration at her endless deceit, Royce jerked her into his arms and kissed her, but instead of fighting the hard, punishing kiss, she leaned up on her toes and welcomed it, her hands sliding up his chest and twining around his neck. Her parted lips clung to his, moving tenderly, softly against his mouth, and to Royce's astonishment he realized she was gentling him. And even when he realized it, he couldn't stop it from happening. His hands no longer dug into her arms, they were shifting over her back in a restless, soothing caress, sliding up her nape and holding her lips closer to his hungry mouth.

And as his passion built, so did the awful, guilty premonition that he had been wrong. About everything. Tearing his mouth from hers, he held her clasped tightly to him, waiting for his breathing to even out. When he could finally trust himself to speak, he moved her slightly away and reached down to lift her chin, needing—wanting—to see into her eyes when he asked her. "Look at me, Jennifer," he said gently.

The eyes she raised to his were innocent of guile and strangely trusting. It was not a question, it was a statement: "You didn't know anything about your father's plot, did you?"

"There was no plot," she said simply.

Royce leaned his head back and he closed his eyes, trying to shut out the obvious truth: After forcing her to stand in her own home and endure the barbs of his people, he had dragged her out of bed, forced her to marry him, hauled her across England, and to finish it all off nicely, he had, within the hour, graciously offered to "forgive" her and "let bygones be bygones."

Faced with the choice of shattering her illusions about her father or letting her go on thinking he was a callous madman, Royce chose the former. He was not in a mood to be gallant—not at the expense of his marriage.

Stroking her silken hair, he tipped his chin down and stared into those trusting eyes, wondering why he consistently lost his reason where she was concerned. "Jennifer," he said quietly, "I am not quite the monster you've had good reason to think I am. There *was* a plot. Will you at least listen to my explanation?"

She nodded, but the smile she gave him told him she thought he was fanciful beyond belief.

"When I went to Merrick keep, I fully expected either your father or one of the clans to try to violate the pact that guaranteed my safety while in Scotland for our marriage. I put men on the roads leading to Merrick and left them with orders not to let any group pass without making inquiries."

"And they didn't find anyone trying to violate the pact," she said with quiet assurance.

"No," Royce admitted. "But what they did discover was a caravan of one abbess with an escort of twelve, making what seemed to be undue haste toward Merrick. Contrary to what you have reason to believe," he added with a wry smile, "my men and I are not in the habit of harassing clerics. On the other hand, following my instructions, they made inquiries of the party —by the expedient measure of letting the abbess believe they were there to give her escort. She, in turn, happily confided that she was coming for you."

Jenny's finely arched brows drew together in a puzzled frown, and Royce almost regretted telling her the truth. "Go on," she said.

"The abbess and her party had been delayed by all the rain in the north—which was, by the by, why your father and your 'pious' Friar Benedict dreamt up that nonsensical explanation about the good friar being very temporarily too ill to perform the ceremony. According to the abbess, it seemed that one Lady Jennifer Merrick had decided to cloister herself as the result of an unwanted marriage. The 'husband,' she understood, was determined to stand in the way of the lady's decision to pledge her life to God, and so she had come to assist Lady Jennifer by helping her father get her out of Merrick—and out of her husband's godless clutches—in secret.

"Your father had hit upon the perfect revenge: since our marriage had already been consummated before the fact, an annulment would have been out of the question for me. So of course would divorce have been. Without the opportunity to remarry, I couldn't sire a legitimate heir, and so all of this—Claymore and all I have—would have reverted to the king on my death."

"I—I don't believe you," Jenny said flatly, and then with heartbreaking fairness, she amended, "I believe *you* believe this. But the simple truth is that my father would never have locked me away for the rest of my life without at least giving me a choice first."

"He would, and he intended to."

She shook her head, shook it so hard and so emphatically that Royce suddenly realized she couldn't bear to believe it. "My father . . . loves me. He wouldn't do that. Not even to avenge himself on you."

Royce winced, feeling like the Barbarian he'd been called for trying to shatter her illusions. "You're quite right. I—it was a mistake."

She nodded. "A mistake." She smiled at him, a soft, sweet smile that made his heart pick up its tempo because it was not like any other smile she'd given him. It was filled with trust and approval and something else he couldn't quite identify.

Turning, Jenny walked over to the window, staring out at the starlit night. Torches were lit on the battlements and the silhouette of a guard patrolling the wall was clearly outlined against the orange light. Her mind, however, was not on stars or guards, or even her father; it was on the tall, black-haired man standing behind her. He had wanted to marry her, and the knowledge filled her with an emotion so poignant, so consuming that she could scarcely contain it. It was so overpowering that feelings like patriotism and revenge became paltry.

She reached out, idly following the handsome tracings on the cold glass with a fingertip, remembering all those sleepless nights at Merrick keep when she could not tear him out of her mind, when her body felt empty and overheated and cried out for his. Behind her, she heard him start toward her, and she knew what was going to happen between them as surely as she knew she loved him. God forgive her, she loved her family's enemy. She had known it at Hardin, but she had been stronger then—and afraid. Afraid of what would happen to her if she let herself love a man who seemed to regard her as nothing more than a temporary amusement. But as surely as Jenny knew she loved him, she knew he loved her, too. It explained everything—his anger, his laughter, his patience . . . his speech in the bailey.

She felt his presence like a tangible thing even before he slowly slid his arm around her from behind, drawing her back against his body. In the windowpane their eyes met, and Jenny gazed into his as she asked him for the one promise that would free her from all guilt for giving him her love and her life. Her soft voice shaking with emotion, she asked, "Will you swear to me never to raise your hand against my family?"

His answer was an aching whisper. "Yes."

Shattering tenderness swept through her, and she closed her eyes, leaning back against him in complete surrender. He bent his head, brushing his mouth against her temple, his hand slowly sliding upward to caress the fullness of her breast. His mouth trailed a hot path down her cheek to her ear, his tongue exploring each fold as his hand slipped inside her gown, cupping her breast, his thumb rubbing over her hardening nipple.

Awash in a sea of pure sensation, Jenny made no protest when he covered her lips with his, turning her into his arms. She felt no shame or guilt when her gown slid down around her hips or when he came to her in bed, his bare, muscled shoulders gleaming like bronze in the candlelight as he leaned over her, skillfully parting her lips with his tongue. With a silent moan of surrender, she slipped her hand around his neck, her fingers sliding into the curling hair at his nape, holding his mouth pressed fiercely to hers as she welcomed his tongue and gave him hers. Her innocent ardor was more than Royce's ravenous body could withstand. Wrapping his arm around her hips he pulled her into vibrant contact with his straining thighs, molding her body to the rigid contours of his. His other hand cupped the back of her head as he drove his tongue into her mouth again and again, forcing her to give him back the sensual urgency he was offering her.

When she tore her mouth from his, he almost groaned with disappointment, thinking he had frightened her with his unbridled passion—but when he opened his eyes, what he saw on her face was neither fright or revulsion, it was wonder. A knot of tenderness swelling in his chest, he held perfectly still, watching her as Jenny took his face between her hands, her trembling fingertips reverently caressing his eyes, his cheekbones and jaw, and then she leaned up and kissed him with an ardor that nearly matched his own. Turning into his arms, pressing him back into the pillows, her hair spilling across them like a satin veil, she kissed his eyes, his nose, his ear, and when her lips closed over his nipple, Royce lost control. *"Jenny,"* he groaned, his hands rushing over her back and thighs and buttocks. His fingers dug into her hair, pulling her lips back to his fevered mouth. "Jenny," he whispered hoarsely, his tongue plunging into her mouth, tangling with hers as he rolled her onto her back and covered her body with his. "Jenny," he murmured hotly as he hungrily devoured her breasts and stomach and thighs with his mouth. He could not stop saying her name. It played like a melody in his heart when her arms went around him and she lifted her hips, willingly molding herself to his engorged manhood; it sang in his veins as she welcomed the first fierce thrust of his body into hers; it rang through every fiber of his being as she matched his fierce, driving thrusts; and it exploded in a crescendo as she cried out, "I love you," her nails biting into his back, her body racked with wave after wave of ecstasy.

His body straining, desperate for release, Royce dragged his lips from hers and leaned up on his forearms, waiting for her tremors to subside as he gazed down into her beautiful, shadowy face. And then, because he could hold back no longer, he drove into her one last time, gasping her name. His body jerked convulsively again and again and again as he spilled his life into her, holding her hips to his hips and her mouth to his mouth.

Lying on his back, his wife cradled tightly against his side, he waited for the thundering beat of his heart to subside, his hand roving over her satiny skin, his mind still dazed by the explosion of his body. In all his years of aimless sexual encounters and torrid dalliances, nothing had ever approached the shattering ecstasy he'd just experienced.

Beside him, Jenny raised her head, and he tipped his chin down, looking into her eyes. In their slumberous blue depths he saw the same wonder and confusion he felt. "What are you thinking?" he asked with a tender smile at her upturned face.

An answering smile touched her lips as her fingers splayed across his hair-roughened chest.

Only two thoughts had crossed Jenny's mind and, rather than admit that she'd been longing to hear him say he loved her, she confessed to the other thought. "I was thinking," she whispered ruefully, "that if it had been like this . . . at Hardin . . . I don't *think* I'd have left with William."

"If it had been like this," Royce countered, his smile widening to a wicked grin, "I'd have come *after* you."

Unaware that she could so easily stir his desire,

Jenny trailed her fingers down the flat planes of his hard stomach. "Why didn't you?"

"I was under arrest at the time," he replied dryly, then he caught her wandering hand in his, flattening it beneath his palm to prevent it from straying lower, "for refusing to turn you over to Graverley," he added, releasing her hand.

His breath caught as her hand slid down the side of his thigh. "Jenny," he warned hoarsely, but it was already too late, desire was pouring through him, making him rigid. With a smothered laugh at her startled expression, he caught her hips and lifted her, settling her gently but firmly atop his swollen shaft. "Take as long as you like, little one," he teased huskily, "I'm entirely at your service." His laughter faded, however, as his wife leaned down, straddling him, and sweetly covered his mouth with hers.

Chapter Twenty-One

A smile drifted across Jenny's face as she stood at the window of the solar, looking out into the bailey, her heart filled with the memory of last night. It was mid-morning, judging from the angle of the sun, and she'd only arisen less than an hour ago—later than she'd ever slept in her life.

Royce had made love to her long and lingeringly this morning, this time with an exquisite, restrained gentleness that even now made Jenny's pulses race. He had not told her that he loved her, but he did love her—as inexperienced as she was with love, she was certain of that. Why else would he have made such a pledge to her? Or taken such care with her when she was in his bed?

So lost was she in her reflections that Jenny didn't notice when Agnes entered the room. The smile still in her eyes, Jenny turned to the maid who was holding out another hastily remade gown to her, this one of soft cream cashmere. Despite the servant's stern, foreboding expression, Jenny was absolutely determined to break through the barriers and befriend her serfs as well. Surely if she could gentle a wolf, it could not be nearly as difficult to befriend his servants.

Searching for something to say to the maid, she accepted the gown and then noticed the tub in the alcove. Seizing on that as a safe topic, she said, "That tub is large enough to hold four or five people. At home, we either bathe in the lake, or else make do with a little wooden tub that holds only enough water to cover you to the waist."

"This is *England,* my lady," Agnes replied as she picked up the gown Jenny had worn last night. Jenny shot a startled glance at her, uncertain whether her tone had been laced with superiority or not.

"Do all the big homes in England have such enormous tubs and real fireplaces and—" she lifted her arm and made a sweeping gesture that included the luxurious chamber with its velvet draperies and thick mats scattered across the floor, "and things like all this—?"

"No, my lady. But you're at Claymore, and Sir Albert—the master's steward and steward to the old lord, too—is under orders to keep Claymore like a castle fit for a king. The silver is polished every week, and no dust is allowed to get into the tapestries, nor on the floors, neither. And if something gets ruint', 'tis given away and replaced."

"It must require a great deal of work to keep it so perfect," Jenny observed.

"Aye, but then the new master has told Sir Albert what he's to do, and Sir Albert, hard, proud man though he is, will do what he's told—no matter *how* he feels inside about he what's tellin' him to do it."

That last startling remark was so laced with bitterness and resentment that Jenny couldn't believe she'd heard correctly. Her brows drew together as she twisted around fully to look at the maid. "Agnes, what do you mean?"

Agnes obviously realized she'd said too much, because the woman turned white and stiffened, staring at Jennifer in wild-eyed fear. "I meant nothin', my lady. Nothin'! 'Tis proud we *all* are to have our new master home, and if *all* 'is enemies come here, as they surely will, 'tis proud we'll be to give up our crops and our menfolk and children for his battles. *Proud!"* she uttered in a low, desperate voice that was still filled with a trace of angry resentment. "We are good, loyal folk, and hold no ill will toward the master for what he did. An we hope he holds none against us."

"Agnes," Jenny said gently, "you needn't be afraid of *me.* I won't betray your confidences. What do you mean by 'what he did'?"

The poor woman was shaking so hard that when Royce opened the door and poked his head inside to remind Jennifer to join him downstairs for the midday meal, Agnes dropped the velvet gown. Snatching it up, she fled from the room. But as she pulled open the heavy oaken door, she glanced back at Royce, and this time Jennifer distinctly saw her cross herself again.

The cashmere gown forgotten in her hand, Jenny stared at the closing door, her forehead furrowed in a thoughtful frown.

The great hall showed few signs of last night's merrymaking; the trestle tables that had filled the room had been taken down and removed. In fact, the only remnants of the night's revelry were the dozen or so knights who were still asleep on benches along the walls, their snores rising and falling sonorously. Despite the air of bustling efficiency, Jenny noticed with sympathy that the serfs' movements were sluggish, and that more than one was unable to dodge a halfhearted kick from an irate knight on the bench who did not want his slumber disturbed.

Royce looked up as Jennifer came to the table and rose to his feet with that easy, catlike grace that she'd always admired. "Good morning," he said in a low, intimate voice, "I trust you slept well?"

"Very well," Jenny said in a voice that was an embarrassed little whisper, but her eyes were bright and sparkling as she sat down beside him.

"Good morning, my dear!" Aunt Elinor chirped happily, as she looked up from daintily slicing a piece of venison from the tray of cold meats in front of her. "You're looking in fine spirits this morning."

"Good morning, Aunt Elinor," Jenny said, sending her a reassuring smile; then she cast a puzzled look up and down the table at the silent men who were also present: Sir Stefan, Sir Godfrey, Sir Lionel, Sir Eustace, Arik, and Friar Gregory. Aware of the strange silence and downcast eyes of the men, she said with a hesitant smile, "Good morning, everyone."

Five male faces slowly lifted to hers—pale, strained faces whose expressions ranged from glazed pain to befuddled confusion. "Good morning, my lady," they echoed politely, but three of them winced and the other two shaded their eyes with their hands. Only Arik seemed normal this morning, which meant he had no expression at all, and he said absolutely nothing to anyone. Ignoring him completely, Jenny looked at Friar Gregory, who seemed to be in no better condition than the others, and then she looked at Royce. "What's wrong with everyone?" she asked.

Royce helped himself to the white wheaten bread and cold meats laid out on the table, and the men reluctantly followed suit. "They're paying the price of last night's orgy of drunkenness and wenc—er, drunkenness," Royce amended, grinning.

Surprised, Jenny glanced at Friar Gregory, who'd just lifted a cup of ale to his lips. "You, too, Friar Gregory?" she said, and the poor man choked.

"I'm guilty of the former, my lady," he sputtered with chagrin, "but I plead complete innocence of the latter."

Jenny, who'd failed to note the word Royce had swiftly altered, gave the priest a puzzled look, but

Aunt Elinor piped up, "I anticipated just such a malady as this, my dear, and early this morning, I went down to the kitchens to prepare a nice restorative, only to find there was not so much as a snip of saffron to be had!"

The mention of the kitchen drew Royce's instant attention, and for the first time he seemed to study Lady Elinor with great interest. "Do you find my kitchens lacking in other items—items which might make all this—" he gestured to the rather tasteless leftover sops from last night, "more pleasing to the palate?"

"Why assuredly, your grace," she replied at once. "'Twas quite a shock to me to find such a woefully understocked kitchen. There was rosemary and thyme, but no raisins, or ginger paris, nor canel, oregano, or cloves to speak of. And I didn't see a nut in the place, except one poor, wizened chestnut! Nuts are such wonderful compliments to delicate sauces and delicious desserts—"

At the mention of "delicate sauces and delicious desserts," Aunt Elinor suddenly became the focus of undivided masculine attention. Only Arik remained disinterested, ostensibly preferring the joint of cold goose he was eating to rich sauces and desserts.

"Go on," Royce invited her, his speculative gaze riveted on her with rapt fascination. "What sorts of things would you have prepared—assuming you had the necessary ingredients, of course?"

"Well, let me think," she said, her forehead furrowed in a little frown. "It's been decades since I presided over the kitchens in my own lovely castle, but—oh yes—there were baked meat pies with crusts so light and lovely they melted in the mouth; and—take for example that hen you are eating," she said to Sir Godfrey, warming to her new position of culinary expert. "Instead of being cooked on a spit and served dried out and tough as canvas, which it is, it could have been simmered in half broth, half wine, with cloves, mace, fennel, and pepper, then laid upon a trencher so the juices made the bread ever so tasty.

"And there's so much one can do with fruits like apples, pears, and quince, but I'd need honey and almond and dates for the glazes and, canel, too, but as I said, there's little to be found of any of that in the kitchens."

Royce eyed her intently, his cold goose forgotten. "Would you be able to find the things you need here at Claymore or perhaps at the village market?"

"Much of it, one would suppose," Aunt Elinor promptly replied.

"In that case," Royce said in the tone of one issuing a royal edict, "the kitchens are now in your hands, and we will all look forward to excellent meals in future." Glancing toward Sir Albert Prisham, who was nearing the table, Royce arose and informed him, "I've just put the kitchens in the charge of Lady Elinor."

The thin steward's face was carefully blank, and he bowed politely, but the hand on the white cane clenched into a fist as he replied, "As I said, food is of little importance to me."

"Well, it ought to be exceedingly important to you, Sir Albert," Lady Elinor informed him authoritatively, "for *you've* been eating all the *wrong* things. Turnips, fatty foods, and hard cheeses ought never to be eaten by those with *gout.*"

His face hardened. "I do not have gout, madam."

"You will!" Aunt Elinor predicted gaily as she, too, arose, all eagerness to begin foraging about in the gardens and woods for her ingredients.

Ignoring her, Sir Albert said to his lord, "If you are ready to begin our tour of the estate, we can leave at once." And when Royce nodded, he added coolly, "I trust you will not find my stewardship lacking anywhere *other* than the kitchens."

Royce gave him an odd, sharp look, then he smiled

at Jennifer and pressed a polite kiss to her cheek, but in her ear he whispered, "I suggest you have a long nap, for I intend to keep you awake all night again."

Jenny felt the warm flush stealing up her cheeks as Arik arose, obviously intending to remain at Royce's side during the inspection of the estate. Royce stopped him. "Accompany Lady Elinor on her expeditions," he said, and then in an odd, meaningful voice he added, "and see that nothing untoward happens."

Arik's face froze at this flat command to play escort to an elderly lady. He stalked off, positively radiating resentment and offended dignity, while Lady Elinor trotted excitedly at his heels. "We shall have a *lovely* time, dear boy," she said enthusiastically, "although this project will take *several* days, not merely one, for we're sorely in need of ingredients for my medicinals and ointments, as well as spices for food. I shall require clove to comfort the sinews, and mace, of course! Mace prevents colic, you know, as well as body fluxes and laxes—and then there's nutmegs, which are very beneficial for the cold and a bad spleen. And I shall take special care of *your* diet in particular, for you aren't well, you know. You've a melancholy disposition—I noticed that at once . . ."

Sir Eustace glanced around at the other knights, grinning wickedly. "Lionel," he called loudly enough to be heard by the departing giant, "would you say our Arik looks 'melancholy' just now? Or would 'piqued' be a better word?"

Sir Lionel paused in his chewing and studied Arik's rigid broad back, his eyes gleaming with amusement as he replied after a moment's thoughtful consideration, "Arik is vexed."

Sir Godfrey leaned back to have a look for himself. "Aggrieved," he concluded.

"Colicky," Stefan Westmoreland added with a grin. In shared camaraderie, the men looked to Jennifer, inviting her to join in their fun, but she was spared the need to refuse because at that moment, Arik turned and blasted a dark look at his cohorts which could have pulverized rock and would easily have terrified most men. Unfortunately, it had the opposite effect on the knights, who returned his look and then burst into shouts of laughter, their mirth bouncing off the walls and echoing to the timbers, following Arik out the door.

Only young Gawin, who'd arrived just in time to see Arik and Lady Elinor depart, spoke up in Arik's behalf. Glowering at the others as he seated himself at the table, he said, "'Tis no fit job for a knight—squiring an old woman about while she picks herbs and gathers nuts. 'Tis a job for a lady's maid, not a knight."

Lionel gave the boy a good-natured cuff. "'Tis thinking like that which leaves you forever in Lady Anne's bad graces, my boy. Were you to squire her about while she picks flowers, you'd get further with the lady than you do by bristling up and trying to impress her with your manly glower—as you did last night." Turning to Jennifer, Sir Lionel said, "This halfling prefers glowering to gallantry. He thinks it's more manly, you see. And while he glowers, Roderick dances pretty attendance upon Lady Anne and wins the fair maiden's heart. Would you care to enlighten him with a lady's point of view?"

Sensitive to Gawin's youthful embarrassment, Jenny said, "I cannot speak for Lady Anne, but I, for one, did not see anything to turn a lady's head in the person of Sir Roderick."

Gratitude flashed in Gawin's eyes before he turned a smug glance upon his fellows and then dug into his somewhat tasteless fare.

Jenny spent the rest of the morning and part of the afternoon closeted with the seamstresses whom Sir Albert had recruited from the village to assist her in the preparation of garments. The steward was certainly efficient, Jenny thought as she delved down into the trunks that had been brought to her. Efficient and cold. She didn't like him at all, though she wasn't certain exactly why. Based on Agnes's words this morning, all the serfs at Claymore certainly held the thin man in high esteem. Esteem and a twinge of fear. Frustrated with her odd, emotional reactions to everyone here, and with the endless, uneasy silence of the women in the room, she studied the array of rich, colorful fabrics flowing over the bed and draped over the chairs. They lay like bright splashes of liquid jewels—ruby silks shot with gold, silver and gold brocades, amethyst velvets, sapphire taffeta shimmering as if sprinkled with diamonds, and rich, glowing satins in every shade of the spectrum from pearl to emerald to onyx. Beside them lay soft English wools in every imaginable weight and color, from brightest yellow and scarlets to shades of cream, gray, tan, and black. There were cottons from Italy, striped horizontally and vertically; richly embroidered linen for gowns and shirts, sheer, almost transparent linen for chemises and undergarments; shimmering tissues for veils; and buttery leather for gloves and slippers.

Even allowing for complete wardrobes for Royce and herself and Aunt Elinor, Jenny could scarcely conceive of ways to use so much. Overwhelmed by the magnitude of the task that lay ahead, and by her lack of imagination and knowledge of fashion, Jenny turned a little dazedly to the two enormous trunks overflowing with furs. "I think," she said aloud to Agnes as she gathered up an armful of luxurious dark sable, "that this could be used to line a cape made of that dark blue velvet for the duke."

"The *cream satin*," Agnes burst out almost desperately, then she closed her mouth and her face resumed its habitual frown.

Jenny turned to her in relieved surprise that the

woman—whom she'd just learned had been seamstress to the former mistress of Claymore—had finally offered a voluntary word. Trying to hide her lack of enthusiasm for the idea, Jenny said, "The cream satin? Truly? Do you think the duke would wear that?"

"For you," Agnes said in a choked voice, as if forced to speak by some inner fashion consciousness that cried out against the misuse of the sable, "not him."

"Oh," Jenny said, startled and pleased by the combination suggested. She gestured to the white fur. "And that?"

"The ermine to trim the sapphire brocade."

"And for the duke?" Jenny persisted, more pleased by the moment.

"The dark blue velvet, the black, and that dark brown."

"I've little knowledge of fashion," Jenny admitted, smiling with pleasure at the suggestions. "When I was young, 'twas of no interest to me at all, and later— these past years—I've lived in an abbey, and the only fashions I saw were the garments we all wore. But I comprehend already that you've a wonderful eye for how things will look, and I'll gladly take all your suggestions."

Turning, she surprised a startled look on Agnes's face, and something that might almost have been a smile, though Jenny rather suspected it was due more to her admission to having been in an abbey than her compliment to Agnes's taste. The other two seamstresses, both plain-faced young women, seemed to have thawed slightly as well. Perhaps they found her less "the enemy" if she'd been living in peace as a pious Catholic these past years.

Agnes stepped forward and began gathering up the fabrics, including the linen and cottons, which had already been singled out for specific uses. "Can you do the design for the cape and gown?" Jenny asked, bending to scoop up the cream brocade. "I haven't much idea how it should be cut, though I'll help with the cutting, of course. I'm more clever with shears than I am with a needle, I fear."

A muffled sound like a swallowed giggle escaped one of the younger women, and Jenny turned in surprise to find the seamstress called Gertrude suffused in an alarmed flush. "Did you laugh?" Jenny asked, hoping she had, regardless of the reason, for she longed desperately for some sort of female camaraderie.

Gertrude's flush deepened.

"You *did* laugh, didn't you? Was it because of what I said about being handy with shears?"

The woman's lips trembled and her eyes almost popped out as she strained to keep her nervous mirth contained. Without realizing that she was staring the poor woman down, Jenny tried to imagine what the maids could be finding funny about her skill with shears. A thought struck her, and her mouth dropped open. "You *heard* about that, did you? About what I did—to your master's things?"

If anything, the poor woman's eyes widened yet more, and she looked at her friend, swallowed a giggle, then looked back at Jennifer. "'Tis true then, my lady?" she whispered.

Suddenly the desperate deed seemed rather funny to Jenny, too. She nodded gaily. "'Twas a dreadful thing to do—worse than sewing the armholes closed on his shirts and—"

"You did *that,* too?" And before Jenny could answer, the two seamstresses let loose great, gusty shouts of laughter and began to nudge each other in the ribs, nodding with approval. Even Agnes's lips were trembling with mirth.

When the two younger women had left, Jenny went into Royce's room with Agnes to give her samples of his clothes so that she might use them to gauge his measurements for the new ones. There was something strangely intimate and oddly poignant about handling his doublets and cloaks and shirts.

He had amazingly broad shoulders, Jenny thought with a tingle of pride as she held a woolen tunic out to Agnes—and surprisingly few clothes, she noted, for a man of such wealth. What he had was of the finest quality, but it had seen much wear—a silent testimony to a man whose concerns had been with matters far weightier than clothing.

Many of his shirts were slightly frayed at the wrists, and buttons were missing from two of them. He was badly in need of a wife, Jenny thought with a whimsical little smile, to look after such details. No wonder he'd reacted with such pleasure, months ago in camp, when she'd volunteered to do mending. A sharp stab of guilt pierced her for the deliberate damage she'd done to what few articles of clothing he apparently had. Unlike the maids, she no longer found that funny, and the fact that they did puzzled and concerned her. It seemed rather odd, but then there was much about Claymore that struck her as being odd.

Now that the dam of reticence had been broken, Agnes seemed willing to talk at length about how to proceed with all the garments, and when she left, she actually smiled shyly at Jenny, but that, too, bothered Jenny as much as it pleased her.

When the maid left, Jenny stood where she was in Royce's bedchamber, her forehead knitted into a puzzled frown. Unable to come up with any answers, she flung a light mantle over her shoulders and went out to seek answers from the one person with whom she felt free to talk.

Sir Eustace, Sir Godfrey, and Sir Lionel were in the bailey, seated upon a low stone bench, their faces covered in a fine sheen of sweat, their swords dangling limply from their hands—obviously trying to recover their strength after a night of carousing and an afternoon devoted to practice with swords. "Have you seen Friar Gregory?" Jenny asked.

Sir Eustace thought he'd seen the friar talking to the wagoner, and Jenny started off in the direction he indicated, not certain exactly which of the stone buildings clustered around the vast inner perimeter of the castle wall was the one which housed the wagons. The kitchen, easily identified by its high, elaborate chimney structure, was next to the castle itself. Beside the kitchen was the store, the brewhouse, and a lovely chapel. Across the bailey from her was the smithy, where a horse was being shod and where Gawin was busily polishing Royce's shield, ignoring the stacks of armor and weapons waiting to be mended by less exalted hands than his. The wagon shed was beside it, and beyond the wagon shed were the stables, a piggery, and a large dovecote, which appeared to be empty of birds.

"Are you looking for someone, your grace?" Jenny whirled around in surprise at the sound of the friar's voice. "Yes, for you," she replied, laughing at her own jumpiness. "I wanted to ask you about . . . about things," she said, casting a cautious glance at the hundred people about the bailey who were busy at various tasks. "But not here."

"A stroll outside the gates perhaps?" Friar Gregory suggested, immediately comprehending her desire to speak where they'd not be observed or overheard.

When they approached the guards at the gate, however, Jenny received a shock. "I'm sorry, my lady," the guard said with polite implacability, "but my orders are that you cannot leave the castle except in the company of my lord."

Jenny blinked at him in disbelief. "What?"

"You cannot leave—"

"I heard you," Jenny said, controlling a sharp spurt of anger, "Do you mean I'm—I'm a *prisoner* here?"

The guard, a seasoned soldier with vast experience

in battle and none at all in dealing with noble ladies, shot an alarmed glance at the sergeant-of-the-guard, who stepped forward, bowed formally, and said, " 'Tis a question of . . . er . . . your safety, my lady."

Thinking he meant that she might not be safe in the village after what happened yesterday, Jenny made an airy motion with her hand. "Oh, but I don't intend to go further than yon trees and—"

"I'm sorry. My lord's orders were specific."

"I see," Jenny said, but she didn't see at all, and she didn't like the feeling of being a prisoner one bit. She started to turn away, then she rounded on the hapless sergeant. "Tell me something," she said in a low, ominous voice. "Is this . . . restriction . . . against *anyone* leaving the castle, or only me."

His gaze shifted to the horizon. "Only you, my lady. And your lady aunt."

Angry and humiliated, Jenny turned away, and then it occurred to her that Royce had undoubtedly sent Arik with Aunt Elinor—not as her escort, but her guard.

"I know another place," Friar Gregory suggested mildly, taking her arm and guiding her back across the wide bailey.

"I can't believe this!" Jenny whispered angrily. "I'm a *prisoner* here."

Friar Gregory made a sweeping gesture with his hand that encompassed everything in the enormous bailey. "Ah, but what a glorious prison it is," he commented with an appreciative smile. "Beautiful beyond any castle I've seen."

"A prison," Jenny informed him darkly, "is a prison!"

"It's possible," the priest said without arguing her valid point, "that your husband has reasons, other than those which you think, for wanting to keep you within the bounds of his complete protection." Without realizing where he was taking her, she'd followed him to the chapel. He opened the door and stood back for her to enter.

"What sort of reasons?" she asked as soon as they were within the dim, cool confines of the chapel.

Friar Gregory gestured to a polished oak chair and Jenny sat down. "I don't know, of course," he said. "But his grace does not strike me as a man who ever acts without good reason."

Startled, Jenny stared hard at him. "You like him, don't you, Friar?"

"Yes, but more importantly, do *you* like him?"

Jenny threw up her hands. "Until a few minutes ago, when I discovered I cannot leave the bailey, I'd have answered yes."

Friar Gregory crossed his arms, his hands and wrists concealed by the full white sleeves of his robe. "And now?" he asked, cocking one blond eyebrow, "after you've discovered it—do you still like him?"

Jennifer shot him a rueful smile and nodded helplessly.

"I'd say that answers that," he said drolly, sliding into the chair beside her. "Now then, what did you wish to speak to me about in such secret?"

Jenny bit her lip, trying to think how to explain it. "Have you noticed anything—well—odd about everyone's attitude? Not to me, but to my husband?"

"Odd in what respect?"

Jenny told him of seeing the maids cross themselves whenever Royce was near, and also mentioned she'd thought it strange when no one cheered their returning master in the village yesterday. She finished with the story of the maids' amusement when she inadvertently confirmed the rumor about damaging his clothes and blankets.

Instead of being scandalized by Jenny's destructiveness, Friar Gregory eyed her with something akin to amused admiration. "Did you really—cut up their blankets?"

She nodded uneasily.

"You're a female of amazing courage, Jennifer, and I sense you're going to need it in future dealings with your husband."

" 'Twasn't courageous at all," she admitted with a wry laugh. "I'd no idea I'd be there to see his reaction, since Brenna and I were planning to escape the very next morning."

"You shouldn't have destroyed the blankets they needed for warmth in any case, but I'm certain you realize that," he added. "Now, shall I attempt to answer your question about the villagers 'odd' reaction to their new lord?"

"Yes, please. Am I imagining all this?"

Friar Gregory abruptly stood up, wandering over to a bank of candles before an elaborate cross, and idly righted a candle that had fallen over. "You're not imagining anything. I've been here only a day, but the people here have been without a priest for more than a year, so they've been only too eager to talk to me." Frowning, he turned to her. "Are you aware that your husband laid siege to this very place eight years past?"

When Jennifer nodded, he looked relieved.

"Yes, well, have you ever seen a siege? Seen what happens?"

"No."

" 'Tis not a pretty sight to be sure. There's a saying that 'when two nobles quarrel, the poor man's thatch goes up in flames,' and 'tis true. It's not only the castle and its owners who suffer, 'tis also the villeins and serfs. Their crops are filched by defenders and attackers alike, their children are killed in the fray, and their homes are destroyed. It's not unusual for an attacker to deliberately set fire to the countryside about the castle, to destroy the fields and orchards, and even to murder the laborers, to prevent them from being enlisted by the defenders."

Although none of this was completely new to Jenny, she'd never before been at the site of a siege during it or immediately afterward. Now, however, as she sat in the peaceful little chapel that stood on land that Royce had once laid siege to, the picture took on an unpleasant clarity.

"There's no doubt that some of these things were done by your husband when he laid siege to Claymore, and, while I'm certain his motives were impersonal and that he acted in the best interest of the Crown, the peasantry cares little for noble motives when they've been impoverished by a battle in which they have nothing to gain and everything to lose."

Jenny thought of the clans in the highlands who fought and fought, without complaint about the deprivations, and shook her head in bewilderment. "It's different here."

"Unlike the members of your clans, especially the highlanders, the English peasantry does not share in the spoils of victory," Friar Gregory said, understanding her dilemma and trying to explain. "Under English law, *all* the land actually belongs to the king. The king then bestows parcels of this land upon his favored nobles as rewards for loyalty or special service. The nobles choose the sites they wish for their own demesne and then they *grant* the peasant a measure of land for himself, in return for which the vassal is expected to work two or three days a week on the lord's fields or to give manorial service at the castle. Naturally, they are also expected to contribute a measure of grain or produce from time to time.

"In times of war or famine, the lord is morally— but not legally—obliged to protect the interests of his serfs and villeins. Sometimes they do protect them, but usually only if it's of benefit to themselves."

When Friar Gregory fell silent, Jenny said slowly, "Do you mean they fear my husband won't protect them? Or do you mean they hate him for laying siege to Claymore and burning the fields?"

"Neither." Ruefully, Friar Gregory said, "The peasantry is a philosophical lot, and they expect to have their fields burned every generation or so when their lord is embroiled in a battle with one of his peers. But in the case of your husband, it's different."

"Different?" Jenny repeated. "In what way?"

"*He* has made a life of battles, and they fear that all his enemies will begin descending on Claymore one after another to exact revenge. Or that he will *invite* them here to feed his love of war."

"That's ridiculous," Jenny said.

"True, but it will take time before they realize it."

"And I thought they'd be proud because he's—he's a hero to the English."

"They are proud. And they're relieved and confident that he, unlike his predecessor, will be willing and able to defend them if the need arises. His strength, his might, is greatly to his advantage in this instance. Actually, they're completely in awe of him."

"*Terrified* of him, it would seem," Jenny said unhappily, recalling the way the maids reacted to his presence.

"That, too, and for good reason."

"They have no good reason to be terrified of him that I can see," Jenny replied with great conviction.

"Ah, but they do. Put yourself in their minds: their new lord is a man who's called the Wolf—named for a vicious, rapacious animal who attacks and devours its victims. Moreover, legend—not fact, but legend— has it that he's ruthless to anyone who crosses him. As their new lord, he also has the right to decide what taxes to levy upon them, and he will naturally sit in judgment on disputes and mete out punishment to wrongdoers, as is his right. Now then," Friar Gregory said with a pointed look, "given his reputation for mercilessness and viciousness, is he the sort of man *you'd* want deciding all this for you?"

Jenny was irate. "Oh, but he *isn't* merciless or vicious. If he were half so bad as that, my sister and I would have suffered a fate far worse than we did at his hands."

"True," the priest agreed, smiling proudly at her. "Now all that's left is for your husband to spend time with his people so that they can draw their own conclusions."

"You make it sound very simple," Jenny said, standing up and shaking out her skirts. "And I suppose it is. Hopefully, it won't take the people long to realize he—"

The door being flung open made them both turn around in time to see an expression of relief cross Royce's angry features. "No one knew where you were," he said, stalking toward Jennifer, his booted footsteps ringing ominously on the polished wooden floor of the chapel. "In future, do not disappear without letting someone know where you've gone."

Father Gregory took one look at Jennifer's indignant face and politely excused himself. As soon as the door closed behind him, Jenny snapped back, "I wasn't aware I'm to be a prisoner here."

"Why did you attempt to leave the castle?" Royce demanded, not bothering to pretend he didn't understand what she meant.

"Because I wanted to talk privately with Friar Gregory without having every serf in the bailey watching us and overhearing," Jenny informed him darkly. "Now, it's your turn to answer *my* question. *Why* am I forbidden to leave this place? Is this my home or my prison? I will *not*—"

"Your home," he interrupted, and to her complete confusion, he grinned suddenly. "You have the bluest eyes on earth," he added with a low, appreciative chuckle. "When you're angry, they're the color of wet blue velvet."

Jenny rolled her eyes in disgust, momentarily pacified by his answer that this was her home. "Wet velvet?" she repeated wryly, wrinkling her nose. *"Wet velvet."*

His white teeth flashed in a devastating grin. "No? What should I have said?"

His smile was irresistible, and Jenny fell in with his teasing mood, "Well, you *might* have said they're the color of—" she glanced at the large sapphire in the center of the crucifix "—of sapphires," she provided. "That has a nice ring to it."

"Ah, but sapphires are cold, and your eyes are warm and expressive. Am I doing better?" he chuckled when she voiced no further argument to wet velvet.

"Much," she agreed readily. "Would you care to go on?"

"Fetching for compliments?"

"Certainly."

His lips twitched with laughter. "Very well. Your eyelashes remind me of a sooty broom."

Jenny's mirth exploded in a peal of musical laughter. "A *broom!*" she chuckled merrily, shaking her head at him.

"Exactly. And your skin is white and soft and smooth. It reminds me of . . ."

"Yes?" she prompted, chuckling.

"An egg. Shall I go on?"

"Oh, please no," she muttered, laughing.

"I didn't do very well, I take it?" he asked, grinning.

"I would have thought," she admonished breathlessly, "that even the English court required a certain level of courtly behavior. Did you never spend any time at court?"

"As little as possible," he said softly, but his attention had shifted to her generous smiling lips, and without warning he gathered her into his arms, his mouth hungry and urgent on hers.

Jenny felt herself sinking into the sweet, sensual whirlpool of his desire, and with an effort she pulled her mouth from his. His eyes, already darkened with passion, gazed deeply into hers.

"You didn't tell me why," she whispered shakily, "I'm forbidden to leave the castle."

Royce's hands shifted slowly up and down her arms

as he bent his head to hers again. "It's only for a few days . . ." he answered, kissing her between each sentence, "until I'm certain there'll be no trouble . . ." he pulled her tightly to him ". . . from the outside."

Satisfied, Jenny gave herself up to the incredible pleasure of kissing him and feeling his big body harden with desire.

The sun was already starting its descent as they crossed the bailey toward the great hall. "I wonder what Aunt Elinor has in mind for supper," she said, smiling up at him.

"At the moment," Royce replied with a meaningful look, "I find my appetite whetted for something other than food. However, while we're on the subject, *is* your aunt as skilled in kitchen matters as she sounded?"

Jenny sent him a hesitant, sidewise look. "To tell you truly, I can't recall any of my family ever singing her praises in that regard. She was always praised for her curatives—wise women from all over Scotland used to go to her for ointments and preparations of all sorts. Aunt Elinor believes that proper food, properly prepared, wards off all sorts of sicknesses, and that certain foods have special curative powers."

Royce wrinkled his nose. "Medicine with meals? 'Twas not at all what I had in mind." He cast her an appraising glance, as if something had suddenly occurred to him: "Are *you* skilled in kitchen matters?"

"Not a bit," she replied cheerfully. "Scissors are my specialty."

Royce let out a sharp bark of laughter, but the sight of Sir Albert marching toward them across the bailey, his face even sterner than usual, put an end to Jenny's gaiety. The steward's cold eyes, gaunt body, and thin lips gave him a look of arrogant cruelty that made Jenny instantly uneasy. "Your grace," he said to Royce, "the perpetrator of the mud-throwing incident yesterday has been brought here." He gestured to the

355

smithy at the far end of the bailey where two guards were holding a white-faced lad between them, and a crowd of serfs had gathered. "Shall I handle this?"

"No!" Jenny burst out, unable to conquer her dislike of the man.

With a thinly veiled look of dislike the steward turned from Jennifer to Royce. "Your grace?" he asked, ignoring her.

"I've no experience with civil disciplinary measures or procedures," Royce told Jennifer, visibly hedging. They had reached the edge of the rapidly growing crowd, and Jenny turned eyes full of appeal on her husband, her mind still full of all that Friar Gregory had told her. "If you do not wish to handle it, I could do it in your stead," she volunteered anxiously. "I've seen my father sit on Judgment day times out of mind, and I know how it's done."

Royce turned to the steward. "Handle the formalities in the customary way, and my wife will decide on the punishment."

Sir Albert clenched his teeth so hard his cheek bones protruded further beneath his flesh, but he bowed in acceptance. "As you wish, your grace."

The crowd parted to let them through, and Jenny noticed that everyone on Royce's side moved back much farther than necessary to let him pass—well out of his reach.

When they reached the center of the wide circle, Sir Albert lost no time in preparing to mete out justice. With his icy gaze riveted on the stricken lad, whose outstretched arms were being held by two burly guards, Sir Albert said, "You are guilty of maliciously attacking the mistress of Claymore, a crime of the most serious nature under the laws of England—and one for which you should have received your just punishment yesterday. 'Twould have been easier on you than waiting until today to face it again," the steward finished harshly, leaving Jenny with the fleeting thought that he'd just made Royce's reprieve seem like a deliberate torment.

Tears streamed down the boy's face, and at the edge of the circle a woman, who Jenny instantly guessed must be the boy's mother, covered her face with her hands and began to weep. Her husband stood beside her, his face frozen, his eyes glazed with pain for his son.

"Do you deny it, boy?" Sir Albert snapped.

His thin shoulders shaking with silent weeping, the lad dropped his head and shook it.

"Speak up!"

"N—" he lifted his shoulder to rub away the humiliating wetness from his face on his dirty tunic. "No."

"'Tis best you don't," the steward said almost kindly, "for to die with a lie on your soul would damn you for all time."

At the word die, the boy's sobbing mother tore loose from her husband's restraining arm and hurtled herself at her son, wrapping her arms around him, cradling his head against her bosom. "Do it then and be done with it!" she cried brokenly, glaring at the sword-wielding guards. "Don't make him be scared," she sobbed, rocking the boy in her arms. "Can't you see he's scared—" she wept brokenly, her voice dropping to a shattered whisper. "Please . . . I don't want him to be . . . scared."

"Get the priest," Sir Albert snapped.

"I fail to see," Royce interrupted in an icy voice that made the boy's mother clutch her son tighter and sob harder, "why we need to have a mass said at this unlikely hour."

"Not a mass, but a confession," the steward put in, not realizing that Royce had deliberately misunderstood his reasons for sending for Friar Gregory. Turning to the boy's mother, Sir Albert said, "I assumed that your miscreant son would naturally want to avail himself of the Church's final sacraments?"

Unable to speak through her tears, the woman nodded helplessly.

"No!" Royce snapped, but the hysterical mother screamed, "Yes! 'Tis his right!—His right to have the last sacraments before he dies!"

"*If* he dies," Royce drawled coldly, " 'twill be from suffocation at your hands, madam. Step back and let the boy breathe!"

A look of tormented hope crossed her face, then wavered as she looked around at the grim faces of the crowd, and she realized no one shared her fleeting hope for a reprieve. "What are you going to do to him, milord?"

"It's not my decision," Royce replied tightly, his anger renewed as he considered the names they'd hurtled at his wife yesterday. "Inasmuch as it was my *wife* who suffered at his hands, 'twill be up to her."

Instead of being relieved, the mother clapped her hand over her mouth, her terrified eyes riveted on Jenny, and Jenny, who could no longer stand seeing the poor woman tortured with uncertainty, turned to the boy and said quickly, and not unkindly, "What is your name?"

He stared at her through tear-swollen eyes, his entire body shaking. "J-Jake. M-my l-lady."

"I see," Jenny said, thinking madly of how her father would handle such a thing. Crime could not go unpunished, she knew, for it would breed more crime and make her husband seem weak. On the other hand, harshness wasn't in order either, especially given the boy's tender years. Trying to offer the child an excuse she gently said, "Sometimes, when we're very excited about something, we do things we don't mean to do. Is that what happened when you threw the dirt? Perhaps you didn't mean to hit me with it?"

Jake swallowed twice, his Adam's apple bobbing up and down in his long, skinny neck. "I—I—" he looked at the rigid face of the duke and chose against lying—"I always hit what I aims at," he admitted miserably.

"Really?" Jenny said, stalling for time and thinking madly for some solution.

"Yes, mum," he admitted in a glum whisper. "I can hit a rabbit 'atween the eyes with a rock and kill him dead if'n he's close enough to see. I don't never miss."

"Really?" Jenny repeated, impressed. "I once tried to hit a rat from forty paces and I killed it."

"You did?" Jake asked, mutually impressed.

"Yes—well, never mind," she amended hastily at Royce's look of dry rebuke. "You didn't mean to kill *me,* did you?" she asked, and lest the foolish child admit that, she added hastily, "I mean, you did not want the sin of murder to stain your soul for all time?"

He shook his head emphatically at that.

"So it was more a matter of the excitement of the moment, wasn't it?" she urged, and to her immense relief, he finally nodded.

"And of course you were proud of your skill with throwing and perhaps even showing off a bit for everyone?"

He hesitated and then nodded jerkily.

"There, you see!" Jenny said looking around at the taut, waiting crowd and raising her voice with relieved conviction, "He meant no serious harm, and the intent is as important as the crime itself." Turning back to Jake, she said severely, "'Tis obvious some form of atonement is called for, however, and since you are so very good with your throwing arm, I think it should be put to better use. Therefore, Jake, you'll spend each morning helping the men hunt for game for the next two months. And if there's no need for fresh meat, you'll come to the castle and help me here. Excepting Sundays, of course. And if your—"

Jenny stopped in shock as the boy's weeping mother threw herself at her feet, wrapped her arms around Jenny's legs and wept, "Thank you, milady, thank you. 'Tis a saint yer are. Bless you, thank you—"

"No, don't do that," Jenny pleaded desperately when the overwrought woman picked up the hem of Jenny's skirt and kissed it. The husband, cap in hand, came to retrieve her, his eyes shining with tears as he looked at Jenny.

"If your son is needed to help in your own planting," she said to him, "he can perform his . . . er . . . penance in the afternoons instead."

"I—" he said in a choked voice, then he cleared his throat, straightened his shoulders, and said with touching dignity, "will keep yer in my prayers ever' day of my life, milady."

Smiling, Jenny said, "And my husband, too, I hope."

The man paled, but he managed to look the fierce, dark man standing beside her in the eye and to say with meek sincerity, "Aye, an' you, too, milord."

The crowd disbanded in eerie, wordless silence, casting surreptitious glances over their shoulders at Jenny, who was wondering if perhaps two months had been too long a time. On the way back into the hall, Royce was so silent that she cast him an anxious glance. "You looked surprised," she said apprehensively, "when I mentioned two months."

"I was," he admitted with ironic amusement. "For a while, I thought you were going to congratulate him on his excellent aim and invite him to join us for supper."

"You think I was too lenient?" she said with relief as he opened the heavy oaken door of the hall, standing to one side for her to precede him.

"I don't know. I've no experience in dealing with peasants and maintaining order. However, Prisham should have known better than to talk of a penalty like death. 'Twas out of the question."

"I don't like him."

"Nor do I. He was steward here before, and I kept him on. I think 'tis time to look for another to replace him."

"Soon, I hope?" Jenny urged.

"At the moment," he said, and Jenny missed the wicked gleam in his eyes, "I have more important matters on my mind."

"Really, what are they?"

"Taking you to bed and then eating supper—in that order."

"Wake up, sleepyhead—" Royce's lazy chuckle brought Jenny awake. "'Tis a glorious evening," he told her as she rolled onto her back and smiled languorously at him. "A night made for loving and now—" he nipped her ear playfully "—eating."

By the time Royce and Jenny came downstairs, many of the knights had already finished eating and the trestle tables had already been dismantled and propped neatly in their appropriate place against the wall. Only those knights who were privileged to dine at the main table on the dais seemed to want to linger over each course.

"Where is my aunt?" Jenny asked them as Royce seated her beside him at the center of the table.

Sir Eustace tipped his head to the archway on his left. "She's gone to the kitchens to instruct the cooks to prepare a greater quantity of food for tomorrow. I don't think," he added with a grin, "that she realized what monstrous appetites we'd have if offered tasty food."

Jenny looked around at the platters on the table, most of which were already empty, and breathed a silent sigh of relief. "It is—tasty then?"

"Fit for the gods," the knight exaggerated with a grin. "Ask anyone."

"Except Arik," Sir Godfrey said with a disgusted look at the giant, who had systematically stripped an entire goose down to the carcass and was finishing the last few bites.

At that moment, Aunt Elinor bustled into the hall, her face wreathed in a smile. "Good evening, your grace," she said to Royce. "Good evening, Jennifer, dear." Then she stood at the foot of the table, beaming her complete approbation at the occupants of the table, the empty platters, and even the serfs who were clearing away the debris. "Everyone seems to have had a veritable feast on my dishes."

"If we'd known you meant to come down and enliven our meal with your presence," Stefan said to his brother, "we'd have saved you more."

Royce gave his brother an ironic glance. "Really?"

"No," Stefan said cheerfully. "Here, have a tart, 'twill improve your disposition."

"I'm sure we have something tasty left in the kitchen," Aunt Elinor said, clasping her small hands in sublime pleasure at this reception of her efforts. "I'll have a look while I get my poultice. Tarts will improve anyone's disposition, except Arik's."

Casting an amused look at his fellows, Stefan added, "There's naught that can improve his disposition—not even pine boughs."

The mention of pine boughs made all the others grin as if they were sharing some particularly delicious joke, but when Jenny glanced at Royce, he seemed as perplexed as she. Aunt Elinor provided the answer as she bustled in with a serf carrying platters of hot food as well as a small bowl and cloth. "Oh my, yes, Arik and I brought back all sorts of them today. Why, by the time we returned, his arms were positively laden with lovely branches, weren't they?" she said brightly.

She paused to cast a puzzled look at the knights, who were suddenly seized with fits of strangled laughter, then she picked up the bowl and cloth from the serf's tray, and to Jenny's alarm, the elderly lady began advancing on Arik with her poultice. "You didn't have a pleasant time today, did you?" she crooned, putting the bowl beside Arik and dipping the cloth in it. "And who can blame you?"

Emanating compassion and guilt, she glanced at Jenny and said sadly, "Arik and I encountered the most *evil-natured* spider I've ever had the misfortune to meet!"

Arik's expression turned thunderous as he watched her dip the cloth in the bowl from the corners of his narrowed eyes, but Aunt Elinor continued blithely, "The vile little creature bit poor Arik when he did nothing at all to provoke it except to stand beneath the tree where it had its web. Although," she added, turning to the glowering giant and shaking her finger at him as if he were six years old, "I think 'twas very naughty of you to retaliate the way you did."

Pausing to dip the cloth into the bowl, she told him sternly, "I could understand why you smashed the *web* with your fist, but I do not think 'twas sensible to blame the *tree* as well and cut it down with your axe!" She tossed a bewildered look at Sir Godfrey, whose shoulders were shaking with mirth, and then at Sir Eustace, whose shoulders were also rocking and whose blond hair was nearly in his trencher as he tried to hide his laughing face. Only Gawin looked truly alarmed as Aunt Elinor said, "Here, dear boy, let me just dab this on your fac—"

"NO!" Arik's meaty fist slammed on the heavy oaken table, making the platters dance. Shoving away from the table, he stalked out of the hall, his body rigid with wrath.

Stricken, Aunt Elinor watched him march out, then she turned to the occupants of the table and sorrowfully said, "He'd not be so very testy, I'm sure, if only he'd *eat* according to my suggestions. 'Twould solve his bow—his *digestive*," she amended hastily for the sake of the diners, "problems. Which I thought I explained to him very clearly today."

After supper Royce fell into a discussion of manly topics with his knights—topics that ranged from how many additional men should be assigned to help the castle armorer with his added burden of repairing the helmets and chain mail of the men-at-arms who'd returned with Royce, to whether or not the big catapult on the battlement had an adequate supply of stones laid by.

Jenny listened attentively, loving the quiet authority with which Royce spoke and generally enjoying the unexpected pleasure of being part of a family of her own. She was thinking how warm it felt and how strange, when Royce called a halt to the discussion of catapults and turned to her with an apologetic smile. "Shall we walk outside? 'Tis a pleasant night for October—much too pleasant to spend it discussing things that must seem very boring to you."

"I haven't been bored," Jenny said softly, unconsciously smiling into his eyes.

"Who would have guessed," he teased huskily, "that the selfsame woman who once tried to carve my initials on my face with my own knife would be so agreeable a wife?" Without waiting for an answer, Royce turned to the knights as he politely helped Jennifer arise. After reminding them to assemble in the bailey after breakfast for a practice session at the quintain, Royce escorted Jennifer from the hall.

After they left, Sir Eustace turned to the others and said with a grin, "Have you ever known Royce to indulge in moonlight strolls before?"

"Not unless he was anticipating a nocturnal visit from the enemy," laughed Sir Lionel.

Sir Godfrey, the eldest of the group, didn't smile. "He's been expecting one since we arrived here."

Chapter Twenty-Two

W here are we going?" Jenny asked.

"Up there to see the view," Royce said, pointing to the steep steps that led up to the wall-walk, a wide stone ledge adjoining the castle wall that ran through all twelve of the towers, enabling the guards to patrol the entire perimeter of the castle.

Trying to ignore the guards, who were posted at regular intervals along the walk, Jenny looked out across the moonlit valley, the breeze blowing her hair about her shoulders. " 'Tis beautiful up here," she said softly, turning to him. "Claymore is beautiful." After a minute, she said, "It seems invulnerable. I can't imagine how you ever managed to seize it. These walls are so high and the stone so smooth. How did you manage to scale over them?"

His brows lifted over amused gray eyes. "I didn't scale them. I tunneled *under* them, shored them up with beams and then set fires in the tunnels. When the beams collapsed, so did the wall."

Jenny's mouth opened in shock, and then she remembered something: "I heard you did that at Castle Glenkenny. It sounds dangerous in the extreme."

"It is."

"Then why did you do it?"

Brushing a stray lock off her cheek, Royce said lightly, "Because I can't fly, which was the only other way to get into this bailey."

"Then 'twould seem," she remarked thoughtfully, "someone else could get in here the same way."

"They could try," he said with a grin, "but 'twould be foolhardy. Just beyond us, a few yards from the walls, I had a series of tunnels constructed, ones that will collapse on invaders should any of them decide to try what I did. When I rebuilt this place," he said, putting his arm around her waist and drawing her against his side, "I tried to redesign it in a way that even *I* couldn't breach it. Eight years ago, these walls were not of such smooth stone as they are now." He nodded at the turrets that rose high above the walls at regular intervals. "And those towers were all square. Now they're round."

"Why?" Jenny asked, intrigued.

"Because," he said, pausing to brush a warm kiss upon her forehead, "round towers have no nice corners for men to use to climb them. Square ones, like those you had at Merrick, are especially easy to climb, as you well know . . ." Jenny opened her mouth to issue a deserved reprimand for bringing up such a subject, only to find herself being kissed. "If the enemy can't climb the walls or tunnel beneath them," he murmured against her lips, as he kissed her again, "the only other thing to do is to try to set fire to us. Which is why," he whispered as he drew her against him, "all the buildings in the bailey now have tile roofs, instead of thatch."

Breathless from his kisses, Jenny leaned back in his arms. "You're very thorough, my lord," she teased meaningfully.

An answering smile drifted across his tanned face. "What is mine, I intend to keep."

His words reminded her of things of her own she had not been able to keep—things that should have belonged to their children.

"What's wrong?" Royce asked, watching her expression turn somber.

Jenny shrugged and lightly said, "I was merely thinking that it's natural you'd want children, and—"

Tipping her face up to his, Royce said quietly, "I want *your* children." She waited, praying he would say 'I love you,' and when he didn't she tried to tell herself that what he *had* said was nearly as good as 'I love you.'

"I had a great many things—jewels and things—" she continued wistfully, "things of my mother's that by rights should have belonged to our children. I doubt my father would give them to me now. I wasn't dowerless you know, if you read the betrothal contract."

"Madam," he said dryly, "you're scarcely dowerless now."

Feeling truly belittled by the sudden realization that she'd come to her marriage with only the soiled garments she wore, she turned around in his arms, gazing out across the valley. "I have nothing. I came to you with less than the lowest serf, without so much as a single sheep as dowry."

"No sheep," he agreed dryly. "Your only possession is the most beautiful little estate in all England, called Grand Oak—because of the giant oaks that guard its gates." He saw her startled look and added with a wry smile, "Henry gave it to you as a bride gift. 'Twill be your dower house."

"How . . . how nice . . . of him," Jenny said, finding it extremely difficult to speak so of the English king.

Royce shot her a sardonic, sidewise glance. "He took it from *me.*"

"Oh," Jenny said, nonplused. "Why?"

" 'Twas a forfeit levied on me for actions pertaining to a certain young Scottish girl captured from an abbey."

"I'm not so certain we were on the grounds of the abbey."

"According to the abbess, you were."

"Truly?" she asked, but Royce didn't hear her. Suddenly he was staring intently at the valley, his body taut and alert.

"Is something wrong?" Jenny asked, peering worriedly in the direction of his gaze, unable to see a single thing out of the ordinary.

"I think," he said coolly as he stared out at a nearly invisible speck of light far beyond the village, "our pleasant evening is about to be interrupted. We have guests." Six more tiny pinpoints of light bobbed into view, then a dozen more and then twice that many. "At least a hundred, possibly more. Mounted."

"Guest—" Jenny began, but her voice was drowned out as a guard far off to her right suddenly raised his trumpet and blew an earsplitting blast on his clarion. Twenty-five other guards, stationed at intervals along the wall-walk, turned in his direction, and a moment later, after confirming what he saw, they lifted their own clarions and suddenly the peaceful night was split with the ominous blasts of trumpets. Within seconds men-at-arms were pouring into the bailey with weapons at the ready, some of them dressing as they ran. Frantically, Jenny turned to Royce. "What's wrong? Are they enemies?"

"I'd say they're a contingent from Merrick."

Sir Godfrey and Sir Stefan bolted up the steps of the wall-walk, strapping on long swords, and Jenny's whole body began to tremble. Swords. Bloodshed.

Royce turned to issue orders to the captain-at-arms, and when he turned back to Jennifer, she was staring out at the flickering lights, her fist pressed to her mouth.

"Jennifer," he said gently, but the eyes she raised to

him were wild with terror, and he realized at once he had to get her away from the scene of what obviously looked to her to be preparations for a full-scale battle.

Hundreds of torches were being lit in the bailey and on the castle wall, and the whole scene was already aglow with eerie yellow daylight as Royce took her arm and led her, down the steps and into the hall.

Closing the door to his bedchamber, he turned to her, and she looked at him in numb anguish. "Should you not be out there—with your men?"

"No. My men have been through this drill a thousand times." Putting his hands on her rigid shoulders, he said to her in a calm, firm voice, "Jennifer, listen to me. My men have orders not to attack without a command from me personally." She shuddered as if the word "attack" had been all she heard, and Royce gave her a slight shake. *"Listen* to me," he commanded sharply. "I had men posted in the woods near the road. In a few minutes, I'll know exactly how large a group is approaching. I don't think it's an army unless your father is a greater fool than I think he is. Moreover, he hasn't had time to put out a call-to-arms to your hotheaded Scotsmen and raise a fully equipped army. I think it's merely a group from Merrick, including Lord Hastings, Lord Dugal, and your father. Considering the awkward position I put him in when I snatched you from Merrick, it's natural he'd want to bluster in here and put up a pretence of innocent outrage. Moreover, he'll save a little face if he's able to gain entrance to Claymore even if it takes a flag of truce and an Englishman from the court of the Star Chamber to get him in here."

"And if it is a peaceful group," she cried frantically, "what are you going to do?"

"I'm going to lower the drawbridge and invite them in," he said dryly.

Her fingers bit into the muscles of his upper arms. "Please—don't hurt them—"

"Jennifer—" he said tightly, but she wrapped her arms around him, pressing herself against him. "Don't *hurt* them," she cried hysterically. "You gave me your word! I'll do anything you ask of me . . . anything . . . but don't hurt them."

Exasperated, Royce moved her away from him and grasped her chin. "Jennifer, the only wound that's going to be inflicted tonight is to my pride. It galls me beyond measure to have to raise my gate, lower the drawbridge, and let your father strut into my hall."

"You didn't care about *his* pride," Jenny argued wildly, "when you breached Merrick's tower and took me from there. How do you think that made *him* feel. Is your own pride so great you can't put it aside, just for a few hours, just this *once?*"

"No."

The single word, spoken with such quiet conviction, finally snapped Jenny from her mindless panic. Drawing a long, steadying breath, she leaned her forehead against his chest and nodded. "I know you won't harm my family. You gave me your word."

"Yes," he said reassuringly, gathering her into his arms for a swift kiss. Turning to the door, he paused with his hand upon the handle. "Stay in here, unless I send for you," he ordered implacably. "I've sent for the friar to bear witness that we're well and truly married, but I imagine the emissaries from our kings will want to see you to ascertain that you're safe and unharmed."

"Very well," she agreed and quickly added, "Father will be in a dreadful mood, but William is gentle and seldom loses his temper. I'd like to see him before they leave—to talk to him and send a message to Brenna. Will you let him come up?"

He nodded. "If it seems wise, I will."

Masculine voices raised in anger thundered in the hall, carrying to the bed chamber, where Jenny paced, waiting, listening, praying. Her father's voice, blustering and furious, was joined by the angry voices of her brothers, as well as Lord Hastings, and Lord Dugal. Royce's deep voice, hard and authoritative, rose above the din, and then there was silence . . . eerie, foreboding silence.

Knowing she could observe what was happening if she left the bedchamber and went out onto the gallery, Jenny walked to the door and then hesitated. Royce had given her his oath not to harm any of her family, and all he had asked of her in return was that she remain in here. It seemed wrong not to honor his wish.

Snatching her hand away from the door, Jenny turned away from it, then she hesitated again. She could, however, honor his wish and still be better able to hear by simply opening the door a bit without leaving the bechamber. Cautiously, she turned the handle, opening the door a scant two inches . . .

"Friar Gregory has verified that the couple is wed," Lord Hastings, the English emissary from King Henry's court was saying. " 'Twould seem Claymore adhered to the letter of the agreement, if not precisely to the spirit of it, while you, Lord Merrick, by plotting to hide your daughter away from her rightful husband, broke faith with the agreement both in spirit and in fact."

The Scottish emissary mumbled something soothing and conciliatory, but Jennifer's father's voice rose in fury. "You English swine! My daughter *chose* to enter a cloister, she *pleaded* with me to send her away. She was prepard to make the marriage, but 'twas her holy *right* to choose God as her lord if she wished. No king can deny her the right to pledge herself to a life of seclusion and devotion to God, and you know it! Bring her down here," he shouted. "She'll tell you 'twas her own choice!"

His words slashed Jenny's heart like a jagged sword. Evidently, he really had intended to lock her away for the rest of her life, and without ever telling her what he meant to do; he'd been willing to sacrifice her life for revenge against his enemy. When it came down to it, he had more hatred for a stranger than he had love for her.

"Bring her down here! She'll tell you I speak the truth!" her father thundered. "I demand she be brought down! The Barbarian objects because he knows his wife loathes him and that she'll confirm what I say."

Royce's deep voice was filled with such calm conviction that Jenny felt tenderness blend with the pain of her father's betrayal inside of her. "Jennifer has told me the truth, and the truth is that she never collaborated in your scheme. If you have any feeling for her at all, you will not force her to come down here and call you a liar to your face."

"He's the liar!" Malcolm bellowed. "Jennifer will prove it!"

"I regret the need to cause your wife unhappiness," Lord Hastings interrupted, "but both Lord Dugal and I agree the only way to get to the bottom of this is to hear what she herself has to say. No, your grace," he said instantly, "under the circumstances, 'twould be best if Lord Dugal and I escort the lady down here— to . . . er . . . prevent the claim of coercion by either party. Kindly direct Lord Dugal and me to her chamber . . ."

Jenny closed the door and slumped against it, laying her cheek against the iron banding, feeling as if she was being torn asunder.

The hall was filled with tension and hostility as she walked forward between her two escorts. Men-at-arms from Merrick, Claymore, and those from King Henry and King James lined the walls. Near the fireplace, Jennifer's father and her brothers stood across from Royce, and all of them were watching her.

"Your grace—" Lord Hastings began, turning to Jennifer, but her father interrupted impatiently. "My dear child," he said, "Tell these idiots that 'twas your *wish* to flee to the solace of a cloister, rather than endure life with this . . . this *bastard.* Tell them you asked me, *begged* me to let you do it, that you *knew*—"

"I knew *nothing,*" Jenny cried, unable to endure the feigned look of honesty and love on his face. "Nothing!"

Jenny saw Royce start forward, saw the look of quiet reassurance in his gray eyes, but her father wasn't finished.

"Hold!" he roared, advancing on Jennifer with a mixture of fury and disbelief on his face. "What do you mean, you knew nothing of this? The night I told you you were to wed this beast, you begged me to let you go back to Belkirk abbey." Jenny paled as her forgotten plea, spoken in terror and dismissed as impossible by her father, screamed through her mind . . . *I'll go back to the abbey, or to my Aunt Elinor, or anywhere you say . . .*

"I—I did say that," she stammered, her gaze flying to Royce's face, watching it harden into a mask of icy wrath.

"There! That proves it," her father shouted.

Jenny felt Lord Hastings take her arm, but she jerked it away. "No, please, listen to me," she cried, her gaze riveted on the drumming pulse in Royce's cheek and the glittering violence in his eyes. "Listen to me," she begged him. "I did say that to my father. I'd forgotten I said it because—" her head jerked to her father, "because *you* wouldn't hear of it. But I never, *never* agreed to any plan to wed him first, and *then* flee to a convent. Tell him," she cried. "Tell him I never agreed."

"Jennifer," her father said, looking at her with bitterness and contempt, "You agreed when you begged me to let you go to Belkirk. I merely chose a safer, more distant abbey for you. There was never any doubt in my mind that you would have to first abide by our king's command that you wed the swine.

You knew that, too. That is why I originally refused your request."

Jenny looked from her father's accusing face to Royce's granite one, and she knew a feeling of panicked defeat that surpassed anything she'd ever felt. Turning, she picked up her skirts and began walking slowly toward the dais as if in a nightmare.

Behind her, Lord Hastings cleared his throat and said to her father and Royce, " 'Twould seem this has been a case of grave misunderstandings between all the parties. If you will be so kind as to provide us with lodgings for the night in the gatehouse, Claymore, we'll depart in the morn."

Booted feet hit the stone floor as everyone filed out. Jenny was nearly at the top of the steps when shouts and a bellow from her father made her blood freeze: "BASTARD! You've *killed* him! I'll kill—" The sound of Jenny's thundering heart drowned out everything as she turned and started running down the stairs. As she raced past the table, she saw men bending over something near the door, and Royce, her father, and Malcolm being held at sword point.

And then the men huddled near the door slowly stood up and stepped back . . .

William was lying on the floor with a dagger hilt protruding from his chest, a pool of blood spreading out around him. Jenny's scream split the air as she raced to the prone figure. *"William!"*

Throwing herself down beside him, moaning his name, she felt wildly for a pulse, but there was none, and her hands rushed over his arms and his face. "William, oh, *please*—" she cried brokenly, imploring him not to be dead. "William, please *don't!* William—" Jenny's eyes riveted on the dagger, on the figure of a wolf etched in its hilt.

"Arrest the bastard!" her father shouted behind her, trying to lunge at Royce while being restrained by the king's man.

Lord Hastings said sharply, "Your son's dagger is

on the floor. He must have drawn it. There's no arrest to be made. Unhand Claymore," he snapped at his men.

Royce came to stand beside her, "Jenny—" he began tautly, but she whirled on her heels like a dervish, and when she came up in a crouch, she held William's dagger in her hand.

"You *killed* him!" she hissed, her eyes alive with pain and tears and fury as she slowly straightened.

This time Royce did not underestimate her ability or her intent. With his eyes riveted to hers, he watched for the moment when she would strike. "Drop the dagger," he said quietly.

She raised it higher, aimed at his heart, and cried, "You *killed* my *brother*." The dagger flashed through the air, and Royce caught her wrist in a vice grip, twisting the dagger free and sending it spinning to the floor, but even then, he had all he could do to restrain her.

Wild with grief and pain, she launched herself at him, striking at his chest with her fists when he jerked her tightly against him. "You devil!" she screamed hysterically as they carried her brother out. "Devil, devil, *devil!*"

"Listen to me!" Royce ordered tautly, grabbing her wrists. The eyes she raised to his were sparkling with hatred and glazed with tears she could not shed. "I told him to stay behind if he wanted to talk to you." Royce let go of her wrists as he finished harshly, "When I started to turn back to take him upstairs, he was reaching for his dagger."

Jennifer's hand crashed into the side of his face as she slapped him with all her strength. "Liar!" she hissed, her chest heaving. "You wanted vengeance because you believed I conspired with my father! I saw it on your face. You wanted vengeance and you killed the first person who got in your way!"

"I tell you, he drew his dagger!" Royce bit out, but instead of calming her, that enraged her—and with good reason: *"I drew a dagger on you, too,"* she cried furiously, "but you took it away as easily as a child's toy! William was half your size, but you didn't take his away, you *murdered* him!"

"Jennifer—"

"You're an *animal!*" she whispered, looking at him as if he was obscene.

White-faced with guilt and remorse, Royce tried once more to convince her. "I swear to you on my word, I—"

"Your *word!*" she hissed contemptuously. "The last time you gave me your *word* 'twas that you'd not harm my family!"

Her second slap crashed against his cheek with enough force to snap his head sideways.

He let her go, and when the door to her chamber slammed, Royce walked over to the fire. Propping his booted foot on a log, he hooked his thumbs into the back of his belt and stared down into the flames, while doubts about her brother's intent began to hammer at him.

It had happened so quickly; William had been close behind him as Royce stood near the door watching his uninvited guests depart. From the corner of his eye, Royce had glimpsed a dagger sliding out of its sheath, and his reaction had been instinctive. Had there been time to think—or had William not been so damned close to his back—he would have reacted with less instinct and more caution.

Now, however, in retrospect, he remembered perfectly well that he'd sized the young man up before inviting him to remain to see Jenny, and that he'd thought him nonaggressive.

Lifting his hand, Royce pressed his thumb and forefinger against the bridge of his nose and closed his eyes, but he could not shut out the truth: either his original instincts about William not posing a threat had been wrong, or else he'd just slain a young man who'd been drawing his dagger merely as a precaution in case Royce was tricking him.

Royce's doubt erupted into almost unbearable guilt. He'd been judging men and the danger they represented to him for thirteen years, and he'd never been wrong. Tonight he'd judged William harmless.

Chapter Twenty-Three

In the sennight that followed, Royce found himself confronted with the first wall he could not find a way to breech—the wall of ice Jennifer had built to insulate herself from him.

The night before last, he'd gone to her, thinking that if he made love to her, passion might thaw her. It hadn't worked. She hadn't fought him, she had simply turned her face away from him and closed her eyes. When he left her bed, he'd felt like the animal she'd called him. Last night, in fury and frustration, he'd tried to confront her about the matter of William, looking for a quarrel—thinking that the heat of anger might succeed where bedding her had not. But Jennifer was past the point of quarreling; in aloof silence she walked into her bedchamber and bolted the door.

Now, seated beside her at supper, he glanced at her, but could think of nothing to say to her or to anyone else. Not that he needed to speak, for his knights were so conscious of the silence between Royce and Jennifer that they were trying to cover it with forced joviality. In fact, the only people at the table who seemed to be unaware of the atmosphere were Lady Elinor and Arik.

"I see you all enjoyed my venison stew," Lady Elinor said, beaming at the empty trenchers and platters, seemingly oblivious to the fact that Jennifer and Royce had eaten very little. Her smile drooped, however, as she looked at Arik, who had just devoured another goose. "Except you, dear boy," she said with a sigh. "You are the very *last* person who should be eating goose! 'Twill only complicate your problem, you know, which is exactly what I told you. I made that nice venison stew for *you*, and you didn't touch it."

"Pay no heed to that, my lady," Sir Godfrey said, shoving his trencher aside and patting his flat stomach. "*We* ate it, and 'twas delicious!"

"Delicious," proclaimed Sir Eustace enthusiastically.

"Wonderful," boomed Sir Lionel.

"Superb," Stefan Westmoreland agreed heartily with a worried glance at his brother.

Only Arik kept silent, because Arik always kept silent.

The moment Lady Elinor left the table, however, Godfrey rounded on Arik in anger. "The least you could have done was taste it. She made it particularly for you."

Very slowly, Arik laid down the goose leg and turned his huge head to Godfrey, his blue eyes so cold that Jenny unknowingly drew in a long breath and held it, waiting for some sort of physical explosion.

"Pay him no heed, Lady Jennifer," Godfrey said, noticing her distress.

After supper, Royce left the hall and needlessly spent an hour talking with the sergeant-of-the-guard. When he returned, Jennifer was seated near the fire amidst his knights, her profile turned to him. The topic of discussion was evidently Gawin's obsession with his Lady Anne, and Royce breathed a sigh of relief when he noticed the slight smile touching Jennifer's lips. It was the first time she'd smiled in seven days. Rather than join the group and risk spoiling her mood, Royce leaned his shoulder against a stone arch, well out of her sight, and signaled to a serf to bring him a tankard of ale.

"Were I a knight," Gawin was explaining to her, leaning slightly forward, his youthful face taut with longing for his Lady Anne, "I would challenge Roderick to meet me in the village jousting matches!"

"Excellent," Sir Godfrey joked, "then Lady Anne could weep over your dead body, after Roderick finished with you."

"Roderick is no stronger than I!" Gawin said fiercely.

"What jousting matches do you mean?" Jennifer asked, trying to distract him a little from the helpless antagonism he felt for Sir Roderick.

"'Tis an annual affair held here in the valley each year after the crops are in. Knights come from far and wide—well, from as far as four or five days' journey, to participate in it.

"Oh, I see," she said, though she'd already heard much excited talk about the lists from the serfs. "And will all of you participate in them?"

"We will," Stefan Westmoreland answered, and then anticipating her unspoken question, he added quietly, "Royce will not. He thinks them pointless."

Jenny's pulse jumped at the mention of his name. Even now, after what he'd done, the sight of Royce's rough-hewn face made her heart cry out for him. Last night she'd laid awake till dawn, fighting the stupid urge to go to him and ask him to somehow ease the ache in her heart. How foolish to yearn to ask the very person who'd caused the pain to heal it, yet even at supper tonight, when his sleeve had touched her arm, she had wanted to turn into his arms and weep.

"Perhaps Lady Jennifer or Lady Elinor," Eustace said, pulling Jennifer out of her dismal reverie, "could suggest something less hazardous to your life as a way to win Lady Anne's heart—other than a joust with Roderick?" Raising his brows, he turned to Jennifer.

"Well, let me think for a minute first," Jenny replied, relieved to have something to concentrate on besides her brother's death and her husband's vicious betrayal. "Aunt Elinor, do you have any ideas?"

Aunt Elinor laid aside her embroidery, tipped her head to the side, and provided helpfully, "I know! In my day there was a custom of long standing that impressed *me* very much when I was a maiden."

"Really, ma'am?" Gawin said. "What would I do?"

"Well," she said, smiling with the memory. "You would ride up to the gate of Lady Anne's castle and shout to all within that she is the fairest maiden in all the land."

"What good would that do?" Gawin asked, perplexed.

"Then," Aunt Elinor explained, "you would challenge any knight in the castle who disagreed to come out and meet you. Naturally, several of them would have to meet your challenge—in order to save face with *their* ladies. And," she finished delightedly, "those knights whom you vanquished would then have to go to Lady Anne and kneel and say, 'I submit to your grace and beauty!'"

"Oh, Aunt Elinor," Jenny chuckled, "did they really do that in your day?"

"Most assuredly! Why, 'twas the custom until very recently."

"And I've no doubt," Stefan Westmoreland said gallantly, "that a great many knights were vanquished by your stalwart suitors, my lady, and sent to kneel before you."

"What a pretty speech!" said Lady Elinor approvingly, "I thank you. And it proves," she added to Gawin, "that chivalry isn't falling by the wayside one bit!"

"It won't help me, however," Gawin sighed. "Until

I myself am knighted, I cannot challenge any knight. Roderick would laugh in my face if I dared, and who could blame him?"

"Perhaps something gentler than fighting would win your lady's heart," Jenny put in sympathetically.

Royce listened more attentively, hoping for some clue as to how to soften *her* heart.

"Like what, my lady?" asked Gawin.

"Well, there's music and songs . . ."

Royce's eyes narrowed in discouragement at the thought of having to sing to Jenny. His deep baritone voice would surely bring every hound for miles to yap and nip at his heels.

"You did learn to play a lute, or some instrument, when you were a page, did you not?" Jenny was asking Gawin.

"No, my lady," Gawin confessed.

"Really?" said Jenny, surprised. "I thought 'twas part of a page's training to learn to play an instrument."

"I was sent to Royce as a page," Gawin advised her proudly, "not the castle of a married lord and lady. And Royce says that a lute is as useless in battle as a hilt with no sword—unless I mean to swing it around over my head and launch it at my opponent."

Eustace sent him an ominous look for further damning Royce in Jennifer's eyes, but Gawin was too intent on the problem of Lady Anne to notice. "What else might I do to win her?" Gawin asked.

"I have it," Jennifer said. "Poetry! You could call upon her and—and recite a poem to her—one you particularly like."

Royce frowned, trying to remember poems, but the only one he could recall went:

> There was a young lass named May
> Ever good for a toss in the hay . . .

Gawin's face fell and he shook his head. "I don't believe I know any poems—Yes! Royce told me one once. It went, "There was a young lass named—"

"*Gawin!*" Royce snapped before he could catch himself, and Jennifer's face froze at the sound of his voice. More quietly, Royce said, "That's not the—er—sort of rhyme Lady Jennifer had in mind."

"Well then, what should I do?" Gawin said. With hope that his idol would think of some more manly way of impressing the lady, he asked Royce, "What did *you* do the first time you wished to impress a lady—or were you already a knight and could show her your mettle on the field of honor?"

With no hope of being able to further observe Jennifer in secret, Royce walked over to the group and propped his shoulder against the chimney piece, standing beside her. "I was not yet a knight," he replied ironically, accepting the tankard of ale the serf handed him.

Jennifer caught the look of amusement that passed from Stefan to Royce and was spared having to wonder about the details by Gawin who insisted, "How old were you?"

"Eight, as I recall."

"What did you do to impress her?"

"I . . . er . . . staged a contest with Stefan and Godfrey so that I could dazzle the maiden with a skill of which I was particularly proud at the time."

"What sort of contest?" Lady Elinor asked, thoroughly engrossed.

"A *spitting* contest," Royce replied succinctly, watching Jenny's profile, wondering if she were smiling at his youthful foibles.

"Did you win?" Eustace laughed.

"Certainly," Royce declared dryly. "I could spit further than any lad in England at the time. Besides," he added, "I had already taken the precaution of bribing Stefan and Godfrey."

"I think I'll retire now," Jenny said politely as she stood.

Royce abruptly decided to tell all of them the news, rather than keep it from Jennifer now that the subject had already arisen. "Jennifer," he said, matching her reserved courtesy, "the annual jousting matches that take place here have been turned into a full-fledged tournament this year. In the spirit of the new truce between our two countries, Henry and James have decided the Scots will be invited to participate." Unlike a joust, which was a contest of skill between two knights, a tournament was a mock battle, with both sides charging each other from opposite ends of the field, wielding weapons—although of limited types and sizes. Even without virulent hatred between the combatants, tournaments were so dangerous that four hundred years before, the popes had managed to have them banned for nearly two centuries.

"A messenger came today from Henry confirming the changes," Royce added. When she continued to regard him with polite lack of interest, Royce added pointedly, "The decision was made by our kings at the same time the truce was signed." Not until he added, "And I *will* be riding in them," did she seem to comprehend the import of what he was saying. When she did, she looked at him with contempt, then she turned her back on him and left the hall. Royce watched her walk away and, in sheer frustration, he got up and went after her, catching her just as she opened the door to her bedchamber.

He held the door open for her and followed her inside, closing it behind him. In front of his knights, she'd kept her silence, but now, in private, she turned on him with a bitterness that nearly surpassed the night of William's death: "I gather the knights from the south of Scotland will be attending this little soirée?"

"Yes," he said tightly.

"And it's no longer to be a joust? It's a *tournament* now?" she added. "And of course, that's why *you're* going to ride in it?"

"I'm going to do it because I've been commanded to do it!"

The anger drained from her face, leaving it as white as parchment and just as hopeless. She shrugged. "I have another brother—I don't love him as well as I loved William, but he should at least give you a little more sport before you kill him. He's closer to your size." Her chin was trembling and her eyes were shining with tears. "And then there's my father—he's older than you, but quite skilled as a knight. His death will amuse you. I hope," she said brokenly, "you'll find it in your heart—find it *possible,*" she amended, making it clear she didn't think he had a heart, "not to murder my sister. *She's* all I have left."

Knowing she didn't want him to touch her, Royce still could not stop himself from pulling her into his arms. When she stiffened but didn't struggle, he cupped her head, holding it pressed to his chest, her hair like crushed satin in his hand. Hoarsely, he said, "Jenny, please, *please* don't do this! Don't suffer so. Cry, for God's sake. Scream at me again, but don't look at me like a murderer."

And then he knew.

He knew exactly why he loved her, and when it had happened: his mind snapped back to the glade, when an angel dressed like a page had looked up at him with shining blue eyes and softly told him, *The things they say about you, the things they say you've done—they aren't true. I don't believe it.*

Now she believed *everything* about him, and with good reason. And knowing it hurt a thousand times more than any wound Royce had ever received.

"If you cry," he whispered, stroking her shining hair, "you'll feel better." But he knew instinctively what he suggested was impossible. She'd been through so much, and held her tears back for so long, that

Royce doubted that anything could force her to shed them. She had not cried when she spoke of her dead friend, Becky, nor had she wept over William's death. A fourteen-year-old girl with enough courage and spirit to confront her armed brother on the field of honor would not cry for her husband whom she hated. Not when she didn't cry for her friend or even her brother. "I know you won't believe this," he whispered achingly, "but I *will* keep my word. I will not hurt your family, nor any member of your clan at the tournament. I swear it."

"Please let go of me," she said in a suffocated voice.

He couldn't help it, his arms tightened. "Jenny," he whispered, and Jenny wanted to die because, even now, she loved the sound of her name on his lips.

"Don't call me that again," she said, hoarsely.

Royce drew a long, painful breath. "Would it help if I said I love you?"

She jerked free, but there was no anger on her face. "Whom are you trying to help?"

Royce's arms fell to his sides. "You're right," he agreed.

Jenny left the chapel two days later after speaking to Friar Gregory, who'd agreed to remain at Claymore until a permanent priest could be located. Royce's knights were practicing, as they did early each morning, at the skills that kept them fit for battle. Hour after hour, they worked their horses, leaping them over ditches and piles of sandbags, springing into the saddle without touching the stirrups. The rest of the time outdoors they spent practicing at the quintain—a post set into the ground with a crossbar so well-balanced that it could be set whirling with a light touch of the hand. On one end of the crossbar hung a suit of armor with a shield. On the other a long, very heavy sandbag. One after the other, over and over again, each knight would back his horse to the far end of the bailey and charge full-tilt, from different angles each time, at the "knight" on the cross bar. Unless their lance struck the "knight" precisely on the breast, the crossbar whirled and the rider was dealt a mighty blow from the sandbag—which never missed *its* target.

Occasionally, all the knights missed, depending upon the angle and the obstacles erected in front of the quintain. All the knights, *except* her husband, Jenny had noticed. Unlike the other knights, Royce spent less time at the quintain and more time working with Zeus, as he was now. From the corner of her eye, she watched Royce at the far end of the bailey, his bare, heavily muscled shoulders glinting in the sun as he took the destrier over increasingly higher jumps, then galloped him flat-out while twisting the horse into the tight figure of an eight.

In the past, she'd been able to ignore this daily practice, but with the tournament looming ahead, what had seemed like mere exercise before, now became a deadly skill which Royce's men were perfecting to use against their opponents. So absorbed was she in surreptitiously watching her husband that she never heard Godfrey come up beside her. "Zeus," he commented, following the direction of her sidewise gaze, "is not yet the horse his sire was. He lacks a full year of training."

Jenny had jumped at his first words, and now she said, "He—he looks magnificent to me."

"Aye, he does," Godfrey agreed. "But watch Royce's knee—there, did you see how he had to move it forward before Zeus knew to turn? Thor would have made that turn with a pressure no greater than this . . ." Reaching out, Godfrey very lightly pressed Jenny's arm with his thumb. Guilt shot through Jenny at the thought of the splendid horse whose death she'd caused; Godfrey's next words didn't ease it: "In battle, having to guide your horse as firmly as Royce will have to do in the tournament, could cost your life."

Eustace and Gawin, who'd just dismounted, came

over to join them, and Gawin—having heard Godfrey's remark, was quick to take umbrage on Royce's behalf. "There's naught to worry about, my lady," he boasted. "Royce is the finest warrior alive—you'll see it in the tournament."

Seeing his men watching him from the sidelines, Royce pulled Zeus out of another turn and then trotted over to them. With Jenny concealed by Godfrey and Gawin, he didn't notice her until he stopped in front of the group and Gawin burst out, "Let Lady Jennifer see you ride at the quintain!"

"I'm certain," Royce declined after a questioning glance at his wife's politely uninvolved expression, "Lady Jennifer has already seen more than enough of that from all of us."

"But," said Godfrey with a meaningful grin as he seconded Gawin's request, "I'll wager she's never seen you *miss* it. Go ahead—show us how 'tis done."

With a reluctant nod, Royce turned Zeus into a tight circle and then sent him leaping forward from a dead stop.

"He's going to miss on purpose?" Jenny asked, cringing in spite of herself at the sickening thud made by the sandbag whenever it struck a knight who missed.

"Watch," said Gawin proudly, "there's no other knight who can do this—"

At that instant, Royce's spear struck a mighty blow on the "knight's" shoulder, not the shield, the sandbag whirled like lightning—and missed as Royce ducked low and to the side of his horse's flying mane. Jennifer barely checked the impulse to clap in amazed surprise.

Baffled, she looked first to Eustace, then to Godfrey for an explanation. "'Tis his reflexes," Gawin provided proudly. "For all his muscle, Royce can move at the blink of an eye."

Royce's smiling voice came back to her, reminding her of what had been one of the happiest nights of her life: *Watch any warrior dodging lances and you'll see dance steps and footwork that will dazzle you.*

"He's just *that* fast—" Gawin snapped his fingers for emphasis "—with a dagger or sword or mace."

This time, Jenny's memory was of the dagger protruding from William's chest, and it banished the other bittersweet memory. "That was a nice trick at the quintain," she said without any emotion, "however, 'twould serve him naught in battle, for he could never lean to the side of his horse like that in armor."

"Oh, but he can!" Gawin crowed, delightedly. Then his face fell as Lady Jennifer politely walked away.

"Gawin," Godfrey said furiously, "your lack of perception frightens me. Go polish Royce's armor and keep your mouth closed!" In disgust he turned to Eustace and added, "How can Gawin be so clearheaded in battle and an utter dolt when it comes to anything else?"

Chapter Twenty-Four

"How many more do ye think are out there, my lady?" Agnes asked, standing beside Jenny on the wall-walk. Agnes had been working so hard for the last week that Jenny had insisted she come outdoors for some air.

Jenny looked out at the incredible spectacle that had resulted from King Henry's order that the Wolf participate in what had once been a "local joust."

Nobles, knights, and spectators from England, Scotland, France, and Wales had arrived by the thousands, and the valley and surrounding hills were now completely carpeted with the brightly colored tents and pavilions that each new arrival had erected for his comfort. It looked, Jenny thought, like a sea of colors splotched with patterns and dotted with banners.

In answer to Agnes's question, Jenny smiled wearily. "I'd guess six or seven thousand. More perhaps." And Jenny knew why they were here: they were here in hopes of pitting their skills against Henry's legendary Wolf.

"Look, there's another group," Jenny said, nodding to the east, where mounted riders and footmen were swarming over the rise. They'd been arriving in groups of one hundred and more for nearly a week, and now Jenny was familiar with the routine of England's riding households. First came a small group, including a trumpeter blasting upon his horn to announce the arrival of his illustrious lord to the vicinity. The job of this first group was to ride to Claymore and announce the imminent arrival of their lord—which now made no difference because every chamber at Claymore, from the sixty in the gate-houses, to the tiniest loft above the hall, were already filled with noble guests. So crowded was the castle that all attendants and servants to the nobles had been obliged to be left outside the gates, where they fended nicely for themselves in the family pavilions.

After the trumpeters and scouts arrived, then came a larger group, including the lord and his lady, mounted on lavishly draped horses. Then came troops of servants and wagons bearing the tents, and every-thing the noble household would require: tablecloths, plates, jewels, pots, pans, beds, and even tapestries.

It had all become a common sight to Jenny in the last four days. Noble families, accustomed to traveling as far as a hundred miles between their castles, thought nothing of coming at least that far to see what promised to be the largest tournament in their life-times.

"We ain't never seen the likes o' this—none of us," Agnes said.

"Are the villagers doing as I bade them?"

"Aye, milady, and grateful forever we'll always be to you for it. Why in one sennight we've all made more coin than we've made in a lifetime, and no one's dared to try 'n' cheat us like they've done every other year when they come for the tournament."

Jenny smiled and lifted the hair off the back of her neck, letting the late October breeze cool her nape. When the first dozen families had arrived in the valley and the tents had begun to go up, livestock had been demanded from the villeins for private use, and a few paltry coins tossed at the heartbroken families who'd raised the animals.

Jenny had discovered what was happening, and now every cottage in the valley, and all the livestock, displayed badges which bore the head of a wolf—badges which Jenny had appropriated from guards, knights, armor, and anywhere else she could find them. The presence of the badge indicated that any object bearing the badge was either the Wolf's or under his protection. "My husband," she had explained as she handed out the badges to the hundreds of serfs and villeins assembled in the bailey, "will not permit his people to be treated in such a vile way by anyone. You may sell anything you wish, *but,*" she advised them, smiling, "were I in your place, with something *everyone* wishes to buy, I'd be careful to sell to those who will offer you the most—not the first person to offer you anything at all."

"When this is all over," Jenny replied, "I'll discover where we can get the new looms I told the women in the village about. If the coin they've made this sennight is put toward things like those looms, then the profits from your looms will make you more profits and more. Come to think on it," Jenny added, "since this tournament is an annual affair, all of you ought to plan to have added livestock and all manner of other things, too, to sell next year. There's great profit in it for you. I'll discuss the matter with the duke and our bailiffs, then I'll help all of you to make plans if you'd like."

Agnes looked at her with misty eyes. "Ye've been a blessing sent here by the Lord himself, milady. We *all* think it, and we're that sorry for the welcome you got from us when you come here. Everyone knows I have yer ear, me being your personal maidservant, and they ask me erry day to make sure ye know how grateful we feel."

"Thank you," Jenny said simply. With a wry smile, she added, "'Tis only fair to tell you, though, that my ideas on the profits to be made from the tournaments and looms and things are those of a Scot—we're a thrifty lot, you know."

"Yer English now, if ye'll pardon me speakin' out 'o turn. Yer married to our lord an' that makes you one 'o us."

"I am a Scot," Jenny said quietly. "Naught will change that, nor do I want it to."

"Yes, but tomorrow, at the tournament," Agnes said with nervous determination, "we're hopin, all 'o us at Claymore and from the village—that ye'll be sittin' on *our* side."

Jenny had given permission for all the castle serfs to attend the tournament either tomorrow, which was the most important day, or the day after, and the atmosphere within the castle walls was positively tense with excitement amongst all who lived or worked there.

She was spared the need to reply to Agnes's unspoken question about where she intended to sit at the tournament by the arrival of mounted riders who were ready to escort her from the bailey. She had told Royce she meant to visit the Merrick pavilion on the western edge of the valley, and he had agreed— because he had no choice, Jenny knew—but only on condition that she be escorted there by his men. In the bailey she saw the "escort" which Royce evidently deemed necessary: all fifteen of his private guard, including Arik, Stefan, Godfrey, Eustace, and Lionel were mounted and armed.

At close range, the valley of brightly colored tents and striped pavilions was even more vivid and festive than it had seemed to Jennifer from the wall-walk. Wherever there was room, practice jousts were taking place, and in front of every tent where a knight was lodged, his banner and spear had been stuck into the ground. And everywhere there was color: tents with broad stripes of reds and yellows and blues; pennants and shields and badges emblazoned with red falcons, gold lions, and green bars—some of them almost completely covered with so many symbols Jenny couldn't help smiling at the display.

Through the open flaps of the larger tents, she glimpsed gorgeous tapestries and snowy linen spread across tables where knights, and even entire families, were having dinner on silver plate and drinking from jeweled goblets. Some families were seated upon plump silk cushions; others had chairs as fine as those in the great hall at Claymore.

Time and again, greetings were called out to one or the other of Royce's knights from friends, but, although her escort never stopped, it still took the better part of an hour to wend their way across the valley floor and up to the western slope. Just as in life, the Scots did not mingle with the hated English, for while the valley was the domain of the English, the northern hill belonged to the Scots. Moreover, the western rise was the province of the French. Because her kinsmen were one of the last to reach Claymore, their tents were pitched to the rear of the northern slope, well above the others. Or perhaps, Jenny thought idly, her father preferred the spot because it put him somewhat closer to the level of the lofty rise where Claymore castle stood.

She looked about her at the "enemy camps," existing for the time being in peace. Centuries of built-up animosity were temporarily set aside as all parties observed the ancient tradition that guaranteed any knight safe passage and peaceful dwelling while attending a tourney. As if he read her thoughts, Stefan said beside her, "'Tis probably the first time in decades that so many people from our three countries have occupied the same territory without fighting over it."

"I was thinking much the same thing," Jenny admitted, startled by his remark. Although he invariably treated her with courtesy, Jenny sensed in Stefan a growing disapproval of her ever since her estrangement with his brother. He thought her unreasonable, she supposed. Perhaps—if he didn't remind her so painfully of Royce each time she looked at him—she might have tried harder to establish the same affectionate relationship she had with Godfrey, Eustace, and Lionel. Those three trod cautiously in the wide gulf between Royce and herself, but it was obvious from their behavior they at least understood her side of the conflict. It was also obvious that they believed the breech between Royce and she was tragic, but not irreparable. It did not occur to Jenny that Royce's brother, far more than his friends, might be much more aware of how acutely Royce felt the estrangement and how deeply he regretted his actions.

The reason for Stefan's warmer attitude today was no mystery to Jenny: her father had sent her word of their arrival yesterday, and Brenna had included a message of her own in it—a message which Jenny had passed along, unread, to Stefan.

Jenny had sent a messenger back to her father, telling him that she would come to him today. She wanted to try to explain, and to apologize for, her overemotional and unjust reaction to his attempt to send her to a cloister. Most of all, she was here to ask his forgiveness for the part she had inadvertently played in William's death. It had been she who had asked Royce to have William stay. And it had undoubtedly been her outburst about the cloister that had upset William and angered Royce.

She did not expect her father, or the rest of her clan, to forgive her, but she needed to try to explain. In fact, she rather expected to be treated like a pariah, but as she drew up before the Merrick tents, she could see at once that this was not going to be the case. Her father came to the doorway of his tent, and before Stefan Westmoreland could dismount and help her alight, Lord Merrick was reaching up for Jennifer's waist himself. Others of her clan emerged from their tents, and suddenly Jenny was being enfolded in hugs and having her hand patted by Garrick Carmichael and Hollis Fergusson. Even Malcolm put his arm about her shoulders.

"Jenny," Brenna burst out when she could finally reach her sister. "I've missed you so," she added, hugging Jenny fiercely.

"And I've missed you," Jenny said, her voice hoarse with emotion over the kindness of her reception.

"Come inside, my dear," her father insisted, and to Jenny's shock it was *he* who apologized for misunderstanding *her* desire to go to a cloister rather than dwell with her husband. Which should have made her feel better, but, instead it made her feel more guilty.

"This was William's," her father said, handing her William's ornamental dagger. "I know he loved you better than he loved any of us, Jennifer, and he would want you to have it. He would want you to wear it tomorrow in his honor at the tournament."

"Yes—" Jenny said, her eyes blurred with tears, "I will."

Then he told her how they'd had to lay William to rest in an ordinary grave in unhallowed ground; he told her of the prayers they'd said for the courageous future lord of Merrick who had been slain before his prime. By the time he was finished, Jenny felt as if William had died all over again—so fresh was it in her mind.

When it was time to leave, her father gestured to a trunk in the corner of his tent. "Those are your mother's things, my dear," he told her as Becky's father and Malcolm carried the trunk outside. "I knew ye would want to have them, especially since you must dwell with the killer of your brother. They will be a comfort to you, and a reminder that you are and will always be the countess of Rockbourn. I have taken the liberty," he added, when it was time for Jenny to leave, "of having your own banner, the Rockbourn banner, flown beside ours on our pavilion at the tournament tomorrow. I thought you would want it there, above you, while you watch us fight your beloved William's butcher."

Jenny was so dazed with pain and guilt she could scarcely speak, and when they walked out of her father's tent in the waning afternoon light, she discovered that everyone she had not seen when she'd arrived was waiting now to greet her. It was if the entire village surrounding Merrick had come, along with every male relation she possessed. "We miss ye, lassie," the armorer said.

"We'll make you proud tomorrow," said a distant cousin who'd never even *liked* her before. "Just the way you make us proud by bein' a Scot."

"King James," her father announced to her in a carrying voice that could be heard by all, "has bade me send you his personal regards and an exhortation that you never forget the moors and mountains of your homeland."

"Forget?" Jenny answered in a choked whisper. "How could I do that?"

Her father hugged her long and tenderly, a gesture so out of character for him that Jenny almost broke down and begged not to have to return to Claymore. "I trust," he added as he guided her to her horse, "that your Aunt Elinor is taking excellent care of everyone?"

"Care of us?" Jenny repeated blankly.

"Er . . ." he amended quickly and vaguely, "that she's making her tisanes and curatives while she's with you? To ensure you stay well."

Jenny nodded absently, clutching Malcolm's dagger, vaguely thinking of Aunt Elinor's many trips to the woods for her herbs. She was about to mount her horse when Brenna's desperate, pleading look finally reminded her of the carefully worded message Brenna had sent to her last night. "Father," she said, turning to him, and she did not have to feign her longing, "would it be——possible for Brenna to return with me and spend the eve at Claymore with me? We'll ride to the tournament together."

For a moment her father's face hardened, then a small smile appeared at his lips and he nodded instantly. "You can guarantee her safety?" he added almost as an afterthought.

Jenny nodded.

For several minutes after Brenna and Jenny had ridden off with their armed escort, the earl of Merrick remained outside his tent with Malcolm, watching them.

"Do you think it worked?" Malcolm said, his icy, contemptuous gaze riveted on Jenny's back.

Lord Merrick nodded and replied flatly, "She's been reminded of her duty, and her duty will overcome whatever lust she has for the Butcher. She'll sit in our pavillion and she'll cheer for us agin' the English while her husband and all his people look on."

Malcolm made no effort to hide his loathing for his stepsister as he asked snidely, "But will she cheer while we kill him on the field? I doubt it. The night we went to Claymore, she practically flung herself at him and *begged* him to forgive her for asking you to send her to an abbey."

Lord Merrick swung around, his eyes like chips of ice. "My blood flows in her veins. She loves me. She'll bend to my will—she already has, though she doesn't realize it."

The bailey was ablaze with orange torchlight and packed with smiling guests and fascinated serfs, who were watching Royce knight Godfrey's squire. For the sake of the six hundred guests and three hundred vassals and serfs in attendance, it had been decided that this part of the ceremony would take place in the bailey, rather than within the chapel.

On the sidelines near the front, Jenny stood quietly, a tiny smile touching her lips as her sorrows were temporarily overcome by the ceremony and pomp that accompanied the ritual. The squire, a muscular young man named Bardrick, was kneeling in front of Royce, clad in the symbolic long white tunic, red mantle and hood, and black coat. He had fasted for twenty-four hours and spent the night in the chapel praying and meditating. At sunrise, he had made his confession to Friar Gregory, heard mass, and partaken of the holy sacrament.

Now the other knights and several ladies who were guests were participating in his ceremonial "arming" by carrying each piece of his shiny new armor forward, one at a time, and laying them beside him at Royce's feet. When the last piece of armor had been laid out, Royce looked over at Jenny, who was holding the golden spurs that were the ultimate symbol of knighthood, since they were illegal for any but knights.

Picking up the long skirt of her green velvet gown, Jenny walked forward and placed them on the grass near Royce's feet. As she did so, her eyes were drawn to the golden spurs on the heels of Royce's knee-high leather boots, and she suddenly wondered if his knighting on the battlefield at Bosworth had been anything so grand as this.

Godfrey smiled at her as he went forward carrying the last and most important piece of equipment: a sword stretched across his hands. When that had been placed beside Bardrick, Royce bent forward and asked him three questions in a low, stern voice which Jenny couldn't clearly hear. Whatever Bardrick answered had evidently satisfied Royce, because he nodded. The traditional accolade came next, and without realizing it, Jenny held her breath as Royce raised his hand in a wide arc and struck Bardrick a resounding slap across his face.

Friar Gregory quickly pronounced the blessing of the church on the new knight and the air was rent with cheers as "Sir" Bardrick stood up and his horse was led forward. In keeping with tradition, he made a running mount of the steed without touching the stirrups, then he rode about the crowded bailey as best he could, tossing coins to the serfs.

Lady Katherine Melbrook, a lovely brunette only slightly older than Jenny, came up to her and smiled as she watched the knight cavorting on his horse to the accompaniment of minstrels. In the past week, Jenny had been surprised to find that she liked several of the English—and even more surprised because they seemed to have accepted her.

It was such a dramatic change from their behavior at Merrick on the night of her betrothal that she had remained slightly suspicious of it. Katherine Melbrook was the single exception, however, for she was so outspoken and friendly that Jenny liked and trusted her from the very first day, when she had laughingly announced: "Serfs' gossip has it that you are something between an angel and a saint. We're told," she'd teased, "that you tore a strip off your own steward for striking one of your serfs two days ago. And that a miscreant lad with an excellent throwing arm was treated more than mercifully."

Their friendship had sprung up from that, and Katherine had regularly been at Jenny's side, helping to ease matters and direct servants whenever Jenny and Aunt Elinor were busy elsewhere.

Now she drew Jenny's attention from Sir Bardrick as she teasingly said, "Are you aware that your husband, even now, watches you with a look that even my unromantic husband describes as *tender*."

In spite of herself, Jenny glanced in the direction Katherine Melbrook was looking. Royce was surrounded by a group of their guests, including Lord Melbrook, but he seemed to be absorbed with the conversation amongst the men.

"He looked away the instant you turned," Katherine chuckled. "He was *not*, however, looking the other way tonight when Lord Broughton was hanging at your skirts. He looked ferociously jealous. Who would have guessed," she rambled on cheerfully, "that our fierce Wolf would become as tame as a kitten after less than two months of being wedded?"

"He is *no* kitten," Jenny said before she could stop herself, and with such feeling that Katherine's face fell.

"I—please forgive me, Jenny, you must be in a dreadful state. We all understand, truly we do."

Jenny's eyes widened with alarm that her private feelings about Royce had somehow become public. Despite their estrangement, they had agreed more than a week ago, when unexpected guests began arriving at the gates for the tournament, that they would not inflict their differences on their guests. "Everyone understands?" Jenny repeated cautiously. "About what?"

"Why, about how difficult tomorrow will be for you—sitting in your husband's gallery at the tourney and giving him your favor with your own kinsmen looking on."

"I've no intention of doing either," Jenny said with calm firm.

Katherine's reaction was anything but calm. "Jenny, you *aren't* planning to sit on the other side—with the Scots."

"I *am* a Scot," Jenny said, but her stomach was twisting into tight knots.

"You are now a Westmoreland—even *God* decreed a woman must cleave to her husband!" Before Jenny could reply, Katherine took her by the shoulders and said desperately, "You don't know what you'll cause if you publicly take sides with his opponents! Jenny, this is England and your husband is—is a legend! You'll make a *laughingstock* of him! Everyone who's come to like you will despise you for it, even while they're deriding your husband for not being able to conquer his own wife. Please, I implore you—don't do this!"

"I—I have to remind my husband about the time,"

Jenny replied desperately. "Before we realized we'd have so many guests, this night was set aside for the vassals to come to Claymore for the swearing of fealty."

Behind Jenny, two of her serfs stared after her as if they'd been slapped, then they rushed over to the smithy who was standing with two dozen Claymore grooms. "Her ladyship," one of the serfs burst out in anxiety and disbelief, "is sittin' with the Scots tomorrow. She's sidin' *agin* us!"

"You're lyin'!" exploded a young groom whose burned hand Jenny had tended and bandaged herself yesterday. "She'd *never* do that. She's one o' *us.*"

"My lord," Jenny said when she reached Royce, and he turned to her at once, cutting off Lord Melbrook in the middle of his sentence. "You said," Jenny reminded him, unable to banish Katherine's words about the way her husband looked at her. It did seem, Jenny thought dazedly, that there *was* something in his eyes when he gazed at her . . .

"I said what?" he asked quietly.

"You said everyone normally retires early on the night before a tourney," Jenny explained, recovering her composure and arranging her face in the same politely impersonal expression she'd tried to adopt with him since William's death. "And if you mean for everyone to do that, then 'twould be wise to get the swearing of fealty over and done with before it grows any later."

"Are you feeling unwell?" he asked, his narrowed eyes searching her face.

"No," Jenny lied. "Just tired."

The swearing of fealty took place in the great hall, where Royce's vassals had all assembled. For nearly a full hour, Jenny stood with Katherine, Brenna, Sir Stefan, and several others, watching as each of Royce's vassals approached him one at a time. In accordance with ancient custom, each one knelt before him, placed his hands in Royce's, humbly bowed his head, and swore him fealty. It was an act of obeisance, oft portrayed in paintings of lofty nobles with their lowly subjects, instantly recognizable by posture alone. Jenny, who'd seen it done at Merrick, had always thought it needlessly humbling to the vassal. So, in a way, did Katherine Melbrook, who quietly observed, "It must be very demeaning to a vassal."

"'Tis meant to be," said Lord Melbrook, obviously not sharing his wife's distaste for it. "But then, I have assumed exactly the same position before King Henry, so you see, 'tis not quite the debasing gesture you ladies obviously find it. However," he amended after a moment's additional thought, "perhaps it feels different where you're a noble bending your knee to a king."

As soon as the last vassal had knelt and sworn his fealty, Jenny quietly excused herself and slipped upstairs. Agnes had just finished helping her into a bedgown of soft white lawn embroidered with pink silk roses when Royce knocked on the door to her chamber and entered. "I'll just go down to the Lady Elinor and see if she needs me," Agnes said to Jenny, then she bobbed a quick curtsy to Royce.

Realizing the linen gown was nearly transparent, Jenny snatched up a silver velvet dressing gown and hastily put it on. Instead of mocking the modest gesture—or teasing her about it—as he might have done when they'd been happy together, Jenny noticed that his handsome face remained perfectly expressionless.

"I wanted to talk to you about a few things," he began quietly, when she had belted the robe. "First of all, about the badges you handed out to the villagers—"

"If you're angry about that, I don't blame you," Jenny said honestly. "I should have consulted with you or Sir Albert first. Especially because I handed them out in your name. You weren't available at the time, and I—I don't like Sir Albert."

"I'm far from angry, Jennifer," he said politely. "And after the tournament I'll replace Prisham. Actually, I came in here to thank you for noticing the problem and for solving it so cleverly. Most of all, I wanted to thank you for not letting your hatred for me show to the serfs."

Jenny's stomach lurched sickly at the word hatred, as he continued, "You've done the opposite, in fact." He glanced toward the door by which Agnes had just departed and added ironically, "No one crosses themselves any more when they walk near me. Not even your maid."

Jenny, who had no idea he'd ever noticed that before, nodded, unable to think of what to say.

He hesitated and then said with a sardonic twist to his lips. "Your father, your brother, and three other Merricks have each challenged me to a joust tomorrow."

The sensual awareness of him that had been plaguing Jenny ever since Katherine had remarked on Royce's alleged tenderness toward her was demolished by his next words:

"I've accepted."

"Naturally," she said with unhidden bitterness.

"I had no choice," he said tautly. "I am under a specific command from my king not to decline if challenged by your family."

"You're going to have a very busy day," she remarked, giving him a freezing look. It was common knowledge that Scotland and France had each picked their two premier knights, and that Royce was to confront them as well tomorrow. "How many matches have you agreed to?"

"Eleven," he said flatly, "in addition to the tournament."

"Eleven," Jenny repeated, her scathing voice filled

with frustration and the endless pain of his betrayal. "Three is the customary number. I take it you require four times the amount of violence as other men to make you feel brave and strong?"

His face whitened at that. "I have accepted only those matches which I was specifically commanded to accept. I've declined more than two hundred others."

A dozen sarcastic retorts sprang to her lips, but Jenny had no heart to speak them. She felt like she was dying inside as she looked at him. Royce turned to leave, but the sight of William's dagger lying upon the chest against the wall suddenly made her feel almost desperate to defend her dead brother's actions. As her husband reached for the door handle, she said, "I have thought it through, and I think William must have reached for his dagger not because he meant to use it, but because he was cautious of his safety while alone with you in the hall. Or perhaps he feared for *my* safety. 'Twas obvious you were enraged with me at the time. But he would never have tried to attack you— never from the back."

It was not an indictment, simply a statement of conclusion, and although Royce didn't turn to face her, she saw his shoulders stiffen as if bracing against pain while he spoke. "I reached the same conclusion the night it happened," Royce said tightly, almost relieved to have it out in the open. "From the corner of my eye, I saw a dagger being drawn at my back, and I reacted instinctively. It was a reflex. I'm sorry, Jennifer."

The woman he had married would not accept his word, nor his love, but, oddly, she accepted his apology. "Thank you," she said achingly, "for not trying to convince me or yourself that he was an assassin. 'Twill make it much easier for us—for you and I to . . ."

Jenny's voice trailed off as she tried to think what lay ahead for them, but all she could think of was what they had once shared—and lost. "For you and I to—treat each other courteously," she finished lamely.

Royce drew an unsteady breath and turned his head to her. "And that's all you want from me anymore?" he asked, his voice rough with emotion. "Courtesy?"

Jenny nodded because she could not speak. And because she could almost believe the look in his eyes was pain—a pain that surpassed even her own. "That's all I want," she finally managed to say.

A muscle at the base of his throat worked as if he were trying to speak, but he only nodded curtly. And then he left.

The moment the door closed behind him, Jenny clutched at the bedpost, tears streaming from her eyes in hot rivers. Her shoulders shook with violent, wrenching sobs she could no longer control; they tore from her chest and she wrapped her arms around the post, but her knees would no longer support her.

Chapter Twenty-Five

Canopied galleries with chairs placed on ascending levels lined all four sides of the enormous tournament field and were already crowded with gorgeously garbed ladies and gentlemen by the time Jenny, Brenna, Aunt Elinor, and Arik arrived. Flags flew from the tops of each gallery, displaying the coats of arms of all the occupants within it, and as Jenny looked about, searching for her own banner, she immediately confirmed that Katherine had been correct: the galleries of her countrymen were not integrated with the others but were set facing the English —locked in opposition even now.

"There, my dear—there is your coat of arms," Aunt Elinor said, pointing to the gallery across the field. "Flying right there beside your father's."

Arik spoke, startling the three women into near panic with the sound of his booming voice, "You sit there—" he ordered, pointing to the gallery flying the Claymore coat of arms above it.

Jenny, who knew this was the giant's order, not Royce's—which she wouldn't have obeyed anyway— shook her head. "I will sit beneath my own coat of arms, Arik. Wars with you have already emptied our gallery of many who should have been there. Claymore's gallery is packed."

But it wasn't. Not quite. There was a large, throne-like chair in the center of it that was conspicuously empty. It had been meant for Jenny, she knew. Her stomach twisted as she rode past it, and the minute she did, all six hundred guests at Claymore and every serf and villager within sight of the field seemed to turn and watch her, first with shock, then disappointment, and, from many, contempt.

Clan Merrick's gallery, flying the falcon and crescent, was between Clan MacPherson's and Clan Duggan's. To add to Jenny's mounting misery, the moment the clans across the field saw that she was riding to their side, an ear-rending cheer went up that continued growing in volume the closer she came. Jenny stared blindly ahead and made herself think only of William.

She took her seat in the front row, between Aunt Elinor and Brenna, and as soon as she was settled, her kinsmen, including Becky's father, began patting her shoulder and calling proud greetings to her. People she knew—and many she didn't—from the galleries around her lined up in front of her to either renew their acquaintance or ask for an introduction. Once she had longed only to be accepted by her people; today, she was being worshiped and petted like an adored national heroine by more than a thousand Scots.

And all she'd had to do in order to accomplish it was to publicly humiliate and betray her husband.

The realization made her stomach cramp and her hands perspire. She'd been here less than ten minutes and already Jenny didn't think she would be able to endure more than a few minutes of it without becoming physically ill.

And that was *before* the people who had crowded around her finally moved away, and she found herself the cynosure of nearly every eye across the field on the English side. Everywhere she looked, the English were either looking at her, pointing at her, or drawing someone else's attention to her.

"Just look," Aunt Elinor said delightedly, nodding at the infuriated, glaring English, "at the wonderful headpieces we are all wearing! It was just as I expected —all of us were quite carried away with the spirit of the day and have worn the sort of thing that was in style in *our* youth."

Jenny forced herself to lift her head, her gaze running blindly over the sea of colored canopies, waving flags, and floating veils across the field from her. There were steeple-shaped caps with veils trailing all the way to the ground; caps that stood out on both sides like giant wings, caps shaped like hearts with veils, like cornucopias with draperies, and even caps that looked as if two square pieces of veiling had been shaken out and hung over long sticks that were standing in the ladies' hair. Jenny saw them without seeing them, just as she was vaguely aware that Elinor was saying, "and while you are looking about, my dear, keep your head high, for you have made your choice—though a wrong one I think—and now you must try to carry it off."

Jenny's head jerked toward her. "What are you saying, Aunt Elinor?"

"What I would have said before if you'd asked me: your place is with your husband. However, my place is with you. And so here I am. And here is dear Brenna on your other side, who I strongly suspect is concocting some wild scheme to stay behind and remain with your husband's brother."

Brenna's head lurched around and she too stared at Aunt Elinor, but Jenny was too immersed in her own guilt and uncertainty to register much alarm over Brenna yet. "You don't understand about William, Aunt Elinor. I loved him."

"He loved you, too." Brenna said feelingly, and

Jenny felt slightly better until Brenna added, "Unlike Father, *he* loved you *more* than he despised our 'enemy.'"

Jenny closed her eyes. "Please," she whispered to them both. "Do not do this to me. I—I know what is right . . ."

She was spared the need to say more, however, by the sudden blast of clarions as the trumpeters rode onto the field, followed by the heralds, who waited until there was a semblance of quiet and then began proclaiming the rules:

The tournament was to be preceded by three jousting matches, the herald cried out, the three matches to be between the six knights judged to be the finest in the land. Jenny held her breath, then slowly expelled it: the first two combatants were a French knight and a Scotsman; the second match was Royce's against a Frenchman named DuMont; and the third was Royce's against Ian MacPherson—the son of Jenny's former "betrothed."

The crowd went wild; instead of having to wait all day and perhaps two to see the Wolf, they were going to see him twice in the first hour.

The rules at first seemed perfectly ordinary: the first knight to accumulate three points won the match; one point was given a knight each time he struck his opponent hard enough to splinter his spear. Jenny assumed it would take at least five passes for any knight to accumulate three points, considering that it was no mean feat to successfully level a lance, take aim atop a galloping horse, and strike an opponent at precisely the right spot to shiver a lance—particularly since the smooth surface of the armor was designed to make the lance skid off. Three points, and the match, were automatically awarded to a knight if he actually unhorsed his opponent.

The next two announcements made the crowd roar with approval and Jenny cringe: the jousts were to be fought in the German style, not French—which meant the massive regular lances would be used, rather than poplar ones—and the deadly spear heads would not be blunted with protective coronals.

The bellows of enthusiasm from the crowd were so loud there was a long delay before the herald could finish by announcing that the tournament would follow the trio of jousts and that the remaining jousts would take place throughout the next two days. However, he added, due to the illustriousness of the knights attending, the jousts that followed the tournement would be organized according to the importance of the knight if such could be determined.

Again the crowd roared with enthusiasm. Instead of having to watch obscure knights joust with even lesser ones, they'd have their greatest pleasure served first.

Outside the ring, the constables had finished checking saddle fastenings to make certain no knight intended to use leather straps, rather than good horsemanship and brute strength, to stay on his mount. Satisfied, the chief constable gave the signal, the heralds trotted off the field, and then kettle drums, pipes, and trumpets began to blast, announcing the ceremonial parade onto the field by all the knights.

Even Jenny was not proof against the dazzling spectacle that followed: six across, the knights paraded onto the tourney field wearing full armor, mounted on prancing warhorses decked out in dazzling silver bridles and bells, colorful headdresses, and trappings of brilliant silks and velvets, that displayed the coat of arms of the knight. Polished armor glinted in the sun so brightly that Jenny found herself squinting as before her eyes paraded tabards and shields emblazoned with coats of arms showing every imaginable animal from noble beasts like lions, tigers, falcons, tiercels, and bears to whimsical dragons and unicorns; others bore designs of stripes and squares, half moons and stars; still others bore flowers.

The blindingly bright hues of color combined with the ceaseless roar of the crowd so delighted Aunt

Elinor that she clapped her hands for an English knight who rode by with a particularly stunning coat of arms bearing three lions rampant, two roses, a falcon, and a green crescent.

At any other time, Jenny would have thought this the most exciting spectacle she'd ever beheld. Her father and stepbrother rode past along with what she judged to be about four hundred knights. Her husband, however, did not appear, and the first pair of jousters ended up riding onto the field to the disappointed roar of "Wolf! Wolf!"

Before confronting each other, each of the two knights trotted over to the gallery where his wife or his lady love was seated. Tipping down their lances, they awaited the ceremonial bestowal of a favor—her scarf, ribbon, veil, or even a sleeve, which she proudly tied on the end of the lance. That accomplished, they rode over to opposite ends of the field, adjusted their helmets, checked visors, tested weights of lances, and finally awaited the blast from the trumpet. At the first note, they dug spurs into their mounts and sent them hurtling forward. The Frenchman's spear struck his opponent's shield slightly off center, the Scotsman swayed in his saddle and recovered. It took five more passes before the Frenchman finally took a blow that sent him crashing to the ground amidst a pile of shining steel legs and arms and the accompaniment of deafening cheers.

Jenny scarcely noticed the outcome, even though the fallen knight was practically at her feet. Staring at her clutched hands in her lap, she waited, listening for the call of the trumpets again.

When it came, the crowd went wild, and despite willing herself not to look, she lifted her head. Prancing onto the field, his horse draped in gorgeous red trappings, was the Frenchman she had particularly noticed during the parade, partially because he was physically huge and also because the couteres that protected his elbows were enormous, pleated pieces of plate that fanned out into points that reminded Jenny of bat wings. Now she also noticed that although he wore a handsome baronial necklace at his throat, there was nothing "whimsical" or beautiful about the gruesome figure of a striking serpent emblazoned on his breast plate. He turned his horse toward one of the galleries for the usual bestowal of a favor, and as he did so, all the noise of the crowd began to die away.

A tremor of dread made Jenny quickly divert her gaze, but even without looking, Jenny knew when Royce finally rode onto the field—because the crowd suddenly became eerily still. So still that the periodic blasts of the trumpeters tolled out into the awed silence like a death knell. Unable to help herself, she lifted her head and turned; what she saw made her heart stop: in contrast to the gaiety and color and flamboyance everywhere, her husband was garbed entirely in black. His black horse was draped in black, its headpiece was black, and on Royce's shield he did not display his coat of arms. Instead there was a head of a snarling black wolf.

Even to Jenny, who knew him, he looked terrifying as he started across the field. She saw him look toward his own gallery, and she sensed his momentary mistake when he saw a woman seated in the chair at the front of the gallery that had been meant for Jenny. But instead of riding toward it, or toward any of at least a thousand women around the field who were frantically waving their veils and ribbons at him, Royce swung Zeus in the opposite direction.

Jennifer's heart slammed into her ribs with a sickening thud when she realized he was coming straight toward her. The crowd saw it, too, and grew silent again, watching. While everyone in the Merrick gallery began to shout curses at him, Royce rode Zeus clear up to within lance's reach of Jenny and halted him. But instead of tipping his lance forward for the favor he knew she would not give him, he did something more shattering to her, something she had never seen done before: He sat there, Zeus shifting about restlessly beneath him, and he looked at her, then he deftly but slowly twisted his lance, setting the end on the ground.

It was a salute! her heart screamed. He was saluting her, and Jenny knew a moment of pain and panic that surpassed everything, even William's death. She half rose out of her chair, not certain what she meant to do, and then the moment was past. Wheeling Zeus around, Royce galloped to his end of the field past the Frenchman, who was adjusting the visor on his helmet, settling it more firmly on his neck, and flexing his arm as if testing the weight of his lance.

Royce spun his horse to face his opponent, lowered his visor, couched his lance . . . and was still. Perfectly still—violence, cold and emotionless; leashed for the moment, but waiting . . .

At the first note from the trumpet, Royce crouched low, dug his spurs into Zeus, and sent him hurtling down the course straight at his opponent. His lance struck the Frenchman's shield with so much force the shield flew off to the side and the knight toppled backward over his horse, landing on his bent right leg in a way that left no chance the leg was unbroken. Finished, Royce galloped to the opposite end of the field and waited, facing the entrance. Unmoving again.

Jenny had seen Ian MacPherson joust before and thought him magnificent. He came onto the field looking as lethal as Royce in the MacPherson colors of dark green and gold, his horse at a ground-eating trot.

Royce, she noted from the corner of her eye, did not move his gaze from Ian MacPherson, and something about the way Royce watched him convinced Jenny that he was judging the future chieftan of Clan MacPherson, and that he was not underestimating Ian's threat. It dawned on Jenny that Royce and Ian were the only two knights in German armor, its starkly angular lines emulating the human body. In fact, the only ornamentation on Royce's armor were two small, concave brass plates the size of a fist, one at each shoulder.

She lifted her sideways gaze to Royce's face and could almost feel the relentless thrust of his narrowed gaze pilloring Ian. So absorbed was she that Jenny had no idea Ian MacPherson had reined to a halt in front of her and was at that moment extending his lance tip to her . . .

"Jenny!" Becky's father grabbed her shoulder, drawing her attention to Ian. Jenny glanced up and let out an anguished moan, paralyzed with disbelief, but Aunt Elinor let out a cry of exaggerated delight: "Ian MacPherson!" she crowed, snatching off her veil, "You always *were* the most gallant man," and leaning slightly sideways she tied her yellow veil on the frowning knight's spear.

When Ian took his place down the field from Royce, Jenny noticed at once the subtle difference in Royce's stance: he was as motionless as before—but now he was leaning slightly forward, crouched, menacing— eager to be unleashed on the foe who'd dared seek a favor from his wife. The trumpet blasted, warhorses plunged, gaining momentum, hurtling forward; spears leveled, adjusted, deadly points glinting—and just as Royce was about to strike, Ian MacPherson let out a blood-chilling war bellow and hit. A lance exploded against a shield and an instant later Ian and his magnificent gray horse were toppling to the ground together, crashing, then rolling sideways amidst a cloud of dust.

An ear-rending roar went up from the crowd, but Royce didn't remain to enjoy the hysterical accolades. With cold disregard for his worthy, fallen foe, whose squire was helping him to his feet, Royce wheeled Zeus around and sent him galloping off the field.

The tournament was next, and it was what Jenny had been dreading most, for even at home, they were little less than full-fledged battles with two groups of opposing forces charging each other from opposite ends of the field. The only thing that prevented them from turning into full-scale massacres were a few rules, but as the herald finished announcing the rules that would cover this tournament, her dread multiplied tenfold. As usual, there was the ban against any weapons with sharp points being brought into the lists. Striking a man whose back was turned or striking a horse was prohibited. It was also forbidden to strike a man who took off his helmet for a period of rest—however, only two such periods would be permitted to any knight, unless his horse had failed him. The winning side was whichever one had the most men still mounted or uninjured.

Beyond that, there were to be no rules, no ropes nor fences dividing the forces once the fighting began. Nothing. Jenny held her breath, knowing there was one more decision to be announced, and when it was, her heart sank: today, the herald cried out, because of the skill and worthiness of the knights, broadswords would be allowed as well as spears, if bated.

Two cavalcades of one hundred knights each—one headed by Royce, the other by DuMont—rode onto the field from opposite ends, followed by squires carrying spare lances and broadswords.

Jenny's whole body began to tremble as she looked over the knights on DuMont's side: her father was there, as were Malcolm and MacPherson and a dozen other clans whose badges she recognized. The field was split between the English on one end and the French and Scots on the opposite. Just as in life, these men were divided into the same sides on the tourney field that they took in battle. But it was not supposed to be this way, her heart screamed; a tournament was fought for individual glory and for exhibition, it was *not* for the triumph of one enemy over another. Tournaments fought between enemies—and there had been some—had been blood baths! Jenny tried to calm her wild foreboding, but without a trace of success; every instinct she possessed was already screaming that something unspeakable was going to happen.

Trumpets sounded three warning blasts, and Jennifer began to pray mindlessly for the safety of everyone she knew. The rope, which had temporarily divided the field in half, tautened; the fourth blast split the air, and the rope was jerked away. Two hundred horses thundered down the field, the earth trembling beneath them as broadswords and lances were raised—and then it happened: twenty of Jenny's kinsmen, led by her father and brother, split off from the charge and headed straight at Royce, wielding broadswords with a vengeance.

Jenny's scream was drowned by the roars of enraged disapproval from the English as the Scots converged on Royce like the Horsemen of the Apocalypse. In the moments that followed, Jenny witnessed the most breathtaking show of swordsmanship and strength she had ever beheld: Royce fought like a man possessed, his reflexes so quick, his swing so powerful, that he took six men off their horses with him when they finally brought him down. And still the nightmare worsened; unaware that she was standing along with everyone else in the galleries, she tried to see into the pile of men and metal, her ears bursting with the clanging, clashing, and clanking of sword on steel. Royce's knights saw what had happened and began hacking a path to him, and then—from Jenny's vantage point—it looked as if the entire outlook of the battle changed. Royce lunged up and out of the heap of men like an avenging demon, his broadsword grasped in both hands as he raised it over his head and swung it with all his might—at her father.

Jenny never saw the twist of Royce's wrists that brought his sword down on a highlander instead of her father, because she had covered her face and screamed into her hands. She didn't see the blood running down beneath Royce's armor from the savage gashes her brother had dug when he rammed his concealed dagger into the vulnerable spot at the neck between Royce's helmet and breastplate; she didn't see that they'd hacked through the light armor at his thigh, or that when they'd had him out of sight they'd hammered at his back and shoulders and head.

All she saw when she uncovered her face was that, somehow, her father was still on his feet, and Royce was attacking MacPherson and two others like a coldly enraged madman, swinging and hacking . . . and that wherever he struck, men fell like savaged metal sheep.

Jenny bolted from her chair, and almost fell over Brenna, who had clamped her eyes closed. "Jenny!" Aunt Elinor cried, "I don't think you ought—" but Jenny didn't pay attention; bile was rising up in her throat in a bitter stream. Half blinded by tears, she ran to her horse and snatched the mare's reins from the startled serf's hands . . .

"Look, my lady!" he burst out enthusiastically, helping her into the saddle and pointing at Royce out on the field, "did you ever see aught like him in yer life?" Jenny glanced up once more and saw Royce's broadsword explode against a Scotsman's shoulder. She saw that her father, her brother, Becky's father and a dozen other Scots were getting up off the ground which was already running with blood.

She saw impending death.

The vision tormented her as she stood at the open window of her bedchamber, her pale face tipped against the frame, her arms wrapped around her middle, trying somehow to hold all the pain and terror inside of her. An hour had passed since she left the tourney, and the jousting had been under way for at least half that time. Royce had said he accepted eleven matches, and he'd already fought two before the tournament. Based on the herald's announcement that jousts following the tournament would begin with the most skilled jousters first, Jenny had little doubt all of Royce's matches had followed the tournament in succession. How much more impressive, she thought with vague misery, it was for King Henry to demonstrate to one and all that even exhausted, his famous champion could defeat any Scot foolish enough to challenge him.

She had already counted five completed matches—she could tell by the awful jeering roar from the crowd when each loser left the field. After four more matches, Royce would be off the field; by then someone would surely have brought her word of how many of her people he'd maimed or killed. It did not occur to her as she reached up and brushed a tear from her cheek that anything might have happened to Royce; he was invincible. She'd seen that during his jousts at the beginning of the tournament. And . . . God forgive her . . . she'd been *proud.* Even when he was confronting Ian MacPherson, she'd been so proud . . .

Her heart and mind ravaged by divided loyalty, she stood where she was, unable to see the field but able to hear what was happening. Based on the prolonged, ugly jeering coming from the crowd—a sound that was becoming more pronounced at the end of each match—they weren't getting much of a show from the loser of each match. Evidently her Scots weren't even worth a bit of polite applause . . .

She jumped as the door to her bedchamber was flung open and crashed into the wall. "Get your cloak," Stefan Westmoreland snapped ominously, "you're coming back to that field with me if I have to drag you there!"

"I'm *not* going back," Jenny countered, turning to the window again. "I have no stomach for cheering while my husband batters my family to pieces, or—"

Stefan grabbed her shoulders and spun her around,

his voice like a savage whiplash: "I'll *tell* you what's happening! My brother is out there on that field, *dying!* He swore he'd not raise his hand against your kinsmen and, the moment they realized that during the tournament, your precious kinsmen massacred him!" he said between his teeth, shaking her. "They tore him to pieces in the tournament! And now he's jousting— Do you hear that crowd jeering? They're jeering *him.* He's so badly injured, I don't think he knows any more when he's been unhorsed. He thought he'd be able to outmaneuver them in the jousts, but he can't, and fourteen more Scots have challenged him."

Jenny stared at him, her pulse beginning to race like a maddened thing, but her body was rooted to the floor, as if she was trying to run in a nightmare.

"Jennifer!" he said hoarsely, "Royce is letting them kill him." His hands bit painfully into her arms, but his voice broke with anguish. "He is out there on that field, *dying* for you. He killed your brother and he's paying—" He broke off as Jennifer tore free from his grip and started running . . .

Garrick Carmichael spat on the ground near Royce as he rode off the field, victorious, but Royce was oblivious to such subtle insults. He staggered to his knees, vaguely aware that the roar of the crowd was slowly and unaccountably rising to deafening proportions. Swaying, he reached up and pulled off his helmet; he tried to transfer it to his left arm, but his arm was hanging uselessly by his side, and the helmet fell to the ground. Gawin was running toward him— no not Gawin—someone in a blue cloak, and he squinted, trying to focus, wondering if it was his next opponent.

Through the haze of sweat and blood and pain that blurred his vision and fogged his mind, Royce thought for a moment he saw the figure of a woman running— running toward him, her uncovered hair tossing

420

about her, glinting in the sun with red and gold. Jennifer! In disbelief, he squinted, staring, while the earsplitting thunder of the crowd rose higher and higher.

Royce groaned inwardly, trying to push himself to his feet with his unbroken right arm. Jennifer had come back—now, to witness his defeat. Or his death. Even so, he didn't want her to see him die groveling, and with the last ounce of strength he possessed, he managed to stagger to his feet. Reaching up, he wiped the back of his hand across his eyes, his vision cleared, and he realized he was not imagining it. Jennifer was moving toward him, and an eerie silence was descending over the crowd.

Jenny stifled a scream when she was close enough to see his arm dangling brokenly at his side. She stopped in front of him, and her father's bellow from the sidelines made her head jerk toward the lance lying at Royce's feet. *"Use it!"* he thundered. *"Use the lance, Jennifer."*

Royce understood then why she had come: she had come to finish the task her relatives had begun; to do to him what he had done to her brother. Unmoving, he watched her, noting that tears were pouring down her beautiful face as she slowly bent down. But instead of reaching for his lance or her dagger, she took his hand between both of hers and pressed her lips to it. Through his daze of pain and confusion, Royce finally understood that she was *kneeling* to him, and a groan tore from his chest: "Darling," he said brokenly, tightening his hand, trying to make her stand, "don't do this . . ."

But his wife wouldn't listen. In front of seven thousand onlookers, Jennifer Merrick Westmoreland, countess of Rockbourn, knelt before her husband in a public act of humble obeisance, her face pressed to his hand, her shoulders wrenched with violent sobs. By the time she finally arose, there could not have been many among the spectators who had not seen what she had done. Standing up, she stepped back, lifted her tear-streaked face to his, and squared her shoulders.

Pride exploded in Royce's battered being—because, somehow, she was managing to stand as proudly—as defiantly—as if she had just been knighted by a king.

Gawin, who had been immobilized by Stefan's hand clamped on his shoulder, rushed forward as soon as the hand released him. Royce put his arm across his squire's shoulder and limped off the field.

He left to the accompaniment of cheering that was nearly as loud as it had been when he unhorsed DuMont and MacPherson.

In his tent on the jousting field, Royce slowly, reluctantly opened his eyes, bracing himself for the blast of pain he knew would come with consciousness. But there was no pain.

He could tell from the noise outside that the lists were still underway, and he was wondering dazedly where Gawin was, when it dawned on him that his right hand was being held. Turning his head, he looked in that direction, and for a moment he thought he was dreaming: Jennifer was hovering over him, surrounded by a blindingly bright halo of sunlight that spilled in from the open tent flap behind her. She was smiling down at him with so much tenderness in her beautiful eyes that it was shattering to behold. As if from far away, he heard her softly say, "Welcome back, love."

Suddenly he understood the reason he was seeing her surrounded by shimmering light, the reason for his lack of pain, and for the incredibly tender way she was speaking and looking at him. He said it aloud, his voice flat, dispassionate: "I've died."

But the vision hovering over him shook her head and sat down carefully beside him on the bed. Leaning forward, she smoothed a lock of black hair off his forehead and smiled, but her thick lashes were spiky with tears. "If you've died," she teased in an aching voice, "then I guess 'twill be up to *me* to go out onto that field and vanquish my stepbrother."

Her fingertips were cool on his forehead, and there was something decidedly human about the press of her hip against his side. Perhaps she was not an angelic vision after all; perhaps he had *not* died, Royce decided. "How would you do that?" he asked —it was a test, to see if her methods would be spiritual or mortal.

"Well," the vision said, bending over him and gently brushing her soft lips against his, "the *last* time I did it . . . I threw up my visor . . . and I did this—" Royce gasped as her tongue darted sweetly into his mouth. He was *not* dead. Angels surely did not kiss like that. His free arm came up around her shoulders pulling her down, but just when he would have kissed her, another thought occurred to him and he frowned: "If I'm not dead, why don't I hurt?"

"Aunt Elinor," she whispered. "She mixed a special potion, and we forced you to drink it."

The last cobwebs in his mind cleared, and with a sigh of bliss, he drew her down, kissing her, his spirits soaring as her lips parted and she kissed him back with all her heart. When he finally let her go, they were both breathless, longing to say words that deserved to be spoken in a better place than here in a tent that shook with the bellows from a crowd.

After a minute Royce asked calmly, "How badly am I injured?"

Jenny swallowed and bit her lip, her eyes shadowed with pain for the wounds he'd suffered on her account.

"As bad as that?" he teased huskily.

"Yes," she whispered. "Your left arm is broken, and three fingers. The wounds at your neck and collarbone, which Stefan and Gawin said are Malcolm's work, are long and deep but no longer bleeding. The gash on your leg is monstrous. But we've stopped all

the bleeding. Your head took an awful blow—
obviously when your helmet was off—and undoubtedly," she added vengefully, "when another one of my
butcherous kinsmen attacked you. Beyond that you're
bruised horribly *everywhere.*"

His brow arched in amusement. "Doesn't sound
too bad."

Jenny started to smile at that outrageous conclusion, but then he added in a quiet, meaningful voice:
"What happens after this?"

She understood at once what he was asking her, and
she rapidly considered the extent of additional physical damage he'd be likely to suffer if he returned for
one more joust, and then weighed that against the
awful damage to his pride if he didn't. "That's up to
you," she answered after a moment, unable to keep
the animosity she felt for her father and brother out of
her voice as she added, "However, out there on the
'field of honor' which my family has disgraced today,
there is a knight named Malcolm Merrick, who issued
a public challenge to you an hour ago."

Royce rubbed his knuckles against her cheek and
tenderly asked, "Am I to infer from that remark that
you actually think I'm so good that I could beat him
with my shield strapped to my shoulder over a broken
arm?"

She tipped her head to the side. "Can you?"

A lazy smile tugged at the corner of his mouth, and
his sensual lips formed one word: "Absolutely."

Standing outside the tent beside Arik, Jenny
watched as Royce reached down to take his lance from
Gawin. He glanced at her, hesitated a split second—a
pause that seemed somehow meaningful—then he
turned Zeus and started to ride toward the ring. It hit
Jenny then what he had hoped for but had not asked
for, and she called out for him to wait.

She hurried into Royce's tent and snatched up the
shears they'd used to cut cloth strips to bind his

wounds. Running up to the black destrier who was restless now, pawing the ground with his front hoof, she stopped and looked up at her smiling husband. Then she bent and cut an oblong piece from the hem of her blue silk gown, reached up and tied it around the end of Royce's lance.

Arik walked up beside her and together they watched him ride onto the tourney field, while the crowd thundered with approval. Jenny's gaze riveted on the bright blue banner floating from the tip of his lance, and despite all her love for him, an aching lump of tears swelled in her throat. The shears in her hand hung like a heavy symbol of what she had just done: from the moment she'd tied her banner on Royce's lance, she had severed all her ties with her country.

She swallowed audibly, then jumped in shock as Arik's flattened hand suddenly came to rest atop her head. As heavy as a war hammer, it stayed there for a moment, then it slid down to her cheek, pulling her face against his side. It was a hug.

"You needn't worry we'll awaken him, my dear," Aunt Elinor said with absolute conviction to Jenny. "He'll sleep for hours yet."

A pair of gray eyes snapped open, searched the room, then riveted with lazy admiration on the courageous, golden-haired beauty who was standing in the doorway of her chamber, listening to her aunt.

"Even without the tisane I gave him," Aunt Elinor continued as she went over to the vials and powders laid out on a trunk, "any man who returns, wounded, to participate in five more jousts would sleep the night through. Although," she added with a bright smile, "he did not take much time routing the lot of them. What endurance he has," she said with an admiring smile, "and what skill. *I've* never seen the equal to it."

Jenny was more concerned with Royce's comfort at the moment than with his feats when he reentered the lists. "He's going to hurt terribly when he does awaken. I wish you could give him more of the potion you gave him earlier, before he went back onto the field."

"Well, yes, it would be nice, but it's unwise. Besides, from the looks of those scars on his body, he's accustomed to dealing with pain. And as I told you, 'tis not safe to use more than one dose of my potion. It has some undesirable effects, I'm sad to say."

"What sort of effects?" Jenny asked, still hoping to do something to help him.

"For one thing," Aunt Elinor said in a dire voice, " 'twould render him unable to perform in bed for as long as a sennight."

"Aunt Elinor," Jenny said firmly, more than willing to sacrifice the pleasure of his lovemaking for the sake of his comfort, "if *that's* all there is to worry about, then please fix more of it."

Aunt Elinor hesitated, then reluctantly nodded, picking up a vial of white powder from the top of the trunk.

" 'Tis a pity," Jenny observed wryly, "that you couldn't add something to it—something to keep him calm for when I tell him Brenna is here and that Stefan and she wish to be wed. He did so want a life of peace," she added with a tired chuckle, "and I doubt he's ever been through more turmoil than he has since he set eyes on me."

"I'm sure you're right," Aunt Elinor unhelpfully replied. "But then, Sir Godfrey confided to me that his grace has never laughed as much as he has since he's known you, so one can only hope he enjoys laughing enough to compensate for a life of upheaval."

"At least," Jenny said, her eyes darkening with pain as she glanced at the parchment on the table that had been delivered to her from her father, "he will not have to live in daily expectation of my father attacking him in order to set Brenna and me free. He has disowned us both."

Aunt Elinor glanced sympathetically at her niece, then she said philosophically, "He has always been a man who was more capable of hate than love, my dear, only you never saw it. If you ask me, the one he loves best is himself. Were that not so, he'd have never tried to marry you off, first to old Balder and then the MacPherson. He has never been interested in you except to further his own selfish goals. Brenna sees him for what he is because he is not her true father, and so she is not blinded by love."

"He disowned my children, too—any I ever have—" Jenny whispered shakily. "Imagine how much he must hate me to disown his own grandchildren."

"As to that, 'twas not what you did today which hardened him to your children. He never wanted any if they were sired by the duke."

"I—I don't believe that," Jenny said, unable to stop torturing herself with guilt. "They would have been my children as well."

"Not to him," Aunt Elinor said. Holding a small glass up to the light, she squinted at the amount of powder it contained, then she added a pinch more. "This powder, if administered in small amounts for a few weeks, has been known to render a man completely impotent. Which is why," she continued as she poured some wine into the glass, "your father wished me to accompany you to Claymore. He wanted to be certain your husband would not be able to get you with child. Which, as I pointed out to him, meant that you, too, would be childless, but he cared naught about that."

Jenny's breath froze, first in horror at her father's actions and then at the thought that Aunt Elinor might have been following his instructions. "You—you haven't been putting any of it in my husband's food or drink, have you?"

Unaware of the tense, thunderous gaze leveled on her from the bed, Aunt Elinor took her time stirring

427

the mix with a spoon. "Heavens no, nor would I have. But I cannot help thinking," she added, carrying it carefully toward the bed, "that when your father decided not to send me to Claymore after all, he must have arrived at some better plan. Now go to bed and try to sleep," she ordered sternly, unaware that she had just added to Jenny's pain by convincing her that her father had, indeed, intended to lock her away in a cloister for the rest of her life.

Aunt Elinor waited until Jenny had gone into her chamber. Satisfied that her niece would get some badly needed rest, she turned to the duke, then gasped, her hand flying to her throat in momentary alarm at the ominous way he was glaring at the glass she held. "I prefer the pain, madame," he said shortly. "Take that powder out of my chamber. Out of my *demesne*," he amended implacably.

Recovering from her brief alarm, Lady Elinor slowly smiled her approval. "Which is exactly what I thought you would say, dear boy," she whispered fondly. She turned to leave, then turned back again, and this time her white brows were drawn together into a stern line. "I hope," she admonished, "you will have a care for those stitches of mine tonight—while you are making certain my potion has not already done its worst to you."

Hampered by his bound left arm and fingers, it took Royce several minutes to struggle into a gray cashmere robe and tie its black belt around his waist. He opened the door to Jenny's bedchamber quietly, expecting her to be either in bed asleep—or, more likely, sitting in the dark, trying to come to grips with everything that had happened to her today.

She was doing neither, he realized, arrested in the doorway. The tallow candles were lit in their wall sconces and she was standing serenely at the window, her face tipped up slightly, seemingly looking out across the torchlit valley, her hands clasped behind her back. With her delicately carved profile and red-gold hair spilling over her shoulders, she looked, Royce thought, like a magnificent statue he'd seen in Italy of a Roman goddess looking up at the heavens. As he looked at her, he felt humbled by her courage and spirit. In one day, she had defied family and country and knelt to him in front of seven thousand people; she had been disinherited and disillusioned—and yet she could still stand at the windows and look out at the world with a smile touching her lips.

Royce hesitated, suddenly uncertain about how best to approach her. By the time he finally came off the jousting field today, he'd been near collapse, and there'd been no chance to speak to her until now. Considering everything she had sacrificed for him, "thank you" was scarcely adequate. "I love you," sprang to his mind, but just bursting out with the words didn't seem entirely appropriate. And if, by some chance, she wasn't thinking about the fact that she'd lost family and country today, he didn't want to say anything to remind her of it.

He decided to let *her* mood make the choice for him, and he stepped forward, throwing a shadow across the wall beside the window.

Her gaze flew to him as he walked toward her and stopped beside the window. "I don't suppose," she said, trying to hide her worry, "that 'twould do the least bit of good for me to insist that you go back to bed?"

Royce propped his good shoulder against the wall and restrained the urge to agree to go back to bed—providing she came with him. "None whatsoever," he said lightly. "What were you thinking about just now while you were looking out the window?"

To his surprise, the question flustered her. "I—wasn't thinking."

"Then what were you doing?" he asked, his curiosity aroused.

A rueful smile touched her inviting lips, and she shot him a sideways look before turning back to the window. "I was . . . talking to God," she admitted. " 'Tis a habit I have."

Startled and slightly amused, Royce said, "Really? What did God have to say?"

"I think," she softly replied, "He said, 'You're welcome.' "

"For what?" Royce teased.

Lifting her eyes to his, Jenny solemnly replied, "For you."

The amusement fled from Royce's face and with a groan he pulled her roughly against his chest, crushing her to him. *"Jenny,"* he whispered hoarsely, burying his face in her fragrant hair. "Jenny, I love you."

She melted against him, molding her body to the rigid contours of his, offering her lips up for his fierce, devouring kiss, then she took his face between both her hands. Leaning back slightly against his arm, her melting blue eyes gazing deeply into his, his wife replied in a shaky voice, "I think, my lord, I love you more."

Sated and utterly contented, Royce lay in the darkness with Jenny cradled against his side, her head on his shoulder. His hand drifted lazily over the curve of her waist as he gazed across the room at the fire, remembering the way she looked today as she ran to him across the tourney field, her hair tumbling in the wind. He saw her kneeling before him, and then he saw her standing again, her head proudly high, looking up at him with love and tears shining unashamedly in her eyes.

How strange, Royce thought, that, after emerging victorious from more than a hundred real battles, the greatest moment of triumph he had ever known had come to him on a mock battlefield where he'd stood alone, unhorsed, and defeated.

This morning, his life had seemed as bleak as death. Tonight, he held joy in his arms. Someone or something—fate or fortune or Jenny's God—had looked down upon him this morning and seen his anguish. And, for some reason, Jenny had been given back to him.

Closing his eyes, Royce brushed a kiss against her smooth forehead. *Thank you,* he thought.

And in his heart, he could have sworn he heard a voice answer, *You're welcome.*

Epilogue

January 1, 1499

"Iis an odd feeling to have the hall this empty,"
Stefan joked, glancing about at the twenty-five people,
including the fifteen men who comprised Royce's
private guard, who'd just finished eating a sumptuous
supper.

"Where are the dancing bears, tonight, love?"
Royce teased, putting his arm around the back of
Jenny's chair and smiling at her. Despite his joking
about the bears, Royce had never enjoyed a Christmas
season the way he had this one.

"I look," she laughed, her hand pressed against her
abdomen, "as if I swallowed one."

Despite her advanced pregnancy, Jenny had insisted that Claymore and all its inhabitants should
celebrate the fourteen days from Christmas Eve to
Epiphany in the traditional manner, which meant
keeping "open house." As a result, for the past eight
days, feasting had continued without abatement, and
any travelers who arrived at Claymore's gates were
automatically welcome to join the family. Last night,
the castle had been the scene of an enormous celebration put on especially for the delight of Royce's serfs

and villeins, as well as all the villagers. There had been music and carols provided by hired minstrels, performing bears, jugglers, acrobats, and even a nativity play.

Jenny had filled his life with laughter and love, and, at any hour, she was due to gift him with their first child. Royce's contentment was boundless—so much so that not even Gawin's antics were annoying him tonight. In keeping with Jenny's decision to celebrate the season to its traditional fullest, Gawin had been given the role of the Lord of Misrule—which meant that for three days, he presided at the high table, where his role permitted him to mimic his lord, issue outrageous commands, and generally manage to do and say things for which Royce would have otherwise banished him from Claymore.

At the moment, Gawin was lounging back in Royce's chair at the center of the table, his arm draped over the back of Aunt Elinor's chair in a comic imitation of the way Royce was sitting with Jennifer. "Your grace," he said, imitating the clipped tone Royce used when he expected instant obedience, "there are those of us at this table who are wishful of an answer to a puzzle."

Royce quirked a brow at him and resignedly waited for the question.

"Is it fact or falsity," Gawin demanded, "that you're called the Wolf because you killed such a beast at the age of eight and ate his eyes for your supper?"

Jenny bubbled with irrepressible laughter, and Royce sent her a mock-offended look. "Madam," he said, "do you laugh because you doubt I was strong enough to slay such an animal at such a tender age?"

"No, my lord," Jenny chuckled, sharing a knowing look with Godfrey, Eustace, and Lionel, "but for a man who prefers to skip a meal rather than eat one that is poorly cooked, I cannot ken you eating the *eyes* of anything!"

"You're right," he grinned.

"Sir!" demanded Gawin, "an answer if you please. What part of the beast you ate matters not. What does matter is your age at the time you slew it. Legend puts you at everything from four to fourteen."

"Is that right?" Royce mocked drily.

"I thought the story was true," Jenny said, eyeing him quizzically. "I mean the part about you slaying a wolf as a child."

Royce's lips twitched. "Henry dubbed me the Wolf at Bosworth Field."

"Because you killed one there!" Gawin decreed.

"Because," Royce corrected, "there was too much fighting and too little food to keep flesh on my bones. At the end of the battle, Henry looked at my lean frame and my dark hair and said I reminded him of a hungry wolf."

"I don't think—" Gawin decreed, but Royce cut him off with a quelling look that clearly said he'd had enough of Gawin's antics for the evening.

Jenny, who'd been carefully concealing the recurring pains assailing her, glanced at Aunt Elinor and nodded imperceptibly. Leaning close to Royce, she said softly, "I think I'll rest for a little while. Don't get up." He squeezed her hand and nodded agreeably.

As Jenny arose, so did Aunt Elinor, but she paused beside Arik, her hand on the back of his chair. "You have not opened your present, dear boy," she told him. Everyone else had exchanged gifts today, but Arik had been absent until supper time.

Arik hesitated, his big hand atop the small, silk-wrapped item beside his trencher. Looking sublimely uncomfortable to be the focus of so much attention, he awkwardly unwrapped it, glanced at the heavy silver chain with a small, round object dangling from it, then covered it with his hand. A curt, uneasy nod expressed his "profound gratitude," but Aunt Elinor was not put off. As he started to arise from the table she smiled at him and said, "There's dried grapevine blossom within it."

His heavy brows drew together, and even though he spoke in his lowest tone, his voice boomed. "Why?"

Leaning close to his ear, she whispered authoritatively, "Because serpents loathe grapevine blossom. 'Tis a fact."

She had turned to accompany Jenny, and so she did not see the odd thing that happened to Arik's face, but nearly everyone else at the table noticed, and they gaped in fascination. For a moment, Arik's face seemed to stretch tight, and then it began to crack. Crevices formed beside his eyes and pouches developed beneath them. The straight line of his stern lips wavered, first at one corner, then the other, then white teeth appeared . . .

"God's teeth!" Godfrey burst out, nudging Lionel and even Brenna in his enthusiasm. "He's going to smile! Stefan look at that! Our Arik is—"

Godfrey broke off as Royce, who'd been watching Jennifer, thinking she'd intended to sit by the fire, suddenly lurched out of his chair, still holding his tankard of ale, and strode swiftly to the foot of the stairs leading up to the gallery.

"Jennifer," he said, his voice sharp with dawning alarm, "where are you going?"

A moment later, Aunt Elinor looked down from the gallery above and cheerfully replied, "She is going to have your baby, your grace."

The serfs in the hall turned to exchange smiling glances, and one of them dashed off to spread the news to the scullions in the kitchen.

"Do *not*," Aunt Elinor warned in direst tones when Royce started up the stairs, "come up here. I am not inexperienced in these matters, and you will only be in the way. And do not worry," she added breezily, noting Royce's draining color. "The fact that Jenny's mother died in childbirth is nothing to be concerned about."

Royce's tankard crashed to the stone floor.

Two days later, the serfs, villeins, vassals, and knights who were kneeling in the bailey were no longer smiling in anticipation of the arrival of the heir to Claymore. They were keeping a vigil, their heads bent in prayer. The baby had not come, and the news filtering down from the frantic serfs within the hall had been increasingly bad. Nor was it regarded as a good sign that the duke—who rarely set foot in the chapel—had gone in there four hours ago looking tormented and terrified.

Faces lifted in hope as the doors to the hall were flung open, then they froze in alarm as Lady Elinor went racing into the chapel. A moment later, the duke burst past the doors, running, and though no one could tell from his haggard face what news there was, it was not regarded as a good omen.

"Jenny," Royce whispered, leaning over her, his hands braced on either side of her pillow.

Her blue eyes opened, smiling sleepily at him as she whispered, "You have a son."

Royce swallowed audibly, smoothing her tousled curls off her cheek. "Thank you, darling," he said helplessly, his voice still raw from the two days of terror he'd lived through. He leaned down and covered her mouth with his own, his tender-rough kiss eloquent of love and profound relief that she was well.

"Have you seen him?" she asked when he finally lifted his lips from hers.

Standing, Royce walked over to the wooden cradle where his sleeping infant son lay. Reaching down, he touched the tiny hand with his finger, then he glanced over at Jenny, his brow furrowed with alarm. "He seems—small."

Jenny chuckled, recalling the heavy broadsword with a ruby embedded in its hilt that Royce had ordered made as soon as she had told him she was with child. "A little small at the moment," she teased, "to wield his broadsword."

Amusement lit his eyes. "He may never be able to *lift* the one Arik is having made for him."

Her smile became a puzzled frown as she turned her head to the window and realized that, although it was nearly dusk, hundreds of torches were lighting the bailey. "Is something wrong?" she asked, recalling the way torches had been lit the night her father had first come to Claymore.

Royce reluctantly left his son and went over to the window, then he crossed to her bed. "They're still praying," he said, looking slightly confused. "I sent your aunt down there to tell them all is well. She must have been waylaid." Ruefully he added, "Considering the way I ran from the chapel when she came to get me a few minutes ago, they aren't likely to believe her in any case."

Smiling, Jenny raised her arms to him, and Royce understood. "I don't want you getting cold," he warned, but he was already leaning down, lifting her from the bed, fur coverlet and all. A moment later, he carried her out onto the parapet.

In the bailey below, the smithy pointed to the parapet and called out. The prayerful and the tearful slowly stood up, their smiling faces turned up to Jenny, and suddenly the air was split with deafening cheers.

Lifting her hand in a reassuring wave, Jennifer Merrick Westmoreland looked down upon her people, and none of them found her wanting. They cheered louder as her husband lifted her higher and closer to him, and it was obvious to anyone watching that the duchess of Claymore was greatly loved by all whom she loved.

Jenny was crying as she smiled back at them. After all, it's not every day a woman is given a kingdom of dreams.

Breathtaking romance from

JUDITH McNAUGHT

A Gift of Love
(A collection of romances from Judith McNaught,
Jude Deveraux, Andrea Kane,
Kimberly Cates, and Judith O'Brien)

A Holiday of Love
(A collection of romances from Judith McNaught,
Jude Deveraux, Arnette Lamb, and Jill Barnett)

Almost Heaven

Double Standards

A Kingdom of Dreams

Night Whispers

Once and Always

Paradise

Perfect

Remember When

Something Wonderful

Tender Triumph

Until You

Whitney, My Love

POCKET BOOKS

3010-01

POCKET BOOKS
PROUDLY PRESENTS

*SOMEONE TO WATCH
OVER ME*

JUDITH McNAUGHT

Now available in paperback
from
Pocket Books

**Turn the page for a preview of
Someone to Watch Over Me. . . .**

An exclusive abridged excerpt from
Someone to Watch Over Me

"Miss Kendall, can you hear me? I'm Dr. Metcalf, and you're at Good Samaritan Hospital in Mountainside. We're going to take you out of the ambulance now and into the emergency room."

Shivering uncontrollably, Leigh Kendall reacted to the insistent male voice that was calling her back to consciousness, but she couldn't seem to summon the strength to open her eyelids.

"Can you hear me, Miss Kendall?"

With an effort, she finally managed to force her eyes open. The doctor who had spoken was bending over her, examining her head, and beside him, a nurse was holding a clear plastic bag of IV fluid.

"We're going to take you out of the ambulance now," he repeated as he beamed a tiny light at each of her pupils.

"Need . . . to tell . . . husband I'm here," Leigh managed in a feeble whisper.

He nodded and gave her hand a reassuring squeeze. "The State Highway Patrol will take care of that. In the meantime, you have some very big fans at Good Samaritan, including me, and we're going to take excellent care of you."

Voices and images began to fly at Leigh from every direction as the gurney was lifted from the ambulance. Red and blue lights pulsed frantically against a gray dawn sky. Uniforms flashed past her line of vision—New York State Highway Patrol officers, paramedics, doctors, nurses. Doors swung open, the hallway flew by, faces crowded around her, firing urgent questions at her.

Leigh tried to concentrate, but their voices were collapsing into an incomprehensible babble, and their features were sliding off their faces, dissolving into the same blackness that had already devoured the rest of the room.

When Leigh awoke again, it was dark outside and a light snow was still falling. Struggling to free herself from the effects of whatever drugs were dripping into her arm from the IV bag above her, she gazed dazedly at what appeared to be a hospital room filled with a riotous display of flowers.

Seated on a chair near the foot of the bed, flanked by a huge basket of purple orchids and a large vase of bright yellow roses, a gray-haired nurse was reading a copy of *The New York Times* with Leigh's picture on the front page.

Leigh turned her head as much as the brace on her neck would allow, searching for some sign of Logan, but for the time being, she was alone with the nurse. Experimentally, she moved her legs and wiggled her toes, and was relieved to find them still attached to the rest of her and in good working order. Her arms were bandaged and her head was wrapped in something tight, but as long as she didn't move, her discomfort seemed to be limited to a generalized ache throughout her body, a sharper ache in her ribs, and a throat so dry it felt as if it was stuffed with gauze.

She was alive, and that in itself was a miracle! The fact that she was also whole and relatively unharmed filled Leigh with a sense of gratitude and joy that was almost euphoric. She swallowed and forced a croaking whisper from her parched throat. "May I have some water?"

The nurse looked up, a professional smile instantly brightening her face. "You're awake!" she said as she quickly closed the newspaper, folded it in half, and laid it facedown beneath her chair.

The name tag on the nurse's uniform identified her as "Ann Mackey, RN. Private Duty," Leigh noted as she watched the nurse pouring water from a plastic pitcher on the tray beside the bed.

"You should have a straw. I'll go get one."

"Don't bother about that right now. I'm really thirsty."

Smiling sympathetically, the nurse started to hold the glass to Leigh's mouth, but Leigh took it from her. "I can hold it," Leigh assured her, and then was amazed by how much effort it took just to lift her bandaged arm and hold it steady. By the time she handed the glass back to Nurse Mackey, her arm was trembling and her chest hurt terribly. Wondering if perhaps there was more wrong with her than she'd thought, Leigh let her head sink back into the pillows while she gathered the strength to talk. "What sort of condition am I in?"

Nurse Mackey looked eager to share her knowledge, but she hesitated. "You really should ask Dr. Metcalf about that."

"I will, but I'd like to hear it now, from my private duty nurse. I won't tell him you told me anything."

It was all the encouragement the elderly woman needed. "You were in shock when you were brought in," she confided. "You had a concussion, hypothermia, cracked ribs, and suspected injuries to the cervical vertebrae and adjacent tissue—that's whiplash in laymen's terms. You have several deep scalp wounds as well as lacerations on your arms, legs, and torso, but only a few of them are on your face, and they aren't deep, which is a blessing. You also have contusions and abrasions all over your—"

Smiling, Leigh lifted her hand to stop the litany of injuries. "That's too much detail. Is there anything wrong with me now that will need surgery?"

Nurse Mackey looked taken aback by Leigh's dismissive attitude, and then she looked impressed. "No surgery," she said with an approving little pat on Leigh's shoulder.

"Any physical therapy?"

"I wouldn't think so. But you should expect to be very sore for a few weeks, and your ribs will hurt. Your burns and cuts will require close attention, healing and scarring could be a concern—"

Leigh interrupted this new deluge of depressing medical minutia with another smile. "I'll be very careful," she promised, and then she switched to the only other topic on her mind. "Where is my husband?"

Nurse Mackey faltered and then patted Leigh's shoulder again. "I'll go and see about that," she promised, and hurried off, leaving Leigh with the impression that Logan was nearby.

Exhausted from the simple acts of drinking and speaking, Leigh closed her eyes and tried to piece together what had happened to her since yesterday, when Logan kissed her good-bye in the morning.

He'd been so excited when he left their East Side apartment, so eager for her to join him in the mountains and spend the night with him there. For nearly two years, he'd been looking for just the right site for their mountain retreat, a secluded setting that would complement the sprawling stone house he'd designed for the two of them. On Thursday, he'd finally found a piece of property that met all his exacting qualifications, and he'd been so eager for her to see it that he insisted they should spend Sunday night—their first available night—in the existing cabin on the land.

"The cabin hasn't been used in years, but I'll clean it up while I'm waiting for you to get there," he promised, displaying an endearing enthusiasm for a task he normally diligently avoided. "There isn't any electricity or heat, but I'll build a roaring fire in the fireplace, and we'll sleep in front of it in sleeping bags. We'll have dinner by candle-light. In the morning, we'll watch the sun rise over the tops of the trees. *Our* trees. It will be very romantic, you'll see."

His entire plan filled Leigh with amused dread. She was starring in a new play that had opened on Broadway the night before, and she'd only had four hours of sleep. Before she could leave for the mountains, she had a Sunday matinee performance to give, followed by a three-hour drive to a cold, uninhabitable stone cabin, so that she could sleep on the floor . . . and then get up at dawn the next day.

"I can't wait," she lied with an affectionate smile, but what she really wanted to do was go back to sleep. It was only eight o'clock. She could sleep until ten.

Logan hadn't had any more sleep than she, but he was already dressed and eager to leave for the cabin. "The place isn't easy to find, so I drew you a detailed map with plenty of landmarks," he said, laying a piece of paper on her nightstand. "I've already loaded the car. I think I have everything I need—" he continued, leaning over her in bed and pressing a quick kiss on her cheek, "—house plans, stakes, string, a transom, sleeping bags. I still feel like I'm forgetting something—"

"A broom, a mop, and a bucket?" Leigh joked sleepily as she rolled over onto her stomach. "Scrub brushes? Detergent?"

"Killjoy," he teased, nuzzling her neck where he knew she was ticklish.

Leigh giggled, pulled the pillow over the back of her head, and continued dictating his shopping list. "Disinfectant . . . mouse traps . . ."

"You sound like a spoiled, pampered Broadway star," he chuckled. "Where is your sense of adventure?"

"It stops at a Holiday Inn," she said with a muffled giggle.

With a laugh, he pulled the pillow from her head and rumpled her hair. "Leave straight from the theater. Don't be late." He stood up and headed for the door to their bedroom suite. "I know I'm forgetting something—"

"Drinking water, candles, a tin coffee pot?" Leigh helpfully chanted. "Food for dinner? A pear for my breakfast?"

"No more pears. You're addicted," he teased over his shoulder. "From now on, it's Cream of Wheat and prunes for you."

"Sadist," Leigh mumbled into the pillows, but she was smiling. A moment later she heard the door close behind him, and she rolled onto her back, smiling to herself as she gazed out the bedroom windows overlooking Central Park. They'd both been very young and very poor when they married. Back then, their only assets had been Logan's brand new degree in architecture and Leigh's unproven acting talent—that, and their unflagging faith in each other.

With those tools, they'd built a wonderful life together and strengthened it over the next thirteen years. During the last few months however, they'd both been so busy that their sex life had become almost nonexistent. She'd been immersed in the pre-opening craziness of a new play, and Logan had been consumed with the endless complexities of his latest, and biggest, business venture.

As Leigh lay in bed, gazing out at the clouds gathering in the November sky, she decided she definitely liked the prospect of spending the night by a blazing fire, with nothing to do but make love with her husband.

She'd hoped to leave the theater by four o'clock that afternoon, but the play's director and the writer both decided to make minor changes after watching the matinee performance, and then they argued endlessly over which changes to make, trying out first one variation, then another. As a result, it was after six when Leigh and the rest of the cast finally left the theater.

Patchy fog mixed with light snow slowed her progress out of the city. Leigh tried to call Logan twice on his cellular phone to tell him she was going to be late, but he'd either left his phone on the charger in his car or else the cabin was beyond range of his cellular service. She left voice-mail messages for him instead.

By the time she reached the mountains, the snow was falling hard and fast, whipped into a frenzy by the wind. Leigh's Mercedes sedan was heavy and handled well, but the snow was deep and coming down so fast, she could only see a few feet beyond her headlights. The driving was treacherous; the visibility so poor that it was difficult to see road signs, let alone spot the little landmarks Logan had noted on his map. Roadside restaurants and gas stations that would normally be open at ten P.M. were closed up, their parking lots deserted. With nowhere to stop and ask for directions, Leigh kept driving. Twice, she doubled back, certain she'd missed a landmark or a road. ·

When she should have been within a mile or two of the cabin, she turned into an unmarked driveway with a fence across it and switched on the car's map light to study Logan's map and directions again. She was almost positive she'd missed a turnoff a mile back, the one Logan had described as being "two hundred feet south of a sharp curve in the road, just beyond a little red barn." With at least six inches of snow blanketing everything, what had seemed like a little barn to her could just as easily have been a large black shed, a short silo, or a pile of frozen cows, but Leigh decided she should go back and find out.

She put the Mercedes into gear and made a cautious U-turn. As she rounded the sharp curve she was looking for, she slowed down even more, searching for a gravel drive, but the drop-off was much too steep, the terrain far too rugged, for anyone to have put a driveway there. She'd just taken her foot off the brake and started to accelerate when a pair of headlights on high beam leapt out of the darkness behind her, rounding the curve, closing the distance with terrifying speed. On the snow-covered roads, Leigh couldn't speed up quickly and the other driver couldn't seem to slow down. He swerved into the left lane to avoid plowing into her from the rear, lost control, and smashed into the Mercedes just behind Leigh's door.

The memory of what followed was horrifyingly vivid—the explosion of air bags, the scream of tortured metal and shattering glass as the Mercedes plowed through the guardrail and began cartwheeling down the steep embankment. Tree trunks rammed at the car, metal collapsed, and heavy objects tore at her flesh and slammed into her head. She remembered the explosive jolt as 5,000 pounds of mangled metal finally came to a bone-breaking stop.

Suspended from her seat belt, Leigh hung there, upside down, like a dazed bat in a cave while light began exploding around her. Bright light. Colorful light. Yellow and orange and red. Fire!

Stark terror sharpened her senses. She found the seat belt release, landed hard on the roof of the overturned car and, whimpering, tried to crawl through the hole that had once been the passenger window. Blood, sticky and wet, spread down her arms and legs and dripped into her eyes. Her coat was too bulky for the opening, and she was yanking it off when whatever had stopped the car's descent suddenly gave way. Leigh heard herself screaming as the burning car pitched forward, rolled, and then seemed to fly out over thin air, before it began a downward plunge that ended in a deafening splash and a freezing deluge of icy water.

Lying in her hospital bed with her eyes closed, Leigh

relived that plunge into the water, and her heart began to race. Moments after hitting the water, the car began a fast nosedive for the bottom and in a frenzy of terror, she started pounding on everything she could reach. She found a hole above her, a large one, and with her lungs bursting, she pushed through it and fought with her remaining strength to reach the surface. It seemed an eternity later before a blast of frigid wind hit her face and she gulped in air.

She tried to swim, but pain knifed through her chest with every breath, and her strokes were too feeble and uncoordinated to propel her forward more than a little bit. Leigh kept thrashing about in the water, but her frozen body was going numb, and neither her panic nor her determination could give her the strength to swim. Her head was sliding under the surface, when her flailing hand struck something hard and rough—the limb of a partially submerged fallen tree. She grabbed at it with all her might, trying to use it as a raft, until she realized that the "raft" was stationary. She pulled herself along it, hand over hand, as the water receded to her shoulders, then her waist, and finally her knees.

Shivering and weeping with relief, she peered through the falling snow, searching for the path the Mercedes would have carved through the trees after it plunged off the ridge. There was no path in sight. There was no ridge in sight either. There was only bone-numbing cold, and sharp branches that slapped and scratched her as she clawed her way up a steep embankment she couldn't see, toward a road she wasn't sure was there.

Leigh had a vague recollection of finally reaching the top of the ridge and curling her body into a ball on something flat and wet, but everything after that was a total blur. Everything, except a strange, blinding light and a man—an angry man who cursed at her.

Leigh was abruptly jolted into the present by an insistent male voice originating from the side of her hospital bed. "Miss Kendall? Miss Kendall, I'm sorry to wake you, but we've been waiting to talk to you."

Leigh opened her eyes and gazed blankly at an unfamiliar man and woman who were holding thick winter jackets over their arms. The man was in his mid-thirties, husky, and prematurely bald. His expression was pleasant, but businesslike. The woman was somewhat younger, slightly taller, and very pretty with long dark hair pulled back into a ponytail. Her expression was also businesslike, but her brown eyes were filled with sympathy.

"I'm Detective Harwell with the New York City Police Department," the man said, "and this is Detective Littleton. We have some questions we need to ask you."

Leigh assumed they wanted to ask about her accident, but she felt too weak to describe it twice, once for them and again for Logan. "Could you wait until my husband gets back?"

"Gets back from where?" Detective Harwell asked.

"From wherever he is right now."

"Do you know where he is?"

"No, but the nurse went to get him."

Detectives Harwell and Littleton exchanged a glance. "Your nurse was instructed to come straight to us as soon as you were conscious," Harwell explained, then he said, "Miss Kendall, when did you last see your husband?"

An uneasy premonition filled Leigh with dread. "Yesterday, in the morning, before he left for the mountains. I planned to join him there right after my Sunday matinee performance, but I didn't get there," she added needlessly.

"Yesterday was Monday. This is Tuesday night," Harwell said carefully. "You've been here since 6 A.M. yesterday."

Fear made Leigh forget about her battered body. "Where is my husband?" she demanded, levering herself up on her elbows and gasping at the stabbing pain in her ribs. "Why isn't he here? What's wrong? What's happened?"

"Probably nothing," Detective Littleton said soothingly. "In fact, he's probably worried sick, wondering where you are. The problem is, we haven't been able to contact him to tell him what happened to you. "

"How long have you been trying?"

"Since early yesterday morning, when the New York State Highway Patrol requested our assistance," Harwell replied. "One of our police officers was dispatched immediately to your apartment on the Upper East Side, but no one was at home." He paused for a moment, watching her as if to make certain she was following his explanation. "The officer then spoke to your doorman and learned that you have a housekeeper, so he asked the doorman to notify him as soon as your housekeeper arrived."

Leigh felt as if the room was starting to rock back and forth. "Did your officer talk to Hilda?"

"Yes." Harwell flipped open his notepad and consulted his notes. "As soon as Miss Bruner arrived at work, Officer Perkins returned to your apartment and spoke with her. Miss Bruner didn't know exactly where you and your husband had gone on Sunday, but she gave Officer Perkins your husband's cellular phone number. He called that number from your phone at the apartment. Your husband didn't answer, but his voice-mail picked up the call, so he left a message for him. Officer Perkins also asked Miss Bruner to check the messages on your answering machine. There were twenty-three messages, but none of them were from your husband. Until now, we haven't been able to do much more than that."

"But," Littleton interjected kindly, "Captain Shrader wants you to know that the NYPD will assist you in every way we can. That's why we're here."

Leigh eased back against the pillows, her mind falling over itself as she tried to come up with logical explanations for a terrifyingly bizarre situation. "You don't know my husband. If he knew I was missing, he'd do a lot more than call the apartment! He'd call the State Highway Patrol and every police department in the surrounding areas, then he'd start looking for me himself. I have a phone in my car, but he didn't try to call me on it."

"You're making too many assumptions," Detective Littleton interrupted gently. "He might not have been able to use a telephone or go looking for you. The blizzard knocked out telephone and electrical service in a fifty-mile radius. In some areas, it still hasn't been restored."

"Logan had his cell phone," Leigh said. "The cabin doesn't have electricity."

"But he wouldn't have been able to recharge the phone's battery unless he could get to his vehicle, which is probably buried under a snow drift. Snow drifts are eight feet high in places, and the plows have only been able to clear the main roads. Some of the side roads and most of the private roads are still completely impassable."

"They are?" Leigh said, clinging shamelessly to the possibility that Logan was safe and warm and simply unable to use his phone.

"Yes, they are."

Harwell opened his notebook and removed a pen from his jacket pocket. "It's also possible your husband went out looking for you and got stranded," he added. "Now, if you can tell us where this cabin is, we'll go out there and look around."

Leigh gazed from Harwell to Littleton in renewed

alarm. "I don't know exactly where the cabin is. It doesn't have an address. Logan drew a map so I could find it."

"Where is the map?"

"It was in my car."

"Where is your car?"

"It's at the bottom of a lake, or a pond, or a quarry, near wherever I was found! I can draw you another map," she added quickly.

Harwell handed her his notebook and pen.

Weakness and tension made Leigh's hand shake as she drew first one map and then another. "I think that second one is right," she said. "Logan wrote notes on the map he drew for me," she added as she turned to a fresh page and tried to write the same notes for the detectives.

"What sort of notes?"

"Landmarks to help me know I was getting close to the turnoffs."

When she was finished, Leigh handed the notebook to Harwell, but she spoke to Littleton. "I might have gotten the distances a little wrong. I mean, I'm not sure whether my husband's map said to go eight tenths of a mile past an old filling station and then turn right, or whether it was six tenths of a mile. You see, it was snowing," Leigh said as tears choked her voice, "and I couldn't—couldn't find some of the landmarks."

"We'll find them, Miss Kendall," Harwell said automatically as he closed his notebook and shrugged into his jacket. "In the meantime, the Mayor, the Chief of Police, and our captain all send you their regards."

Leigh turned her face away to hide the tears beginning to stream from her eyes. "Detective Harwell, I would appreciate it very much if you would call me Mrs. Manning. Kendall is my stage name."

Samantha Littleton waited until the hospital elevator doors closed before she spoke. "You shouldn't have mentioned that her husband might have gone looking for her and gotten stranded somewhere in the mountains. She has enough to worry about without that."

Harwell shot her a derisive look. "I didn't think she'd believe for long that he's too lazy, or too stupid, to get from his front door to his vehicle so that he could use his cell phone."

The lobby of Good Samaritan Hospital was deserted except for two maintenance men who were polishing the terrazzo floor. Harwell put his shoulder against the exit door, and the blast of arctic wind nearly blew both of them back a step.

On the third floor of the hospital, a young doctor was standing at the foot of Leigh's bed, reading her chart. He left quietly, closing the door behind him. The additional morphine he'd ordered was already seeping through Leigh's veins, dulling the physical ache that suffused her body. She sought refuge from the torment in her mind by thinking about the last night she'd spent with Logan, when everything had seemed so perfect and the future had seemed so bright. Saturday night. Her birthday. And the opening night of Jason Solomon's new play. Logan had given her a party afterward to celebrate both occasions. . . .

Leigh closed her eyes, trying to concentrate on that night, but all she could think about was this one. "Oh darling," she whispered, "stay safe for me. Please, please be safe."